Seraphine

Seraphine

A Provincetown Story

Julie Papetsas (signature)

Written and Illustrated by

Julianne Papetsas

authorHOUSE®

AuthorHouse™
1663 Liberty Drive
Bloomington, IN 47403
www.authorhouse.com
Phone: 1-800-839-8640

First published by AuthorHouse   11/11/2011

ISBN: 978-1-4685-0033-2 (sc)
ISBN: 978-1-4685-0032-5 (hc)
ISBN: 978-1-4685-0031-8 (ebk)

Library of Congress Control Number: 2011960278

Printed in the United States of America

Any people depicted in stock imagery provided by Thinkstock are models, and such images are being used for illustrative purposes only.
Certain stock imagery © Thinkstock.

This book is printed on acid-free paper.

This Book is Dedicated To:

My family

And Provincetown, my home

Contents

Book II: The Changing Tide

Author's Note

Our lives are comprised of a series of stories, snippets of memories that highlight major events but that are rarely told in a sequential order. The best stories are those told with the coming of a sudden recollection, when we see or taste or smell something that brings to mind a long-forgotten happenstance. Hidden in the midst of birth, death, marriage, and all other milestones in one's life are the little tales that are only considered important enough to tell as a joke over a cup of coffee or as a side-note to a more pressing conversation. It is these stories, these personal legends that never quite fit into the chronological sequence of a memoir, that make up the meat of our lives. As we reminisce about our pasts, the average person does not think in terms of first, second, third, but rather, "Did I ever tell you about the time . . ." But of course nobody really knows when the time was, and really, does it matter? All that matters is that this is one story, amongst many, that makes up that person's life.

It is important to listen to the stories told around us. In casual exchanges are some of the best stories we could ever hope to hear. The key is to believe that no story is lacking in importance and that every story deserves to be told. So it is my mission to tell these stories, to give these personal tales a form so that they can no longer be forgotten, because these little tales are the most beautiful, the most special, and the most telling.

I am a fifth generation native of Provincetown (or at least that is as far as I can trace back), born and raised here and a graduate of Provincetown High School. I am related to, probably, half the town in some capacity. My grandmother is full Portuguese, her mother a Taves and her father a

Cabral. My great-grandfather, Bill Cabral, was a dory fisherman, and my great-great-grandfather, Seraphine Taves, is the man in the cover photo and the namesake of my novel. My family and ancestors have been an integral part of the native population of Provincetown, and if you were to ask around, you would find that some of the most colorful local characters have been part of my family. Who they were and what they did would be another book in itself. Throughout my life in Provincetown, I have listened to many stories with great attention that have inspired me to write this novel.

In this book, I have taken as many Provincetown tales as I could find and remember and attached them to one, fictional character. I have attempted to condense a hundred years of Provincetown history into approximately one decade. I did a goodly amount research, but I do, by no means, intend for my readers to think that this is an accurate history of Provincetown. I do not want my fellow locals to lash out, "This is not how that really happened!" or cry, "Why, her timeline is all wrong!" or shout, "But the real so-and-so never looked like that or did those things!" because a textbook history of Provincetown was not my intention. The characters are all fictional and not intended to resemble any one person. I used recognizable family surnames at random, but I modified all Provincetown nicknames despite how amusing the originals were. If any of my names match up with a real person, I am sorry—that was not my intention. I know many people, but certainly not everybody.

All of the events in my novel, though many are based on true occurrences that I have heard of, read about, or experienced, are entirely fictionalized. Many will be very recognizable to those familiar with Provincetown legend. Books such as Mary Heaton Vorse's *Time and the Town, The Cape Cod Pilot* by Josef Berger, Howard Mitcham's *Provincetown Seafood Cookbook, The Provincetown Book* by Nancy W. Paine Smith, and *Provincetown or, Odds and Ends from the Tip End* by Herman A. Jennings were valuable sources for well-known Provincetown lore, as were the Portuguese Festival pamphlets, interviews with Provincetown elderly on the local television station, and of course, the stories that were told to me by friends and family, particularly my Great-Uncle Robert Cabral and my late Great-Aunt Yvonne Cabral. Many of my favorite stories in this book came from her, and I wish she were here to see that the humorous tales she interrupted Uncle Bobby's serious account of Provincetown history with are immortalized.

And as for the stories in this piece of writing that seem to have come from nowhere, simply accept them as having come from the imagination of one who grew up in Provincetown and was ever enamored with the mystical, legendary, and romantic quality of this town. I know I am not the only one who has felt this way. It's why people always come back, whether they grew up here or just came for a visit.

It is my intention to capture what I feel is the essence of Provincetown and to somehow immortalize a town and a time and a people through a nostalgic narrative. The best analogy I can draw is that of a painting. When we look at a painting of, say, a house, we do not get angry because the lines are not all perfectly accurate and the color is a bit off. No, we see it as an impression of that house, and more importantly, we see the meaning of that house. Writing is not so different. This novel is an impression of Provincetown and its people and its history, all of which were scrambled around in my mind and transferred onto paper in the hope of deriving a greater meaning. Provincetown is the catalyst for what, I hope, will be a greater message, a tale that all people, no matter where they are from, can relate to. But I will give no more away. My disclaimer is complete. Read with pleasure this work of very inspired fiction.

Book I

Still Waters

I

The Portrait of a Fisherman

The first glimmer of light filtered through the bedroom window, highlighting a small patch of the unfinished wood floor. Seraphine's eyes fluttered open at the gentle call of morning, and he carefully rose from the creaking bed so as not to wake his wife. Reaching over, he pulled his heavy pants from the back of a rickety, wooden chair that sat in the corner, too brittle for anyone to safely sit in but the perfect rack for his one set of well-worn work clothes. He stood to button his pants and cinch a dried-out, cracking, leather belt under his round gut that "done-lopped," as he liked to jokingly point out, over his belt buckle in such a dignified manner as to further exemplify the overall sturdiness and strength of his physique. His wife carefully hemmed the cuffs of all his pants (by "all," meaning two) so that they were the perfect length for his short, stout legs, and the sleeves of his flannel shirts that were equally too long for him, were always rolled up to the elbow, revealing his muscular, brown, fairly hairy forearms.

Seraphine walked toward the window where a mild breeze blew into the room causing the sheer, yellowing curtains to billow softly. He looked down onto the soon-to-be bustling Front Street and then sent his gaze out to where the harbor sat blue and serene, the clean morning light reflecting off the water's glassy surface. It was "flat-ass calm" today, and Seraphine breathed in the sweet, warm air. There was no need for a jacket today.

He went to the basin on the washstand and splashed some water on his face, brushed his teeth, and quickly shaved the thick stubble on his chin that would be nearly completely grown in by mid-afternoon. The only bathroom in the house was on the first floor, but Seraphine was so accustomed to life without running water that he was content to use the washstand instead. He quickly ran his fingers through his thick, wavy hair, beginning to show hints of gray through its original darkness, before shoving the black, wool fisherman's cap on his head and retreating from the brightening bedroom.

As he headed down the hallway, he caught a glimpse of himself in the mirror that hung on the wall. He quickly drew his attention away but found himself unable to fully disregard the image despite his efforts. After a hesitant pause, as though digging for some great courage inside of him, Seraphine bravely faced the mirror square-on and looked himself directly in the eyes. Seraphine rarely studied his own face and had long ago decided that his physical appearance was not a quality on which he would base his sense of self worth. But on this morning, for whatever indeterminable reason, he allowed himself to stop and examine the features that he, himself, admired little.

Seraphine was not an overly attractive man. A blunt person would say he was downright homely. His nose was large and crooked, jutting out from a weathered face, hard and worn from a life of working in the most brutal of elements. His dark, piercing eyes were framed by heavy lids and deep crow's feet, evidence of his perpetual need to squint against the glare of the water with the utmost wariness and alertness. His lips were thin, and his small chin blended into his round, pitted and pocked face. Deep lines cut across his forehead, and a pronounced crevice lay between his bushy eyebrows. His skin was dark and leathery, and his cheeks were plagued by an irregular redness that no doctor had been able to diagnose and no ointments seemed to cure. The toil and wear of the ocean had prematurely aged him so that anyone who did not know better would say he had reached his sixtieth birthday and then some. He was just shy of fifty.

But there was nothing strange or extraordinary about Seraphine's rugged appearance. He was a product, an encapsulation, of the life he lead, as were all the men who found their livelihood on the sea. His face was aged, but his shoulders were broad and strong, his forearms thicker than most men's calves, and his chest round as a barrel. The palms of his powerful hands were callused from pulling on ropes and lines, his knuckles large and swollen, and his thick fingers, at rest, were always curled from continually having them clenched in a strong grip. The pinky on his right hand was a mere stub from being cut off to the second knuckle the time he caught it in a snare and lost the end in the water to feed the fish he would soon be catching himself, and all over, his hands were covered with white, jagged scars from rusting hooks, careless knife blades, and angry sea creatures. He stood with his legs noticeably bowed, his wide feet set far apart from years of stabilizing himself on a rocking boat, and even when he was on land, he had a rolling, swaying gate like the motion of a boat on a gentle wave.

Life on the ocean was not kind to the body of a man, but so weren't many things; war, for instance. The Great War, specifically, was written on his body in the form of a large, jagged scar across his right shoulder from a flying piece of shrapnel and a rippled burn mark that covered nearly a quarter of his thigh from the flames when a bomb struck his naval ship. These scars he kept carefully concealed under his clothing, never taking off his white undershirt, even on the hottest of days, and always wearing long pants. Some things he preferred to keep to himself.

He put his hands in his pockets, unable to draw his eyes away from the mirror. There was a time in his life when he would have been repulsed by the sight of his face. He would have shrunk away in disgust and bitterness that he was made this way. But the wisdom of age had told him that a face does not make a man, just as clothes do not, and that a face no matter how beautiful or how ugly can lose its luster or its grotesqueness once a person's character is revealed. To Seraphine, his body was nothing more than a map on which every journey of his life could be traced. With every step he took and would take, another mark would be made, another line would be etched, and another scar would be burned. His body, his face, was a record of his life, a normal life, a simple life, an ordinary life, but a life that was his. No, he no longer considered himself a monster. As he looked at himself on this morning that was no different than any other, he regarded himself as nothing other than a man.

Seraphine turned away from the mirror and eased himself down the creaky, stairs to find Fluke, his dog, lying on his side at the very bottom, wedged between the last stair and the front entrance, allowing himself to catch the pleasant, cooling breeze through the screened-in storm door that was never locked and to be the first to greet Seraphine in the morning. The dog still appeared to be sleeping but the steady *thump, thump* of his tail against the floor revealed that this was not the case, along with the eye that cracked open and looked up at Seraphine.

"Mornin', Fluke," Seraphine said, keeping his voice low as the dog finally rose to greet him, and patted him on the head. By this time, Mary was already rising out of bed, but Seraphine preferred to spend the early morning hours alone and opted to assemble his own breakfast, much to Mary's chagrin.

"Why don't you ever let me make you breakfast!" Mary would, every so often, exclaim to him in the evenings when he came home from work.

"I can manage," he would say with little production. Everything Seraphine said was simple, concise, and without flourish.

"Bah!" she'd cry, having the more animated of the two dispositions. "It's no extra sweat for me to make you breakfast. I've got five kids to do it for anyway." But Seraphine never let her, and though she knew the argument was futile, Mary still persisted on occasion for the sake of conversation.

Fluke's wagging tail thumped against the banister as he watched Seraphine reach outside the front door to grab the glass bottle of milk from off the stoop, still delivered daily by a man with a farm out in the high hills of Truro. It had only been a few years since he had foregone the horse and cart for a grumbling, red, Ford pickup truck that appeared to struggle up hills more than the horse ever did, but the milk had not changed a bit. People from out of town often complained that the milk had a fishy taste, which was attributed to the fact that the local cows always ate grass fertilized with fish carcasses and seaweed. Nobody local ever noticed, perhaps because they'd drunk fishy milk their whole lives, and just as likely because everything in the town was permeated with salt and sea and the fresh clean odor of fish and seaweed, including the folks themselves.

Taking the milk into the kitchen, Seraphine cracked open the glass bottle and poured a small cup for himself. From the tin on the counter, he removed the large loaf of sweet bread and broke off two hunks, a big one for him and a small one for Fluke. After chewing, or gobbling without tasting in Fluke's case, they both stole out the door without anyone in the house noticing, only narrowly escaping Mary's footsteps down the stairs, and failing to stir the five children still sleeping in their rooms.

The sun had almost completely risen by this point, though the street was shady and the air was still cool. There was nothing like a June morning when the air was clean and crisp, warm enough to shed heavy jackets and sweaters, but cool enough to be comfortable. The salty breeze from the ocean mingled with the scent of the damp earth and freshly blooming trees and flowers in perfect harmony before the sweltering summer heat and oppressive humidity could put a damper on the lovely ease of returning life.

Budging himself from the brick walk of his wife's budding garden, Seraphine unlatched the white, picket gate and stepped onto the board sidewalk. It was time to go to work, and off strode Seraphine with the dog following closely behind him.

II

The Town at the End of the World

Seraphine walked along the narrow, plank sidewalk toward the wharf. His home was in the West End of the three-mile long town, and rarely did he venture into the East End; it contained a very different population of people. The local, year-round Azorean Portuguese were concentrated in the West End, creating their own little village in an already miniature town. The East End harbored the artists and the summer folk who came for inspiration and left once they had had their yearly fill for bigger and livelier places, as well as the Portuguese population that had come primarily from Lisbon and mainland Portugal.

Seraphine needed no buildings scraping the sky, no fast cars, nor bustling stores. He was content to inhabit this minute piece of a very large world, and he was satisfied by the comfort he received from knowing every corner, every tree, and every loose board in the sidewalk of his little half of this little town. He knew who lived in the houses that abutted his. He knew everyone who lived on his road. As a matter of fact, he knew everyone in every house from his home to the wharf. This was not because he was a social person, eager to make friends and meet new faces. He simply knew because it was unavoidable. It is the nature of a small town that everybody knows everybody else's business without even trying.

He took his time walking to work. There was no need to rush. He could enjoy the quiet before the town came alive with the hustle and bustle of people doing their daily errands, dropping bills off at the post office, cashing checks at the bank, picking up cans of paint from the hardware store. The small roads swarmed with people, warm and greeting each other as though it had not just been the day before that they had spoken. It was pleasant to see the town come to life, but Seraphine preferred to keep to himself. He had few words to contribute to small talk, or much of any talk for that matter.

This time of day there were fewer people for him to have to converse with, aside from the early risers he was accustomed to seeing nearly everyday; the same people who had their daily regiments that required waking at the crack of dawn and preparing themselves for the busy day ahead. He felt a special bond with these people, the only ones who seemed to know what the town looked like this early in the morning. It was a secret that only they understood. Only they knew what it was like to walk down the center of the road without having to think twice about a car coming, or a reckless bicycle, or a herd of excited children. Only they knew the way the houses cast a pleasantly cool shadow on the road before the bright sun could beat down and heat the pavement. Early in the morning, one could take in the true beauty of the town with no distractions or interruptions.

Seraphine's house was not directly on the water, but on the other side of the road, the "Front Street." His house still had a clear view of the harbor, and the beach, and the point of land that hooked around and provided safety and protection like the arm of a mother shielding her child. That strip of land was the end of the world, the very extremity, the very last stop. At that point, you could go no farther. You had reached the end, and your only options were to be happy you were there, turn back in the direction from which you had come, or jump into the water. The Point was marked by a simple, white lighthouse, Long Point Light, and a couple shallow, grassy hills that were the only markers of what had once been two Civil War forts. The rest was little more than a sandbar that never completely submerged, and it glimmered at the water's surface like a sandy mirage.

The water sparkled a deep blue now that it was high tide, but when the tide went down, it seemed that, in places, one could walk across the harbor from the town to the Point without ever getting in water past knee height.

Expanses of flat sandbars were exposed, puddles, streams, and rivulets of salt water still gracing them as they pillowed all that the falling tide had left behind. Empty clam shells, fish carcasses, patches of seaweed, and ships' moorings had been hidden beneath the water's surface and now lay naked for all the town to see. And just a short distance away rose the Point, much more tangible than it appeared when the tide was high, like an iceberg that had just uncovered the extent of its mass hidden underwater.

Now that the tide was nearly high, all that could be seen was the dry, sandy shore, in some places riddled with colorful beach glass, barnacle-covered stones, and dried patches of black, grassy seaweed. A quick glance at the moored boats in the harbor told Seraphine that the wind was blowing from the east. There was enough of a breeze to ripple the water, but there were no choppy seas today, no whitecaps to be had. The boats rolled peacefully on their moorings, their shiny, painted sides an array of color. Buoys marked clam beds, lobster pots, and unoccupied moorings, donning color patterns that distinguished to whom they belonged. Seraphine turned from the cool, blue harbor, sparkling and serene, to enjoy his bit of time on solid ground. He experienced enough of the ocean not to dwell so much on its awe-inspiring beauty.

The houses crouched along the shore, just teetering on the edge of falling into the harbor, and wharves were numerous, reaching out into the depths of the harbor. Railroad Wharf, the town pier, was the longest and stretched nearly to the heart of the harbor where before it, running perpendicularly, rested a long stone breakwater to protect the valuable wharf from the onslaught of crashing waves. The wharves had to be long or else the boats could not get to them during low tide when the harbor was considerably drained of its water.

The streets of the town were narrow and difficult for outsiders to navigate, disbelieving that certain roads were capable of being two-way, but it mattered little to the natives, for few actually had cars. They recalled a time when there were no roads, and everyone got from place to place by boat, stopping off at any of the numerous piers and landings, weaving between sand and beach grass. They made paths through the sand from their houses to the shore where their little boats would be waiting for them. Even when the town put in roads, sidewalks were unheard of, and when they were finally built, the townsfolk rebelled by refusing to use them. Though, these days, they were more accustomed to the presence of the sidewalks, they still tended to walk in the street, not out of obstinacy, but more from sheer habit.

There were two main roads, Front Street and Back Street, that stretched the length of the town with a series of smaller streets connecting them the entire distance. On each street the houses crouched close to one another, huddled with very little space between them, sharing yards, trees, and fences. A fire on a windy night would certainly mean shared destruction as well.

The houses were small, neat, and humble, the majority faced with white, painted clapboard, black shutters, a black, shingled roof, and a little, red chimney. The miniature yards were fenced in with either white, picket fences or thick, green hedges, a tree at the corner, shared by two yards, and hanging over the sidewalk, and bursts of wildly cultivated flowers peering out from behind. There appeared to be no particular system or fussy taming of the yards, yet it was obvious that the people who lived in those houses cared for their flowers and made sure that they grew lush and bright. Nearly every family had a vegetable garden in the back, loaded with kale, tomatoes, and various other necessities. The sweet fragrance of damp earth, flowers, and trees mingled harmoniously with the salty sea air.

It was remarkable that gardens overflowed with such lush foliage when the town was built on pure sand with barely a hint of soil. In the spring, the crocuses, daffodils, and tulips dotted color along the dank earth. Slowly the trees began to come into bloom, the shad bushes staying white for less than a week, their white petals falling like unmelting snowflakes. Townsfolk quickly planted pansies in window boxes so that huddles of colorful faces sat in front of nearly every house. Cherry blossoms came and passed, and the lilac trees that existed in almost every yard bloomed large bunches of flowers whose sweet scent overpowered everything else. Goldenrod bushes, irises, and lily of the valley burst into bloom. Women planted hardy geraniums, petunias, marigolds, and impatiens, while clematis and ivy vined along fences and up the sides of houses, and the occasional great tree cast a shadow on a certain corner of the yard, though large trees were rare on a sandy peninsula, and most of the tall trees that had once existed centuries before had been cut down by passing ships to replace broken masts. Everything was finally beginning to come into bloom and fill in the gaps that winter had left behind.

Seraphine passed the occasional woman shaking out a doormat and responded to her friendly wave with a polite nod. Another passerby touched the brim of his hat and said, "Mornin', Cap'." Seraphine always nodded or saluted with a couple of fingers, or once in a while he would return the "mornin'" in a low voice.

As he came closer to the center of town, the residences became fewer and shops more numerous. Wooden signs were nailed above the doors declaring "Liquor Store," "Pharmacy," "General Store," "Florist," and whatever else one wanted or needed. The windows displayed shoes and clothing, netting and buoys, dried fish, and during holidays everybody had a display of Christmas lights, or Easter eggs, or pumpkins, or paper hearts for Valentine's Day. The windows were always changing, but the same person stood outside sweeping the stoop every morning or polishing the panes of glass. Not many stores were open this early in the morning, but everyone was getting ready for another busy day, some store neighbors standing and chatting about how business was going, but usually discussing the weather.

Nearly every person Seraphine passed on his way to work acknowledged him for he was one of those local figures that everyone knows, and, in his case, respects. They all recognized him as one of the most prominent captains in town. These people, who had lived on the water their whole lives and had, in most cases, worked on a fishing boat themselves, understood the struggle, sacrifice, and peril of finding one's livelihood on the sea. They knew the courage it took to take a boat out to George's Bank and then fish out of little dory boats, susceptible to fog and rough seas. They understood that it was thanks to the fishing industry that this town even existed, and thus Seraphine was a very revered man.

It was not an unfamiliar sight for them to see Seraphine walking down the road with his rolling gait and knew that his odd manner of walking was not due to a gimp. They knew to expect little comment from his mouth, and respected it as simply being part of his humble, introverted nature. The simplicity of his appearance with his rubber boots and his worn pants and shirt was countered by the pride he portrayed with his steady gaze and his sturdy posture. And they found his dog to be equally extraordinary, following closely behind his master with no leash, just a rope collar spliced around his neck and a name tag Seraphine had made from a flattened soda pop cap. They saw these two figures every morning, but for many, it was difficult to not stop and watch.

Before going to the wharf, Seraphine had one stop he always made. He had made it to the center of town in not much time at all and approached the pharmacy door, the best coffee in town, five cents a cup. He laid his hand right above Fluke's head, not quite touching it, and said quietly, "You wait here." There was no need to say this for Fluke always stayed. They were two creatures of habit, unable to break from their daily routines and their unwavering practices. Fluke sat right in front of the shop window, looking out at the road, and waited patiently, the occasional person passing by patting him on the head.

Seraphine went into Adams and stood by the counter. The pharmacy was to the back, but along the left wall there was a long counter, with high, pivoting stools and a soda fountain. They served ice cream, coffee, hot chocolate, and frappes. The children rushed down after school every afternoon for sundaes and soda pop, and the old timers sat around the counter all day sipping black coffee, reading the newspaper, and hashing out local gossip and nostalgic stories of the good old days when whaling was prominent, all fish caught was salted and dried, and dory men were not a dying breed. Most of the early morning regulars were already there, and each acknowledged Seraphine with a "Good morning," a nod, or a wave.

"What'll it be, Cap'n'? The usual?" Dotty asked him in her loud, jolly way. She was a petite woman who wore heels high enough to help her to see over the counter and a blue apron that always had chocolate stains on it. She had curly, dark brown hair that she wore cropped to just below her ears and a round, smiling face.

"Yep," Seraphine replied, and gave a shy smile before sitting on a stool to wait for her to get his coffee.

Joe Silva, a local lobsterman, who was more commonly known as "Potts" sat next to Seraphine, and turned to have a brief talk. Everyone in town had a nickname, and it was an extraordinary habit. Some of the names, to outsiders, sounded foolish, but here everyone went by their nicknames, and people would often forget what others' real names were. If a person said, "Did you hear that John Taves died?" Most would look at him funny and say, "Who?"

"You know, Boofa."

"Oh yeah, him," they would say in sudden, grave recollection, not giving the slightest laugh or snigger at the knowledge that *boofa* was the Portuguese word for a fart. The nicknaming was mostly due to the fact that the old-world Portuguese could not pronounce the English names that the younger generations began giving their children in an effort to Americanize, along with the fact that there were so many duplicate names, in an effort to avoid confusion, the Provincetown Portuguese became skilled nicknamers to create distinction. Once a person was tagged with a nickname that person was stuck with it for life. Even entire families would be labeled with a certain nickname by which they were known, as opposed to their real family name.

"So Cap'," Potts turned to Seraphine, clutching his cup of coffee in his hands, "The fish biting?"

"Oh sure," he responded, but sensing that a bit more was expected of him, he reluctantly continued, "But we're just working on the boat today."

"You got a big trip coming up?" Potts asked eagerly.

"Soon," Seraphine reached for the steaming cup of black coffee Dotty handed to him across the counter, "But we've still got a lot of work to do."

"You don't need to tell me about work, Cap'. I hear you loud and clear. My pots haven't been full to the brim lately, but they still weigh a ton! Imagine if they were chock full! I tell ya, my back has been killing me these days. All I do is lift pot after pot after pot. Take the lobsters out, put the bait back in, drop them down and pull them back up, day after day. You don't need to tell me about hard work, Cap'. I'll be doing it til the day I die."

Seraphine steadily looked down at the paper cup he held tight between his hands, letting the burning heat seep into his skin, but not feeling much more than a dull pain from it. His hands had experienced the extremities of hot and cold and little bothered them anymore. Dotty watched the pair with her arms crossed over her chest and an amused smirk on her face as she leaned against the back counter.

Seraphine straightened and put his hat back on. "Well, best be goin'. My dog's waiting outside. Don't want him to run off."

"Pleasure talkin' to you, Cap'. You have a nice day, now."

Seraphine nodded with a slight smile in thanks to Dotty, and touched the brim of his hat, in a goodbye, to Potts.

As soon as Seraphine was out of earshot, Dotty shook her head at Potts and scolded, "What's the matter with you? Don't you realize that man doesn't speak more than five words at a time?"

"Just trying to be friendly, that's all." Potts shrugged his shoulders and took a sip of his cold coffee.

Fluke was still waiting when Seraphine stepped outside the door, and eagerly followed him to the benches in front of Town Hall. There,

Seraphine was able to sit and sip his coffee in peace and quiet while enjoying the pleasant morning. He was able to see the people stroll by as the streets, already, were beginning to get busier. Pigeons pecked at his feet, and the breeze rustled the large trees that grew behind him, lining the short walk to the stately clapboarded Town Hall with its natural wood door and high steeple. Seraphine was disappointed to not have anything to feed the pigeons, so he told himself to bring a hunk of stale bread with him tomorrow.

"Eh, Cap'!" Seraphine was pulled from his reverie. He turned to his left and saw a scraggly looking fellow shambling toward him, a grimy cap pulled down over his greasy, black hair, concealing his deeply creviced forehead, but failing to completely disguise his sunken cheeks and tight, peeling lips. He gave a large, yellow toothed smile which he held, as he moved from the bench he had been dozing on to Seraphine's. He flopped down, comfortably, a body's distance away, close enough for Seraphine to see, and smell, the filthy state of the man's worn clothing.

"Morning, Cap'. How goes it?" He flashed his decaying smile again, and sprawled his arms across the back of the bench.

"Morning, Ernie. Not so bad. You?" Seraphine sounded and appeared indifferent to the man, though it was obvious they were acquaintances.

"Oh, I'm fine. Just fine. I'd be a hell of a lot better, though, Cap', if I had a quarter. You don't have a quarter, by any chance, do you, Cap'?"

"Nah, Ernie, I don't have a quarter."

"Ah, but Cap', I'm hungry."

"Ernie, if I give you a quarter, I know you're not gonna buy yourself food with it."

"How do you know? You've never given me a quarter." Ernie wasn't frustrated or angry; he saw it more as a game, a challenge to win Seraphine over, which he tried nearly every day and always failed.

"And I'm never going to," Seraphine said definitively.

"Aw, Cap', I thought you were a church-going man. That ain't very gracious of you," and he let out a cackle.

17

"Don't say I've never offered you anything. How about I buy you a cup of coffee and a cake from Adams so you can get some food in you?" This was the sort of compromise Seraphine always offered to Ernie, and Ernie always responded with, "Nah, Cap', I'd rather have the quarter."

"Sorry, *Pahd*, I'm not gonna give you one. I'd feel better if I knew you were getting a hot meal instead of putting more booze in you."

"Ah come on, Cap'! You like an ole swig from the bottle too!" Ernie exclaimed throwing up his hands as though what he had been asking for was the most natural thing in the world.

"Sure, but I also put food on the table."

"I ain't got no family."

"Thank God for that."

"Well, now what am I supposed to do?" Ernie flopped his hands down on the tops of his knees.

"Why don't you come with me to the dock, and you can help paint my boat. Get in a good, honest day's work. You'll make more than a quarter," Seraphine proposed, but Ernie wanted no part of this. "Nah, Cap'. Thanks for the offer, but I've got bigger fish to fry." Seraphine knew this meant scrounging up a bottle of whiskey, and lounging on the beach with it, propped up against an overturned rowboat the entire afternoon.

"So do I, *Pahd*. Best be going," and Seraphine rose from his seat, summoning Fluke, who had been lying patiently at Seraphine's feet, to go with him to the wharf. The stores were beginning to open, and the bells of Town Hall rang seven times. It was time to get to work.

III

On the Wharf

On his arrival at the pier, most of Seraphine's crew was already there. "What took you so long, Cap'?" Bill Buckets, Seraphine's long-time mate, asked.

"Ernie Gobo." Those two words were enough to explain everything.

"That old drunk! Christ, Serry, you can't get away from him!" Bill was the only person that called Seraphine by the shortened form of his name and was likely the only person Seraphine would permit it from.

"I don't know why. It's not like I ever give him anything. If I give him money, he's just going to spend it on booze and cigarettes. It ain't worth it," Seraphine sighed and shook his head helplessly as he checked the ropes that attached the boat to the wharf and began to step on board.

"Ernie's losing his mind. He lost it a long time ago, but it seems to be getting worse and worse every year. He walks around talking to himself now."

"True, but you'd be surprised. He makes a lot of sense once you start talking to him. Sometimes, anyway."

"The bum's *tederka*!" Bill exclaimed pointing to his head.

"Yep."

Bill was considerably larger than Seraphine, though his stature was more oafish than sturdy and muscular. The wool cap that was always jammed on his head concealed the sparseness of his hair, and the faded black cloth seemed more natural than the thickest mane would have been. He was a bit fairer than Seraphine, his father having been a Yankee, but he was raised primarily by his mother, and in mind and spirit, he was one hundred percent Portuguese. Bill had a jollier personality than withdrawn Seraphine, always compensating for Seraphine's introversion with a continual onslaught of jokes and colorful stories.

There were three other men working on the boat that day, but the dynamic of Seraphine's crew often changed, and the only one who consistently worked with him was Bill. Most men had a favorite boat to work on, a favorite captain, but they tended to come and go as they needed the work. One boat could be leaving on a trip, and if a man needed money at that time, he opted to work on the boat heading out to George's Bank rather than continue on the one still at port.

Much like the changing tides, the transforming sand dunes, and the growing and shrinking shores, the people changed. They were free spirits, not tied down by anything, not their job, not their house. They moved around within the little town in whatever way pleased them and in whatever way key to their survival. The only steadfast loyalty anyone had was to his family, and if his kids needed new clothes for school, you could guarantee that that man would be on the next boat out to sea. If a new baby was being born in the spring, that man would be out on a rickety ladder, building a lean-to style addition on his house, in the oddest of places, to accommodate the new addition to the family. Sometimes one would go so far as to roll his entire house down the road for a more desirable spot.

All the men on the wharf today had been working with Seraphine, on and off, since he'd been a captain, and they all knew how to busy themselves. Seraphine turned to Paul Careiro, a man in his early thirties, short, with three children and a wife who barely spoke a stitch of English. "Start repainting the name on the back of the boat. Then work on the trim. She got a bit shabby after the last storm we were in."

"Aye Cap," Paul said, and lowered himself down into a little boat that he rowed to the back of the fishing vessel and began painting over the faded white letters that spelled out *Halcyon*.

The *Halcyon* was a modest but rugged vessel that Seraphine had been the captain of for nearly twenty years. It had been brand new when his father-in-law bought it and was the first motored fishing boat in the harbor. She was a beautiful combination of modernity and tradition, propelling herself with a state-of-the-art engine while carrying her family of dory boats. But these days, 1942, all fishing boats had motors, and the *Halcyon* had become something of a relic. Dory fishing was becoming a thing of the past, trawling a more efficient, thus popular, form of fishing, and the once marvelous engine was now rusted and constantly in need of repair.

Seraphine had worked on the *Halcyon* when he was just a teenager, and the boat had become for him a second home. It was his house, his shelter, when he was out at sea for days, sometimes weeks, at a time. The boat was no longer strong enough to handle the extremely long excursions that it had once undertaken when it was a salt fish boat that went out to the Grand Banks. Now, it was predominately a fresh fishing boat going out to George's Bank and coming back in time to deliver the fish fresh to the ice houses. Few ate salt fish anymore with the refrigeration technologies that were considerably more advanced than the days of the *Halcyon's* youth.

While Seraphine had Paul Careiro and Frank Medeiros, a man who lived three doors down from him and whose father owned the general store, painting the *Halcyon*, and Steve Lisbon patching the hulls of the dories with tar, he and Bill set to mending the longline trawls, checking for weaknesses in the line, putting on new hooks, and replacing missing ones. It was a tedious task, but he and Bill were deft and efficient at it. Never once had it occurred to Seraphine to convert the *Halcyon* into anything other than a dory fishing vessel.

Across the way was docked a weir boat, the *Mary Morning* with her crew mending nets and coating them with tar to be laid out to dry atop the blueberry bushes in the dunes or in the lot behind the icehouse. The weir boats, also known as trap boats, remained in the harbor trapping schools of small fish in their nets, though they often found surprises much bigger.

Usually the fish went to the ice house for storing until the Bankers came back, a flag raised, signaling that they needed fresh bait, since, often, the fish were too small to sell or were what the Portuguese called "trash fish." Seraphine got along very well with the trap boat men. They relied on each other.

"Hey Mealy!" Bill hollered.

A leathery man with a shock of curly black hair that fell into his eyes looked up and waved. "Buckets, get a look at this!" He proceeded to hold up a five foot long shark with a brownish gray back and a white belly. "Found this guy in my weir this morning. Had a hell of a time getting him out and nearly destroyed my whole rig. Sonofabitch."

"Seems early for sharks," Seraphine said.

"Water's pretty warm. Had a few hot days already, but, yeah, I was pretty surprised. Ain't the first shark I've caught, but it's sure a pain in the ass to deal with. Had to gaff the damn thing so he wouldn't bite my hand off, and the bastard was so spooked, he got all tangled up in the nets. What a fucking mess."

"Too bad," Seraphine said, sympathetically, while Bill let out a loud laugh, "Well you got yourself one hell of a trophy! Go stuff it and hang it on your wall."

Mealy gave a low chuckle, "I'll throw it in the yard for the kids to play with." This may or may not have been a joke. Mealy threw down his catch and went back to repairing his trophy's damage.

Afternoon had quickly arrived. The men had had their coffee break, though Bill drank whiskey and Seraphine smoked his clay pipe. He began to light an old one he'd been using for quite some time now, but after examining it more closely, noticed a fine crack that was impeding its ability to work. Nonchalantly, he tossed the pipe overboard, into the harbor, and rummaged through his pockets for a new one, a spare that he always kept handy. The harbor was full of discarded clay pipes, just tossed off the sides of the boats like any other rubbish, and usually ended up washing up on shore in a dozen little irreparable pieces.

JULIANNE PAPETSAS 2011

Lunch had already passed as well. Most of the men had brought lunch with them, but Seraphine waited for his wife to come. Mary had been in the habit of doing this since she was a young girl bringing lunch to her father every afternoon, and she'd not given it up since marrying Seraphine.

"Hellooo!" she called from the wharf as though they were all a mile away. Everyone paused in their work and gave her a greeting. "Where's my beloved?" she said in her usual teasing way. She had an engaging personality, always ready with a blunt, direct response to any comment and with a sense of humor that many cultures may have deemed crass for a woman. She was straight to the point, always got done what needed to get done, and never took any lip from anybody.

"Down in the engine room," Frank said.

"Well, can somebody please go get him for me? I've got a big mouth, but sometimes I wonder just how good that man's hearing is."

"You know men's hearing is selective," Peter laughed.

"Except when you get called for dinner. There he is!" Seraphine had just emerged from the cabin, and walked toward Mary who was holding up the brown paper bag and shaking it as though luring a fish. "You're favorite—a linguica roll."

Seraphine raised his eyebrows with approval, as he opened the bag and looked in. "What? You didn't believe me? I made kale soup for dinner tonight and had a piece of linguica left over. There's an apple in there too."

"Thanks," Seraphine said clutching the paper bag and thermos of coffee that always accompanied it. "No cake left?"

"Cake! We're having the rest for dessert tonight. You don't need to be eating all of that sugar in the middle of the day. An apple's much healthier."

Seraphine's face fell, almost imperceptibly, but Mary spotted it. "Well, if I don't look out for your health, who will? Now, I've got to get home before the kids do or else they'll eat us all out of house and home! Make sure you're home by six, okay?" Mary said before leaving, knowing that Seraphine had the tendency to work longer than he originally intended. "Eat your apple!" Seraphine walked back to the boat and tossed the apple to Paul as he stepped on board, a ritual that had long been in place.

As they finished eating their lunches and were getting back to work, a fishing boat was pulling into port, the wet, seaweed covered nets tightly wound around the prominent wheel at the stern. As soon as they docked, the men began offloading fish into giant bins and crates stocking them to be put on the train that went to the end of Railroad Wharf, and carted the fish off to be delivered inland.

Murray Shrug called from aboard the trawler, "Eh, Cap'!. You still patching' the bottoms of those dory boats?"

Seraphine slowly nodded. "Yep."

Shrug was known to be a big mouth and blowhard. He was in his late twenties, unmarried, and had the maturity level of somebody a decade or more younger. He was not particularly well-liked, but he was an able seaman and easily found fishing jobs. "Cap', you're too old fashioned. Don't you realize that ain't the way it's done anymore?" He sprung off the side of his boat onto the dock, a gleeful smile on his face.

"There ain't no right way," Seraphine said apathetically. "I still fill my boat."

"Yeah, but it takes twice as long. You should at least put motors on your dories."

As soon as Bill heard Shrug's voice, he was out on the wharf, red in the face. "We don't troll, we jig, you lousy sonofabitch, and it ain't none of your goddamn business anyhow. You fish your way; we fish ours."

"I don't mean nothing by it," Shrug said with mock hurt. "Just trying to give the captain some advice."

"He don't need no advice from you. We've been fishing since you were still puking and shitting yourself. We don't need to hear none of your talk about how it should be done. You don't have a real love for fishing. You just take those big nets and scrape the bottoms of the ocean clean. You don't give a goddamn what you catch as long you fill up your boat. That ain't the sort of fishing we do, *Pahd*."

Seraphine gave a very subtle motion for Bill to let it go, but as he was doing so, the persistent young man said, "Your kind of fishing is as outdated as that shitty old boat you've got."

At this comment, Bill was furious, "You rotten bastard! Nobody here gives a rat's ass what you think! You oughta get a clue before you start talking about shit you don't know nothing about. I'd like to see you out there in the middle of the ocean trying to row a dory full of fish. You couldn't handle it! You don't fish; you stand around and watch machines fish for you, and then you come here and try to tell people how to do it. You know what would smarten you up? A good, swift kick in the ass, that's what!" By this point, Seraphine had his hand on Bill's shoulder, prepared to hold him back if he'd made any real sign of lunging at Shrug, and hoping that Shrug wouldn't open his foolish mouth again since he knew that there would be no hope for him after that.

"You go along now. We'll keep minding our business; you keep minding yours." Seraphine kept his arm in front of Bill's chest. He was agitated, but it showed little.

"Keep living in the past," Shrug shot one last dig before going back to his duties, and it took all of Seraphine's strength to hold Bill back who was red in the face with eyes wild with fury. "I can't believe that sonofabitch! You're the best captain in these parts, and the *Halcyon's* caught more fish than all these boats put together. What an insulting bastard!"

"Ah, don't think nothing of it. He was just feeling good 'bout they came back with a full load."

"It's gotta bother you too, Serry, don't it?"

"Nah. He doesn't know any better. People are cocky when they're young like that—think they know everything. Dory fishing's becoming a thing of the past, but it's my way, and I'm sticking to it."

"That's it? That's all you're gonna say?"

"There ain't nothing else to say."

"Serry, I don't think I've ever seen you get mad before. It ain't natural, especially not for a *Portugee*. We're stubborn sonsofbitches."

"I never said I wasn't stubborn. I just don't let some kid get the best of me."

"Well, you're a better man than I am, I guess," Bill conceded.

"He kinda has a point, though," Paul said, having overheard the entire confrontation. "It would be a lot easier if you, at least, had motored dories."

"It's the way we've done it, and it's the way we're always going to do it," Bill said. "Ain't that right, Serry?" and he gave Seraphine a jab with his elbow.

"That's right," Seraphine replied. "You gotta be a little stronger, a little more patient, and a little bit crazy. But it's worth it in the end. We do it for the love of fishing."

"Damn right!" Bill chimed. Thus ended the conversation.

IV

Birth

As the steamboat cut through the churning waves of the Atlantic Ocean, black smoke billowing from its stacks, Josephine, heavy with child, leaned on the railing of the deck, looking as far as she could over the vast expanse of dark blue water. She was making the long journey from Portugal to America with no companion other than her unborn child. It had been her husband's goal since adolescence to leave the Azores for a small town called Provincetown that his whaleship had been based out of. While she still did not feel fully prepared to leave behind her familiar life and begin afresh in a place that was nothing more to her than a name, Josephine understood when she married Carlos that she would be estranged from her whaleman husband for long periods of time, and that someday she would have to move away from her home. She clutched the letter in her pocket that she had received from Carlos only two weeks earlier telling her that he had jumped ship in Provincetown and was sending for her to come. He sent her some money to start, but told her that she was to sell everything they owned to pay the rest of the boat fare and, hopefully, give them a little something with which to get started.

Josephine and Carlos had lived in her family's small home since their marriage three years earlier. Her father, a widower, had died a year and a half later and left them the primitive clay and stone cottage, which she now reluctantly had to sell. She sold it to the captain and owner of a Grand Banker who declared that he would use it to store fish and supplies in, leaving her even more crushed, but Carlos assured her that they would have a house twice the size and with more modern necessities once they moved to America. Josephine sold the chickens and the pigs, what little furniture there was in the house, and all her cookware, bedding, and excess of clothing, though excess there was not. Josephine sadly visited the graves of her parents for what would be the last time. There was no longer anything for her here, and she prayed for a better life to come that would erase any longings for Portugal.

Josephine, growing weary of standing, sat down on the deck of the ship and began rustling through the small burlap sack of provisions she had brought with her, consisting of such necessities as sewing needles and thread, twine, matches, a small knife, a bar of soap, and her iron frying pan. In another, larger satchel, she kept an assortment of necessary clothing, her important papers, and a crazy quilt her mother had stitched together with various pieces of cloth and an array of embroidery, within which was wrapped a framed portrait of her mother and father and her wedding license. She looked with glassy eyes at the sepia photograph as she leaned back and gnawed on the hunk of stale bread she had just removed from the sack.

Josephine's nose was large and her lips were thin, but her atypically tall stature greatly assisted in giving her a striking appearance. Her skin was dark and smooth, a deep olive complexion, and her thick, wavy hair hung down to the small of her back in a shining, black braid. Her eyes were a piercing, rich brown, captivating in both their gentleness and strength, and she had the long graceful fingers of a musician, though the only instruments she played were the washboard and frying pan.

Her entire family was of the same dark complexion and found themselves outcast from the rest of the village because the townsfolk accused them of being gypsies. Josephine's family admitted that over a hundred years ago they did have gypsy ancestors, but even after many generations had passed, the townsfolk still chose to travel miles away to have their shoes repaired than go to Josephine's father's shop, a reputable business he had struggled to keep afloat. Though most everyone living in the Azores was poor, Josephine's family was of a lower tier and found that they could never rise above it not matter how hard they tried.

Josephine was thankful to have met Carlos, who was enamored with her from the moment he set foot off the whale boat of his first, three-year-long, voyage, a ship captained by a yankee from Provincetown that Carlos has stowed away on in an effort to escape the Portuguese mandatory military service in South America and, he hoped, return to the islands as a rich man. He, at first, thought she was mysterious and striking, and this intrigue led him to speak to the quiet girl who helped about her father's shop and seemed to never rest from her chores. What he discovered was a kind, generous woman, who loved her family, worked hard, and was the epitome of strength and loyalty. When difficulties arose, she worked harder to make things better, and when things were easy, she did whatever she could to help everyone else. She had a backbone made of steel, yet she was subdued in a way that gave her a sort of refinement, though she had no formal education, and her family was at the very bottom of the social hierarchy.

On hearing the news that Carlos desired to marry Josephine, the gypsy girl, his mother was furious. "How can you do this to your family?" his mother cried, blessing herself and wringing her handkerchief. "Your poor father must be rolling in his grave right now! What about your children? Do you want them to be outcasts too? Do you want them to be spit at and called heathens and live a life of rags and filth?"

"Heathens?" Carlos frowned at the ridiculousness of the comment. "You sound foolish. Listen to what you're saying. You're making yourself out to be as ignorant as everyone else in this town." He had little tolerance for his mother's hypocritical words, for the truth was, they were dirt poor as well, even poorer than Josephine's family. And three years at sea had given him enough audacity to speak against his mother's outcries. "She is a Catholic just like you and me. Our children will not be poor or looked down upon because they will work hard and be respectable people. That is what Pa always told us. He said it didn't matter how much money a person had, just how hard a person worked. Josephine and her family are only poor because nobody dares set foot in her father's shop. Just a couple weeks ago, somebody smashed one of the front windows with a rock. I don't understand how you people can go around calling yourselves 'Catholics' as you treat your neighbors like this."

"*You people*. How dare you insult me like that! You're going to separate yourself from your own mother? You meet some low-life girl, and you are suddenly better than your family, better than the rest of the town? I'm your flesh and blood. I sacrificed so that you could be here today!"

Carlos did not flinch. He did not let his shoulders slump or his voice falter. He did not retreat a step or hang his head in shame. Instead, he looked his mother straight in the eye, with the disdain of a son who had grown to be a man and could now read all of his mother's faults and flaws; a son who knew he had become a better person than his mother had ever been. "Well, Mother, I am sorry you feel that way, but I am not like you, regardless of how much blood we share. I choose to judge people based on their character, not on the prejudices of a bunch of old fools. I will marry Josephine whether you are ashamed by it or not, and you can choose if you want to be a part of our life." With that he turned, and left the home he was born in, his mother standing speechless behind him. She did not come to the wedding, but on her deathbed, only two years later, she summoned Carlos and said that she regretted what she had done. She wanted Carlos and Josephine to take the family home, and bring their own children up there. Carlos cried heartily the day his mother died, but the house no longer meant anything to him, and he allowed the eldest of his five sisters to have it instead. Home was with Josephine and nowhere else, and he had decided that as soon as the opportunity presented itself, they would make their home elsewhere and rid themselves of this world that had never given them a fair chance.

Carlos's devotion to Josephine, so strong that he would turn against his own mother, was enough to make Josephine confident in his decision for them to emigrate, and though she was apprehensive, there was no question in her mind that Carlos had their best interests at heart and that, when all was said and done, he would be right. The days on the boat were long and tedious for Josephine, as well as for the entire boatful of hopeful people. There was nothing to do but sit and look out on the expanse of blue water and blue sky, talk of their futures, and eat their rations prudently. As each day passed, the passengers became more and more restless, anxious to pick up where they had ended. Josephine wondered how many, if any, were going where she was.

The sun had finally gone down after what felt like an eternally long day, and Josephine prepared to rest. Before she retired, an old man approached her and stood facing the water. He had patched, brown pants on, a frayed button-down shirt, partially concealed by an old dress coat with a patch on the left elbow, and a misshaped, beaten, old derby hat from under which tufts of white hair stuck out. His deeply wrinkled face was covered with gray bristle, the gauntness accentuated by the red silk handkerchief he had tied around his neck, and his thin, long fingers clutched the rail of the ship as his furrowed gaze directed itself toward the horizon. "It don't bode well," he said, half to Josephine, half to himself.

Josephine was surprised when he spoke to her in Portuguese because he did not look at all Portuguese to her. "What do you mean?"

"My bones, they ache. And my old mangled hands are throbbing. See those dark clouds on the horizon?" he pointed. "A storm's a-coming."

"Do you really think so?" Josephine said, tension in her voice, and the old man nodded his head. "Maybe you're wrong. Maybe it'll miss us."

"No, nice girl," he said gravely. "I'm an old seaman, and an old seaman's always right about these things."

Josephine no longer questioned him. "Do you think it is going to be a bad one?" she asked, her eyes wide and hopeful that his response would be "no".

"Yes, I think so," he said with certainty.

Josephine's head fell slightly, thinking about her child and the husband waiting for her so many miles away.

Seeing the small movement, the old man turned to her and looked her in the eye for the first time. Josephine was shocked to see that from under the worn hat peered two watery blue eyes that seemed far too sparkling and clear for one of his apparent age. He gave her a gap-toothed smile, his remaining teeth old and worn. "Don't you worry, nice girl. The Lord won't strike down this ship. Not when you've got extra baggage, and I'm not talking about that little old sack you've got next to you. Your son is blessed."

Josephine, who had been staring down at her fat belly, looked up with a start, but before she could question him, the man walked away, leaving Josephine to wonder why on earth he would assume her child would be a son. She went inside the boat and settled herself as comfortably as she could against a wall, propping herself up against her sacks as a pillow. She looked around at the people all huddled together like flocks of birds on a chilly shore. There was little speaking and little movement, and Josephine felt saddened that this was what hope for the future looked like. Everybody appeared worn and disheartened, and though the trip had been long and uncomfortable, she could not understand how people could lose faith so easily. She leaned her head against the cold wall, and tried to close her eyes and forget about where she was.

The old man was not wrong in his judgment. The storm hit hard, and it hit fast. Without a moment's notice, the boat was engulfed by howling winds and treacherous waves. The boat rocked violently from side to side, and down in the dark hold, the passengers clung to whatever they could. They pressed themselves against the walls, the only light a couple of lamps violently swinging from the ceiling, flashed across the fearful faces lost in the shadows; a wailing child, a ghostly white woman, a trembling man. People who had spent their lives on the water were vomiting, as best they could, into buckets, as wooden crates, barrels, luggage, and even people slid from one side of the boat to the other as the helpless vessel was pummeled by the vicious sea.

The storm had barely begun when Josephine felt a stabbing pain, so sharp and sudden that she let out a cry. Clutching her swollen abdomen she felt the pains come one after another, and then realized that her dress was damp. "Oh Lord," she thought to herself, "Why now?" But there was no stopping it. She could not tell the child to crawl back inside of her and wait a few days or for the boat to turn around or for the storm to stop. All she could do was lie back and hope for the best. A woman sitting near her realized that something was wrong, and came to her side, asking her something in a language she did not know. Realizing that they did not speak the same language, the woman asked no further, and hurried into action. It was plain what the problem was, and the woman was determined to help.

The color had drained from Josephine's face, and she was dripping with sweat mixed with the salt water that was washing into the hold. The woman laid her on her back as gently as she could, positioned the sack of clothing under her head, and tried to shield Josephine with her body from hurtling objects. With every contraction, Josephine squeezed the woman's hand until her knuckles turned white, and the woman looked kindly and encouragingly upon her, though Josephine was sure her hand must be aching. The woman's hand was warm and dry and calm and comforting, and Josephine could not believe the infinite kindness this woman was showing her. They had never met before, but here she was helping Josephine deliver her child. The pain was great, but Josephine suffered so silently that no one else on the ship appeared to realize that there was a woman in labor. Everyone was concerned with their own plight as the storm grew more and more vicious, and even when the woman stumbled around begging for somebody to help her, since she was no midwife, nobody did, either because they could not understand her or because they did not want to.

The hours passed, and the storm raged on, as did the birth pangs. The sweat ran down Josephine's face and her hair was matted to her damp temples. She bit on her tongue, not wanting to draw attention to herself, though her cries would draw little attention over the raging storm and the sound of crashing luggage and provisions. She gripped onto the woman for dear life so that she would not slide to the other side of the boat with every swell. The pain of the labor was aggravated by the uncomfortable environment, the burlap sack under her head, the crates and unidentifiable objects that would only miss her by inches, the wet, cold, slippery floor. The woman did a good job of shielding Josephine, but it was hard enough for her to keep herself from being flung away, and she took many painful hits from flying objects. Water was seeping down into the hold and becoming more torrential every moment as bigger waves crashed over the boat. The lights had all crashed down and been put out, so they were in the pitch black. It was impossible to know what were the causes of the cries and whimpers and loud clatters. The storm raged on for three terrifying hours until, finally, the wind began to subside, ever so slightly, as Josephine gave her final heave.

The woman took the little body in her arms and had barely handed it to Josephine when the storm ended as quickly as it had begun. The violent rocking and shaking of the boat stopped. The wind no longer howled. The water stopped rushing through the deck. It was over. The storm had gone, and a baby was born. The old man was right; it was a boy.

Josephine held the child in her arms, swaddled in the crazy quilt she had brought, specifically for this purpose. It was still too dark in the hold to see the baby clearly, and Josephine felt around to make sure all his limbs were in the right place and that he had all of his fingers and toes. The woman lit a lamp she found and held it near the bundle of quilt so that Josephine could see his face. There was nothing unique about this baby. He looked as all newborns do, peering eyes and skin yet to adjust to its normal color. His head was covered with a dark tuft of hair, and he was a healthy weight.

The woman smiled reassuringly down at her and squeezed her shoulder, and Josephine smiled back, the only thank you she knew how to express. The woman slid back to where she had been formerly sitting, and though

Josephine looked for her, she never saw her again during the few days that remained of the voyage.

The rest of the journey was calm. No storms, hardly even any wind. Josephine was able to sit on the deck with her child and nurse him. She feared the stale air of the hold would make him sick, and spent as much time as she could outdoors with him. As careful as she was about preventing his exposure to direct sunlight, it was impossible to completely evade the strength of the sun's rays while on the water, but it was a sacrifice she was willing to make for a cleaner environment. She immediately noticed that his face had developed a redness she assumed was from the sun, but could not be sure it was not something he had been born with. It resembled a rash more than a sunburn, and the hold had been too dark to detect it when he was born.

As she looked down at his oddly red face peering up at her through his swaddling cloths, she knew precisely what to name him.

"I am going to name you *Seraphine*," she said to the child that was her one source of company. "Your face is red like the angels that are closest to God." She lifted him from his blanket and held him up to face the great expanse of blue sky and water. "You see this. This is your world. This is your home. Never fear the ocean. You were born of the sea."

And with that, she wrapped him up again, tightly, and held him the rest of the way to America.

V

The Gale

Seraphine was only three years old when he lost his father in the gale of 1898. Carlos, retired from whaling since his family's arrival in America, was out on a fishing trip to the Grand Banks when the unexpected gale struck and swept him and hundreds of other fishermen away, burying them in the depths of the churning ocean, the watery grave of hundreds of thousands that came before them.

Josephine did not need his dead body to be salvaged from the waves, for months to go by with him missing, or for word that his ship had sunk from the howling winds to know that he was never going to come home. As soon as she saw the first gusts of wind fiercely bend the helpless trees in front of her house and the skies grow as dark as lead, she had committed herself to widowhood and realized that it was time to focus on the welfare of herself and her child.

The gale was blowing southeasterly with hurricane force winds at high tide, and it was certain that the little town was in great peril. As it was, the water's edge at high tide nearly touched the foundations of the houses that sat directly on the shore. With the wind pushing pounding waves upon them and torrential rainfall, flooding was inevitable.

The Coast Guard and town officials fought through the first gusts of the storm to warn those living on the Front Street to move to safer ground and advise them to wait out the storm with friends or family who lived on the back roads. But many old, stubborn Portuguese with salt water in their veins, remained rooted to where they were, braving the storm from the comfort of their own homes. Women who had men currently out at sea wanted to remain in the houses their fathers, husbands, or ancestors had built, the homes where their children were born, where their homemade jarred preserves were stored, where they expected their husbands to return in only a couple days' time. They, too, refused to move, stoked a fire, and put on a pot of soup. And when the storm blew in their doors, shattered their windows, and flooded their kitchens, they gathered their few most prized possessions, huddled their children toward them, and pressed themselves against the howling wind, pulling shawls and afghans tight over their faces, to find some security in their neighbor's home, hoping it stood tighter to the weather than their own.

Josephine still lived in the small apartment Carlos had taken when he first arrived in Provincetown. It belonged to a whaling captain's widow, one of the last of her kind, Mrs. Francis, a woman in her early sixties and so full of vigor, few doubted she was tougher than even her late husband, having spent much of her married life alone and self-sufficient. After her husband passed away and her children left to make their own lives, the house was too big for her to inhabit alone, so she had a part of it made into its own quarters. The rent money brought her a small income with which to pay the bills, and the companionship of her renters helped to fill the void her departed family had left.

Mrs. Francis's house was on the Front Street on the side of the road opposite from the shoreline houses. Josephine and Carlos' apartment was comprised of two rooms. The larger room had windows facing the street and served as a living room, dining room, and kitchen, with two chairs at the front, one being a rocking chair Carlos had built, a little wooden table in the middle, and a stove and sink setup in the back. A door beside the kitchen area opened into a tiny room that served as a bedroom with a mattress on the floor, a rickety bureau, and a small stool. Seraphine's simple cradle, a hand-me-down from the attic of Mrs. Francis, was also in the bedroom, though he was close to outgrowing it. At three years old, he was in need of a more substantial bed. But Seraphine loved that little, wooden cradle, gripping the sides as he used the momentum of his own body to rock it. Josephine would often brace him with her hands in fear of him flipping over, but he never did no matter how violently the cradle rocked.

Josephine sat in the rocking chair, holding Seraphine, and looking out the window. The glass in the windows rattled, the shutters clapped against the side of the house, and the entire frame of the building strained against the force of the wind. Josephine pulled a shawl tightly around her body to shield herself from the terrible draft, and watched the black sky and pounding rain. Tears began to trickle down her face, but her hand roughly dashed them away. In an effort to maintain her courage and keep her mind off her certainty that her husband was dead, she went to the entrance of Mrs. Francis' side of the building and gave the door a hard knock, which was responded to by a miniature, white curly haired old lady with keen brown eyes and a stern look on her face. But when she saw that it was Josephine, her features softened and she said, "Oh hello, dahlin'. I was afraid you were one of those goddamn officials trying to kick me out of my own house." Mrs. Francis spoke to her in Portuguese because she knew that Josephine hardly spoke a word of English. Mrs. Francis was a second generation native and had grown up speaking Portuguese.

"I just wanted to make sure you were all right. The storm is terrible."

"Oh no. I'm just fine. I've seen storms ten times as bad as this. I'm cured with so much salt, they could stick me in the ground, and I'd come back looking like my old self a hundred years later!" She gave a loud cackling laugh. "Come in, come in. You'll catch a cold standing out there in that drafty hallway." Mrs. Francis went directly to her green armchair by the fire, sat comfortably down, and picked up her knitting as though she hadn't a care in the world. Josephine remained standing.

"Sit down, sit down. Stay awhile. Here, have a cookie." She pushed a plate toward Josephine. "I'm just going to end up eating them all myself, and that wouldn't be too good for this trim, youthful waistline I've got!"

Josephine gave a weak smile and sat down across from Mrs. Francis, placing Seraphine on her knee and sharing a cookie with him. "Ain't he *cunnin*," Mrs. Francis said as she peered over her knitting. "I know a good doctor who I think can fix that skin of his."

"I don't know. I've already tried everyone in town. Nobody seems to be able to come up with something that will help."

"Hmm," Mrs. Francis wrinkled her mouth. "Well, I'm used to it anyhow."

She turned back to her knitting, and Josephine reclined in the chair in silence and looked around the old lady's quarters. Mrs. Francis' room was much cozier than her own apartment with lamps on the tables and artwork and photographs on the wall. There were a few books on a shelf near the fireplace and a ships bell clock on the mantle. Josephine stared down at the top of Seraphine's dark head.

"You don't usually say much, but you're particularly quiet tonight." Mrs. Francis paused because she knew the reason behind this graveness, but was unsure of how to continue. "He could still come back. Stranger things have happened, believe me."

Josephine's eyes remained downcast. "No. He's gone."

Mrs. Francis sighed. She was a straight-shooter and a realist, and she struggled to maintain the façade of one with hope. "I'm not too good at being encouraging, I'm afraid. The truth is you're probably right. I can't sit here and lie to your face. It's just the way this life is. It's the gamble we take. You knew what you were signing up for when you married that man; we all do. We do so in hope that we will never have to spend a sleepless night, that our husbands will always come back home, and that there will always be food on the table, but the fact of the matter is, that never is the case, and we know it. You've just got to be strong. You've got to be self-reliant. All that's left is you and your child, and that is a tragedy that many women are experiencing at this very moment, same as you. You've got to be strong. You've got to be the glue that holds what's left of your family together. That's the life of a seaman's wife . . . a seaman's widow. It ain't pretty, and it ain't fun but you gotta do what you gotta do."

Josephine faced Mrs. Francis trying to blink the tears out of her eyes. "I'll try."

"Trying isn't good enough. You won't survive. You've got to *do* it."

Josephine looked down and nodded her head. "I will."

Mrs. Francis' hard face softened, and she put out her arms. "Come here, dahlin'. Everything will be all right. Don't you worry." Josephine rose from Mrs. Francis' embrace, and said, "I better head back."

"Sure. You be careful now, and come and get me if you need anything. If things get real bad we can go up to my daughter's house on Pleasant Street. She'll let us in . . . I think," Mrs. Francis let out a little chuckle. "But I intend to ride out this storm like every other one that's tried to knock my door down. They haven't budged me yet!"

"Yes," Josephine gave a half-hearted smile, and bowed her head a little as she backed out the door. "Goodnight."

The storm had greatly increased in intensity since she had first gone to Mrs. Francis's. The wind howled like a locomotive and the trees whipped violently from side to side. Every gust made the house shake and rattle until it seemed it would collapse in on itself. She could hear the sand beat against the windows, pitting the glass, and various unidentifiable objects blowing over themselves.

Josephine was just about to head into the bedroom to put Seraphine to sleep when a gust of wind blew so strongly that the sand shattered the already worn down windows. The glass burst, and Josephine, reflexively, flung herself to the floor on top of her child so as to shield him from flying shards of glass with her body and the painfully pitting sand.

She clutched him to her body with one arm, and crawled to the bedroom on her hands and knees, water and sand beating against her by the howling wind that came through the empty window panes and the buckling door. She had no idea that the tidewater had already encroached upon the road, the waves and wind beating the ocean farther onto the land. Josephine was

41

concerned as to whether Mrs. Francis was all right, but it was impossible for her to get over there at this time. Her first concern was to protect her child.

After what seemed like a mile's trek across her living room floor, she finally made it to the bedroom, drenched from the salty spray. Still clutching Seraphine close to her, she pushed the door shut against the rain and wind with all her might. She had to put her full weight against it to get it closed before managing to latch it shut. She quickly placed Seraphine in his cradle, wrapping his blankets snuggly around him and moved toward the bureau to push it in front of the door in order to prevent it from blowing in.

But as she turned away from the cradle, a mighty gust of wind blew, and the door flung in on its hinges. Without any time to react, Josephine was struck hard across the side of the head by the solid wooden door, and fell back, unconscious, onto the floor.

When she finally awoke, she was surrounded by a pool of black water and unaware of how long she had been unconscious. The whole house was flooded with nearly six inches of water, and all the windows and doors were gone. The wind, though, had subsided; the storm was passing.

Josephine quickly sat up, flinching at the splitting pain in her head, but ignored it as she bolted toward the cradle. It was gone! Frantically, she looked around the room, wading through the icy cold water on her hands as knees as though the cradle were hidden in some corner of the empty bedroom. She shakily got to her feet and stumbled to the other room, hoping to find Seraphine there, but the room was cleaned of all of its contents except for Carlos' rocking chair. Panic-stricken, she clumsily waded through the water out the front door of her house, head splitting, her clothes soaked, her dark hair matted against her face and neck.

She could not believe her eyes. Though it was still very dark out, there was light enough to see that Front Street was completely flooded. There was no more beach, no more yard, no more road. The houses, or what was left of them, were surrounded by water, and it was impossible to tell where the harbor ended and the town began. The roofs of the houses had gaping holes in them. Some had no roofs at all. All the houses had broken windows and blown-in doors. The paint had been stripped from the clapboards by the furiously spraying sand, and in spots, the siding was completely gone. There were no signs of yards or fences, and many trees were up-rooted while the rest had broken limbs and had lost all of their leaves. Debris floated past her; metal buckets, tin cans, pieces of wood, children's toys, whatever you could imagine. There was the wreckage of boats that had been blown off their moorings and onto the shore, crushed by the force of the waves.

Josephine, stood in horror, knee-deep in water, overwhelmed by this world that looked nothing like the town she'd known. She began to wade frantically, the water getting deeper with every step, screaming, "Seraphine!" hysterically, tears coursing down her face. How could she find him in all of this? He could be anywhere. He could be out in the middle of the ocean by now or drowned before he even made it to the front door, his little body whisked away with the undertoe. The water was almost up to her waist, and the futility of her effort was evident. She could barely move, she was frozen to the bone, her head was aching so badly she could barely see, and her torn clothes clung to her body. The town was devastated and countless people had died on this day. This storm had left nothing but broken homes, widows, and fatherless children.

Josephine came to a lamp post and clung to it as though it were going to save her life. She rested her head against the cold iron and sobbed. How could God take away her husband and her son with just the fury of one storm? It was bad enough that her husband had perished while trying to provide for his family and begin a new life. Her son, too, only three years old and yet to experience life, had been snatched away, leaving her with nothing. This was what she had left her home for? She was a stranger to this land. She had no friends. She had no home to call her own. She could not speak the language. And now, she did not even have a family. She had nothing.

The pain was too much, and she sunk down, doubling over onto herself, finding a stone wall hidden beneath the water that she rested her weary body on, the water still settling at her thighs. The wind had decreased to only a whisper, a light breath against her face, and the sun began to appear, an eerie yellow color through the departing gray skies.

Josephine was hiding her misery in the palms of her hands when she heard a cry; no, not a cry, a giggle. A child's giggle. She dismissed the sound as a part of her imagination; she had to have had a severe concussion from the door hitting her.

But she heard it again, and this time it was undeniable. She looked up, not seeing where it was coming from, and stood, turning in a circle and scanning the distance around her. The world whirled by in an indistinguishable blur until, finally, her eyes landed on a tree toppled and partly submerged in the water. Caught in between its leveled branches and floating in the flood water was the wooden cradle. Or was it just a wooden box? Josephine was afraid her mind might be playing tricks on her again, but, no, it had to be the cradle. Even such a rough piece of workmanship was better quality than a simple wooden box.

She moved closer to it, afraid to see what was inside. Even if it were the cradle, perhaps it was empty, perhaps the child was dead inside, perhaps the giggle was only the mocking whisper of the receding storm through the branches of the fallen tree. But as she neared it, her senses were alerted by a movement from within, and over the side of cradle, popped Seraphine's unmistakable face with its ruddy cheeks. And he was *giggling*, smiling like a fool, happy as though exhilarated by the thrill of an adventure! He was happy to see his mother, but reacted to her presence as though nothing more than a mere trifle had separated them.

JULIANNE PAPETSAS 2011

Josephine rushed to the tree that held the cradle in its great arms and pulled her child out from the little ark and pressed him to her chest, bursting into another great wave of tears. He was very damp, but there wasn't a scratch on him. She could barely believe her eyes. It was a miracle! How could this child survive being lost in such a storm? It was impossible, but it had happened, and all Josephine could do was lift her tear-stained, bruised face to the clearing sky and accept the deliverance of her child back to her as a heavenly phenomenon.

She cradled Seraphine against her chest as she waded through the water, back to the house to see if Mrs. Francis was all right. The front door to her quarters was gone, like all the rest, and the house was still flooded despite the receding tide. There was no sign of Mrs. Francis in her living room. Her armchair was tipped backward and waterlogged, and the rest of the furniture in the house was broken or toppled.

"Mrs. Francis!" Josephine called, over and over again, fearing the worst. "Mrs. Francis!"

There was no sign of her in the entire house, and Josephine resigned herself to the idea that that the old woman had escaped to her daughter's house, or more likely, was pulled out to sea by the storm, her little, creaking body unable to protect itself from the winds and gushing water. She was about to turn to go out the door when she heard a banging and hollering coming from some unidentifiable place.

"Mrs. Francis? Is it you?"

"Who do you think it is, the mailman? Course it's me." Josephine heard the strong, but muffled voice. "Get me out of here!"

"Where are you?"

"In the closet!"

"The closet?" Josephine followed the banging and finally noticed a door vibrate as though there were a mad bull on the other side trying to bust its way out. There was a large trunk pushed in front of it, so the infuriated kicking and punching was hardly worth the effort.

"I see! Stop banging before you hurt yourself." Josephine bent over, Seraphine in one arm, and used her other to pull on the trunk with all her might. One final bang from inside flung the door open and sent the old woman tumbling out in a heap on the submerged floor. She was disheveled, her white, curly hair matted to her forehead, her wet clothes clinging to her body, but otherwise, she was in one piece.

"Mrs. Francis. Are you okay?"

"Sure I am. Thought I was going to lose my mind, though, if I stayed in that damn closet any longer." She sat her weary body on the trunk and rested her hands on her knees.

"What happened?" Josephine asked concernedly.

"Well, I was just fine, until the wind blew my windows and the door in. I knew I wasn't going to get these crackling old bones up the street to my daughter's house without falling flat on my ass and being sucked into the harbor like a useless old turd. With the way the wind and sand and water were blowing, I knew I would never even make it to your side of the house. So I crawled, pulled, rolled, flopped, whatever you want to call it, to the closet, and closed myself in. I tell ya, it was like there was a thousand horses stampeding right past that door, the way it rattled and shook and the loud banging noises that were going on outside. I've seen a lot in my days, but that had to have been one of the most frightening things I've ever experienced. Don't tell anyone, but I nearly peed my pants! I managed to hold my own in that little place, but it sure was damp and dark and cold as hell. You can bet I was relieved when the storm sounded like it was letting up, but wouldn't you know, after all that, I was trapped in that goddamn room! With no food or water or dry clothes or nothing! I thought I was going to be stuck in there for weeks, and you'd all find me in there, shriveled up like a scully joe. I think I must have dozed off for a bit, 'bout I woke up to hear you calling me, and nice girl, that was the sound of an angel if I ever heard one."

Josephine stood before the woman, bedraggled, her black hair falling in dripping strands over her face and down her shoulders, and her clothes, muddy and torn. A rivulet of blood was coursing down the side of her face, which, when mixed with the salty water, appeared like a profuse amount. A deep blue bruise was forming at the corner of her forehead. She stood, ankle deep in water, since the water level was lowering at last, ever so slightly, with the falling tide, and held the smiling child in her arms, who was, by far, in the best shape of the three of them.

As though noticing for the first time, Mrs. Francis exclaimed, "My lord! What happened to you?"

Josephine, in all the excitement, had forgotten all about the splitting pain in her head, but at the reminder, the aching welled right back up, and she flinched a bit. "I-," she faltered.

"Don't tell me now. There's plenty of time for that. We need to get that head of yours taken care of. Let's see if we can get these tired old bodies up the street to my daughter's house. Assuming it's still there. You think you can make it?"

"Yes. I'm all right"

"Well, I don't know about all right, but good enough to walk up the road for some food and a dry bed."

The two women supported each other with each exhausted step up the flooded road. They were thankful to see that the house was still structurally sound, though aesthetically, it would certainly need some work. Mrs. Francis's son-in-law had already boarded up the broken windows and was outside trying to put the door back in place when the bedraggled trio arrived. He gave an exclamation of happiness and relief when he saw Mrs. Francis and quickly ushered them into the house. It was damp inside from the rain, but still considerably drier than their flooded house down on Front Street. Mrs. Francis' daughter welcomed them, happy to see that her mother was still alive and gave them dry clothes and blankets. She struggled to make a fire with damp wood and a soup with sandy potatoes. It was the best meal they'd ever had.

VI

Meet the Family

The end of the day quickly arrived, and Seraphine had his crew clean up and put away all the tools they had used in an effort to leave the boat organized. There never seemed to be enough hours in the day to get everything done, but he realized, once he looked toward the Town Hall clock, just how tired he was.

He climbed off the boat, onto the dock, and Fluke was sitting there waiting for him, as he was everyday.

Seraphine gave the dog a small smile and a pat on the head in acknowledgement. "Good boy. Let's go home."

Off they went, down the street, the same way by which they had come to the pier, but this time the sun was beginning to set and the sky was turning a brilliant orange and magenta in the direction of home.

Seraphine unlatched the gate and stepped into his wife's yard, already filled with budding flowers. Once inside the door, he slowly took off his boots and left them on the mat, always conscious not to dirty his wife's clean floors. He did not announce his arrival but walked into the kitchen-dining room to find Mary standing in front of a pot at the stove, stirring it vigorously.

She turned at the sound of his step and gave him a warm smile. "Ready for some soup?"

"Yep. Kale's my favorite."

"Well, it better be because I made a *panalla* big enough we'll be eating it all week." Seraphine went to the sink and thoroughly scrubbed his hands and halfway up his arms, then dried them on a dishrag.

"How was your day?" Mary asked indifferently, turning back to her soup, since she knew what little elaboration she was going to get from him. Posing the question was an unnecessary formality that seemed the better alternative to just sitting in silence. She'd been married to Seraphine for twenty years and her father had been a fisherman. She was very familiar with the work done on a fishing boat.

"Fine," Seraphine responded

"Get much done?" she continued to stir and pulled a loaf of Portuguese bread out of a drawer.

"Not enough." Seraphine was sitting at the table attentively watching what she was doing. He loved watching his wife go about her daily tasks. He enjoyed the way she wiped her greasy hands on her apron, the way her fingers traveled deftly over the needles and yarn of her knitting, and the way her hair fell into her face while sweeping the floor. She casually went about her chores never seeming to notice the way she held him captivated.

"You always say that. How will you ever finish anything if you never get enough done?"

"I guess I'll just have to work harder."

"I guess so!" She looked over her shoulder and gave him a grin. After all these years, Seraphine was still taken aback by her beauty. She was the most attractive woman in town, and that was no exaggeration. She was beautiful, not simply because she was his, but because she truly was. When they were young, every eligible bachelor wanted her for his girl. Every girl wanted to look just like her. Every parent was bitter that she stole all the attention from their daughters or that she had their sons tripping over themselves only to be treated with indifference. She had the sort of beauty that could win her the world if she dared to use it.

Mary had always had a stunning figure in her youth, and even now, in her early forties and having given birth to five children, she was still lovely to behold. She had filled out a bit across the middle, but her legs and work-worn fingers were still slender, as was her youthful neck and shoulders. Her face was round with a straight nose and large blue eyes framed by thick, dark lashes that were longer and fuller than any fake ones that could be bought at the drug store. Her blue eyes were her crowning attribute, since any color other than brown was an extreme rarity among the Portuguese. They contrasted well with her mahogany hair that lit up with cherry highlights whenever it came in contact with the sun. It was thick and was cut to shoulder length in the style of the time, the natural wave eliminating any need for a permanent, and her broad, white, straight-toothed smile added warmth and charm to her exquisite appearance.

Seraphine cherished her above all things, and it was not simply because she was beautiful but because such a woman could love him. She could have had her pick of any man in town, but she chose him, and though he had once struggled with self-doubt as to why she did this, he respected her all the more for it. A woman like Mary was rare, and not a single day went by that he took her for granted.

"All right, dinner's just about finished. Let me call the kids." Mary wiped her hands on her apron one final time and walked to the foot of the stairs. "Dinner's ready! Come down now. Wash your hands first!"

There was a rumbling of bodies rolling off beds, feet beating on the floor, shut text books, and the clattering of toys. The two youngest children came barreling down the stairs first. Small and dark, Joseph was nine and Sally was seven. Sally was a pretty little girl with long, brown hair that reached to the middle of her back and a moon-shaped face with two, round dark brown eyes that held wisdom beyond their years. Joseph's facial features were very much the same with the button nose of childhood and smooth, olive skin. He was built like a dory plug, short and chubby, barely taller than his younger sister and twice as broad.

"Ma, what's for dinner? I'm starvin'!" Joseph cried.

"Kale soup."

"Mmm. I'm gonna eat the whole pot myself!" He puffed out his belly and slapped it a couple of times. Joseph was always the epitome of enthusiasm and his mother's greatest champion.

Sally stood beside her brother, hands clasped behind her back. Sally tended to be quiet and shy, but she was tough and never took any lip from anyone, a result of always hanging around her older brother. When circumstances necessitated it, she could have as big a mouth as anybody.

"You hungry too, Miss Sally?" Mary leaned down so they were face to face.

"Mhm," she said softly.

"Good. Now what do you say to your father?"

"Hi, Dad!" they both cried in unison, their faces lighting up as if they hadn't even noticed him sitting at the table. They each went over and gave him a hug and then sat at their places at the table. Mary smiled to herself. If only that childhood affection lasted forever.

Next came Sarah, the fifteen year old. She came down the stairs carefully, hardly making a sound, and patted her father on the shoulder as she came into the dining room.

"Hi, Dad. How was work today?"

"Good, good." Sarah was already taller than Mary, and while the other children tended to favor their mother, she was undeniably her father's daughter with a prominent nose and a heavy brow. Her thick hair was long and almost black in color, and her deep brown eyes were large and perceptive.

"Do you need help with anything, Ma?"

"Not really. You can set the table, I suppose, and take out butter for the bread."

Sarah, silently, went about her business, while Jimmy, the oldest, came into the room. He was seventeen and a sturdy young man, broad shouldered with a handsome face and dark hair cropped close to his head.

"Did you get your homework done, Jimmy?" Mary asked without turning from the stove.

"Just about."

"You know you have to keep your grades up if you want to stay on the football team."

"I know. I know. I'm just so sick of school."

"Well, it's almost over and you'll be back on the boat with your father. We'll see just how sick of school you are then!"

Jimmy didn't comment and sat in the seat closest to his father, giving him a nod of acknowledgement. He wasn't much more vocal than Seraphine. All the children were atypically quiet, except for the fifth and final child who favored the other extreme.

"Jimmy, where's Tommy?" Mary asked, already assuming the worst.

"He was reading a comic book when I left the room."

"Comic book? That boy should be doing his homework!" She walked exasperatedly to the bottom of the stairs, and called up again. "Tom! Get down here! Now! Dinner is on the table!" She stormed back to the stove, picked up the pot, and dropped it heavily on the wooden table, some of its contents splattering out. Then she sat down at the other head, across from Seraphine, and nodded for the family to begin filling their bowls. By the time everyone had served themselves, Tommy still had not come down.

"Tom! Get down here this instant! Dinner is getting cold. You want to spoil it for everyone?" Mary yelled from her seat.

When there was still no response, she looked at Jimmy and said, "Go get your brother."

Jimmy sighed, and grudgingly stood from his seat, slowly going up the stairs. There was a yell, and Jimmy came back down the stairs, as calm and collectedly as he had gone up with Tommy flung over his shoulder, kicking and flailing violently. Jimmy dropped Tommy right by his chair, like a sack of potatoes, and then went over and sat back in his own seat. Tommy glared at him and then sat down.

He was a skinny kid with a tanned face and arms from being outside all the time. He always had dirt under his nails and holes in his clothes. He was almost thirteen and was adverse to anything that was healthy or safe—a mischievous boy from sun up to sun down.

"Ugh, kale soup again!" He scrunched up his nose in disgust at the soggy green leaves floating in the yellow broth.

"Be quiet. You love kale soup," Mary said dismissively.

"No I don't!"

"Since when?"

"Since we started eating it three times a week." He crossed his arms over his chest and scowled.

"Well, it's what we're having for dinner three times this week, too, so eat it or starve, 'bout you ain't getting anything else."

Joseph and Jimmy gave subtle scoffs, while the rest acted as though they heard nothing. Sarah stopped Joseph's hands as he tried to pick out pieces of linguica with his fingers and pop them into his mouth. Tommy sulked in between throwing digs back and forth with Jimmy, while Mary tried to mediate. Sally chewed on a hunk of well-buttered bread and sipped at her glass of milk, so big for her that she had to hold it tight between two hands, then went to wipe her mouth on the back of her arm before being stopped by Mary thrusting her napkin at her. Jimmy went back for seconds while Tommy snapped, "Jeeze, Jimmy, eat it all, why dontcha?"

"What do you care? You don't like it anyway."

"Boys, will you cut it out? There's plenty to go around," Mary interjected.

"Maybe if you eat enough, Jimmy, we won't have to have it for dinner tomorrow."

"Oh we're having it for dinner tomorrow, don't you worry, Tommy. Whatever Jimmy eats comes out of your ration," Mary said without a glimmer of irony on her face.

"What!" Tommy exclaimed as though a great injustice had been exercised upon him. Joseph giggled through a mouthful of potato and threatened to throw a piece of bread at Tom which Sarah quickly snatched out of his raised hand and put back on the table by his bowl. Tommy kicked Jimmy under the table, and Jimmy raised a hand like he was going to smack him until a glare from Mary halted him halfway through the motion.

Seraphine observed his family's antics, an audience more than a player at his own dinner table. He enjoyed watching the way his family interacted, having such little time to spend with them that he sat memorizing their faces and gestures, the way they moved and chewed their food, what they said, how they talked, and their various expressions. He always studied them as though it was the last time he would ever see them. He ran his index finger along a crack in the solid wood table, traced the line back and forth, as was his habit, the wood around the crack growing shiny and worn from the oil and friction of his hands. Fluke sat under the table, his chin resting on Seraphine's foot. The room was warm with a soft, dim light, and the food was good as usual. It all made life worth living.

Seraphine was snapped from his reverie by the loud clap of Mary slapping her hand on the table. "That goddamn bird!" Mary cried.

"What is it?" Sarah asked.

"That seagull's been on the roof all day banging away. It must be trying to open an oyster or something. I swear, if I could shoot a gun, I'd go up there and shoot that *cadeesh*!"

"What's it doing on our roof?" Joseph queried.

"It's your father's fault. He's always feeding the gluttons! Them and those goddamn pigeons. The rats of the sky!"

Seraphine straightened in his chair, a surprised look on his face.

"Don't even try to deny it," Mary continued. "I know you're always out there throwing out food for the animals."

Seraphine shrugged. It was the truth. There was nothing to argue with nor was he going to stop. "It'll be gone soon."

"Easy for you to say. You haven't been in the house all day going crazy from it."

When dinner was cleared and the children sent to their rooms to get cleaned up and finish their schoolwork, Seraphine went to the living room and played his violin, while sitting in his father's rocking chair by the fireplace. It was his only hobby, and he was quite good at it for someone with no formal training, though nobody, outside of the family or a passerby on the road, ever got to hear him. His violin was simple with a dull, honey finish and a bow strung with horsehair. He stored the instrument in a black leather case that was cracking from age. Mary once bought Seraphine a new case as a gift, but he refused to use it, keeping his violin in the old one and using the new case to store tackle. He played a slow, soft melody that washed over the listener like the sound of waves lapping on the shore, while Mary sat in a chair opposite him, knitting and listening.

He put his violin away and went to bed at his usual early hour, on heels of the sun's departure. He climbed up the steep staircase in his stockinged feet, changed out of his work clothes, and crawled into bed for the night, pulling a blanket up to his chest and closing his eyes to prepare for another day of work.

VII

The Floater House

Mary stood in the narrow strip of yard that ran along the side of her house, a giant basket of laundry at her feet and a long line stretched above her head. With a household of seven, it seemed she was always doing laundry, the children getting their play clothes soiled after just one day's use and always in need of having clean, pressed clothes for school. She looked forward to the summer when she could tuck the good clothing away to be used only on Sundays and let the kids run around in their play clothes (or hardly any clothes at all), getting as dirty as they wished.

Jimmy would be back on the *Halcyon*, working with his father, which meant, thank God, more talk at the dinner table. Sometimes the silence was agonizing, and as much as fishing talk bored her, having spent her whole life listening to it, Mary preferred it to the sound of crickets chirping through meals. Working together gave Jimmy and Seraphine plenty to talk about and Mary would do her best to urge them on, posing more questions just to get them using those weak vocal cords. Mary loved her husband and son more than anything, but having to carry conversations with them was a tiring feat. She always noticed an increased energy in Seraphine when Jimmy was working with him, always having something new to show him and teach him. He enjoyed the companionship and comraderie, and though Jimmy still had a great deal to learn, they made an excellent team.

Mary would have Sarah home to help her with chores and looking after the younger children, thank God for that too, though she tried not to burden Sarah too much. She was, after all, a teenager, and an introverted one at that. While Jimmy was quiet simply out of sheer lack of desire to talk, Sarah was quiet out of shyness, and this made Mary nervous because Sarah didn't seem to have as many friends as the average teenager nor the desire to go out and have fun. She liked staying inside and reading, was a good student, and never argued against helping Mary around the house. Thus, Mary tried not to ask for help too often and tried to encourage Sarah to enjoy herself now and then, an opportunity never offered to Mary by her own mother.

But then there were the younger children, particularly Tommy, who made summer life for Mary considerably more difficult. It seemed the house was constantly in disarray, and as soon as she picked up one toy or swept one track of sand off the floor, there was another in its place. Sally and Joseph were, for the most part, very well-behaved children, but they were young and needed extra attention. Tommy was another story entirely, and she knew that he was responsible for the gray hairs that she kept carefully concealed with bottles of dye from Adams. He was a good kid, but he never listened, and this absolutely infuriated her. Everything with him was an argument, like he didn't believe a word she said, and would do just the opposite of what she asked just to spite her. The good thing was that he was usually out gallivanting, causing God-knows-what trouble, but at least he wasn't home doing it. Mary cringed at the thought of what poor soul had fallen into the path of the incorrigible Tom.

No, no, that was an exaggeration. Mary scolded herself for the frustrated thoughts running through her head as she hung Tommy's tattered play clothes on the line for drying. She was too hard on him. Tommy never meant any harm; he was just a *cadeeshka*, a harmless trouble maker. He didn't like being constrained in any fashion, and thus he squirmed behind his desk at school, he squirmed at the dinner table, and he squirmed at church. The only way to avoid his discomfort was to let him go uninhibited, and when that happened, he was happy, and everybody else was relieved.

Mary let out a pleased sigh of relief as she clipped on the final clothespin, the final sock. The beds were made, the house was cleaned, and dinner was prepared, ready to be popped in the oven. The younger children had just gotten home from one of their final days of school, and were upstairs changing out of their good clothes. Sarah and Jimmy wouldn't get back from school until later, especially Jimmy who was probably going to go off with some girl before his afternoons would have to be spent with his father. As if she didn't know he was up to such things!

Mary could finally get to her own afternoon plan which was to do some long-anticipated work in her garden. She had an old dress on, even older than the ones she wore when she simply cleaned, and some flat shoes that she usually kicked off. She had a small spade and fork, a metal bucket of soil, several packets of seeds, and a tin watering can. She had already done the boring work of clearing out all the dead leaves and last year's annuals and was ready to do some intensive planting.

As she was about to plunge her hands into the cold earth, Mary heard heavy, trotting footsteps approaching and the sound of crunching branches and leaves. Remaining on her knees, she peeked over the fence and looked down the road. She had already guessed that it was Tommy, naturally, thirty minutes later than his siblings. She watched as he rushed into the neighbors' hedges bouncing off their bushes, body blocking imaginary opponents. Mary shook her head. It took Tommy three times as long to get anywhere because every bush he saw, he had to run into it, preparing himself for the junior high football team next year.

As he clattered and stumbled through the gate, Mary said, "Ready for the football team?"

"Close. Real close," he responded breathlessly and hurried straight into the house.

Mary just laughed to herself and shook her head.

She was pleased to see the bulbs she planted last year sprouting. The daffodils were already passing, and she'd have tulips soon enough. Her perennials were all turning green again—lilies, irises, black-eyed susans, rhododendrons, hostas, and so on—and the lilacs and cherry blossoms were budding. Even though the sun was stronger in the front yard, she kept her vegetable garden behind the house full of kale, herbs, beans, tomatoes, and carrots. She preferred the entrance to her house to be aesthetically pleasing with bursts of colorful flowers as opposed to green, leafy vegetable plants. She dug her fingers into the soil, enjoying the feeling of the damp earth beneath her nails and not thinking about the time she would have later cleaning it all out.

It hardly seemed a moment since he had arrived home when Tommy came bolting out the door, letting it slam behind him in a whirlwind of energy.

"See ya later, Ma!" he called without a falter in his stride.

"Where are you going?" She looked up.

"I'm going to play baseball up at the field with Art, Ronny, and Jiggy." They were a few of the neighborhood boys that Mary was very familiar with. "Oh yeah, and I think Johnny's coming too."

"Which Johnny?"

"Ah, I don't know his last name. Calhoun or something weird like that."

"Who is he?"

"Just a summer kid."

"A summer kid here already? Doesn't he still have school?" Mary asked with genuine curiosity.

"Nah. He goes to one of those fancy private schools for smart kids," Tommy said shrugging his shoulders a bit, and not looking overly concerned. "I think they get done really early."

"Huh."

"I guess they're so smart they don't need to stay in class for very long. Can I go now?" Tom's tone quickly changed from cooperative to impatient.

"Oh, all right. Have a good time. Stay out of trouble."

"Sure, Ma," he responded, hardly listening to her, and sprinted out the gate.

"Be back in time for dinner!" she called, though he was already two houses down the road. She knew he hadn't heard her, and if he had, he had selectively blocked it out.

Mary sighed and went back to her work, digging little holes and placing a couple geranium seeds in each one. She mixed some new, rich soil from her compost heap out back and seaweed from the beach with the mineral depleted dirt of the front yard. From years of planting, the ground was more soil than sand, but she still liked to make sure her plants were well nourished. She deadheaded the flowers that were already growing and trimmed wayward branches so they wouldn't poke one of the children in the eye. She moved small stones to create borders around her flower beds and gave the new seeds some fresh water.

There was another clatter of the door, and she heard Joseph call. "Ma! I'm bored. Can I go play?"

"Of course you can. Did you clean your room?"

"Yep."

"Well, fine then. The afternoon is yours."

"Can I go play with Tommy and his friends?" Mary did not like the idea of Joseph getting involved with that unruly gang of boys. They were nice kids, but a bit too old for Joseph to be hanging around with. Plus, she knew Tommy would be mortified at having his little brother shadowing him all afternoon.

"Why don't you take Sally with you to the beach, instead? Go right in front of the house here, so I can keep an eye on you two."

"Aw, Ma. Do I hafta? Why do I always have to watch Sally?"

"Because you're a responsible, young gentleman. Now take her with you. It's low tide. See what kinds of treasures you can find."

"Yeah, let's go, Joe." Sally was looking through the screen of the storm door.

"Fine," Joseph gave in without any further argument, and the two of them went off across the street together to see what kind of adventures they could find on the beach.

Mary smiled. All was quiet now, and she could finish her gardening in peace. Eventually, she leaned back underneath the mid-sized cherry tree that grew in the corner of the yard and looked up at the house.

The yard was small, enclosed by a white, picket fence on the front and green hedges on the side that she made sure to keep neatly trimmed. A narrow, brick walkway went from the gate on the sidewalk to the three brick steps and stoop that led to the front door.

The house was a small Cape style, sided with painted white clapboard and black shutters, as was the trend with many of the houses in town. Within the front door was the steep staircase to the upstairs, while the living room was to the left and the kitchen/dining room was to the right. The floors were made out of dark, aged mahogany, and the walls were covered with whitewashed wainscoting. The baseboard and casings were left natural so that they matched the dark color of the floor, and the old, drafty windows were eight-paned.

There was a coal stove in the kitchen that used to be their primary cooking appliance until they updated to a modern kitchen with a real range and even an icebox! The stove was still used for heat on very cold nights, though the narrow brick fireplace in the living room was the main source of heat. In the back of the house, Mary and Seraphine had recently put in a bathroom with running water and flushing toilets, a large improvement over outhouse system they'd had before, frigid on winter nights and not nearly as sanitary. It was, possibly the nicest room in the house with its wainscoted walls, porcelain, claw footed tub, and pedestal sink. The changes recently made to the house and the modern conveniences they added were a reflection of the prosperous year of fruitful catches Seraphine had recently had.

On the second floor of the house were the bedrooms. To the front of the house was Seraphine and Mary's bedroom with windows that overlooked the harbor. Toward the back of the house were the two bedrooms in which the children slept. Sarah, Joseph, and Sally shared the room on the left and Jimmy and Tommy shared the room on the right, each with windows that looked onto the next door neighbors' houses, hardly more than five yards away.

In the open ceilings, one could see the thick wooden beams that supported the roof. They were nailed into place by hand-chiseled wooden pegs, not the galvanized nails carpenters used these days, since the house was very old. The basement consisted of a round cellar that had once been used to hang and store fishing tackle, and the supports that held the house on its foundation were made from the masts of old ships since lumber was very scarce on this windblown, sandy peninsula. If one were to kick the packed dirt at the bottom of the cellar away, right below the surface would be revealed a shiny green bottle. And if one were to continue digging one would find many more bottles in an array of shapes, sizes, and colors, an old bottle dump left behind by one of the house's previous owners.

What made this house different from other buildings in the town was that it was a "Floater House." Long ago, this house had been part of a small colony of about sixty buildings on the Point, clear across the harbor from where it was now, but storms had threatened to wash the little village away. The most reasonable solution to this problem was for the inhabitants of the Point to simply float their houses on rafts, made of wrecking barrels used to float sunken ships to the surface, across the harbor to the more protected stretch of land on which they now existed. The houses floated across the harbor, since Provincetown seamen did not see their homes as stationary but able to move and change and *float* just like their vessels. Legend had it that women stayed inside their homes and cooked dinner as they were floating across the harbor, seeming not to notice the difference between being in a grounded house or a floating one. These "Floaters" came to make up a large portion of the West End.

Mary was proud to live in a house that had made such a unique journey. It had a history and a character that none but the other floaters could say the same for. It was unique and charming in its simplicity with its modest trim and little, red chimney poking out of the roof. Mary had no desire for marble floors, smoothly plastered walls, and luxurious carpeting. Her house was built from wood that had traversed the globe. The salt of the sea and the sand of the shore were imbedded in every board and shingle. The house had withstood gales, hurricanes, and Nor'easters, unshakably rooted to the land that harbored it, but also capable of picking up and moving should necessity require it to do so. No West Coast mansion could replace her unassuming home which had a personality and a vitality of a very different kind.

Off the back right corner of the house was a shed where Seraphine stored most of his fishing equipment. Nets, trawls, hooks, and ropes all hung from the ceiling and walls. Paints, tar, brushes, nails, and various tools lined the floor and some rickety shelves Seraphine had built. He always kept a dory in there that he would work on from time to time, making sure it was sealed to water and weather before putting it on the boat and bringing another damaged one in. Mildewed tarps were messily draped over wooden crates and barrels, and colorful buoys hung, here and there, along the walls, in between everything else.

Every time Mary went in the shed, she felt like she was stepping onto the boat itself. She loved the way the shed smelled, not overpoweringly fishy or damp, but smelling of paint and salty wood, a rich, natural, clean smell. It smelled of sea and the labors of a hard working man, and Mary could see a story in every tool and every tarp that sat quietly in its place. These ordinary objects had seen and done things that were extraordinary, and they waited patiently to be taken out to sea for yet another adventure, bored with the quiet peace of the shed and recounting their stories with each other as they anticipated their time to go.

Mary felt, in the silence, she could hear what these objects said, she could read, smell, feel their stories, things that her husband never told. Mary would run her hand along the hull of the dory Seraphine had just brought in from the ship, lying bottom up on a couple of wooden horses, and feel the rough, corroding surface. She could see the cracks, the buckled pieces of wood, the chipped paint, the rusting nails, the rough barnacles and dried out seaweed. This boat had gone so far, so much farther than she had ever gone or would ever go, and she wondered at its story.

The shade felt nice after the hot sun beating on her back. Mary rubbed her hand over the little patch of grass she lounged on and admired her handiwork. This yard was her own, as well as this house on this little patch of land. She had found a little spot in the world that she cultivated and made her own. While others longed to go on excursions, see distant lands, go on adventures, and travel the world, she was content to remain rooted where she was. Not the sea, nor the sky, nor anywhere else in the world did she belong besides here in this yard, her house, her home, her town, and she vowed she would never leave.

She looked at the other houses clustered around hers like a family and toward the harbor at the shimmering flats. From here the world did not seem so great. The thin peninsula cradled the town and its harbor, creating a self-sufficient little world. The people here did not fear the ocean though the town teetered on the edge, just inches from being swallowed whole. The ocean was their friend, their livelihood, and in many ways, their protector. It separated them, almost completely, from the rest of the world with only one direction in which one could go by land.

People came from all over to experience this town at the end of the world, and they were welcomed, warmly, by the townsfolk. They were invited to enjoy the town, the cool water and sandy beaches, the brilliant sunsets and pleasant hospitality. The visitors were free to do what they wanted, and in no way did the townsfolk interfere, though the town belonged to them.

The people who came and loved the town enough to stay were labeled by the natives as "washashores." They were welcomed into the community, but unless one lived here from the first breath to the last, one never quite belonged. It was difficult for some to accept that they did not have the same innate attachment to the land that the natives seemed to have, and though they may have spent the majority of their lives in the town, they could never quite acquire this attachment or shake the label of "washashore".

But despite the fact they were not natives, the washashores had as much a right to this town as the natives, and many appreciated it more. The two groups of people lived together, for the most part, in harmony, except of course in the cases when a washashore angered a native neighbor by tearing down *his* fence or cutting down *his* tree—in this case, the native would have no qualms with using the washashore's non-native status as ammunition. But all disputes, native versus washashore, native versus native, washashore versus washashore, typically blew over, and everyone continued loving the land for their own reasons. One group realized how fortunate they were to have found this unique land of such unparalleled beauty and was grateful to be a part of it. The other group simply had it in their blood.

VIII

Mary

Mary was born and bred in Provincetown, never having ventured outside of its borders and never intending to. Her father was a successful sea captain, one of the only Portuguese immigrants of his time to own and captain his own boat. He was a proud, stubborn man, but he liked a good joke as well. His name in the old country had been Ferdinand, but most people knew him as Glory.

Mary spent the majority of her time helping her crotchety mother do chores around the house and take care of her six younger siblings. She had a small group of girlfriends with whom she was occasionally permitted by her mother to get ice cream at the pharmacy, but she was never very close to the girls in town, since, deep down, she could sense that they all envied her and was certain that even her closest friends said cruel things about her when she was not around. For this reason, her attractiveness was more a burden than a blessing. Though she had an animated, outgoing personality that made her character enjoyable, she was never quite sure what motivated acquaintances to be around her. The girls were either exaggeratedly friendly to her or downright ignored her, the young men were all polite and tripped over each other to have the opportunity to dance with her at dances at the Masonic Lodge, and the mothers would greet her curtly because they were bitter that she was more attractive than their own, and because, other than her physical splendor, nobody had a good reason to resent her.

This all bothered her immensely because she was not vain, snooty, conceited, or arrogant. She did not gloat in her beautiful features, and she did all she could to be nice to people. She worked hard and never flaunted herself so as to make other girls jealous. She just lived her life as averagely as any other girl in the town, but she still could not seem to shake gawking eyes and cold daggers, and it made her feel terribly alone.

Her favorite part of each day was when her mother would send her down to the wharf to give her father his lunch. She loved being able to get out of that dark, little house, away from her demanding mother and screaming siblings, and into the warm sunshine and fresh air. She strolled down the street, smiling, and greeting people she knew since most found her charming despite her petty peers and their mothers.

Everyday she would bring her father his lunch and everyday his crew would tease and banter with her, most of them having known her since she was a little girl. They were like a second family to her. They respected Glory, and they loved his daughter, and she knew that they would look out for her as they would one of their own.

"Mary! What did you make for lunch today?" John Blarmey yelled down to her.

"Nothing you'd be interested in!"

"Aw, don't you know I love your cookin'?"

"Yeah, Mary, what'd you bring us?" Rickie Cabbage asked, though, he knew there was nothing for them.

"Rickie, if I had to feed all you fellas, there'd be no more food left in the house! Now where's my father?"

"In the wheelhouse. I'll get him," Blarmey said. "Hey, Cap'! Special delivery!"

Only a minute later, Glory came onto the deck of the boat and stepped onto the wharf, slowly, not gracefully, but with perfect ease. He was a large man, nearly six feet tall, and burly. His face was covered with a thick, salt and peppered beard and mustache, and his nose was wide and round.

His eyes looked out from under his cap like two, tiny, round pieces of coal, and he was dressed in a heavy oilskin jacket and pants, even though it was a warm day, the cuffs of the pants tucked into tall boots.

"Mary! What are you doing here?" he cried ironically in a heavy Portuguese tongue.

"Funny," she dryly dismissed him in English. "Here's your lunch." She shoved the sack of food toward him, and he chuckled as he took it from her, as though he had just cracked the greatest joke he'd ever heard. For years Glory had been studying English but failed to speak more than a few broken phrases, though he understood it quite well.

"Thank you. Everything all right at the house?"

"As good as it can be." Mary did not try to conceal her rolling eyes.

"Your mother running you ragged, I suppose?"

"Just the usual."

"Well, a little hard work never hurt anybody. Makes you stronger." He was not scolding her, just trying to give her a bit of support, knowing how domineering Philomena could be.

"I know. I just wish she didn't have to yell so much," Mary sighed, frustrated.

"Well, just think. One day you'll have your own children to abuse."

"Can't wait!" And they both laughed.

They said their goodbyes, and Glory walked slowly back to the wheelhouse, already taking a peek at what his lunch consisted of. Giving "hmph!" of satisfaction, he closed the bag back up, and stepped inside.

Mary was given enthusiastic good-byes from all the crew before she left—all except for one. Everyday she came, while the others took it as an opportunity for a short break and some amusing conversation, this one man kept his head down, busy with his work, steadfast and diligent, but so much as to seem strange. Mary had never seen anybody work so hard, especially not while she was around.

Mary was intrigued by this young man. He was a bit older than her, but clearly the youngest man on the crew. He never spoke to her or to anybody, from what she could tell, and though he always pretended to be too busy at his work to notice her, she saw, from the corner of her eye, him glance up quickly at her and then back down before she could catch him. Mary did catch him, though, and smiled at his shyness.

One day, as she was joking with her father's men, she turned to Seraphine who was up on the cabin, patching the roof, and said, "And what about you? Are you going to be polite and say hello to me today?"

He looked up, startled, his face red, though she knew not whether this was from blushing or from something else. "Good afternoon," he nodded courteously, though his voice was barely loud enough to hear. He went straight back to his work, and Mary did not bother to further trouble the man. But that night at dinner, Mary decided to ask her father about the mysterious laborer who appeared to have no desire to give her the time of day.

"Dad, who is that man that works for you?" Mary asked in English. Glory always insisted she speak English in his presence.

"Who?" Glory asked in Portuguese.

"The quiet one. The one that barely says a word."

"Oh, Seraphine!" Glory cried. "He's a local boy. Lived here his whole life."

"Really? I've never seen him before—well, except for on the *Halcyon*, of course."

"Hm. I'm surprised. He lives right up the street. He's actually been working for me for quite a while now. Started before the war when he was only a teenager, and then started right back up again when the war ended."

"He fought in the war?"

"Yep. The navy. I'm pretty sure he was one of the first to enlist."

"He seems too quiet to fight in the navy. He acts kind of," Mary searched for an appropriate word, "meek."

"Meek? Oh no! That boy is tough as steel. One hell of a worker too. He's got skills like you wouldn't believe, and what he doesn't know, he learns quickly. That young man's a fine fisherman. He can sense where the fish are almost as well as I can, and he brings those trawling lines in with a fish on each hook every time."

"Now you're exaggerating," Mary feigned skepticism, though she hung on her father's every word. "But he sure does seem to keep himself busy."

"Well, I think it's all he really knows how to do—work that is. You know, he was orphaned at a very young age."

"Orphaned?"

"Yep. His father died in the gale of 1898 when Seraphine was just a little fella, and for many years, he had to take care of his mother especially after she got sick. He was just a little kid, but he had to go out and work doing, oh I don't know, paper routes and soda jerking and sweeping houses and whatever else he could find to do at such a young age. His mother died—of pneumonia or tuberculosis or something like that—when he was only, oh, twelve or thirteen. I don't think he has any family here, or many friends, seems to me, so he lives in a tiny studio just a few doors up the street from us."

"Poor guy," Mary shook her head solemnly.

"I wouldn't worry too much. He seems to be doing just fine for himself," her father said as he rose to retire to bed. He responded to her questions with a tone of ambivalence, leading Mary to believe that he was ignorant to her interest in Seraphine, though as he headed up the stairs, he chuckled slyly to himself.

Outside the little house on Conant Street slowly walked a quiet, lonely figure. His jacket was pulled tightly around him and his fishing cap down low over his eyes. He paused by the great lilac bush in the front yard, as he did most evenings, and listened to the clatter of plates, Philomena giving orders, hollering children, and the sound of Glory's fist angrily slam against the wooden table followed by a string of Portuguese curses. The sky showed its last hints of orange through the deep purple and blue of rapidly approaching nightfall, and he stood in semi-darkness, gazing at the warm yellow light glowing through the windows and smelling the scent of a home cooked meal.

Seraphine stayed there little more than a moment before continuing up the road to a crumbling house just a few doors down and climbed up the rickety outdoor stairs to his small, studio apartment on the top floor to the back of the house. It was one room, with a tiny bed in the corner, one flattened pillow and a thin, gray, wool blanket folded at the end. He had a small, iron stove that provided both heat and a place to cook, and he had a sink but had to pump the water outside. There was no bathroom either, but there was an outhouse in the back yard, and he kept a washbasin near his bed with a comb and razor. In the center of the room there was a square, wooden table with one chair at it, and in another corner there was the humble yet sturdy, wooden rocking chair his father had built. Besides these few belongings—a couple pairs of pants, two shirts, a hat, a jacket, a pair of boots and a pair of shoes, one of each a bowl, plate, mug, and eating utensils, and one pot and frying pan—the room was bare. There was no art on the walls, no books, no little artifacts that add personality to a space, not even a mirror. He lived the most meager life possible.

There was only one other object in the room besides his bare necessities, and that was his violin, which he had found in the wall of an old house he had helped to tear down and rebuild when he was only an adolescent. After eating a simple meal of beans and potatoes—on good days he would cook fish he had brought back with him from the wharf at the persuasion of the Captain—Seraphine would sit in his rocking chair, looking out his small window, down the street toward Mary's house, and play on his violin. The sound rose from it, soft and melancholy, and the melody filled the room with the voice of a lonely, unknown soul.

But the soul was not alone because Mary felt it. She could feel that soul move through her bones, as she heard the sound come in her open bedroom window. She rose out of bed, and kneeled down, folding her arms on the window casing, and leaning her head out into the warm night. She heard this beautiful music every night, and every night, she sat by her window and listened intently until it stopped, prompting her to crawl back into bed and go to sleep. Mary knew it had to be Seraphine who played this violin every night. He had to speak somehow.

One night as Seraphine stood by the lilac bush, Mary came racing out the front door with a bucket of table scraps in her hand to be dumped in the compost heap out back. He quickly hid himself beside the bush so that she could not see him, his heart racing with fear that she may discover him and think he was some kind of lunatic, loitering outside her home. "Maybe I am," he thought to himself. "Maybe I am crazy." When she had gone back inside, he quietly stole down the road, trying to suppress his nervous breathing.

He spent every morning anxiously anticipating the time when Mary would come to the wharf to bring her father lunch and always took note of her plain but pretty housedress, her black flats, and the gray cardigan she wore on cooler days. The breeze blew mahogany strands of hair into her face, her hair cut in a bob so it hung to just above her shoulders. When he felt it safe to get a good look at her, he was stricken by her clear, blue eyes. He had never seen a Portuguese girl with blue eyes before. Then he turned back to his work, putting his face down before she could get a good look at him and feeling ashamed and guilty for looking so longingly at something so beautiful.

It was a warm evening in the middle of the summer. Seraphine was departing from his bush—the house was particularly quiet tonight—and was heading up the road, when he heard a voice behind him call, "Seraphine!" He froze in sudden terror.

"Seraphine. That is you, isn't it?" Mary knew very well that it was him.

He swallowed hard. "Yes," he said, his low, deep voice still managing to carry to Mary's ears.

"Well, aren't you going to say good evening to me? You know, my feelings are a bit hurt. I'm beginning to think you don't like me at all."

"Oh no!" he cried as he turned around to face her, and then catching himself, he returned to his typical monotone and said, "I—I like you—very much."

"Well, that's a relief," Mary said with a twinge of laughter in her voice, her eyes still trained uwaveringly on him. "Beautiful evening, isn't it?"

"Yes, very."

"Would you like to take a walk?" Mary realized she was going to have to do all the work with Seraphine, while most men would be jumping out of their shoes to take her by the hand and lead her away.

"Walk? Why—no. I mean, I can't. I—I have some work to do." He quickly searched for some excuse, and weakly puffed himself up with rehearsed confidence and self-importance that was far from convincing.

"What kind of work? Violin playing?" Mary said challengingly, a smug look on her face.

Seraphine looked quickly down in embarrassment.

"No," her voice softened. She took a step toward him, holding up her hands as though to stop him before clasping them demurely in front of her. "I love your music. It's beautiful. I listen every night from out my window."

"You do?" he looked up surprised.

"Yes. I just wish that you would play for *me* sometime."

There was a long pause as they looked expectantly at each other. It was the first time, Mary noted, that Seraphine had looked her directly in the eyes. "I always play for you," he said at last, sounding and appearing much bolder than Mary ever would have thought possible of him. The air she'd been holding in her lungs in anticipation released through her nose in a short burst, and her shoulders relaxed. Mary walked slowly toward him, putting out her hand and linking her arm with his.

"Let's go for a walk."

Seraphine looked down at the slender hand gripping his arm and then faced forward to walk with her up the road. They found a low wall to sit on, arms still linked, and said little as they looked up at the nearly black sky, spotted with white dots of stars, and felt at once overwhelmed and empowered by the immensity of the universe. They listened to rustling trees and smelled the air, fragrant with salt and flowers as they rubbed the soles of their shoes against the rough pavement. Seraphine and Mary did this every night from that moment on, quickly overcoming their shyness with each other. Mary had no fear of telling him good-humored, animated stories about her nagging mother, her bratty siblings, and her trials and tribulations of the day, and Seraphine sat quietly and listened, though he was no longer timid in her presence. He, at times, would tell her a tale of his childhood, or the war, or life on a fishing boat, stories he never told to anybody. Mary broke down the wall that he had so carefully built around himself, but on the other side, there was still little more than silence. Being in each others' presence was enough. No words needed to be said.

Their nightly visits continued for months. Twice Mary had tried to coax Seraphine into going with her to a dance at the Masonic Lodge, but he declined, and she knew better than to try to force him. They were content to simply be alone with each other, and no dances or dinners or nights on the town were needed to make the two fall in love. On the *Halcyon*, Seraphine spoke and laughed more, he worked with more vigor and energy, and his face was no longer hidden in whatever job he was doing.

"What's this? The quiet man speaks!" the shipmates would holler and laugh, pleased to finally be able to communicate with him and integrate him into their socialization.

"What brought your voice back, Seraphine?" Blarmey laughed.

"I got a thought," Bill Buckets said.

"What's that, Buckets?" Blarmey coaxed him along.

"I think it's a woman."

"A woman!" Blarmey guffawed and pretended to nearly fall over the side of the boat. "Who's the lucky lady, Serry?" But Seraphine just smiled at them and kept working. He never told, and they never suspected, all except for Glory. He was nobody's fool. He had not missed his daughter's absence every evening at the very same time, the subtle glances and smiles she would flash at Seraphine when she brought his lunch, the way she whistled while she did her chores and didn't even argue with her mother. The two's change in demeanor was far too coincidental to go unnoticed.

But like Seraphine, he never said anything, and always pretended not to notice, realizing that they would both be more comfortable if the relationship were kept a secret. He had no objection to a union between the two and did nothing to discourage it. He knew that Seraphine was an honorable man and a hard worker. He knew that he would love his daughter and provide for her better than any other man in the town could, and he was thankful that Mary was wise enough to love him. Seraphine was a hell of a lot better than those other bums hanging around town who would certainly take her for granted.

One day on the wharf, a large pleasure boat came to unload passengers from the city. A thin man with a gentlemanly mustache stepped off the vessel. He was dressed in a tailored black suit, with a black fedora, black patent leather shoes, and the gold chain of a pocket watch hanging out of his vest. He stood with a stylish cane and walked toward the *Halcyon* without its assistance.

"Might I enlist one of your men to help me with my luggage?" he appealed to the captain.

"Sure, gov'na." Glory summoned Seraphine over, and Seraphine willingly went to fulfill the request.

As he lifted the cumbersome wood and iron trunk, laden with what felt like a hundred pounds of bricks, one of the handles on it broke, and it crashed to the dock with a with a loud clank. The latch broke and the lid flew open, spilling the contents all over the pier—mostly books, some clothing, and other odds and ends that Seraphine was picking up too quickly to note. He was on his hands and knees in an instant, apologizing for the mishap and piling everything back into the open trunk as efficiently as he could.

The gentleman cried at the sight of his belongings strewn upon the wharf and glared down at Seraphine, his face red with fury. "You ignorant Portuguese. I can't trust you to do a damn thing. Take your dirty hands off of my belongings and get your homely face over to your stinking piles of fish where you belong."

Seraphine dropped the items in his hands and stood up slowly. He straightened himself to his maximum height so that he seemed to be looking down at the man who was actually a bit taller than him. He glared at him with his piercing eyes, and the gentleman's angry face dropped at the unexpected shock of this Portuguese man's humbling presence.

Seraphine did not say a word, but turned and walked proudly back to the boat, letting the man pick up his belongings himself. Everyone on the dock watched him foolishly gather the scattered possessions, and no one budged to help him after witnessing the insult he had dealt on Seraphine as well as the entire Portuguese race.

Seraphine went back to his work as his shipmates gave him reinforcing slaps on the back and told him he was twice the man that city bastard was. Seraphine could not care less about that other man, but he still had an unsettled feeling. As he walked past the wheelhouse, he caught his reflection in one of the windows, and a great sense of guilt came over him. His crooked nose, his ruddy face, the crowsfeet already creasing the corners of his eyes—he truly was a homely man. How could Mary, so beautiful, tolerate such a face? She could have anyone she wanted; why would she choose such an ugly man who stunk of fish? He looked down at his rough, blackened hands and was certain that they must feel no better than sandpaper rubbed against her soft skin. These hands worked and toiled but he still had no money, no home, and no education—he had little to offer Mary and nothing that she deserved.

That night, he took the long way home so as not to pass her house.

It was seven o'clock, their usual time, and Mary was surprised not to find Seraphine waiting for her beside the lilac bush and even more surprised to find him not coming up the street. She stood in the yard for a good while, finally sitting on the stone wall, her sweater wrapped tightly around her, wondering where he was when he had never yet missed a night. She waited for a full hour and then went sadly inside up the stairs to bed. She sat by the window listening for the violin music that never played and feared that something bad had happened to him. It was a quiet lonely night, and Mary's guts churned.

"Did Seraphine tell you he had any plans last night?" she asked her father the next morning, throwing all caution to the wind.

"No, he didn't say anything. Not that he ever does." Glory shrugged.

"Did he seem all right?" she asked.

"Same as usual. He had a run-in with some uppity bastard yesterday, but something like that wouldn't bother Seraphine. I don't really think he gives a damn what anybody thinks."

Mary just stood there, finding no solution to her problem, and when she later brought her father his lunch, Seraphine was nowhere to be seen working around the *Halcyon*. That night she waited again, but he did not arrive. "Dad," she asked her father again, "was Seraphine at work today?"

"Of course. He's never missed a day."

Mary's head lowered, and she walked silently up to bed.

Night after night she waited, but he never came, and everyday she went to the *Halcyon*, he had mysteriously disappeared. Mary had never been the crying sort, but finally her disappointment became so unbearable that she rested her face against her knees and felt her skirt become damp with her tears. Seraphine must not love her anymore. But why didn't he just tell her? Why would he allow her to sit here feeling so miserable without any idea of why he left?

Two weeks had passed before it finally occurred to her to walk the only other route she knew of to get to Seraphine's house in the hope of intercepting him. She had to know the truth. As she walked briskly up the narrow road, she saw his figure in the distance, slowly walking home. She hurried on tiptoes until she was only a short distance behind him.

"Seraphine," her voice cracked. She saw him startle and then put his head down, keeping his back to her.

She took a few steps closer. "Seraphine. Where have you been?" She tried to make her voice sound angry, but there was no hiding that it was hoarse with sadness as she choked back tears.

He did not respond; just kept looking at the ground.

"Please, Seraphine speak to me." Mary was frustrated now. "You just disappeared! I had no idea what happened. I've missed you so much, but now I just feel like a fool! If you didn't want me anymore, you could have at least *told* me."

There was still silence, but she saw his shoulders shaking. She took another cautious step closer.

"Look at me, Seraphine. See how much you've hurt me." Tears were now coursing down her face. "I've been so lonely without you."

It seemed that ages passed before he finally turned around, his face wilted with sorrow.

"Please, tell me what's *wrong*. Don't you love me anymore?"

His voice, dry, like the rustle of fall leaves, whispered, "What do you want with me?"

"I—I love you. You know that."

He shook his head in doubt.

"What? Do you think I'm *lying?*"

"You deserve better."

"Better than what?" Mary asked bewildered and infuriated.

"Better than me."

"You? But I don't want anybody else. Don't you see that? How can I do better when you are the only man I want?" She was practically yelling at him.

"But look at me!" he cried.

"Is that what this is all about?" A look of relief and disbelief came over her face. "Do you really think that the way you look is important to me?"

She gave a bit of a laugh. "I have never met such a vain fisherman before! Do you honestly think that the world revolves around how you look?"

Seraphine sighed and looked at his hands. "I just—I want you to be happy."

"But *you* make me happy, Seraphine," Mary said as she finally closed the gap between them. "There is nobody in this world I would rather be with than you. Seraphine, you give yourself such little credit. You don't realize how special you are." She placed her hand on his jaw and lifted his face to meet hers. "I love you for how hard you work, your kindness, your gentleness. I love you for something I can't explain. I can't see it, I can't touch it, but I feel it inside. Every time I look at you, I know there is someone much more than a man standing in front of me. I don't know what it is. I can't put my finger on it, but it is like I am just a few steps closer to God."

Seraphine's eyes were filled with tears, but he couldn't hide them from her because she had his hands clenched in a strong grip. Finally, he wrapped his arms around her and pulled her to him, kissing the side of her face, and they stayed like that, their tears running down each others shoulders. He breathed in the smell of her hair, and she clung to his rough jacket, her face against his shoulder. The air was cool and dry and filled with the earthy autumnal scent of burning leaves.

They were married just a week later.

IX

Tommy and the Summer Kid

Finally, school was dismissed for the summer holiday. No more homework, no more being trapped indoors, and no more stiff, starched, uncomfortable clothes . . . except on Sundays.

Tommy, his *coompard*, Art, and the summer kid, Johnny Calhoun, stormed down the street toward the moors. They sped along, not in any particular rush, but with the vigor of boys setting themselves upon some adventure. Tommy and Art moved agilely and quickly through the familiar streets, while Johnny Calhoun struggled to keep up, unaware of where they were going or what they were up to but joining after his mother urged him to get out and meet some local children. They were going to be in Provincetown all summer until school began, and Johnny must find ways to get out of the house.

The two dark boys did not pay much attention to blonde, freckle-faced Johnny Calhoun.

"Hey guys," Johnny said breathlessly, tripping behind them. "Where are we going?"

"The breakwater," Tommy said without turning from his forward march.

"Where's that?

"It's by the moors."

"What's those?"

"You don't know what the moors are?" Art said disgustedly. "Haven't you ever been anywhere?"

"Oh, I have been to lots of places," Johnny said proudly.

"Well, if you haven't been to the moors, you haven't been anywhere," Art snipped, deflating Johnny's pride.

"So, what *is* the breakwater?" Johnny asked, unsatisfied by the responses he was getting.

"Will you shut your trap?" Art said. "By the time I'm done explaining it, we're gonna be there already."

Art lived up the street from Tommy in a little, ramshackle house with his mother and father. He had a stiff, brown face that always seemed to be frowning and dark hair that was worn long and shaggy from lack of a timely cutting. Art's father was a veteran of the Great War, and he claimed he'd been stationed down in the trenches of France. But the trenches didn't seem to bother him much as long as he could use them as an excuse for his excessive drinking. The townsfolk didn't place much credence in his stories, but nicknamed him "Frenchie". Art's mother was a frail lady with weak, fragile bones. The family was nearly destitute, or as most folks would say, "they didn't have a pot to piss in or a window to throw it out of." Frenchie was a clammer, but he was so inebriated the majority of the time that he never seemed to fill his bucket.

Tommy had known Art since they were very young, being neighbors and all, and they were in the same grade in school, but Mary was always a bit skeptical about her son hanging out with such a boy. Her sympathy for his mother was the only reason she tolerated their friendship as much as she did. "That poor woman with that drunken bastard for a husband and that gallivanting, foul mouthed child of hers!" she would cry and bless herself. "It's a wonder it's her bones deteriorating and not her sanity."

Johnny Calhoun was of another breed entirely, and neither he nor his mother knew just what he was getting himself into hanging out with this gang. He was a short, chubby boy with pale features that couldn't handle the sun very well. All summer the local kids would giggle because his skin color never changed from lobster red even though he spent most of the day sitting in the shade on the covered porch of his family's summer home. He lived with his mother, who was an artist, and his father who was a banker, or a lawyer, or something like that. All the townsfolk knew was that they had a lot of money and could afford to be on vacation three months out of the year.

Poor Johnny was a studious little boy who went to private school in the fall and preferred to stay inside and read than go running around getting his nice white shirt muddy or his knees skinned. He always did as his mother said and was never getting himself into scrapes as these boys were.

Shortly, they were at the moors and the breakwater.

"Oh, *now* I know what the moors are. It's those big, grassy things."

"Big, grassy things?" Tommy remarked. "You talk like you've never seen them before."

"Well, I haven't. Only when I come here."

"You mean you don't have moors where you live?"

"No, no beaches either."

"No beaches!" Tommy nearly jumped out of his skin from shock. "Then where do you go swimmin'?"

"There are lots of ponds and some really rich people have pools."

"I thought *you* was rich. How come you ain't got a pool?" Art asked.

"I'm not rich. My parents have quite a bit of money, but not as much as some as some of my friends' parents," Johnny said shrugging his shoulders. The others shook their heads and began to weave through the beach grass and sandy shoulder of the road, down onto the banks of the moors.

It was about half tide and the water was not very high around the tufts of grass that formed the moors that stretched far to the sand dunes in the distance. The moors were one vast maze of grass, sand, and water. Sometimes the water was up to the very tips of the grass so that they stuck just above the surface of the water like the face of a man with a five o'clock shadow. Other times, the beds were completely dry, revealing circles of soggy sand. It was a salt marsh teaming with life, and the long breakwater, made of its massive stones that stretched the distance from the town to the Point, separated the moors from the harbor.

With their first step from the shore into the shallow water, Johnny's legs were sucked down into soft mud up to the middle of his calves. He leapt backwards onto the hard sand as quickly as the suction of the mud would allow him.

"It's quicksand!" he cried.

"It ain't quicksand you dumbbell," Tommy said. "All you gotta do is move fast. A little mud isn't gonna hurt you."

As Johnny eased into the center of the pool where the firmer sand was, Art added, "Yeah, what you really gotta worry about is those damn fiddler crabs. One of those suckers will pinch your big toe right off."

"Oh dear!" Johnny cried. "Then I don't want to go in there."

"Ah, don't be such a sissy," Tommy scolded.

Johnny continued, but took every step with extreme caution until they made it to the side of the breakwater. When the tide was not high, the rocks appeared tall and daunting, at least to Johnny, for the other boys had seen them plenty of times. Water rushed in between them at a steady flow, and as Johnny followed his friends out farther, waist deep in water and looking at the rocks in awe, he suddenly stepped onto nothing, and went down into water over his head. He scrambled and splashed back to the surface, frantic from the surprise, and sputtering because his swimming skills were not top notch.

"Hey, what happened, Johnny, old boy? You get some water in your nose?" Art mocked him.

"I guess I should've warned you about those holes by the rocks." Tommy looked on without making any sign of giving aid.

Johnny blew water out of his nose and wiped it from his eyes. He waded to higher ground, looking like a drowned rat, and was even more cautious with every step he took. He clung to the sides of the rocks, wary of further hidden holes. His face was pressed so close to the breakwater, it was easy for him to note the creatures growing along the side of the rocks and asked, "Hey, you can eat these, can't you?" pointing to the blue black mussels.

"Yeah, you can eat them, but we ain't here to pick mussels," Tommy responded.

"Well, what is it we're here for? Swimming? It seems like a good place."

"Yeah, it's good, until the tide goes out. The current becomes so strong the water'll pull you right under and out to sea. So I wouldn't suggest you go bringing your foolish summer-kid-behind down here after the tide has changed or else the whole town's gonna be looking for you, and you're just gonna be stranded out at New Beach like a beached whale." After Tommy finally finished giving his considerate guidance, he answered the true nature of the boy's question, "But we aren't here to go swimming. We're here to catch rats."

"Rats?!" Johnny gasped.

"Yeah, they live in the rocks."

"In the rocks?" Johnny gulped.

"Yeah, they're the size of cats."

"They're that *big?!*" he shrieked and turned as though to run off.

"Oh come on," Art grabbed him by the back of his shirt. "There ain't nothin' to worry about. Tommy's got his slingshot."

Johnny looked at the Y-shaped piece of wood without confidence, and slunk along beside the boys, subjecting himself to the destiny of becoming rat food. He stayed at what he hoped was a safe distance while he watched Tommy and Art jab sticks into the rocks. They stuck them in at the sides, and they climbed to the top and stuck the sticks downwards. Frustrated, Tommy began to shoot rocks into the crevices, but seeing how rocks were scarce, he began to rip mussels off the rocks and shoot those. They didn't fly very well, though, due to their irregular shape, and Tommy eventually gave up.

"I can't believe this. We've been trying to force rats out for hours," (it had only been about twenty minutes), "and we still haven't found any. Let's face it, rats only come out when there's a storm during high tide."

Johnny's whole body filled with relief, but he did his best to look as disappointed as the other two. "I won't come within a mile of this place when there's a storm," Johnny thought to himself, and he never did, not even on cloudy days.

"*Now* what are we gonna do?" Art flung himself down on a smooth rock, his arms crossed upon his chest sulkingly.

"I don't know," Tom responded, lying on his back and looking blankly up at the crystal blue sky. Above him circled a little bird, and he quickly sat up. "I got an idea! Let's go tern egg hunting!"

"Yeah!" Art cried, and leaped up, beckoning Johnny to follow. "Come on, Summer Kid, let's go." Johnny figured that searching for eggs couldn't be all that bad; he did it every year in the churchyard on Easter.

They ran clear across the breakwater, the whole way to the other side, jumping from stone to stone with needlessly grandiose leaps. Once they got to the sand, they began to traipse through the beach grass, where the tide doesn't reach, in search of eggs.

Now, anybody who knows anything about terns realizes that these birds are extremely protective of their eggs. As soon as they see a person within ten yards of their nests, they circle and prepare for attack. Tom and Art knew better than anyone that this was the nature of the terns. They'd disturbed nests many times before, nearly being pecked to death and loving every painful minute of it. They could care less about the eggs. The amusement was all in the challenge.

Tom and Art went step by step through the grass, until they saw a tern begin to fly over them. "Look! There's one overhead. We must be close." Tom was exhilarated by the thrill of the hunt, but he noticed that Johnny was standing safely on the beach, outside the line of beach grass. "Hey, Johnny. Come on. Help us get some tern eggs."

"I—I'd rather not," Johnny clasped his hands before him.

"Well, why not?"

"The terns never did anything to bother me. I think it would be best if I didn't bother them."

"Your loss, then, Summer Kid," Art snapped and kept going. "Hey look I found-" he said, but before he could finish his statement, a tern came diving down and pecked him on the shoulder, only to swoop back up to safety. Then he dove again and again. Art covered his head with his arms and ran to the beach, away from the nest he had practically stepped on.

There were three of them now, an army of terns taking turns diving and pecking at him.

"Ah!" he screeched. "Ah! Eee! Ow! Ooch! Ouch! You sonsofbitches!" He ran in circles, he flung himself on the ground in a fetal position, he dove into the water, he waved his arms and attempted to bat them away. It was utterly hopeless. The birds were merciless.

"You guys! Help me! Help! Ouch! Do something! Ah! Don't just stand there you lazy sacks of shit! Do—Ow!"

All this time, Tommy and Johnny were rolling over with laughter, staying a safe distance away so as not to be attacked as well. But, beginning to feel bad for Art, Tommy finally said, "Art, come on! There's only one thing we can do."

"Wh-what? Ouch! What?!"

"Run!" And off the boys ran along the shore as fast as their legs could carry them. They ran and ran and ran until they were as far away from the nest as they could get before falling into the water at the Point. They'd lost the terns, finally. The birds would not abandon their nest for some foolish kids. It was not about principal with them.

"Oh man. Those bastards," Art gasped. They were all out of breath. Art had red marks all over him. In some places the terns had even drawn blood, and other places they'd put tiny holes in his clothing. "I've never been attacked so bad in my life."

The boys began to make the long trek back across the peninsula home, Art swearing and cursing all the way about the birds, among many other things. Finally, Johnny felt the need to interject.

"Gee wiz, Art, you sure swear a lot. My mother says it's a sin to curse."

"Yeah? Well my ma says it's just fine," Art sneered.

"Yeah, so does mine," Tommy chimed in, though Mary had no tolerance for her children cursing in any way.

They were nearly to the Front Street when Tommy cried, "Hey! It's almost three o'clock. That's the Boston boat coming into the harbor over there."

Art immediately knew what Tommy meant, but Johnny asked, "What's at three o'clock?"

"We gotta go jump off the wharf," Tommy said picking up his pace.

"Off the wharf? But doesn't that hurt?"

"Only if you do a belly flop," Tommy replied.

"Or land on your head at low tide," Art added, and chuckled at his morbid sense of humor.

"But what for?"

"A. It's fun, and B. It's good money. The tourists coming off the boat throw money into the water, and we dive down and get it. Sometimes, if we do a fancy trick, they give us twice the amount once we get back to the top."

"Yeah, Buggy Burns once climbed to the top of a fishing boat mast and jumped off. He got a whole buck for that!" Art enthusiastically added.

Johnny stopped, red in the face from running and from sunburn. His clothes were wet and salty, he was starving, and he was downright exhausted.

"What is it?" the two turned to look at him, surprised to see him anchored to his spot in the middle of the sidewalk (which Johnny could not believe the other boys never used), his arms lifeless at his sides and his beet red face drooping from emotional and physical discomfort.

"I can't do it anymore, guys. You two just have to go along without me. It's been fun, but I'm ready to go home. Maybe another day." Without even saying goodbye, he turned and hobbled back toward his house, no intention of ever jumping off that wharf or hunting for rats and tern eggs again. He'd had his fill and was ready for a bath, a good meal prepared by his mum, and a comfy chair with *Robinson Crusoe* in his hands and his cat in his lap. That was his idea of a good time.

The other boys shrugged and continued toward the wharf at a rapid clip without saying goodbye.

Five houses later, Tommy said, "He's not so bad."

"Yeah, for a summer kid," Art added, and the subject was pursued no further.

Once they'd gotten to the wharf, the passengers were already coming off the boat. There were kids in a skiff floating beside the steam liner, waving to people as they got off, while other kids were perched on the edge of the wharf, prepared to go diving for loose change.

People who had been before knew the drill, and others were so impressed that they willingly joined in the fun too. They chucked change into the harbor, and watched as the children dove from the pier into the water with perfect form, the light color of their bodies gliding under the water's greenish brown surface. Some would submerge themselves multiple times, trying not to miss anything. The kids climbed back up the ladder to the wharf and spit out the mouthfuls of change they had retrieved while under water, coins that had been jammed into their cheeks like squirrels hoarding nuts in order to keep their hands free for swimming.

Many times a youngster would go up to a gentleman and say, "What kind of dive would you like to see today, sir?"

"Cannonball," the gentleman would say.

"That'll be ten cents, then," the boy would respond and then do his dive and come back up with an open palm and dripping wet.

"For twenty-five cents, Ma'am, I'll do a flip right off of this here wharf."

And naturally, the woman would willingly pay to see the feat accomplished.

On an average day, a youngster could make upwards of a dollar, but on a great day, some kids were rich with several dollars worth of coins filling their pockets. The best swimmers and divers made the most money, because they could get to the coins first when they were underwater, and they could do the most expensive tricks.

The money they earned from diving off the wharf could purchase them an ice cream soda or frappe at Adams Pharmacy, an ice cream cone, a bag of penny candy, or sometimes even a coveted toy like a yo-yo, marbles, or jacks. Some kids who were very smart and economical saved their money until they could buy something like a bike or a new baseball mitt. But these types of children were quite a rarity.

Tommy and Art knew all of the kids down at the wharf from school or from the neighborhood, socializing as kids do between making their candy money. By the time they were both sufficiently waterlogged, their pockets were full of coins, and they were ready to spend it.

"Tommy, I could really go for a coffee frappe at Adams," Art said.

"Yeah, me too," but then Tommy realized what time it was. It was getting close to dinner. "Um, maybe I better not."

"What do you mean? That money's gonna burn a hole in your pocket."

"I know, but last time my Ma gave me such hell for coming home with a full stomach, I think it might be better if I wait til tomorrow."

"Tomorrow? But it ain't even dinner yet."

"I know, but my hide still hurts. I better give it a rest."

"Well, all right then. I suppose I'll see you tomorrow."

"Yeah, see you then," and off Tom walked down the road toward home, his money jingling in his pocket.

X

Vovo

Every Sunday morning Mary had her entire family dress in their best clothes to go to church. A devout Catholic, she never missed a Sunday service unless one of her children was extremely ill. The house was a flurry of energy as the children struggled with their clothes, Sally missing the ribbon to her dress, Joseph unable to tie his tie properly, and Tommy with a spot of jelly on his white shirt. Mary barely had time to get herself ready, but Sarah helped as best she could between trying to get a brush through her own hair and washing her face. Jimmy, naturally, was no help at all as he sat at the table chewing on toast, appearing not to notice the younger ones running circles around him, while Seraphine sulked nearly as much as Tommy did over going to church. He'd never been one for organized religion.

Seraphine's mother had been more religious than even Mary was, but she had died when he was young, and he never had anybody to force him to go to church every Sunday or to say his prayers before meals and at bedtime. It wasn't that Seraphine didn't believe in God (he wasn't sure what he believed in besides hard work), but he was sure that if there were a God, He would not strike Seraphine down for missing a church service. Still, he went to appease his wife.

The family, as ready as they were going to be, paraded out the door and walked up the Front Street and then up the hill to the church.

It was a beautiful church, white with a gray door and steeple. It sat on a shallow hill with a lawn in front, and the stained glass windows that

93

lined the walls depicted biblical scenes with intricate detail. They heard the bells toll 11:00 and organ music beginning to play as they went up the front walk. Church was the only event the family was ever late for, and they were consistent about it, primarily because it was the only function they all went to together, scrubbed and dressed in something other than work or play clothes. As devout as Mary was, she did not grumble about being late, because walking through a packed church seconds before the service was to begin was the perfect opportunity to draw attention to Mary's exquisitely coifed appearance. She wore a simple, black cotton dress with red flowers on it, patent leather heels, and a black shawl even though it was the middle of summer. Her hair was done up gracefully, and she even put on a bit of rouge. Sunday morning mass was the only time most people saw her, especially so well put together. Every housewife deserves a moment of glory.

Mary made sure each person genuflected before sliding into the pew, and then reverently watched the mass unfold on the altar in front of the mural of Saint Peter walking on water that took up the entire back wall.

The church was roasting on that sweltering summer morning, and the women fanned themselves with *Today's Missal*s, and some even thought to bring Chinese paper fans. The children tugged on their ties and dress shirts and squirmed around in their seats until they received reprimanding smacks from their mothers. The rustle of clothing persisted throughout the entire service as people gradually shed layers, and sounds of sneezes, yawns, and crying babies filled the stifling air.

Mary's attention was trained on the altar, as a good Catholic's should, until she heard a snort beside her. Mary turned to see Seraphine sitting with his eyes closed and his chin on his chest. He was snoring! She kicked him in the ankle, and he straightened himself up, confused for a second as to where he was and then disappointed once he found out. Mary shot Tommy a vicious look that halted his foot that had been repeatedly kicking the back of the pew in front of him, and she lifted Joseph by his collar into sitting position just as he was falling asleep, sprawled on the pew.

Mass was finally over, and everybody filed out of the church, wilted in their Sunday best. They huddled into groups on the lawn and said hello to each other, asked about health and weather, and other such small talk. It was a good time to socialize, but Seraphine and the children were itching to go home, so they went.

Once in the door, Mary had Tommy, Joseph, and Sally change out of their best clothes into their *second* best clothes. They had to go visit their grandmother, and Mary did not want her mother to accuse her of letting her children run around looking like slobs. At the same time, she did not want them to go out in their good clothes, because God knows what messes they could get into along the way.

"Can't I put my real clothes on, Ma?" Tom complained once he was given his first order.

"Those are your real clothes," Mary frowned at him.

"No, my comfortable clothes. The ones that don't make me feel like I'm being strangled." He was on the cusp of whining.

"Not yet. You have to visit Vovo first."

Tom's eyes widened in horror, and his chest seized as though he'd stopped breathing.

"Do I hafta?"

"Oh come on, it's not that bad."

"Yes, it is," Joseph came to his brother's assistance after overhearing the conversation. "She's mean."

"And she smells funny," Sally chimed in.

Mary sighed knowingly. "You still have to go, and I don't want to hear anymore complaining from you. She's a lonely old lady and your grandmother. She's not even well enough to leave the house to go to church. The least you can do is go visit her."

"Well why don't *you* go?" Tom challenged.

"Because I have to cook." Mary was ready with an excuse.

"Why can't Sarah go?" Joseph whined.

"Because she has to help me."

"What about Jimmy?" Tom asked.

"Because he's helping your father."

"Do what? Sleep on the couch?" Tommy quipped.

"Now don't get *sassy* with me," Mary pointed at him. "Yesterday I made an apple pie and some soup. You three take this to her, and you be nice to her, and you show her what little *dahlin's* you are." Tom rolled his eyes, and Joseph followed his cue.

Once they had reluctantly changed, they took the packages from their mother and went out of the house, Fluke joining them for the sake of a pleasant jaunt. Down the sidewalk they went, single file, Tom in the lead, walking briskly, and Joseph close behind taking long steps so as to keep up. Sally was never within a few yards of them, scurrying as best she could, while Fluke either trotted beside boys or behind Sally, bringing up the rear.

The group saw their mother's childhood home with dread. It sat close to the road, in dire need of repair. The white paint on the shingles was peeling off, and in areas, the white was green from mold. The wall that separated the yard from the street was crumbling, as was the cement walkway, the slabs cracked and filled in with weeds. A similar growth had sprung out of the chimney that jutted crookedly from the swaying roof, most likely caused by birds dropping seeds on the decaying bricks. The windows were foggy with a thick film, and the yard was unruly, with weedy grass and wild bushes. The window boxes were unplanted, and even a shutter was hanging off its hinge. The only nice part of the entire scene was the lush, green lilac tree in the front yard. As bad as the house looked from the outside, the children knew that what lay in store for them inside was much worse, and they apprehensively walked up to the side entry. Tommy lifted his hand and gave a couple knocks on the storm door.

"Who is it?" a loud, screeching voice hollered from inside as though thoroughly inconvenienced by the presence of visitors.

At the sound of her voice, Fluke cowered down, his tail between his legs, and his ears pulled back.

"It's us," Tommy called back, his voice quavering. "Your grandchildren."

"Tom, Joseph, and Sally," Joe added, trying to be brave.

There was no response but an irritated huff and the creak of a chair. The children heard the ominous sound of a cane clumping and Vovo's slippered feet shuffling along the wood floor. Fluke cowered a little lower before turning and trotting down the street toward home.

"Scaredy cat," Joseph muttered in Fluke's direction.

The children heard the click of the latch before a withered old hand opened the door and a wrinkled old face stuck its nose out. She sniffed a bit and looked down at the uneasy children. "What's all this?"

"Pie and soup. Ma made it," Tommy answered.

"What'd she think I'd want that for?" the old lady snapped, but motioned for them to come in. "Put it on the table in the kitchen," she commanded as she eased herself into a rocking chair that creaked at each roll of its rockers.

The three kids cringed at the damp, moldy, old lady smell, mixed with what was probably the odor of cabbage soup.

"Smells like farts," Joseph whispered to Tommy.

"Shhh, quiet!" Tom retorted under his breath while giving Joseph a severe look.

"Sit down. Sit, sit. Don't stand their gawking at me like a bunch of boiled scrod."

The children squeezed themselves onto an undersized loveseat that was rigid and uncomfortable but what Vavo claimed to be a valuable antique and thus her primary piece of furniture. They waited uneasily for her to say something, but she just stared them down with her black, beady eyes, rocking ever so slowly, back and forth, back and forth, creak, crick, creak, an afghan in her lap.

Reaching for something to say, Tommy asked Vovo how her health was.

"My health? How do you think it is? I sit alone in this dingy house day in and day out. I'm in vile shape. I can't even walk."

"I'm sure it will get better, Vovo," Sally said barely above a whisper.

"Better?" Vovo let out a roaring cackle revealing a few crooked teeth in her dark, gaping mouth. She wiped some spit off her face as she continued, "This body's all shot to hell. Just put me out of my misery now."

The children squirmed in their seats.

"Do you still knit and crochet?" Tommy asked hoping to hit on a safer subject.

"Please," she snarled, "with rheumatism like I've got! No knit stockings for you folks this Christmas, if that's why you're asking." The children were somewhat relieved by this for they hated those socks. They were thick and itchy and in ugly colors.

There was more silence. Not a sound besides the creaking chair and not a change in the old lady's appearance besides the dribble of drool that was oozing out the corner of her mouth and down her jowls.

"Have you done anything fun lately, Vovo?" Joseph gave one last, halfhearted attempt at creating conversation.

"I throw rocks at cats from out my window," she snipped with bitter sarcasm. "I scare off the neighborhood children. I call the cops on people illegally parked outside my window. What do you think I do penned up in this house all day? Nothing! And I like it too, so you can save your pity for somebody else."

"We don't pity you, Vovo."

"Oh you don't, do you? What, you think I have it so good here? Since your cursed grandfather died, I don't have anybody to talk to . . ." ("Or yell at," Tom thought.") ". . . And your mother won't come visit me but every two weeks. Nobody talks to me. I'm rotting here. Put me in my grave."

The children did not quite know how to react to this. They wanted to say something, but were scared of what her response might be. They just sat there, their shoulders pressed tightly against each other. Vovo continued to look at them, her sharp gaze unwavering.

"Want a cookie?" she asked, unexpectedly, and almost sounding nice.

"Sure," Joseph said, pleased to have the opportunity to break the silence and do something.

"They're in the jar on the counter. One for each of you, and don't let me see you sneaking a crumb more." The children no longer wanted the cookies after this statement, but went anyway to get out of the room. They brought their cookies back to their seat, and began to nibble on the soft, stale cookies. As usual, the humidity of the summer had wreaked havoc upon the food, making it soggy, but the children could tell that these cookies had been sitting around for a very long time. Their consistency wasn't simply due to the weather. They nibbled, politely, unable to stomach too much of a cookie that nauseatingly resembled the scent of mothballs in flavor. The old woman rocked back and forth and back and forth, never removing her eyes from them.

"So how's your father?"

"He's fine," Tommy replied.

"Run that boat into the ground yet, has he?"

"Course not, Vovo!" Sally was indignant at the jibe at her father. "He's a great fisherman and a great captain. He takes the best care of that boat. Better than anybody!"

"I'm sure. Well, it's easy to make ends meet when everything is just handed to you for free."

"Dad didn't get nothing for free," Tommy said, his eyes narrowed. "He got it because Vovoo wanted to give it to him when he died."

"And I've never understood why. That man had two sons, why'd he leave it to a stranger?"

"Dad's not a stranger. He's married to Ma," Joe argued.

"Besides," Tommy added, "Uncle Zookie and Uncle Finx don't fish. Zookie clams and Finx runs a convenience store. They never worked a day on that boat!"

"Hush, hush. No need to get all worked up, kids. I was just making sure the boat's still running, that's all. If it weren't for your grandfather leaving that boat to your father and mother, you kids wouldn't have two nickels to rub together."

Tommy stood up. He couldn't bear it any longer. He was angry and red in the face and had stuffed the rest of his stale cookie in between the cushions of the antique settee. The rest of the children followed his lead.

"Well, we have to get going, Vovo. Ma wanted us to be back in time for dinner."

"It's not even two o'clock," she seemed surprised.

"Um, well, we have to pick some things up for her at the general store."

"Yeah, but we'll see you soon," Joseph chimed in.

"If I'm not dead by then," she grumbled.

"Enjoy your pie, Vovo," Tommy said as they turned to leave.

"What kind is it, apple? Better not have too much nutmeg in it. I hate nutmeg," but the children did not answer the question. They just waved and said goodbye and stepped out the door.

As they walked down the street they heaved great sighs of relief that their weekly torture was finished. How they hated Sundays! Visting Vovo was the worst kind of penance.

Once they got to the corner, they found Fluke waiting for them. "Thanks a lot, Fluke. Some help you are," Tommy said bitterly. The troop marched back home trying to force the memory of their grandmother's bitterness out of their heads.

XI

Fluke

Nobody could say exactly what kind of dog Fluke was. For the most part, he resembled a Labrador retriever, but his eyes drooped slightly, resembling a bloodhound's, and he had a patch of fur on his chest shaped like an upside down heart of the same brilliant whiteness as the spots on the bottoms of his paws and the tip of his tail. Aside from these markings, he was a golden honey color, too light to be a chocolate lab and too dark to be a yellow lab. He had a taller and ganglier build than the typically stocky figure of most labs, and he weighed far more than most of his assumed breed. Still, he was an admirable looking dog with rich brown eyes, so dark they appeared to be black, and his head was blocky and wide between the ears. Despite his long, athletic legs, he had a big, barrel chest, and his tail was thick and otter-like, though it was crooked in several places from numerous accidents.

Fluke had a warm disposition. He never growled, and he rarely barked. He never lashed out at his owners, and he allowed children to crawl all over him, tug on his ears, pull on his ruff, and yank on his crooked tail. He never bothered much with the game of fetch, watching the thrown stick with his usual indifference to such banal activities; but when food was at stake, he was quick to jump to action.

Even more unique than his appearance was how Fluke came to Seraphine's family. Nobody knew how old Fluke was, and the even greater mystery was from where he came. The best way Seraphine could answer the question was, "from the fog."

Seraphine had been a dory man the entirety of his fishing life. Even as a veteran captain, he still went out in the dories that fished away from the mother ship, because, to him, there was no more natural way of fishing. He did not bother with weir boats or trawlers because he enjoyed the intimacy of fishing with a hook and line; his ability to feel that he himself had rightfully caught each fish he pulled in. He did not scoop them up by the thousands in large nets, raking the bottom of the sea, but rather, he selected each, individual fish. He kept the big ones, got rid of the small, and every fish that flopped into his boat had been touched by his own hands. He loved floating in the middle of the wide expanse of ocean with merely a little wooden dory, no more than fifteen feet long, separating him from the waves.

Motored dories were fashionable and becoming much more affordable, but he preferred the use of oars. The motors scared the fish away, he felt, and there was nothing more soothing than the sound of the splash of the wooden paddles hitting the water and scooping through it. He enjoyed the steady motion of rowing, the circling of the hands, the back and forth of the arms and body. The strenuous activity had an oddly relaxing effect on him; the rhythmic motion entrancing him and taking his mind to a place separate from his daily cares.

Floating around in his wooden dory was when Seraphine felt closest to the ocean and most at home. He was surrounded by silence besides the lapping of water on the sides of the boat. On windier days, the dory rocked and rolled over the waves, lifted up and down, but with hardly any water splashing over the side as long has he kept the boat from pointing into the waves. It was possible to survive in nature as long as one knew how to work with it, and this was something Seraphine had spent his entire life doing.

It was a day late in October when Seraphine found Fluke, or rather, Fluke found him, and the days were finally beginning to get colder. There was need for a mid-weight flannel jacket, but no scarves or gloves. Seraphine enjoyed this kind of weather best, because he hated feeling as though he was being cooked in the scorching sun of summer, and winter required him to wear gloves which were cumbersome when trying to bait his hooks. He rarely wore them, and preferred to let the frost nip at his skin than lose control of his line. His hands had toughened to the cold, and he preferred the pleasant, moderate temperature of the fall.

The one drawback of October, and this was no small matter, was the frequency of sudden fog. Out on the Banks, the fog would roll in and engulf them with hardly a moment's warning, leaving the dory men unable to gauge how far from the main ship they were or to see what other perils were approaching.

Dory men typically fished two to a boat, and Bill had always been Seraphine's mate since the days when they were young and fishing for Glory. Bill's long arms were good for reaching down into the water, but he was not quite as strong as Seraphine. Once he'd latched onto the line, Seraphine did most of the heavy pulling, while Bill yanked each fish off its hook throwing it either into the boat or back into the water as he went, one by one. The two of them spent a good deal of time baiting each hook on their trawl. There were hundreds of hooks on the long line, and baiting them with squid, or sand eels, or whatever bait was most readily available, was tedious work that the men had grown accustomed to. They fed the baited trawl into the water, and all that they could do was sit and wait until it was full of fish.

Seraphine and Bill looked around them at the two other dories floating nearby, and Seraphine hunkered down into the bow of the boat, resting on some burlap sacks. He pulled out his clay pipe from his jacket pocket, and began to pack it with tobacco.

"You still smoke from one of those things?" Bill asked wrinkling his nose.

"Yep," Seraphine responded without pulling his attention away from his pipe.

"Haven't you seen those nice wooden pipes? They're all shiny and sophisticated looking; like something a rich man would smoke."

"Well, I ain't a rich man." Seraphine sucked the end of his pipe, beginning to get some smoke out of it.

"Yeah, but those clay pipes are ancient. Nobody smokes them anymore."

"I do."

"Well, for Christmas, I'm gonna buy you a nice, shiny, new, wooden pipe. All classy and such."

"I don't want a wooden pipe. I like my clay."

"Why?" Bill asked bewildered, unable to grasp how Seraphine could be so unwavering where his habits were concerned.

"The wooden pipes don't burn as hot. And they don't hold the flavor like clay." Seraphine dragged on his pipe, the white clay well-blackened from several uses. Suddenly he fumbled the pipe and dropped it into the hull of the dory, the hot clay cracking. "Damn!" Seraphine grumbled, and he stamped the tobacco out before it could cause much damage and picked up the broken pipe.

"See what I mean!" Bill cried. "A wooden one wouldn't have cracked like that!"

Seraphine frowned at the broken pipe and nonchalantly tossed it overboard. Then he dug into his coat pocket and pulled out a brand new pipe. "Happens. I always carry an extra. They're cheap as dirt. I have a whole box at home." The corner of his mouth turned up at one corner, the hint of a smug smile.

"You're one stubborn bastard," Bill said, tossing up his hands.

A short time later, after Seraphine had gotten a good light on his new pipe and was puffing away, Bill said, "Hey, did I ever tell you the story about the sea monster?"

"Yep."

"I have not!" Bill cried adamantly.

"Course you did. Probably a hundred times."

"That ain't true. I've never told you that story before."

"Well, it changes every time anyways, so go ahead."

Not catching the sarcasm, Bill plunged into his tale. "Well, I was walking by the shore at New Beach one day. It wasn't a special day. Sunnier than this, so there was no mistaking what I saw. Suddenly, the water began to bubble—there wasn't any wind either that day—and I see the back of some creature rise out of the water. I saw the end of the tail come up, and then the head. The thing must have been fifty yards long and twelve feet thick—like half a football field, I tell ya! I see the head, as big as a two hundred gallon cask come out of the water, and it was the most god-awful thing I've ever seen. It opened it's mouth and I saw four rows of razor-sharp, white teeth, and it had six eyes that stuck out three feet from its head, all looking in different directions and red and green like port and starboard lights. It had blue, green, and red scales as big as the lid of a fish barrel all over it. His body slithered through the waves like a big, green, ugly-as-all-hell, snake. Well, I tell ya, I was shaking in my boots, and I runned and dived right behind a blueberry bush. I don't think the monster saw me because he moved into shore, hardly making a sound. He was so quiet that there was a group of seagulls that didn't even hear him. Suddenly his long, purple tongue shot out and licked up nearly the whole bunch of them before they even knew what they were hit by. They stuck right to his tongue like glue, the whole lot of them, and he sucked that slimy thing into his mouth and ate the whole load of them at once, feathers and all! Then he went back out into deep water, and disappeared under the surface. I thought he was gone and was about to get out from behind the bush, but suddenly his head comes back up, and he lets out a roar that shook the whole beach. I fell over and put my hands over my ears, like this!" Bill clapped his animated hands to the sides of his head. "But the worst part was the smell! Christ, what a stink! It smelled like sulfurous shit. Then he went back under water leaving a bunch of bubbles at the surface. The water foamed and gurgled like a submarine had just sunk there, and I never saw him again. You can imagine I wasn't about to stay around and wait for him to come back, so I hightailed it down the beach, and ran all the way back to town. I've never run so fast in my life.

I ran all the way to the Old Colony, and would you believe it, not a soul believed a word."

"Probably because you were stinkin' drunk," Seraphine muttered, taking the pipe from his mouth.

"Was not!"

"You're always drunk."

"I," Bill began to argue vehemently, but then reconsidered, "well . . . still, I know what I saw."

Seraphine laughed softly, and shook his head.

"And I wasn't the only one that saw strange creatures. They say there was an earthquake under the water a few years back, and it stirred up all kinds of crazy creatures that live deep down there where nobody goes. Giant squids and such."

"Who says?"

"They do!"

"Who?"

"The people who say things about that kind of stuff! I ain't no scientist!"

"I suppose you're gonna start talking about mermaids next."

"Don't be foolish. There ain't no such thing," Bill dismissed the statement, and then reached into his coat to pull out a flask of whiskey and took a good, long swig. "Ah. That's better. I was getting a bit cold." They sat in silence a moment or two, and Bill looked up and around him. "I'll be damned, Seraphine, sure looks like the fog's beginning to roll in."

"Yep. No good."

"We won't be able to see a goddamn thing in just a few minutes."

And he was right. Within a matter of moments they were engulfed in dense, white fog, so thick they could barely see each other or the water that surrounded them. They could not see their fellow dories or the *Halcyon* at all, and Bill stood up in the boat, and cupped his hands around his mouth. "Hulloo!" he called, but nothing other than an eerie silence returned to him.

"I didn't think they were that far away," Bill sat back down in the boat with a perplexed frown on his face.

"Who knows how far we'd drifted while you were telling that foolish story of yours." Seraphine was a lot calmer than Bill who was visibly agitated.

After giving Seraphine a half-hearted scowl, Bill asked, "Well, now what'll we do?"

"Only thing we can do is wait it out."

So they sat in the misty silence, seeing nothing, hearing nothing, but the white of the fog and the lapping of the calm water. There was hardly a breath of air, allowing the water to be abnormally still, which, combined with the fog, created an ethereal atmosphere. Even Bill had ceased his talking. The fog left a damp, dewy feeling on their skin, and it was so thick it seemed they could reach out and grab a handful of it. They sat for what felt like an eternity, though it was probably a couple of hours. Suddenly Bill straightened up. "What's that?" he asked.

"I don't know." Seraphine had heard it too and was looking around. It was a splashing sound that seemed near, but the stillness and the fog had warped their senses.

"Probably just some fish coming to the surface," Bill tried to assure himself.

"Nah, it's different." Seraphine was gripping the side of the boat, squinting into the dense, cottony fog.

The steady paddling sound was coming closer and closer, becoming louder and louder and more distinct.

"It's something swimming."

"Yeah, that's what I said," Bill said with annoyance.

"No, not a fish. It's too choppy. Too heavy. It's an animal or something. Like a deer," Seraphine concluded.

"All the way out here? There ain't no land for miles and miles."

Seraphine was on his knees, leaning over the side of the dory, and looking into the water. Before they could wonder any further, the sound, continuing to grow louder, revealed itself as a wet, furry face that appeared at the side of the boat. In the water floated a damp, golden head, and out of the fog pushed a shiny black nose.

"It's a dog!" Serpahine exclaimed. He reached into the water to pull the treading animal into the boat.

"What're you doing?" Bill cried.

"We gotta get it into the boat."

"No way. That dog's the devil." Bill's voice was grave.

"It's just a dog."

"You leave that creature right where it is. It ain't natural for an animal like him to be floating around in the middle of nowhere. That dog could be the devil or something evil. We don't know where he came from."

"He probably just jumped off some other boat that's lost in the fog and found us."

"There ain't any other boats around!"

"You don't know that. We've been sitting in the fog for hours. One could have pulled near us."

"I want nothing to do with that dog. You do what you want, but I ain't touching it."

So Seraphine, with some difficulty, reached down and lifted the dog himself. He was used to hauling fish into the boat, but this dog was large, and his flailing paws did not make it any easier. Seraphine fell back into the boat, his arms wrapped around the wet dog, it falling down on top of him.

The dog shook itself once, and then pressed its nose in Seraphine's face and let Seraphine run his hands along the slick fur.

"See, he's a friendly fella. Look, he's got webbed feet."

Bill pulled back and crouched in the stern of the boat as far as he could. "I told you, I don't want nothing to do with that animal." Seraphine scowled and let the dog sit beside him, where he lay for quite some time, when all of a sudden, he stood up and began barking in an alarming fashion.

Seraphine immediately became alert, understanding that this was some sort of a warning. He began to feel the waves swell and hear the gentle sound of something slowly plowing through the calm water.

"Quick!" Seraphine called to Bill, "Put her hard over."

They grabbed the oars and as soon as they veered the dory and pulled it back a few yards, a giant ocean liner cut through the fog. It missed them by mere inches, and they could have reached out and touched the side of it as it steamed by. It had been moving so slowly, it hardly left a wake, and barely made a sound. As close as vessel was, the fog still hung over it, making it appear like a ghost ship that suddenly appeared from another dimension, the men only able to make out the gray metal that slid right alongside them. Their hearts pounding and gasping for breath, the two men sat back down, and the dog relaxed as well.

"Whew! That was close," Bill said in disbelief.

As though Seraphine hadn't heard what he'd said, he reached out and wrapped his arm over the back of the dog, who was now sitting again.

"This dog ain't no devil. This dog's some kind of an angel."

In barely enough time for the men to ease their quaking nerves, the fog rolled out as quickly as it rolled in, and there in plain view was the *Halcyon* and the other dories, as though they had never been separated by the fog. All the men waved to each other, relieved to see that everyone was accounted for and in one piece. But there were no other ships in sight.

"Where did you come from?" Seraphine uttered baffledly under his breath as he stroked the dog who stood and turned and looked with his black eyes directly into Seraphine's. Seraphine held the dog's face in his hands and his expression warmed with gratitude toward the beast. "You're gonna come home with me. You can look after my wife and children. We'll take good care of you."

"Where the hell you guys been?" Bill hollered at the others. "I been calling and calling, and not a damn one of you answered."

"We called for you too, but we didn't hear nothing," Paul Careiro said. "Frank and Posey shouted back to us, but I didn't hear a damn thing come from your direction. We thought we'd lost you!"

"Well, from the looks of it, we've been here the whole time. I think you need to clean some potatoes out of your ears."

"Seems to me, you've got some problems with your hearing too, old man."

"Yeah, yeah, old man my ass," Bill grumbled as he began to reach for the line.

It was time to return to the *Halcyon* for the night and pull the trawl lines in, coiling in them into their round tubs. As Seraphine pulled the line in, hand over hand, each hook had on it a big, plump, silvery fish. They plopped into the dory, sliding over one another, slick and shiny, glistening in the light of the setting sun, the orange in the sky turning their scales golden. By the time they'd reached the end of the line, the boat was filled with fat, beautiful fish, a pile of silver and gold. Not a hook was empty, and not a single fish did they throw back.

As Seraphine and Bill rowed closer to the *Halcyon* and the other dories, Paul asked, "Hey, what's that you got there?"

"A dog," Seraphine responded.

"I can see that. Where'd he come from?"

"I don't know. Some nearby boat, I suppose."

"Wow! That's the craziest thing I've ever seen."

"Ain't crazy. Crazier things than this happen all the time on the ocean."

Paul looked at him skeptically. "You gonna keep him?"

"Sure," Seraphine replied simply as though he hadn't given it much thought either way.

"What're you gonna call him?"

"Not sure."

The third dory moved closer, and Posey called, "That's quite a catch you got there, eh? A real fluke!" He laughed loudly.

"He sure is," Seraphine smiled back. "Ain't ya, you Fluke?" And he patted the Christened dog on the head.

They rowed slowly back to the ship with a plentiful catch, the biggest they had had in ages, if not ever. The dog stood in the bow of the boat, looking proudly ahead like a commander over the fish, and the sea, and the dory men of George's Bank.

XII

Joseph, Sally, and the Squid

The sky was a clear, brilliant blue on this day that fell during the height of the summer. There was no haze, and the air was dry and fresh. Days like this were rare, as the summer heat usually had a steamy quality to it, a damp stickiness that made it uncomfortable everywhere but on the beach, chest-deep in water. Since the tide was low, all were grateful that the weather did not necessitate a good soaking in the harbor, as the best one could do was to find a shallow pool of salt water amid the flats, or to walk out far past the wharves to wade in water up to one's knees.

Joseph stomped through the hot sand with Sally scurrying to keep up, close to his heels. They spent the majority of their time barefoot, and never for a second did they have shoes on at the beach. Their brown, little feet were toughened against burning sand, rocky shores, and bits of beach glass. They did not cringe at the feeling of seaweed beneath their feet, and the nip of a crab hidden under the sand resulted in nothing more than a giggling yelp. The brother and sister skipped across the parched, burning sand near the road until they reached damp, cool sand near the shore. What treasures could they find today?

The two were skilled swimmers, and the lack of water to play in on low tide days brought with it minor disappointment. They loved to swim the length of a wharf and back or pick out a moored boat in the distance, touch it, and race back to shore. They would stay under water for shocking periods of time, trying to sneak up on one another, jump off stones serving as miniature breakwaters that broke up sections of the shore, and splash around like two, little, white sided dolphins.

As disappointing as it was to not be able to enjoy such pleasurable activities, the low tide brought plenty of surprises with it as well. Joseph and Sally began by flopping themselves down at the point where the beach no longer sloped toward the water and the really wet sand began. They started to dig a large hole with their hands and feet, picking out any stones they happened across until it became a pool of water nearly five feet in diameter. With the excess sand they built a damn in front of it to ward off the incoming tide, though the water would not become a threat for at least four more hours. Thus, Sally and Joseph abandoned their hole for a more exciting game, since there is a limited amount of fun in building a wall of sand without rising water to endanger it.

They began to meander between the pilings of the wharf, the sand damp and cold on their feet from being left in the shadows. A third of the way up the pilings grew hard, white barnacles. They appeared to be merely shells that stuck out just far enough to scratch one's skin, but hidden within each crusty peak lived a tiny animal that remained a curious mystery to the children. They had no qualms about taking a stick or a stone and prying those pesky creatures off the wooden pilings. They loathed the barnacles since it was not rare for Mary to have to nurse scrapes all along their arms and legs and backs when they got home from the beach from rubbing up against them while swimming or diving. Once a barnacle had been forced off its piling, the children stuck their fingers in the sticky slime at the back that had been hidden from eyesight and attempted to inflict the same torture they themselves has endured at the hands of the, now victimized, barnacle.

The barnacles were not the only creatures that were harassed by the children. They scraped off the little, black and brown *conker-rinkles*, as the Portugees called them, that climbed up the pilings over the barnacles, deriving enjoyment from releasing the suction the snails had made and listening to the series of thuds as they dropped in a pile on the sand.

The children derived even more enjoyment out of the *sweetmeats* that were so fat, they could barely squeeze all the way into their shells when poked at. They were not nearly as shy as the conker-rinkles, and kept their white, slimy bodies wriggling outside of their pearly grey-blue shells. The children rubbed the sweetmeets' soft flesh all over their arms and hands, an aloe of the sea, and, if they were patient enough, waited to let the sweetmeats pull themselves little by little up the children's extremities, leaving sticky trails behind. The best way to find sweetmeats was to follow the meandering trail they'd make on the sandbars until one came to the end where there was often a lump that, when dug up, usually revealed a sweetmeat.

In the little streams that separated the sandbars, the children found hermit crabs and held them in their hands, waiting patiently until their little, antennae-like eyes peeked out from their shells. Sometimes Sally and Joseph would toss them in a bucket with sand and carry them around the beach until the water got hot, and they dumped the crabs back into the water within moments of losing their lives. Other times the children would take a net and try to catch minnows which would meet the same, sometimes worse, fate, as they were less hearty to the rapidly warming water than the hermit crabs.

Joseph and Sally would stand in the gentle currents of the little streams, very still, until they could feel tickle fish walking on their toes. At the first giggle, the tickle fish would be off in a flurry, only to come back again as soon as the children were still. Sometimes they would sit themselves down in the water, their palms open on the sand, waiting for an unsuspecting tickle fish to land there, but the tickle fish were virtually impossible to catch.

Other amusements came not from harassing the living creatures, but from finding inanimate objects lying on the beach. When the water went out, all kinds of treasures could be found washed up on the shore. They found pieces of old, clay, smoking pipes that men threw off the sides of the boats and pieces of worn down beach glass, soft with no sharp edges and a foggy color from being rolled around in the waves and sand. Green, white, and brown were the most common colors, but once in a while they would find blue, and these they hoarded like Indian wampum. They would find clay and glass marbles, tea cup handles, and pieces of pottery with a variety of pretty designs. Sometime they would find porcelain pieces of doll faces, arms, and legs, but these were rare as were other treasures such as reading glasses, jewelry, the soles of shoes and wooden spools. The children's bedroom was filled with their treasures from the beach, and Mary, though she wanted to, didn't dare to throw them out.

Joseph and Sally, as they moved through their daily beach routine, eventually took note of a brown lump in the distance and immediately suspected it was a stranded horseshoe crab. In the height of the summer, horseshoe crabs were rarer than during the early parts of the summer, their mating season, when they could be seen in clusters of two and three. The children loved to pick them up by their tails and look at the many legs hidden under their hard shells grapple at the air. The horseshoe crabs were Joseph and Sally's favorite sea creature. Once they got closer, they could see that its shell was already drying in the sun, the horseshoe crab unable to bury itself completely in the cool, damp sand.

"Poor horseshoe crab," Sally shook her head. "We have to save it!"

Inspired by the importance of their imperative task, Joseph and Sally immediately began their rescue. Joseph pulled it out of the sand, while Sally splashed water on its heated shell.

"This fella's big!" Joseph moaned and he lifted it up. "Would ya look at that!"

"I never saw one so big before."

"Me either." Joseph held it in his two hands in front of him

"Hurry!" Sally cried, "He's sick. He might die if we don't get him to water fast!" The two took off across the flats, out toward the nearest and deepest stream of water they could find. As soon as they came to it, Joseph placed the crab in the water and let it go. The horseshoe crab was still a minute and then suddenly sped off, revived by the cool water. It half floated, half walked across the ocean floor as it was carried partly by the current, partly by its own volition, out to deep water.

The two brushed their hands off, pleased with their work, and then began walking out farther on the flats, seeing if there were any other helpless creatures that needed saving. They had walked no more than ten yards when they noticed an unusual sight. Stranded on the flats were dozens of squid.

"Joe, look! It's squid!" Sally squealed in excitement. "Are they alive?"

Joseph bravely walked up to one, bent over, and wrapped a hand around its rubbery body. He had barely lifted it up when it waved its tentacles and stuck its little suction cups to his hand and wrist. Joseph quickly dropped it, shaking the tentacles off, while Sally laughed.

"It scared you!" she giggled.

"No it didn't," Joseph protested, pretending not to have been startled, and picked up another to prove his bravery. They both skipped around picking up squid and laughing every time the tentacles clung to their hands.

The bodies were sprinkled all over the flats, about ten inches long, perfect eating size. As the squid's bodies warmed, their skin color changed from a shimmering purple to a mother of pearl color. They shimmered and each dot of pigmentation could be seen changing from one color to the next. Their black eyes turned a cloudy purple, and the children could tell that they were quickly dying.

"We should tell Ma," Sally urgently said to Joseph.

"Yeah, these squid are good eatin'. We should get them before they die!"

So the two filled the one, small, metal pail they had brought with them and rushed off across the street to their house. Mary was bent over in the front yard shaking out the door mat, when Joseph and Sally arrived.

"Ma! Ma!" the children hollered as they ran down the street as fast as their little legs would carry them.

"What? What is it?" Mary asked, startled and concerned.

"Ma," Joseph said breathlessly, "there's squid on the beach."

"Lots," Sally added.

"Come quick before they die!"

"Yeah, Ma. They would feed us for the rest of our lives."

Mary briskly went into the house, and grabbed two large buckets. Then she and the children, and Fluke as well, for he had been sleeping in the shade of the tree, hurried down to the beach and began to fill the buckets as quickly as they could.

Each live squid they picked up, flung its tentacles back and latched onto their hands in self defense but causing no harm to its enemies. The buckets were filled to the top, and there were still plenty of squid to spare, most, surprisingly, still alive. Mary decided that she would clean the squid right there on the beach instead of taking them home, that way they could get as many as they wanted and could leave all the guts behind.

"Joseph, run back to the house and get your sister to help me. I'll never get this all done by myself. And tell her to bring a sharpened knife." Joseph ran toward the road.

It was only a few occasions in a lifetime that squid would get caught in the falling tide and stranded on the flats like this, but Mary was an expert at cleaning them, for squid was something they ate regularly. She carefully detached the heads, pulling them so that all the innards came out in one piece, leaving a nice empty tube. From that she pulled a thin, clear piece of cartilage that served as the spine of the squid and rinsed out any remaining guts in the water before attempting to peel off the thin skin in one piece. Then she took a small knife and cut the tentacles from the head, throwing the head and the inside of the body away and making sure that the hard, beak-like mouth was removed from the circle of tentacles. Once the two pieces, body and tentacles, were rinsed clean, she threw them into the rinsed out bucket and moved to the next.

Within a few minutes, Sarah came along the beach, her skirt hiked up over her knees, and sat down on the grounded float beside her mother. She only needed to be shown once the proper protocol for cleaning squid.

Mary and Sarah cleaned at least a hundred squid that day, but as they went they became more and more deft and efficient at it. Once in a while, one of them would puncture the inside of the body, and black ink would go everywhere, which made Joseph and Sally squeal in delight, and then run off to scavenge more.

Seagulls quickly discovered the squid guts and busied themselves by eating those since the children labored to keep them away from the whole squid. Fluke also helped in this task as he joyfully ran circles on the flats, spraying water and sand behind him and plowing through the flocks of gulls. The birds dove down, one after another, snatching squid heads from the flats and lifting them back into the air with them before settling on the ground with the rest of the flock to gobble down the remnants and fight away any who attempted to steal his share. The gluttonous birds left not a single scrap behind, but Mary was thankful there would be no stench of rotting fish, and the seagulls were happy to have full bellies with minimal effort.

By the time they had finished, the tide had already moved in around their feet, under the raft that Mary and Sarah had been sitting on. The water had at last reached Sally and Joseph's long forgotten damn, but they did not look twice at it as they helped their mother carry the squid home.

Before they went in the door, Mary made them brush the sand off their feet with a dirty towel, and then sent them up the stairs to get themselves washed up. She went into the kitchen and immediately began preparing dinner. She made a pile of all the squid she knew she would need to make her pot of stew, and the rest she had Sarah put into little containers and bags, whatever she could find, and stuck it in the icebox. What a useful contraption that new icebox was! She was glad she chose that over a car.

Mary cut up onion and celery and sautéed it in the bottom of her pot with some oil. Then she added several cans of tomatoes and a spicy mixture of herbs before adding the squid. She dumped all the tentacles in whole, and then the bodies which she cut across widthwise, making rings out of each one that shrunk and curled as they cooked in the hot sauce. The stew boiled and created a spicy odor that wafted through the house. She stirred it with a wooden spoon seeing the translucent, white rings of the squid turn a solid, pinkish color. It was quite a *caserla*.

Mary was taking her first taste as the kids came down and huddled around her legs, pulling on her skirt.

"Wow, Ma! Smells great!" Joseph said enthusiastically since squid was one of his favorite delicacies. Both children especially liked the tentacles for the way they felt as they rolled them around in their mouths feeling the tickle of each one and the tiny bumps of the lifeless suction cups. Sally and Joseph were not squeamish at all.

"Wait 'til Dad comes home. He's gonna be so happy," Sally grinned, hooking her fingers over the counter and looking up at her mother.

The door slammed, and in stormed Tommy, looking for something to make a fuss about. "What's cookin'?" he asked loudly.

"Squid stew."

"Squid?" He stood by the dining table and rolled his eyes toward the ceiling as though he were carefully considering whether or not he liked squid today. But finding no qualms with it, he settled and said, "Sounds good," before running up the stairs.

Mary was rather surprised, but decided she had better enjoy the positive reinforcement while she could.

An hour or so later, Seraphine and Jimmy came home from the boat, and were thrilled to find a giant pot of stew waiting for them and not one, but *two* loaves of bread, quite a luxury.

It was arguably the best squid they'd ever had. The rings were thick and not too tough, and the children were satisfied with the length of the tentacles. Tom stuck his tongue through the middle of one and taunted his siblings until his mother snapped at him to stop.

The stew lasted three days, and the frozen squid took them into the winter.

XIII

The Dory Race

Seraphine and Jimmy stood in the shed looking down at the freshly painted dory they had been working on every Saturday and Sunday afternoon for the past three weeks, stripping away a skin of old paint and weathered wood to reveal a golden newness hidden beneath the surface. They patched any weak spots and sanded the entire dory so that the boards were as smooth as a frosty piece of beach glass. The inside, benches and oars, were coated with a high-gloss urethane and the hull of the boat was painted forest green. The trim that circled the entire top edge of the boat was a bold red color and the ribs of the bow and stern were a clean, glossy white. She was fitted with new brass rungs for the oars and even the small trailer that she lay on was given a fresh coat of black paint. The two men looked down at their work approvingly after giving the dory a final buff before heading to the event.

"I don't see how we can't win that race with a boat like this," Jimmy said proudly. Seraphine nodded slowly in agreement, a satisfied smile on his face.

"The race starts at noon. Why don't we go grab some breakfast at Tip's?" he suggested.

"Sounds good. But wasn't Ma going to make us breakfast?" Jimmy began wiping his hands off on a clean rag.

"Nah. I told her to take a vacation. It's a special day."

"Yeah, she's busy making her chowder for the soup tasting contest, anyway."

"More reason to leave. I've never eaten so much chowder in my life."

"I don't understand why she keeps changing the recipe," Jimmy said as the men began to leave the shed.

"She's determined to beat Elsa Costa this year, but I'm the one suffering for it. Every time I come home, she's got a new spice she's just added and another bowl for me to eat."

"Well, which one has been the best?"

"How the hell should I know? It all tastes the same to me."

Jimmy laughed.

It was a perfect day for the dory race. The sky was blue, the sun was warm, and there was barely a gust of wind. The Blessing of the Fleet was a four day long festival with numerous activities; parades, block dances, soup tasting contests, fishing derbies, swimming challenges, and dory races. Aside from the blessing itself when all of the fishing boats, bedecked in colorful flags, lined up and paraded to the pier to be blessed with holy water by the bishop, the dory race was the highlight of the weekend.

They raced, two to a dory, from the end of Railroad Wharf to a marker over near the Grozier House, about a quarter of a mile. Some boats were manned by father and son duos, others by friends from school or mates on the same fishing boat. All the dories were beautifully refinished and painted in signature ways so that the team could be identified from afar.

Seraphine and Jimmy sat at a table in Tip's and Roda Cabral came to take their order.

"Ready for the race today, fellas?" she asked pulling a small notebook out of her greasy apron.

"Yep," Jimmy replied.

"It's your first race, ain't it, Jimmy?"

"Yeah, Dad's too."

"You've never been in a dory race, Seraphine?" Roda raised her eyebrows.

"Nope."

"Well then this competition's been missing out. We can't have a dory race without the last dory fishing family in it."

Seraphine nodded. "Now that the boy's been working with me for a few years, I figure he's ready for the race."

"I guess so! Look at the shoulders on you, nice boy. You're a man!"

Jimmy gave half a smile, embarrassed by the attention he was getting. Roda grinned and changed the subject. "So what'll it be today?" They ordered linguica and pancakes, scrambled eggs and home fries, coffee and orange juice, French toast, and anything and everything their hearts desired.

"Geeze, Dad, we sure ordered a lot."

"Well, we got a busy day ahead of us."

"Yeah, but isn't it kinda extravagant eat like this?"

"What's the use of having money if you ain't gonna to spend some of it once in a while? This is a special day. I want to eat like a king."

And they did. There was barely enough room on the table for all the dishes to fit, but the two men didn't leave a crumb behind, and when they were finished, it was almost time to head to the race. They walked back home, got their dory, and wheeled it down to the landing. The two men hopped in as they launched the boat, and each grabbed a set of oars, pulling their way to the wharf. Several boats had already begun to congregate, and the men were exchanging good-humored banter.

"Out of my way, slowpokes!" one young man cried as he and his partner glided past the others. "The race'll be over before you make it to the starting line."

"Aw shut your trap!" an older voice from another boat shouted. "You keep showing off like that, you'll be spent before the horn blows."

"Showing off? Hell, this is just a warm up!"

"What do you say I take you all out for drinks after I win my fifty bucks!"

"*Your* fifty bucks?" another voice responded. "You ain't gonna be winning no races with that old shit-box. You'll be ass deep in water, and we'll have to call the coast guard to bail you out."

"At least my boat ain't painted whore red." There was uproarious laughter had by all as the banter continued until the signal for the boats to line up was given. The twelve boats lined up while crowds of people stood on the wharfs and sat in little boats surrounding the race route. They all cheered on their favorite team, and Jimmy and Seraphine spotted the rest of their family. The horn sounded and the boats were off. The three winners would go to a championship round.

"Let's pace ourselves, Jim," Seraphine said, "We only need to be in the top three to qualify. We should do that no problem. Better to save ourselves for the next race."

The boats cut through the calm water, the oars making a gentle splash with every dip as the duos moved in perfect unison. Seraphine and Jimmy effortlessly pulled on the oars of the dory. They were used to rowing dories everyday under much more strenuous conditions than these.

"Come on, Jim. We can't let those trawlers and weir boaters beat us at our own game!" They began in fifth place, letting the more eager competitors get their head start, knowing that they would not be able to sustain such a speed for long. They pulled steadily on the oars, gradually gaining ground on the boats ahead of them. They moved into fourth place, then into third as they neared the finish line. The crowds of onlookers roared and cheered as the dories made it across the finish line, and the winners proudly waved back.

As the three boats looped back around to the starting line, Seraphine and Jimmy heard someone cry to them, "Third place! Is that the best you can do?" The two men looked and saw Bill leaning on the top of a piling at the edge of the pier, smiling good naturedly at them and taking a swig of whiskey.

"Just you wait, Bill," Jimmy called up. "You ain't seen nothing yet!"

"You better be right, else I'm gonna have to hang up my trawling lines and retire."

There was a fifteen minute break before the final race, and Seraphine and Jimmy sat in their boat and talked with Bill. Jimmy leaned back in the stern, his hand gripping the side of the boat and listening to Bill tell an elaborate tale about a fish he caught that won him first prize in the fishing derby, when somebody called, "Look out!"

"Ow!" Jimmy cried. It was too late. His hand had been sandwiched between his dory and a little sailboat, recklessly driven by a few youngsters. The boats quickly separated, and Jimmy snatched his hand away and gripped it between his legs. His face turned red and furrowed in pain. Seraphine scrambled to his side.

"You okay?"

"I don't know. It hurts real bad," Jimmy moaned.

"Let me have a look at it," Seraphine took up the hand and saw that it was already beginning to swell, and two of the fingers hung limply.

"What do you think Dad?" Jimmy choked down his pain.

"I think you might have broke it, son, but I ain't no doctor."

Bill leaned over the side of the pier, as far as he could without falling. "I don't know, Cap'. It don't look too good. Not even from here."

"Oh no!" Jimmy cried. "We gotta win the race."

"Don't be foolish," Seraphine said. "You can't race with your hand like that. You gotta get that to a doctor."

"But, Dad, we worked so hard."

"There's next year."

"Yeah, Jim," Bill said. "It's just a race. You need to get that hand taken care of. You don't want it to be spoiled for football season, now do you?"

"No," Jimmy responded glumly.

Mary came bursting through the crowd. "Seraphine! Is everything all right?"

"I think Jimmy here's hurt his hand."

"Oh my lord! Look at that! I have to get you to the doctor right away," Mary said as urgently as though Jimmy had blood gushing out of a deep wound in his side. Jimmy looked sadly at his father, holding his limp, bluish hand in his lap.

"Go on, son," Seraphine said gently.

"This is so embarrassing. My first race, and I get injured."

"It wasn't your fault, nice boy," Bill said, as he helped Jimmy pull himself up a rickety ladder onto the pier.

"Dad," Jimmy said turning to his father who sat alone in the shiny dory. "Don't forfeit the race."

"Don't be silly, son. I can't finish the race without you," Seraphine scratched the side of his face.

"Course you can! Come on, Dad. That boat wasn't made to sit on the sideline. You gotta race."

"By myself?"

"Why not? Nobody can row a dory better than you can."

Seraphine looked down at his thick, brown fingers in thought, and then looked up. "All right. But you gotta get that hand checked out, okay?"

Jimmy smiled for the first time since the incident and nodded. "Sure will, Dad. Good luck!" and he finally let Mary drag him down the wharf.

Bill shook his head, a small grin on his face. "Well, old man, see you at the finish line."

Seraphine responded with a shake of his head, as though he had no idea what he had gotten himself into, and picked up the oars.

The three boats lined up again, and the men in the other two gave Seraphine a strange look. One of them was Murray Shrug.

"What happened, Cap'? Where's the boy?"

"Had a bit of an accident, that's all."

"Chicken out, did he?"

"My boy ain't no coward," Seraphine said, not looking at him, but maintaining a severe focus on his task at hand.

"You should just throw in the towel, old man," Shrug continued. "You can't row that dory all by yourself. Not against us fellas."

"We'll see," Seraphine said, still not looking at him, and with a note of finality that ceased all conversation.

The horn sounded and the boats were off. Seraphine immediately fell back into third place, but he pulled steadily on the oars, not appearing to be concerned with his position. The two other boats were neck and neck, about a length and a half ahead of him. One began to fall behind, and Seraphine quickly gained ground on it, taking note of the bewildered faces of the two men as he passed by them. He heard the crowd cheer but did not let it distract him. He felt the warmth of the sun beating hot on his damp back. Sweat coursed down his face and into his eyes, but he paid no attention to it. He realized that they were nearing the end, and he began to grip the oars hard and put more of his weight into each row as he tried to pick up speed.

Shrug's boat was about a length ahead of him, and Seraphine's hands ached from the strong grip he was using. He put his whole body into each pull of the oars, feeling them slice through the water faster and faster. Under the strain, he clenched his eyes shut and put every ounce of himself into propelling the dory until finally he heard a loud cheer. He opened his eyes and looked around not knowing whether he'd won or lost, but amidst the roaring applause he heard his name being cried. He glanced over at his competitors both looking rather subdued, and he knew he had won.

Seraphine rowed his dory back to the pier where he was given a trophy, fifty dollars, and a coupon for dinner at Cookie's Tap. People clapped him excitedly on the back, and his picture was taken for the newspaper.

"So, Cap, did you ever think you'd win that race on your own?" one man asked him.

"I didn't do it on my own."

"What are you going to do with that fifty dollars?"

"It's up to my boy."

Seraphine tried to push through the crowd. He wanted to see how Jimmy was doing. Bill met up with him and took his trophy, holding it up in the air as though he were the proud trainer of the heavy weight boxing champion of the world. "Wait til Jimmy gets a load of this, eh?"

He looked over the edge of the wharf, to see Shrug bitching at his dory mate. "Hey!" Bill cried down, holding the trophy out toward them. "How do you like that, you trawler assholes!" Bill and Seraphine walked off before they could hear the men's responses, laughing.

Tommy, Joseph, and Sally rushed over cheering and wrapping their arms around Seraphine's legs. Seraphine hoisted Sally up into his arms and set her on his shoulders while he let Joseph hang onto his hand. Bill gave Tommy the trophy to hold, and declared that he had to be going. "Congrats, Cap'. One hell of a job. I'll see you for the Blessing tomorrow. Mary loading the *Halcyon* with food?"

"Sure is."

"Better be making those stuffed clams I like."

"You bet."

"Well, the *Halcyon's* looking mighty pretty with the flags and such. We proved today, Serry, it don't matter how old you are to still get the job done. It'll be a good blessing." Bill took a sip of whiskey and headed in his own direction.

Seraphine and the children walked home together, proud as peacocks. "How's Jimmy doing?" he asked.

"I don't know," Tommy said. "Mom called the doctor. I wish Jimmy could have seen the race."

"I wish he could have been *in* the race, but there's always next year."

"What are we going to do now?" Joesph asked.

"Well, how about we get some ice cream?" Seraphine proposed.

"Yeah!" they all chimed.

"Or what about some *malasadas*?" Tommy asked.

"Or what about both?" Joseph suggested.

"We can get both, but you won't have any room for your mother's chowder at the festival."

"Oh . . . that's okay," Tommy said trying to sound slightly disappointed.

Seraphine laughed. "Yeah, I'm sick of chowder too."

The children ate their ice cream and fried dough the rest of the way home where they found Jimmy lying on the couch, a large bandage on his hand.

"How're you feeling son?" Seraphine asked, but Jimmy did not answer his question as his glum face lit up at the sight of the trophy.

"You won?"

"Don't sound so surprised."

"Nah, I'm not surprised. Just wish I was there."

"Well, if you feel up to it, the winner is supposed to be in the parade. Why don't you and the other three show off our trophy and that fine boat we built. I never would have won the second round if we hadn't finished the boat so good. Sliced through the water like butter." The three young ones considered this to be a marvelous idea, and Jimmy agreed.

A few hours later they had retrieved the dory and pulled it out of the water onto its trailer. They had just finished wiping it down and adorning it with streamers and balloons when Mary and Sarah returned from the chowder contest lugging a giant pot. Sarah greeted them pleasantly and remarked at the trophy, but Mary seemed not so happy.

"Oh rub it in, why don't you?"

"What's wrong?" Seraphine asked, having some idea as to what the problem was.

"What else? Elsa Costa won again. Can you imagine? All that work, and I lost to her again."

"Ma, second place isn't so bad," Sarah said and pointed to the red ribbon on the side of the pot for the others to admire.

"I guess so," Mary sighed. "Well, even if the town doesn't agree, at least I know my family likes my chowder." She brightened.

Seraphine and the kids all shot each other sideways glances.

"As a matter of fact, why don't we eat the leftovers for dinner? There's just enough left." They all held back groans and plodded into the kitchen.

XIV

Glory

Glory immigrated to the U.S. with his family when he was seventeen years old. He was the first Portuguese captain in Provincetown to both successfully own and run his own vessel, the *Halcyon*. But Glory always claimed that it was a crucial quirk of fate that had allowed him to lead his auspicious life.

Glory, was the second to youngest of eight sons of Manuel Taves, a native Azorean and former captain of the *Mirage*, a merchant ship that exported and imported goods between Northeastern U.S. and South America until his son, Manuel Jr., took over the position. Glory and all of his brothers worked on the ship and were to set sail on a month-long excursion to Brazil in May of 1879.

It was a sunny morning as the brothers gathered on Railroad Wharf to load cargo and supplies before heading to Boston where they would pick up the bulk of their shipment. Manuel Jr., Glory's oldest brother, informed Glory that he was to stay below deck for the majority of the trip. His post would be in the cargo hold to ensure that the goods did not get damaged by plugging any of the frequent leaks that would spring before they could do harm and arranging and rearranging the crates as they slid around.

Glory, known to have quite a temper even when he was young, reeled back at this order, and cried furiously, "What do you mean I'm below deck? You said I was gonna be a deckhand this time! No more shit jobs! I've done my time!"

"Well somebody's got to watch the goods, and it might as well be you," his brother responded. "Besides, I don't care how many trips you've been on, you're still the youngest."

"I ain't the youngest you shit-for-brains! What about Jose?" Glory retorted. "Why don't you put him down below?"

"Because he's a better sailor than you."

At this, Glory was filled with rage. His face turned a brilliant shade of red. "That little shit's only sixteen! I'm nineteen, and I'm due for a real run on this boat."

Jose, the youngest, offended by the derogatory reference, began to argue against Glory's sailing skills. "Glory, you wouldn't know what a jib was if it fucking smothered you!"

"You cocky little bastard! It's easy to run your mouth when big brother Manny's looking out for you, but I can lay a beating on all of yous, *and* I can out-sail you. Manny, you steered us straight into that last storm we were in! What the hell kind of sailor's sense you got? And Francisco navigated us thirty knots off track killing three days' time. And Mario and Ferdinand are fucking klutzes! I've never seen grown men trip around on a deck like they do!" Glory went on, and in defending himself had managed to individually offend nearly all of all of his brothers, putting himself more and more on the defensive with every statement he made.

An explosive argument erupted on the end of the wharf, sixteen arms flailing and making violent gestures, eight angry voices roaring in Portuguese. It didn't take long before it was Glory against his seven brothers, arguing about things that weren't even relevant to the issue at hand, like how Ronaldo's feet smelled the worst, that Francisco caught the biggest fish at the derby eight years ago, not John, and how it was Ferdinand's stupid idea to name their mutt "Jangles." But aside from these asides, most of the fingers were being pointed at Glory, and finally, he threw up his hands and cried, "That's it! I refuse to set foot on that boat!"

"You refuse? Well who the hell is going to watch the cargo?" Manuel Jr. asked.

"I don't give a damn!"

"We can't sail a man short," Franciso said.

"Course you can, 'bout I ain't no sailor anyway, remember?"

"Aw come on, don't act like such a baby," John, the third oldest said. At this, Glory bit down on his tongue and then brought a hard left fist to the side of John's jaw. John was stunned only a moment before he bounded right back on top of Glory, and the two tussled violently on the wharf until the other brothers managed to pull them, still swinging, apart.

Glory, red, sweating, and rumpled, pointed a finger at them and cried, "You can all go to hell!"

Then he walked home where he sulked for one whole month, then two, then three, when everyone began to wonder what had happened to the *Mirage*? There had been no word from any of the brothers, nor would there ever be. The boat had disappeared into thin air. No wreckage was found, no sightings were reported, nothing. The boat had just vanished like a ghost ship, never to return, though any seamen who knew the story always kept a lookout for the vessel. Some claimed to have seen ships of its likeness docked at various South American ports. One even claimed to have spotted it somewhere on the Indian Ocean. But nobody could prove its existence or its extinction.

Glory always told this story proudly. He was where he was because he had gotten into a fight that, ultimately, saved his life. And when listeners asked him if he felt guilty, his response would always be, "They were all bastards anyway. I put the hex on them. I didn't mean to, but I did. It's become a habit." And it was true; Glory had a habit of hexing people who had affronted him. There was the miserable fat man with the nasty dog who one day bit Glory on the leg, and then the man had the audacity to blame Glory for provoking the runt. Glory pointed a portentous finger at the man and growled, "You fat bastard; I hope you rot in hell." Of course, this was said in the Portuguese, so the man never thought twice to blame Glory as he fell down dead of a sudden heart attack three days later. Then there was the neighbor who was always blocking the front walk to Glory's house with his car. "Who needs a goddamn car in a three-mile-long town, anyhow?" Glory would complain as he huffed back into the house after one of numerous angry exchanges with the neighbor. "He and that goddman car can go to hell!" And it wasn't but a week later that the car was found wrapped around a tree out by East Harbor. And there was also the owner of the inn to whom Glory had lost a game of cards and most of his week's earnings. "You're a goddamn cheat!" Glory cried. "I ain't never lost a game of cards this bad! Ain't no way you play straight, you rotten son of a bitch." The man just gave him a sly smirk that made Glory's blood boil hotter. There was no way he could prove the con, but there was one thing he could do: "You son of a bitch, I hope you burn in hell for the rest of your days and that Satan craps on your head the whole time!" Well, Satan certainly wasn't doing any crapping, at least not for a long while, but the man's inn burned down within a month, nearly consuming the whole rest of the town with it, and ashes raining down all the way up on High Pole Hill. He lost everything.

But those who knew Glory best knew that, deep down, he did feel remorse for the curse he believed he had accidentally put on his brothers. It was a difficult burden to bear but he bore it. Though Glory, as a truly superstitious seaman, believed in the reality of his hexes, he did not let it cripple him and moved on with his life. The lives of seafaring families are rife with loss.

But Glory's ability to put hexes on people was not the entire substance of the man. Another intriguing fact about Glory was his great desire to be an American. Though Glory spent most of his life in America, since his family did not immigrate to the United States until he was well into his adolescence, and having worked with his family on the *Mirage* from that age on, Glory never went to school in America and did not develop fluency in the English language. Though he had tried several times, Glory was unable to pass the test to become an American citizen because his

English was not good enough. It became his primary goal and ultimate passion to one day earn citizenship in the country he most adored.

"What do you care?" Philomena, his wife, would cry as Glory sat in his armchair diligently trying to decipher the English of elementary level U.S. History books. "You were born in Portugal. You are Portuguese. What difference does it make whether you're a citizen here or a citizen there? You're still just going to be a fisherman."

"You don't get it, you stupid woman! You never will," Glory hollered back at her in Portuguese, the only language he ever used when he was mad. "My house is in America. My children were born in America. I have lived and prospered here in America. This is my home. I am an American!"

"You are Portuguese!"

"To hell with Portugal!" Glory boomed and threw up his hands. It was suprising that, at that very moment, the entire country of Portugal hadn't been erased off the map of the world.

"Being Portuguese is who you are."

"It is *not* who I am. It has nothing to do with who I am. I am an American, and every other goddamn immigrant in this country should think so too. Did we come to America to be whatever nationality we were before? Of course not! We came here to be American!" With that he slammed the book shut, threw it on the floor, and stormed up to bed.

When Seraphine was just a young man, sixteen years old, working on Glory's *Halcyon*, the Captain approached him.

"Nice boy. A word," Glory said in Portuguese.

Seraphine nervously approached him, afraid he had done something wrong. He stood with his face turned to the ground awaiting his reprimand.

"Get that look off your face, boy! I'm not going to yell at you!" Then the captain lowered his voice, covertly pulled a rumpled set of papers out of his coat pocket, and showed them to Seraphine as though he wanted nobody else to see. This caught Seraphine's interest, and he looked down to find the study guide for the American citizenship test. Seraphine confusedly looked up at Glory.

"I've taken it four times, and I can't pass it," the captain said under his breath. I can't speak English worth a damn." Seraphine still was unsure of what he was expected to do. "I need you to help me learn English."

Seraphine started in surprise. "Oh, Cap'n, I can't do that. I haven't got more than a sixth grade education."

"You speak English don't you?"

"Yes."

"Well how hard can it be?"

"What about your wife? Doesn't she speak English? I thought she was born here."

"That woman's a beast! All I get out of her is a pain in my ass!"

"But what about your children? They're still in school. They can help you."

"No. I don't want them to help me. I don't want anybody to help me, but I've tried, and I can't do it on my own. You mind your own business, Seraphine. I like that about you. And I think you've got a real head on your shoulders."

"Yes, but I'm in no position to be teaching you English. Hell, I can barely read myself."

"We can do it. We can do it. You can speak the language. That's all I need. You went to school in America. That's the big difference. You've got a hell of a lot better advantage that I've got. Teach me."

"When?"

"Today."

"Today?"

"Everyday."

"I can't."

"Okay, okay, not everyday, but as long as it takes."

Had Seraphine known just how long it would take for Glory to develop a rudimentary proficiency in English, he likely would have risked losing his job and said no. It was as though Glory had a mental block to learning the English language. Perhaps someone better suited to teaching English than Seraphine could have made progress more quickly, but Glory, as always, was a stubborn man and refused to let anyone else near him and his English books. Seraphine and the Captain sat trying to learn English for an hour twice a week after work nearly every week they were in port until Seraphine joined the Navy. It was only a short time after Seraphine returned from the Great War that they started up again, and after Seraphine married Mary, the two men continued their weekly ritual that had always been, and still was, held secretly in the dark forecastle of the *Halcyon*.

Finally, Glory tossed down an elementary spelling book in frustration and said, "I've got to take this test. I'll be dead before I learn English."

Seraphine nodded, understanding his captain's point. Glory was old. He was overweight with high blood pressure, high cholesterol, diabetes, gout, and every other ailment a man pushing seventy and still working like a dog could have. He went, finally, to take the biggest test of his life. He placed his hand over his heart and proudly recited the Pledge of Allegiance with more passion and dedication than any man who had spent his entire life in the U.S.A. He confidently named the three branches of the American government, listed the freedoms granted by the Bill of Rights, recited lines from the Declaration of Independence, answered various questions on U.S. history from who the first president was to what caused the Civil War, and even noted that the only good thing to have come out of the War of 1812 was the "Star Spangled Banner." (This last part was his own, personal touch.) Glory was dismissed and waited in hot anticipation for his results. Sweat dripped from his brow, and he leaned forward in the uncomfortable chair, hardly noticing the fly that buzzed around his head or the clock that ticked on the wall.

When at last Glory learned that he had passed the test and had finally earned his American Citizenship, he took the American flag that he had neatly folded in his pocket, the one that he had had hanging in front of his house (the only flag permitted to be hung in front of his house) and wrapped it around his shoulders like a blanket. When he got off the boat from Boston, he paraded himself down the wharf and through town to his house, proudly wrapped in the colors of his country. At last his life was fulfilled.

Captain Glory died a year later. On his death bed, he requested the presence of Seraphine at his side.

"I'm giving you the *Halcyon*."

Seraphine looked at him, stunned, and as he opened his mouth to object, Glory cried, "Don't argue with me, boy! You're taking her!" a final impassioned burst of energy from a dying man. "You know that boat better than anybody else does. You know how she runs. You've worked on her everyday for the last fifteen years. You are my oldest daughter's husband. You are a hard worker. You deserve to captain that boat."

Seraphine scratched his head. "Shouldn't one of your sons—"

"To hell with my sons!" Glory cried. And then he stopped himself. "The last time I said that I sent my all of my brothers to their deaths. No. Not to hell with my sons. My sons never worked a day on that boat. I never let them. You know why? Because I didn't want to see the ocean swallow them up like the rest of my family. I carry with me enough guilt. That's why. But the *Halcyon* deserves to be captained by a good man. You're a good man. You're a better man than my sons. I love my sons, but you're a better man."

Seraphine looked down at his hands, unsure of how to respond to such an endorsement. "You got for me what I most desired," Glory continued, his voice becoming thick.

"You got it for yourself."

"It doesn't matter. I got it. But you need to promise me one thing. Do for me one thing if I give you this boat."

"Yes."

"Don't you die on it. I don't want to see my sons die on it, but I don't want to see you die on it either. You're like a son to me. And Mary is my prize. Don't you dare leave her."

"I won't," Seraphine said softly, looking into the captain's glassy eyes. "I won't."

He took Seraphine's hand and pressed it to his chest, Seraphine feeling the rise and fall of Glory's final breaths before going to meet his maker.

XV

Rainy Days

For most children, rainy days would relegate them to their rooms, staring longingly through the blurry, rain-rinsed window panes at the damp outdoors. They might take out a book or play board games, but there would be no tree climbing, no bike riding, and no ball playing until the rain subsided.

For the children of Provincetown, rainy days brought as much outdoor enjoyment as sunny ones. There is no greater sensation than swimming while the rain falls, dimpling the surface of the water. The children would run around in their swimsuits, dancing in the falling rain, and diving into the water for a double dose of wetness. The fresh mixed with the salt as they tasted the sprinkling of water on their faces, the clean freshness of the rainwater in some licks and the salty taste of the sea in others. There is no getting dry on days like this, and that was the way they liked it.

The children dove under the water, and floated on their backs, looking up through the surface of the water at the dim, blurry sky above them and the rings made from the splash of every raindrop that hit the ocean. The rain falls and is absorbed into the ocean only after it has made its initial pockmark in the water's surface, replaced by another before the water can mend itself. When the rain is hard, the water is covered with dimples and ripples and splashes, and when the rain is soft, it is easy to see each separate drop make its landing.

Joseph and Sally ran down the street, barefoot, as soon as the rain began to fall. They were wet before they got to the beach, and as they rushed, they ran into other neighborhood children, fleeing the confines of the indoors to the freedom of the beach. Though high tide, the sand was damp and pocked from the falling rain. Their favorite spot was near the icehouse where there was an outfall pipe with water rushing out of it, creating a miniature waterfall that soon became much more appealing than just swimming in the harbor.

The rain had been falling hard and the rushing water from the pipe had created a gully that was beginning to fill with water from both the rain and the rising tide. Joseph, Sally, and two other neighborhood children, Reggie Santos and Maxine Silva elbowed each other to get under the rush of the pipe. They let the dirty water run down their backs, and sometimes it came out so strong that it knocked them over. They flopped around in the trench, laughing, the pressure of the water pinning them down and rushing over them.

Joseph was letting the water run over his head while Maxine and Reggie were falling down in the water of the gully. Sally cried, "Joseph, let me stand under the pipe. You're hogging it!" But when Joseph wouldn't move, she gave him a shove, and surprised by her strength, Joseph toppled over into the water that was about thigh deep. Maxine jumped under the pipe with Sally, and the two splashed each other and laughed hilariously. Sticks and leaves and old tin cans were falling out the pipe and raining down upon the laughing children.

"Hey look!" Joseph cried, pointing to Sally, "You got a turd on your head!"

"A turd?" she asked bewildered and delighted and began to laugh. The others laughed hysterically as they floated on their backs and held in their guts.

"Hey! I want a turd too!" Reggie called and rushed under the pipe.

"Me too!" called Maxine, and the lot of them began to scramble under the pipe, attempting to get their share of the refuse. They elbowed and shoved, fell into the tide on their stomachs, splashed and danced and ran along the beach. Every time one of them appeared to have a turd land on his or her head the children laughed with glee and delight and scrambled for more.

Other children were quick to join the fun, and the beach became a swarm of neighborhood children. They all knew each other. They were like siblings, for they had grown up together as their parents had. They knew whose house was whose, who had a dog, who had the black cat with the white stockings, who had a boat, and who had a baseball bat.

They played all afternoon until their stomachs began to growl with hunger, and the only calling from their amusement was the smell of dinner about to be put on the table or the call of a mom that lived nearby.

"You kids get off the beach. All of you, before your mothers have a fit and your dinner gets cold!" Mrs. Silva called from her front porch, since Maxine lived across the street.

As quickly as they had come down the road, the children ran back up it, through the rain. They jumped in the puddles and let the rain water rinse all the salt off their shining bodies. The clothes of the children, who had come at a moment's notice without putting on swim trunks or suits, clung to them. The little boys were bare-chested, and the little girls' brown ankles showed under their damp skirts. Their hair was matted to their foreheads, and each had a gigantic grin on his or her face.

They arrived at their mothers' doorsteps sopping wet and in desperate need of some soap and a bit of drying out.

There was a time when Tommy, too, enjoyed playing in the outfall pipe, but on this occasion, he had bigger fish to fry.

"Where are you going?" Mary halted him as he began to slip out the door behind her.

"To the breakwater."

"What for?"

"To catch rats."

"What in God's name is your fascination with those rats? You'd best leave those poor creatures alone."

"But Ma, Art's father's gonna shoot them! It's high tide and the wind's picked up. It's some stormy out there and those rats are gonna be pushed right out of their nests. It's prime for shooting rats."

"I don't want you anywhere near guns," Mary scolded him. "You stay right here."

"Aw, Ma, come on! It'll be fine. Art's pa was in the war, remember?"

"And he's a stinking drunk."

"Please, Ma. There ain't nothing better to do! *Please*. I might never get to do this again!"

A lengthy amount of argument went back and forth between them, until Mary finally threw up her hands and gave in.

"I've got to get dinner ready, and I can't spend the whole afternoon listening to you sulk and moan. Go ahead, but you tell Frenchie that if you come home with any holes in you, I know where to find him!"

Tommy took off down the road, his clothes drenched all the way through by the time he was only a few houses up the road.

Art and his father were already coming out the door when Tom arrived at their gate. Frenchie was a thin man with long, unkempt hair, and a haggard face that was more from years of alcohol abuse than age.

"Evening, Sir," Tommy said politely, but was only received with a nod and no change in the deeply creviced face.

The house was gray and dark, almost as though it were nighttime. The clouds that had rolled in were a steely, ominous gray that blocked out the sun almost entirely. The rain was falling in sheets, and the wind picked up, and through the dim light of the window, Tommy could see the slight figure of Art's mother, hunched over and clearing something off of a table.

A moment later, she appeared at the door in a worn, plaid housedress and a stained white apron. She was frighteningly thin, and she stooped considerably, enhancing her appearance as a frail, diminutive woman. She was younger than Tommy's mother, but her face was gaunt. She had deep, black circles under her eyes, and her angular nose protruded from her sunken face. Her lips were thin and drawn, and her light brown hair, pulled back from her face into a bun, was filled with coarse gray hair. Her pale eyes looked sad and lifeless, and her whole demeanor gave an air of desolation and apathy.

"Chuck, where you going?" a mousy voice squeaked through the doorway.

"Going practice shooting. Be back in a bit." He did not turn to face her, nor raised his voice above a grumble.

"Hello Ma'm," Tommy politely greeted her.

"Oh, hello, Tom. How's your mother?" Art's mother gave a weak attempt at a smile.

"She's good. She asks about you from time to time."

"That's nice, dahlin'. Tell her I'm fine. Give her my regards." But Art's mother did not look fine. She looked like she'd just crawled out of the grave. "Well, don't stay out for too long. I'll have dinner done soon," she continued to her husband and son.

"We'll be back soon, I said. Now, get back in the house," Frenchie said abruptly, and his wife slinked back inside and shut the door.

Tommy was feeling rather uptight by this point and was not so sure he wanted to go rat hunting anymore.

They began to make their way down the road, and Art started to discuss the rats. "They come out of the breakwater when the rain pushes the water too high. They wriggle around those stones and swim in the water like a bunch of drowned cats. They're the size of them too! Then Dad, he shoots one and blows the head clean off. He blows them right to nothing but a black stain on the rocks." Art laughed in a way that Tommy felt was rather sinister. "The water just keeps on coming and so does those rats, and we get them one after another. There must be hundreds of them . . ." The excited stream of consciousness would have continued had Frenchie not intervened.

"Shut your mouth," Frenchie growled, and Art immediately stopped talking. Frenchie had his gun clutched down at his side in one hand, and with the other hand, he pulled a flask from his jacket and took a swig.

"How old are you now, Tom?" he asked, making a feeble attempt at conversation, and with a tone so cold, Tommy was reluctant to respond.

"Twelve. Almost thirteen."

"That right?"

"Yeah, he's the same year as me," Art chimed in.

"I didn't ask you," he said coldly, and Art cowered ever so slightly.

Tommy was taken aback by Frenchie's demeanor, especially toward his own son, for Tommy had never been talked to like that by either of his parents.

"I knew you two was the same age, but I didn't know if you two was still in the same grade. My boy here ain't the smartest fella. I figured he'd been held back by now or was kicked out. I should have guessed my boy got more of the smart genes cause he sure ain't got no spine. Just like his mother. He ain't nothing like me. I was only a few years older than him when I went to the war. I've seen lots of things no teenage boy should see, but they make me stronger. I learned about life. I wasn't sheltered from the real world. My boy here, he ain't got no idea about life. Life's cruel. You gotta look out for yourself. Nobody's gonna take care of you. He's used to his mother babying him. He gives me lip, and she sends him up to his room. Hides him. Won't let him deal with me like a man. Meet me face to face." He spit. "I tell ya. I never thought no son of mine would turn out like this. He better pray that those countries in Europe get their acts together, else we're gonna have another war. War would eat him up and spit him out. He wouldn't last a single day, my boy wouldn't. He ain't cut out for the hard life."

Tommy looked over at Art, who had his head down. He thought he might have seen a tear running down Art's cheek, but it was hard to tell with all the rain. Tommy didn't want to leave Art behind with this monster, but he had a knot in his stomach that made him queasy.

"Aw, Sir," Tommy choked. "Art ain't a bad kid. Art's my best friend." And Art glanced at Tommy with a look of either fear or gratitude, Tommy couldn't quite tell. He couldn't understand how Frenchie could be so cruel to his own son. Tommy had always seen him around and knew that he was one of the biggest drunks in town, but he had figured that Frenchie couldn't be all that bad, what with the way Art always glorified his father. "My pop" this and "my pop" that, he'd go on all day, like his father was some kind of a hero. "When my pop was in the war" and "my pop says." Tommy never suspected that a boy could love a father who was so cruel to him and to his mother, as well, but he remembered his own mother always saying that you cannot choose your family. There was nothing Tommy could do.

By this point, he had little desire to go to the breakwater with Frenchie and Art, and stopped short. The two others turned around.

"What is it?" Frenchie scowled.

"Um, well," Tommy fought for an excuse to go home, "I just remembered my ma wanted me to be home early for dinner tonight. I don't want her to be mad at me."

"Didn't you tell her you were coming?" Art asked.

"Uh. No. I forgot."

"Suit yourself," Frenchie said indifferently. "Me and my boy will shoot a boatload, won't we, son?" And he placed a heavy hand on Art's shoulder, causing Art's downcast face to brighten.

"Sure thing, Pop," Art smiled. "You're missing out, Tom"

"Thanks, Art, but I really gotta go. Ma probably has dinner already on the table."

"Okay, then. See you tomorrow, Tommy."

"Bye, Art." And the boys went their separate ways.

When Tommy got home, he was sopping went, and his shoes squeaked as he stepped inside the door. He walked into the kitchen to find his mother at the stove and his father at the table packing his pipe.

"Back already?" Mary looked over her shoulder, surprised.

"Yep."

"Well, dinner won't be ready for a little while yet."

"That's okay. I'll wait," and he sat down in the chair closest to his father.

Mary turned to tell him to go up to his room and change into some dry clothes, but when she saw the unfamiliarly somber look on Tommy's face, she decided against it. Something was bothering him, and she figured she ought to get a chance to find out what.

"Did rat hunting go okay?" she measured her words.

"Yeah. I didn't bother going," he said unenthusiastically.

"Why not?" Mary asked. Seraphine had finished lighting his pipe and was leaning back in his chair, puffing on it, and looking at his son's disheartened expression.

"Just didn't feel like it," he replied, and Mary was surprised because Tommy was never one to give up on an adventure.

"I just thought," he continued, "I'd see what Dad was up to."

Seraphine's expression remained blank, but his eyes seemed to burn right into Tommy. "Well, nothing as exciting as shooting water rats," he said, pretending not to notice anything out of the ordinary.

"Ah, those rats are overrated," Tommy said, still looking down at the table. "You gotta work tomorrow, right Dad?" Tommy looked up with a glum expression.

There was a pause, and Seraphine shot a quick glance at Mary who was looking on, still uncertain. "Nah. I was thinking of taking the day off." He rubbed his hands on the edge of the table.

"Really?" Tommy asked, surprised.

"Yep. I'm getting kind of sick of that boat. I need a break from it."

"Well, what're you gonna do?" Tommy asked eagerly.

"I don't know. Maybe you'd like to do something with me?"

"Sure!"

"Cause, when I'm not on that boat, I don't know what to do with myself. Maybe we could go to the movie house."

"Like to see a film?" Tommy's eyes were wide with amazement.

"Sure."

"But you never go to the movies."

"I know, but I think I might like to try it. Something different."

"Great!" Tommy was thrilled.

"Now, why don't you run upstairs and get some dry clothes on and figure out what movie's playing so we know what we're in for."

Tommy jumped from his chair. "Okay Dad!" he cried and then scurried up the stairs.

Mary and Seraphine looked at each other. "So what do you think happened?" Mary said.

"Frenchie."

"You don't think he hurt him, do you?"

"Nah, Frenchie knows better than that."

"Maybe he hit Art."

"I don't think Frenchie would do something like that in front of Tommy, but I've heard that he's pretty rough in the way he speaks to the boy. His wife too."

"Well, as difficult as Tommy can be sometimes, he's no fool. It wouldn't take much for him realize that man's not right."

"Yep."

"I just hope he didn't hit him."

"My guess is that a lick to the face is better than some of the things that man says to his family." Seraphine puffed on his pipe.

"Poor Arthur. Poor Lorraine. That man's a devil," Mary sighed and turned back to the stove. There was silence for a minute or two before she said, "Seraphine, what on earth are you going to do with yourself in a movie house?"

Seraphine's mouth turned up at one corner as he rubbed his finger along the crack in the table. "I don't know."

XVI

The Cat and the Kale

Mary proudly surveyed the lush heads of kale that filled her vegetable garden. "I think I'll make a nice pot of kale soup for dinner tonight," she said to herself and took a walk to the general store to buy some linguica, bean and bacon soup, and potatoes.

She stood in the market with a basket in her hand, examining the tightly packed shelves for a jar of pepper, when Sandy Buckets, Bill's wife, approached her. "Looks like you're making kale soup for dinner tonight."

"I sure am, Sandy. You should see the beautiful kale I have in my back yard. Wow! I've never tried to grow it before. I don't know why. Apparently it's pretty easy because I've got enormous heads of it. It feels so much better making soup with something you grew yourself."

"That's great," Sandy said, "But you better wait to use that kale."

"Why?"

"You have to wait until the first frost. It kills the bugs."

"I haven't seen any bugs on my kale plants."

"They're there. But the frost'll kill them. Then you can eat as much as you want. You better plan something else for dinner."

Mary frowned. She distractedly waved good-bye to Sandy and looked down at her basket. She didn't feel like making something else for dinner. Ever since she had gotten the idea in her head, she had had a hankering for kale soup, and that was what she was going to have. She paid for her groceries and headed home.

Mary knelt down in the soil of her garden near the biggest kale plant she could find. She spread the leaves of the plant apart, closely examining the leaves. "There's no bugs!" Mary exclaimed. "What is Sandy talking about?" With that, she snapped the head of kale out of the ground and took it inside to wash it thoroughly. Still no bugs. Mary grinned to herself. "See, this kale's fine."

Mary sautéed the linguica in the bottom of her big iron *panalla* until it browned. Then she added the cans of bean and bacon soup, pealed and cubed the potatoes, and added just enough water to let it all simmer. She stripped the kale off its thick stems and shredded it into the pot, closing the lid so that the kale could cook down. After some time, Mary lifted the lid and smelled the aroma of the half-cooked soup, noticing that the kale, though wilted, was still dry, and added more water until the kale was just covered. As the water level rose to the top of the pot, to the surface also rose several black dots.

"What on earth?" Mary said as she squinted her eyes to take a closer look, starting back once she realized that the little black dots were small bugs. "Oh hell!" Mary rarely swore, but this occasion greatly warranted such an exclamation. She dipped a spoon into the water, attempting to skim off the dead bugs, but to no avail. She could get a couple of the big ones, but the rest were too small. Mary looked helplessly as the bug-littered pot of soup and clenched a dishrag. She decided that there was nothing she could do about the bugs. "Well I'll be damned if I throw out a good pot of soup!" Food was too expensive, and she had labored to grow that beautiful kale, bugs and all.

So when the family sat themselves around the table, Mary plopped the giant pot in front of them, and served each member herself. She settled herself into her chair at the head of the dinner table and took the first brave bite. "Mmm. Good, huh?" she said, which was out of character for her, as Mary never commented on her own cooking. Jimmy and Sarah nodded.

"Ma, what's those little black things?" Joseph asked.

"It's pepper!" Mary snapped, startling everyone in their seats. They dared not ask anymore questions and continued to eat.

When Seraphine walked in the door of the house one evening, the two youngest children were huddled together on the floor in the living room, laughing and giggling and whispering to each other. Seraphine took a brief glance at the scene but did not bother to investigate the situation. He sat on the bench and began taking off his work boots, when the kids finally spotted him and rushed gleefully to his side, something nestled snuggly in Joseph's arms.

"Dad! Look what we got!" they cried in unison, Joseph opening his arms to reveal a grayish brown cat. Seraphine started up in his chair.

"What's that?"

"It's a cat."

"Yeah, I see, but what's it doing in the house?"

"We saved it," Sally said.

"From where?"

"From the rocks on the beach. It was hiding and was all cold and wet, and we fixed it up and brought it home with us and gave it milk and some fish and it's all better now, see?" Joseph nodded along with Sally's narration.

"That's nice, but you gotta take that cat somewhere else."

"Why?" they asked in unison.

"Because I don't like cats."

"Why?"

"Because I do."

"But why?"

"Because I don't like the way the climb all over everything and dig their nails into the furniture. I don't like how you can feel every bone in their bodies. And I especially don't like how they ignore you even when you treat 'em good! I got nothin' but scars to show for every cat I've ever met."

There was a slight pause as the children pondered this. Then Joseph said, "But he's got six toes."

"I don't care! I hate cats. All of 'em. Even the six-toed ones. Get rid of it. I want it out of this house!"

"But Dad—"

"No buts. I'm gonna eat dinner, and if that cat's not gone by the time I'm done, I'm gonna take that cat into town and throw it right off the end of the wharf!"

The two children looked at him wide-eyed in horror, astounded at the sudden heartlessness of their, generally, gentle father. They'd never heard their father say anything so terrible in their lives. Then Sally's lip began to quiver, and her eyes started to glass over. Seraphine looked at them, then to the cat held limply in Joseph's hands, then back to the children's crushed faces. His stern expression faltered followed by his shoulders drooping forward in a sign of utter submission. He sighed deeply.

"Keep the cat."

The children burst from their dismay into hops of glee and claps and began to turn to run off, but Seraphine stopped them for one, simple compromise. "But don't let me see that cat again or make me have to take care of it."

"Okay!" They hurried off without even looking back, and Seraphine shook his head, thinking again that perhaps he had made a mistake.

As Seraphine sat eating his dinner, while Mary indifferently fished for insight into his day, Seraphine started, the spoon halfway to his mouth, at the sensation of something rubbing against his ankles. He dropped the soup-filled spoon back into the bowl, and looked under the table to see the cat weaving back and forth between his legs, and then sit to rub the side of his face against Seraphine's shin.

Gripping the edge of the table, Seraphine hollered in the direction of the stairs, "Get this cat out of here!"

Sally and Joseph frenziedly rushed down the stairs, scrambled under the table to get the cat, the cat letting out a screech, and then rushed back upstairs with it in their arms.

Mary, still focused more on her own activity at the stove, said, "Seraphine, don't give them such a hard time."

"I'm not. I just don't want to see that cat."

"Cats aren't so bad."

"Maybe to you, but I hate 'em." He went back to eating his soup.

Later, as he sat in the living room, rocking back and forth in his father's rocking chair, tuning his violin, he looked up to see the cat rubbing itself along the armchair.

"How'd you get in here so quietly?" he said under his breath, in awe at the silent stealth of the cat and a little apprehensive. He went back to his instrument but kept one eye suspiciously on the cat that now leapt onto the settee at the other side of room and began kneading its claws into the upholstery. Seraphine widened his eyes in horror.

He hollered upstairs again, "Will you get this cat the hell out of here? He's ruining the furniture!" But this time there was no response, and the cat was left to do his damage. Finally, unable to witness the destruction any further, Seraphine chucked his bow in the direction of the cat, frightening it off the chair and behind the table in the corner. Seraphine pleased with the result went back to plucking at his violin, until he eventually became tired, and placed it back in the case. He rocked, back and forth, back and forth, the dull creak of the runners relaxing him, and under his heavy eyelids, he gazed down at the worn carpet.

Just as he was about to doze off, he caught sight of the cat's yellow eyes glowing at him from behind the table. Seraphine opened his eyes slowly and looked straight back at the cat. The cat then began to creep out from behind the table, taking only a couple wary steps at a time, pausing to sit, eye-up Seraphine, and consider the safety of venturing out any farther. The staring match continued even as the cat was halfway across the floor. Then the cat was at his feet, and suddenly it was in his lap. Seraphine's hands gripped the arms of the chair, and finally he unclenched one hand and let it hover, shakily above the cat's back. Then he slowly let it come down and glide along its fur.

Sure, he could feel every vertebra in the cat's spine but he marveled at how silky soft the fur was; how it changed color when he moved his hand in the opposite direction. The cat nestled itself in his lap, rubbed its face against his belly. Maybe it wasn't so bad, for a cat. It was kind of nice having something he could hold in his lap. Fluke was much too big. And his fur wasn't as soft. And he didn't smell too good a lot of the time. Seraphine supposed that there must be some benefits to having a cat after all.

Then Serephine jolted in his chair as he felt a sharp pain is his thighs. "Aaah!" he cried and threw the cat off of him just as it had begun to knead its nails through his trousers. "Get out of here you filthy cat!" The cat disappeared immediately, and Seraphine decided it was time for bed.

In the middle of the night, he was awakened by something tickling his nose, and opened his eyes, to find the cat lying on his chest, its tail brushing across his face. Seraphine let out another annoyed cry and pushed the cat onto floor.

"What's wrong?" Mary mumbled, her back to him.

"The kids have to get rid of that cat," Seraphine grumbled and went back to sleep. He arose again, just before dawn, to go to the bathroom, and as he groggily made his way down the hall, he stepped on something soft, and heard a screech come from the cat. Seraphine nearly jumped out of his skin, and the cat scampered down the hall to the stairs. His heart in his throat, Seraphine made a vow that he would get rid of that cat first thing in the morning.

The cat rubbed along the backs of his legs as he stood at the counter chewing on his sweetbread. Seraphine tried to kick it away, but the cat just kept coming back. "Don't you realize I don't like you?" he glared down at it. Fluke sat at his usual post waiting for a morsel of bread to fall, but the cat seemed to have no effect on him. He watched it from time to time but, otherwise, did not allow it to interfere with his usual routine. The cat then jumped onto the counter to lap from Seraphine's milk, and Seraphine yanked the glass away before crying, for the very last time, "Get this cat out of here!" And for the very last time, there was no response. That was it. The kids had lost interest already, and he could no longer tolerate this creature in his home.

He grabbed a burlap potato sack from behind the pantry door, snatched the cat, underfoot, by the scruff of its neck, and dropped it into the bag. It clawed around for a few moments before submitting, and Seraphine determinedly clutched the bag at his side before heading out the door. Fluke wanted to follow, as he usually did, but Seraphine told him to stay. Today there would be a brief detour from the usual routine.

He strode down to the beach, where he always kept a rowboat turned upside-down, flipped it over, tossed the bag into it, pushed it out into the water, and climbed in. As he began to row into the harbor, he noted that the burlap sack was moving again, and somehow the cat had managed to work itself out of the opening. It sat there and stared and him, as Seraphine rowed. It licked its paw, raised it to clean its face, yawned, and then did the other side. Seraphine's rowing began to slow as he watched. He gave a brisk shrug and then said, "That's it, Cat. Don't think your gonna make me feel bad."

Once he got to the Point, he shuffled the cat back into the sack and carried it onto the beach where he opened it back up and shook the cat out onto the sand. "There you go, Cat. This is the end of the road for us."

The cat sat there and blinked up at him. "I'm leaving now. Have a good life, Cat." It continued to just sit and blink. So Seraphine climbed, with the heaviness of a guilty man, back into the boat and pushed off, rowing directly to Railroad Wharf.

By the end of the day, he'd practically forgotten about the cat, and strode home with Fluke at his side, whistling, not sure why he felt so happy. But as he unlatched the gate and stepped into the front yard, the whistling came to an abrupt halt. The cat was sitting on the stoop, looking right at him.

Seraphine thought he had seen a ghost. How on earth had it gotten all the way from the Point back to the house? "Is this some kind of joke?" he demanded as he crashed through the door. Mary, in the kitchen looked over her shoulder. "What are you yelling about?"

"The cat! The cat! What is it doing here?"

"You said the kids could have it."

"But why's it back here?"

"Back? I didn't know it ever left."

"I . . . but . . . I . . ." Seraphine groaned and then collapsed on the bench, absolutely bewildered and defeated. The cat hopped into his lap and helped itself to a seat. He was too baffled to even care.

"Gee, Dad, what a nice cat," Sarah's voice said from above him, and she picked it up. "I thought you hated cats."

"I do," Serephine said weakly.

"Is this the one Joseph and Sally found?"

"Its ghost."

"Huh? Well this seems like a really nice cat. Look, he has six toes. Do you know that's good luck?"

"Yeah, luck."

Sarah just laughed. "Well, I like him. I'll take care of him. You know Joseph and Sally won't."

"Do what you want," Seraphine said feebly, but added without much command, "Just don't let me see it again."

"You won't," Sarah responded, and he didn't . . . not much, anyway.

Julianne Papetsas 2011

XVII

The Last Days of Summer

The summer was nearing its end for the boys on the beach, but they did little thinking about the cooler weather and the school year ahead. They enjoyed their last days of stumbling around barefoot, their clothes wrinkled and dirty, their skin brown from the sun, before their mothers would stuff them into stiff, starched shirts and jam their feet into uncomfortable shoes in an effort to make them look presentable for their teachers. They had no interest in new notebooks and freshly sharpened pencils, and they loathed the idea of being stuck behind a desk in a hot room, listening the droning voice of the teacher, and gazing out the window as another sunny day was passing by. For now, these last days of freedom, they would ignore the encroaching days of school and enjoy the outdoors to the very fullest.

Tommy was playing baseball on the sand lot behind the cold storage building where the fishing nets were tarred. Rudy had a baseball bat, Art brought the ball, and most of the others had their own gloves. They ran easily through the sand, jumped, dived, slid. They got sand in their pants and an entire beach in their hair, and they laughed and jeered and egged each other on all the while.

Jarrod Cunningham, a summer kid, slid to what was designated as first base just as Art was catching the ball thrown to him by Tom.

"You're out!" Art declared.

"What do you mean I'm out? You blind? I was safe by a long shot!" Jarrod stood up, sand stuck all over his body, his pale skin red from both heat and anger.

"No way, I had the ball way before you got there." Art's dark hair was damp with sweat, long, and hanging into his face as it usually was for lack of proper maintenance.

"Yeah, but your foot wasn't on the base." Jarrod hadn't even bothered to brush himself off.

"Yes it was!" Tommy yelled from home.

"Shut your mouth! You're too far away to see it. You kids don't even have a real base."

"What you talkin' about?" Art wrinkled his nose bitterly.

"Don't you folks have a real field to play on?"

"Course we have a real field," Rudy jumped in. "But playin' on the beach is better."

"Yeah, what d'you know about baseball anyways, Summer Kid?" Art challenged.

"A lot more than you do. I may be a summer kid, but where I come from, we know how to play baseball the right way."

"So do we!" Rudy protested

"Yeah, you can't handle playing on the beach. You need some fancy field to make you play well. You're just full of excuses 'bout you can't get to the base in time," Art snipped.

Jarrod glared at him, "I bet you ain't even seen a real Red Sox game before either."

"I've heard it on the radio," Art curtly replied.

"That don't mean anything. You don't know anything about baseball until you've seen the Red Sox play for real."

"You stuck up, summer snob, I oughta—" Art clenched his fists and stepped heavily in Jarrod's direction, and Jarrod reached out and grabbed the front of Art's shirt. Before any of the other boys could react, the two were rolling around on the sand, angrily wrestling each other, though neither of them ever appeared to get any serious shots in.

As the tussel continued, a voice from the dock called down to them. It was Sou'east, one of the more legendary fishermen in town. "Hey boys, you cut that out, or I'll hafta come deal with you myself. You gonna waste the whole day fighting like a couple of fools when there's dolphins in the harbor?"

The boys immediately ceased their fighting, and all turned to look at the old salt standing upon the dock. "Dolphins?" several of them cried.

"Yeah. Go see for yourself. It don't happen every day."

The boys scrambled to their feet and turned to Luke Days who had the boat. It was a little skiff with a sail, entirely sufficient for a rag tag bunch of boys. He never kept it far away, because they never knew when they would need it, and they hustled down the dock to get it and untied it from its piling. They loaded in and shoved off.

In the distance, they could see the steel gray dorsal fins cutting through the water. They pulled the sail in, catching as much of the light wind as they could, and leaned forward toward the bow, urging the little vessel forward alongside the swiftly moving school of dolphins. There were nearly a hundred of them, their sleek bodies leaving a rippling wake behind them. The boys traced their fingertips through the water, trying to touch the shiny backs, but they could't quite reach.

"Luke! Try to get in front of them!" Tommy called.

"Pull the sail in more!" Luke responded. "Lean forward!"

"There ain't enough wind," Art said, but Tommy noted that the pod looked like it was beginning to turn.

"Wait! Come about, Luke! The dolphins are going to go in the other direction."

So Luke pulled the tiller hard and brought the boat around, Rudy quickly pulling the sail in, and the other boys ducking and then resituating their weight. The boat suddenly took off as it caught a gust of wind, and they were able to get in front of the circling pod of dolphins.

"Stop the boat!" Tommy cried, and Rudy slacked the rope allowing the sail to luff in the breeze and the boat to stand still. The boys quickly rushed to the sides and leaned over, gazing down into the water. The dolphins were quickly upon them and they swam under and around the boat, incorporating the tiny vessel into their group. The boys watched the bodies of the dolphins dip under the water and remain submerged as they swam beneath the boat, their steely gray backs outlined under the rippling water. Occasionally one would roll over onto its back revealing a brilliant underside, the whiteness masked only slightly by the yellow-green color of the water. The boys dipped their hands into the water, and Jarrod was lucky enough to have his fingertips brush the smooth, slippery surface.

"I touched one!" he cried with glee, and the others, not to be outdone, leaned even farther forward over the side of the boat, dangerously close to falling in. The boat was surrounded by the swiftly moving dorsal fins that glided in perfect unison. The boat did nothing to break up the dolphins' rhythm, and Tommy was filled with the sensation of being carried along with them. So mesmerized were they that it came as a shock to the boys when the last dolphin swam by. With that they all sat up and leaned back in the boat, sighing.

"Wow! That was great," Luke said.

"Yeah," Art conceded.

"We could do it again," Rudy proposed.

There was a pause.

"Nah, I've had enough," Tommy said. "Let's go in, and get something to eat."

"Yeah, I'm hungry," Art agreed, so he pulled in the sail, and Luke took hold of the tiller, and the little boat sailed back to the beach.

"I don't want to go back to school," Tommy moaned when they were halfway there.

"Don't even talk about it," Jarrod said. "At least you get to stay here all year. I've got to go back to Western Mass."

"Well, it ain't any fun around here either," Art added.

"What do you mean? Course it's more fun than where I'm at. Least you get to go the beach."

"Not when it's snowing," Art responded, more defensively than was necessary.

"Snow?" But before pursuing the question further, Jarrod paused and thought about it and then nodded. "Yeah, you're right. I never thought about that. I always forget you guys get cold weather too. It's just 'bout I'm only here in the summer."

"That's right. It ain't so different from where you live," Rudy said.

"True. But I sure would rather be here than at home right now."

"Yeah," Tommy said. "There ain't no dolphins in Western Mass. Say," he continued after a pause, "since we don't have many days left, why don't we camp out on the beach tonight? You know, make a bon fire."

"And eat *conkerinkles*!" Rudy exclaimed.

"Conkerinkles?" Jarrod furrowed his face inquisitively.

"Snails," Tommy and Art responded together, and then they all cheered at the idea.

The boys went home to gather their things and make a show to their mothers that they were still in one piece. Some snuck a square meal that they would never admit to, and others attempted to assemble a larger group, a task that was not overly difficult. Art, Rudy, and Jarrod, were in charge of gathering driftwood and seaweed for the bon fire while Tommy and Luke both rushed to their homes to get the paint cans, stopping each youngster they passed along the way to inform him of the event. Tommy spotted little Johnny Calhoun sitting in a wicker chair on the front porch of his house reading a book. Johnny had been scarce since his outing with Tommy and Art earlier in the summer. From the paleness of his skin, it was obvious that he had not gone on any adventures beyond the pages of *Robinson Crusoe*.

"Hey-a, Johnny. Watcha been up to?" Tommy hollered jovially and paused outside of the white, picket gate. He saw Johnny cringe at the sound of his name and slide even deeper into his chair on seeing that it was Tommy.

"Oh, hello Tom," he said, not very demonstratively.

"We're having a bon fire. Wanna come?"

"Oh, no, I don't think so."

"Oh come on! It'll be a great time!" Tommy waved him along.

"No. Really. I'm—busy."

"Doing what? Reading? Come on. You've got all winter to do boring stuff like that!"

"No. Um. I—have a dentist appointment." Johnny gave a little shake of his head and a dismissive turn of his shoulder, but the worried look on his face negated all conviction he tried to assume.

"Johnny. I know you ain't going to the dentist at five o'clock at night. What you scared of?"

"I'm not scared," Johnny retorted unconvincingly.

"Well, then come. I'm not gonna see you for a long time after this."

"Like you care."

"Well, sure. I get sick of seeing the same people all the time."

"You're full of malarkey."

"No I ain't."

"If you like having me around so much, why do you make me do terrible things and call me 'Summer Kid' and make fun of me all the time?"

"I don't make you do terrible things."

"Yes you do!"

"Like what?"

"You make me hunt for rats and get my toes bitten off by crabs. You make me walk through the nests of killer birds, and then you expect me to jump off a wharf that is really high!"

"Johnny, who you foolin'? You didn't do half those things."

"That's not the point. You expected me to, and then you made fun of me when I didn't."

"We was just having fun."

"Well, your idea of fun is a little different from mine." Johnny, who had risen a bit from his seat in the heat of his annoyance, sank back down with a pout and folded his arms crossly over his chest.

Tommy scratched his head, not sure of how to proceed. "Well, all right then. See you next summer, I guess." As Tommy turned to go away, Johnny's eyes fluttered a bit, breaking up the stoniness of his expression. He looked at the book folded in his lap, and then turned behind him and peered around the high back of the chair at Tommy traipsing down the street. He looked back at his book, lifted it close to his face, lowered it back down, looked over his shoulder one last time, and then tossed the book to the side. He hopped down from the chair and hurried to catch up to Tommy, his short legs doing double the work.

"Tom! Wait!" Tommy heard the voice behind him, and slowed his already measured steps. "Wait, Tom!" Johnny panted again once he got to Tommy's side, his face bright red and gasping for air. "I—I change—ma—my mind. I—I think—"

"It's okay," Tommy said and slapped him on the shoulder. "Did you tell your ma?"

"Oh, why, no." Johnny straightened, realizing that, in acting on impulse, he had also forgotten all proper protocol.

"We can tell her on the way back from my house. Don't want her to think you got kidnapped or something."

By the time Tommy had given Mary a quick holler through the storm door that they would be having a bon fire that night, snuck a few empty paint cans from the shed, reported to Johnny's mother the full details of the night ahead (with some slight adjustments), and made it back to the beach, the other boys were almost finished building the bon fire. The group had already grown to double the size it was before, and it was bound to get bigger. Some boys were hunting along the beach for wood and other fuel to toss on the growing fire. Others began to scrape snails off the side of pilings and into buckets, while some went out onto the flats of the falling tide and began to dig up little necks and quahogs. One rushed back home to raid his mother's sewing kit for pins and another drew a box with a couple lonely matches from his pocket and struck one, setting the entire pile of salvaged debris into a giant flame.

The sky was beginning to dim and the boys drew near the fire, their eyes glowing, the orange fire reflecting off their faces. A couple jumped up and began to make Indian noises, doing a dance around the fire, the rest quickly joining in. The group of a dozen or so boys and girls jumped and danced and twirled around the fire sometimes tripping and rolling down into the sand, bellowing with laughter. Once the sun was completely gone, they all sat down and began to cook the snails over the heated paint cans. Once they felt they'd cooked up the critters to satisfaction, they stuck the pins into the opening of the shell and dug out the salty, chewy flesh.

"You know. In France, they call this escargot," Johnny said.

"Es car who?" Art frowned.

"In Provincetown we call it good eatin'," another boy added.

They cooked clams as well and the shells began piling up. It took a lot of snails and clams to satisfy the ever increasing group of youths. When the eating was done, they all sighed with pleasure, lying back in the sand and staring up at the stars. The contrast of the orange flames made the sky look even blacker than usual, and each star was like a spark from the crackling wood.

"I got an idea," one boy proposed. "Let's tell ghost stories."

"Aw, do they have to be ghost stories?"

"Well, any kind of stories."

"I got all kinds of good stories that my dad tells me."

"It's gotta be something scary, though."

"I like to make up my own."

"They're better if they're true."

"Yeah, that's right."

"Who's gonna go first?"

"I will," Timmy Cook said, raising his hand and solemnly straightening his shoulders for the task. The crowd of boys hushed as Timmy's seriousness grasped their attention.

"I have a story to tell, a story that will make your blood turn cold. If any of you are afraid of ghosts, you better leave now. If any of you are scaredy cats, you better go home to your ma. This story ain't for no little kids. This story makes even the bravest shake in their boots." The boys stared at Timmy, mesmerized. Everyone knew that Timmy was the best story teller.

"Everyone knows the Martin House."

"I don't," Johnny Calhoun squeaked.

"Sh!" Tommy shushed him. "Let him tell the story."

"It's an inn and restaurant on the Front Street. It's real old. Built in 1700s," Rudy clarified. He already knew gist of the story, but he continued to listen politely.

"Well," Timmy continued, unshaken by the interruptions, "my dad used to work there, and he told me that the place is *haunted*."

"Yeah, yeah, we all know it's haunted," Art yawned.

"Yeah, but you ever actually seen a ghost?" Timmy challenged.

"No."

"Well my dad has. Many times. And it was all while he worked there. Now, back before the Civil War, there was something called the Underground Railroad-"

"What's this gonna be a history lesson?" Art complained, crossing his arms. "I'll be getting enough of that in three days."

"Shut up, Art. I wanna hear the story," Jarrod Cunningham snapped. Jarrod was from South Boston and wasn't intimidated by Art even slightly.

Timmy continued: "Well, slaves who'd escaped from the South used to hide out there. It was one of the stops. There's this secret little room hidden between two fireplaces. They called it a "snug harbor" where the slaves used to hide out. Well, one night, my dad heard this knocking sound coming from the secret passage, and he went and looked behind the door. Sitting there was the ghosts of a whole family of slaves! They were sitting right there on the floor! They looked all dirty and skinny like they'd been

169

starving. All of a sudden the big one, probably the father, my dad figured, held out a hand like he wanted something, but my dad shut the door real fast before they could grab him or something!"

There was a gasp from the crowd; from all except Art who sat and feigned boredom.

"But that's not all," Timmy resumed his tale. "That's just the beginning. My dad was sweeping the lobby one night when he looked in the mirror hanging on the wall. In the mirror he saw a man walking back and forth. When he turned away from the mirror, he could see a bunch of men pacing around the room with their arms folded behind their backs. It was like they didn't even see each other or my dad! Dad ran up the stairs and asked the owner of the building about them. He said that that room used to be where women had their babies, and those were the dads waiting. He told my dad they wouldn't hurt him. The slaves in the closet wouldn't either."

All the kids made a relieved sigh.

"One night my dad was cleaning behind the bar when he heard a cabinet slam behind him. He turned and saw a little slave girl standing there looking at him. He knelt in front of her and put out his hand. She walked over to him and touched his face with her hands. They were face to face, but he could still see the wall behind her!"

"He could see right through her?!" Luke exclaimed.

"You can see through all ghosts," Tommy said matter-of-factly. The rest nodded in assent.

"Just when he was thinking she was kinda cute, the little girl gave my dad a big smack on the cheek and laughed and disappeared. He could still hear her laughing even after she was gone and feel her cold hand of his face. Some nights, when it snowed real hard and he couldn't get home, he'd sleep in the spare room upstairs and the little girl would come and lie next to him. He could feel her coldness next to him. But then she'd pull his blankets off him and laugh, or pull his pillow out from under his head. I actually think she kinda liked him. The owner said she wasn't evil, just curious and mischievous. The same could be said for the sea captain and his wife. Sometimes my dad would see clouds of smokey stuff appear in front of the fireplace, but the fireplace wouldn't be lit. The smoke would turn into the shape of a man with a big beard. Sometimes my dad would see a woman in a rocking chair, knitting. She was the captain's wife. When my dad asked the owner about them, the owner said, 'Oh, today is the day he died. He always appears on this day.' They used to own the house."

"Wow," Johnny said, wide-eyed. He loved the stories. "These stories actually aren't all that scary. I think I'd kinda like to meet these ghosts."

"Oh please. You'd wet your pants if you saw a ghost," Art scoffed.

"Leave him alone!" Tommy rebuked.

"Oh no," Timmy gravely shook his head. "It gets worse. Much worse." After a dramatic pause, he continued: "There was one room upstairs where the door was always closed and locked. One night my dad thought he heard footsteps up there. He asked the owner if he should clean the room since, obviously, people were staying in there. The owner got a scared look on his face. 'Oh no, don't go in there,' he said. 'There's a ghost in there and you don't wanna meet him. He's a mean one. He's not like the others.' 'Who was he?' my dad asked, but the owner said he didn't know. Nobody ever got close enough to find out. One night, my dad heard a creaking sound and looked up the stairs to see that the door to the room was open. My dad figured he'd better go close it 'bout it was winter, and lots of cold air was coming down. As he went to touch the knob, the lights in the room began to flash on and off. He got real scared, but he couldn't move. It was like he was glued to the spot. He felt something really cold grab his arm and yank him into the room. The lights kept flashing, and wind began to blow even though the windows were closed! Things began to fly all over the room like somebody was throwing stuff. Then the shadow of a man formed right before my dad's eyes in the middle of the room. It made an angry face and held out its hands like it was gonna grab my dad, but my dad hollered at the top of his lungs and fell backward out the door. He slammed the door shut behind him and locked it. As soon as he did the noise stopped. Everything was silent, but my dad had a prickly feeling all over his body."

The boys were all wide-eyed. Nobody said a word.

"What'd your dad do?" Johnny asked.

"Well he sure as hell quit that job!" Timmy said, and the boys laughed nervously.

"So, is the ghost still there?" Frank asked.

"Of course he is!" Timmy exclaimed. "I heard that the only reason why he didn't kill my dad was 'bout he likes to kill little boys instead."

"Little boys?" Johnny yelped. "Like five or six?"

"Oh no," Timmy said. "They got too much baby fat on them. He prefers boys of, oh, about twelve or thirteen. He likes them kinda gangly, so he can chew on the bones."

"Now that's a bunch of bull!" Art argued.

"You're just scared," Timmy snarled.

"No I ain't."

"Nah, Art's right," Rudy added. "That ain't part of the story."

"How do you know?"

"I know this story! I ain't never heard nothing about him eating kids. My ma used to work there too."

"Well-" Timmy was about to argue, but Tommy said, "I think I've had enough of scary stories for tonight."

"Yeah, me too," Jarrod concurred.

"I think I'm ready for bed," Frank said, and the rest agreed. Despite pretending to not be scared, the boys' nerves had been worn thin. They all stood up, throwing sand on the bon fire. It was time to go home to their nice, comfy beds, safe with mom and dad.

XVIII

Back to School

Joseph squeezed a couple fingers under his stiff, new shirt collar and made a tortured face as he scratched his neck.

"Oh, come on, Joe, it's not that bad. Don't you want to look nice for school?" Mary said as she roughly tried to smooth down a chunk of hair that was stubbornly sticking up from the crown of his head. "Look at how happy Sally is with her new clothes."

Sally was twisting around in a new blue dress with shiny, black, patent leather shoes, mesmerized by the way the skirt turned beneath her. Mary had bought it for her, along with a pink dress and white shoes, from a man who was selling clothes from out the back of his truck. Mary and Sally had been in the yard when they saw a small group of people gathered around his truck a couple doors up the street.

"Want to go see?" Mary asked.

Sally nodded enthusiastically and took Mary by the hand. Her eyes lit up at the sight of the two little dresses, simple, but with piping on the sleeves and a thin ruffle around the neckline. "Which color do you want?" Mary asked her, and Sally bit her lip in consideration. She loved them both and struggled with the decision while Mary picked out a new shirt for each of the boys and a pair of slacks for Tommy because he had just put a hole in his good ones hopping a fence after church. She was annoyed about it, but had to admit that they were getting to be a bit short for him. For Sarah she found a navy blue dress with a green floral print and short, loose sleeves. It had a matching tie around the waist and plunged slightly in the neckline, not too much, but enough that Seraphine wouldn't be entirely pleased. She decided that Sarah was old enough now to not have to cover every square inch of her skin. Mary felt it was important for all young ladies to have pretty dresses. For herself, she saw the most beautiful red derby with a simple, black ribbon around the base. It would be perfect to go with the dress she always wore to church, and she adored it the moment she tried it on.

She went back to Sally who was still standing, perplexed, in front of the dresses. "So which one do you like?" Mary asked.

"I don't know," Sally said without removing her gaze.

"Well, you have to decide soon. This nice man has more rounds to do."

Sally hesitated another moment and then snatched the blue one. "Okay. I'll get this one!"

"Good. Let's pay for it." But as they headed to the cab where the salesman was completing a transaction with another woman, Sally shouted, "Wait! I want the pink one instead." So she rushed back to make the switch, but on touching it, she looked at the blue again. "Oh no, actually, I still like the blue one." But then she changed her mind again, holding each up to herself, though there was no mirror to look in. Mary watched as Sally suffered with her decision. She took a peek at the price tags, sighed, and then said, "Let's get both."

"Both? Can I really, Ma?" Sally's face lit up as she crumpled the pink dress against her chest.

"Sure you can. Why don't we get you two pairs of those patent leather shoes, as well; a white pair and a black pair."

"Oh wow, Ma! Thanks a lot!" Sally gave an enthusiastic hop. As they headed back toward the cab, Mary discretely dropped the red derby back on its hook and smiled at Sally's excited jaunt.

"What'll it be for you lovely ladies today?" the wiry man said from behind his bushy, gray mustache. "All this!" he chuckled as they handed him their pile of clothing. "You're my big spenders of the day, I see."

"Well, I've got five kids going back to school tomorrow," Mary smiled.

"Five. Wow. That must put a dent in the ole pocketbook," he grinned.

"Oh, they're good kids. I don't mind."

"Except for Tommy," Sally added.

The salesman laughed loudly. "Tommy. Is that your little brother?"

"Oh no. He's older, but Ma's always gotta yell at him."

"Really? Well, I sure hope he behaves himself after he gets his new school clothes." He winked at Mary. "If not, she can bring it back and get something nice for herself."

Mary laughed. "Oh, that won't happen. New clothes, to him, are more a punishment than a reward." She gave the man the money, and he handed her the clothes in a paper bag.

That night, as she and Seraphine crawled into bed, Mary said tentatively, "I bought the children new school clothes today."

"Good. Did you have enough money to get everything they needed?"

"Oh yes, but I'm afraid I spent a bit too much."

"Don't worry about it."

"But I do. We really can't afford to spend money lavishly."

"The kids need clothes. That's not lavish."

Mary sighed and rubbed her dishpan fingers. "No, it's not, you're right. I wouldn't have bought them if they weren't necessary." Seraphine was already under the covers with his back to her. "It's just so hard when we barely make ends meet. I want to make sure I spend every cent wisely."

"You do just fine, Mary," Seraphine said sleepily. "We're doing just fine. If the kids need new clothes, buy them new clothes. It's fine."

Mary smiled and kissed Seraphine on the cheek before lying down herself.

***

"Tom! Get down here and eat your breakfast. You don't want to be late on the first day of school!" Mary shouted up the stairs. Seraphine had gone to the wharf hours ago, Sarah and Jimmy were already on their way because school started earlier for them, and Sally and Joseph were just slamming the licked-clean spoons on the wooden table and hopping from their chairs. Tommy, as usual, was the last one to be ready.

Joseph and Sally went to school only a few minutes up the street. There were three small elementary schools in the town; one in the East End, one in the West End, and one in the center of town. Since all of the children walked to school, the school system was structured so that the little ones didn't have to go too far. Mary used to walk her children to school in the mornings, but now she felt Joseph was old enough take care of himself and keep and eye on Sally during their short journey. Tommy went to the middle school which was in Town Hall, and Sarah and Jimmy went to the new high school on the hill.

Sally and Joseph hollered goodbye to their mother as they rumbled to the door. "Sally, remember to wait for Joseph at lunch so he can walk you home. Joe, remember to get your sister!" Mary called as the door slammed shut. Tommy finally dragged himself down the stairs, scuffing his feet on the floor and looking gloomy. "Shoot me now and get it over with," he mumbled.

"Oh for crying out loud, Tom! When your father was your age he was working on the boat all day long. He would've loved to have been able to go to school instead of breaking his back. Now smarten up and get going." She put an apple in his hand and pushed him onto the front stoop, closing the storm door behind him.

She stopped two steps from the door and paused, closing her eyes. Silence; a strange bliss.

Sarah and Jimmy usually walked to school together, as well. She was a junior and he was senior, and they frequently ran into each other in the small brick building.

"I can't believe I have Ms. Crane for algebra this year," Jimmy moaned.

"She's not so bad."

"Course you would say that. You're a teacher's pet."

Sarah didn't deny it. She was smart. She liked school. She always had a book open in her lap. She hoped, someday, to go to college.

"If she flunks me, they'll keep me off the football team."

"You won't flunk."

"Yes I will. I'm lousy at math, and Crane's a tyrant."

It was true; Jimmy's weakest subject was math. He preferred history, though he didn't do very well in any subject. "I'll help you study. You'll be okay," Sarah assured him. Jimmy always tried to pawn his homework off on Sarah, but it never worked. Even though it would take a fraction of the time if she just did it for him, Sarah preferred to sit with him and explain everything, taking the time to make sure he knew how to do it himself. She wanted to be a teacher some day.

"How's Vickie?" Sarah asked, changing the subject.

"You're so nosey!"

"God. Don't get so defensive. I'm just trying to make conversation."

"I don't ask you about your love life."

"That's because I don't have one. And believe me, I'm not trying to live vicariously through yours."

"Why you always gotta use such big words with me?"

"What? *Vicariously*? All I'm saying is, I don't really care what you and Vickie do. It's just that she's one of my really good friends, and I hardly see her anymore because she's always running around with you."

Jimmy didn't comment.

"Do you have football after school today?" Sarah asked.

"Yeah."

"What position are you this year?"

"Running back and linebacker."

"How can you play two positions at the same time?"

"I don't. One's offense and one's defense."

"Oh."

"There aren't enough guys. Everyone has to do both—you know that."

"I know. I just wasn't thinking." There was a pause. "You're going to be the star this year, you know."

"I don't know. Maybe. Depends on how well I do."

"Jimmy, you're great. Everyone knows it."

"You're going to pull your nose out of those books for a minute to come see me play, right?"

"Oh, of course," Sarah said.

"You should go out for cheerleading!" Jimmy proposed, half jokingly.

"Absolutely not!" Sarah snapped.

"Oh come on. Don't you want to wear one of those cute little skirts and stand on your head?" Jimmy was laughing at the thought of his serious, book-smart sister doing flips across Motta Field.

"No way!" she frowned and gave him a shove.

They made their way up the granite steps that lead to the heavy wooden front door of the school, which had been built in '31 during the depression as a government funded job opportunity like the Sagamore Bridge over the Cape Cod Canal. It was small, compared to most other high schools that were being constructed, but this was because there were no more than sixty-five students per class. The building was made of red brick with gray granite trim, and paned windows looked across to High Pole Hill and over the harbor. The children could sit in certain classes and watch the fishing boats coming and going around the Point, trying to spy their fathers and seeing the seagulls make lazy circles in the sky.

The principal's office was to the left and the guidance counselor's office was to the right. In front of them were the glass-paned doors to the auditorium separated by rows of narrow, orange lockers. Painted above the lockers was an intricate mural depicting the Pilgrims' landing which none of the students ever noticed, except, perhaps, Sarah. The library and cafeteria were on the first floor, and the gymnasium extended off the main part of the building.

All the students, this being such a small school, were involved in most activities and worked together to keep the school alive. Without participation from all hands, the school's programs would cease to exist, and Jimmy and Sarah were no different. Though football was his favorite and best sport, Jimmy also played basketball in the winter and baseball in the spring. Sarah was not much of an athlete but she was on the student council, wrote for the school newspaper, and stage managed for the theater class that would put on the plays of Eugene O'Neil and Susan Glaspell.

Vickie spotted Jimmy and Sarah as soon as they stepped into the hallway with their locker assignments. "Hey!!" she called as she walked toward them. She was pretty with a head of dark brown ringlets that hung above her shoulders. She tucked any whips behind her ears and held the bangs back with barrettes, revealing her pretty, round face, small, pouty lips, and long, dark lashes. The summer months had browned her arms and given a pleasant pink flush to her cheeks. Or maybe it was just from seeing Jimmy, Sarah thought as she struggled to not roll her eyes.

"Wow, Sarah, I feel like I haven't seen you all summer!" Vickie said cheerily.

"That's because you haven't."

"No. I must have seen you. Didn't I?"

"Maybe once at Adams."

"Yes! That's it. I bumped into you there." Vickie's face lit up at the recollection. She took a sidestep toward Jimmy. "When's the first home game, Jimmy?" she asked, batting her eyelashes a couple times. Sarah wanted to gag.

"Next weekend."

"Great. I'll be there!"

"You're cheering this year, right?"

"Absolutely not!" she exclaimed.

Sarah laughed. She really did like Vickie, though her relationship with Jimmy teetered on the edge of being annoying. Sarah didn't mind that they went out with each other, she just wished they didn't always try to be so secretive about it. Did they think she was blind?

"Jimmy's always trying to get me to be a cheerleader too!"

"Well, he should get over it," Vickie said primly. "If he wants to see me in a girly uniform, he can come watch one of my tennis matches in the spring." She stuck her nose up at him. "What class do you have now?" Vickie asked Sarah. She, too, was in mostly upper level classes, so she was usually in the same room as Sarah.

"Biology."

"Me too! Oh god. I hate biology. Do you have English third period with Mrs. Rogers?"

"Yes," Sarah responded.

"Good. I can only find good things to say when I've got you around to bounce ideas off of."

Jimmy, growing bored with the girls' chatter, spotted some of his friends across the hall and was saying bye to Vickie and Sarah just as the bell rang. They saw him go to the group of boys he'd been friends with since they were little kids and congratulate each other on being Seniors.

"I guess Jimmy's embarrassed to hang out with us little junior girls," Sarah said feigning bitterness.

"Oh phooey," Vickie waved him off. "Let's head to class."

As the girls walked down the hall, Vickie put her arm around Sarah, half hugging her. "I really did miss you this summer."

"I missed you too," Sarah said quietly. She was much less bubbly than Vickie and wasn't quite sure that Vickie meant what she said.

"We really should've hung out more. I'm sorry. I started full-time at Tip's waiting tables, and then on my days off I would just nap on the beach all day."

"And in the evenings you would hang out with Jimmy."

"Sometimes," Vickie responded, a tinge of guilt in her voice.

There was an awkward silence. "You don't mind do you?" Vickie asked with the utmost sincerity in her tone.

"What?"

"Me going out with Jimmy."

"No. Why would I?"

"I don't know. I just thought maybe you did. Because we're best friends and all."

"No. I just wish you two wouldn't sneak around like thieves in the night. It doesn't bother me."

"It's more for our parents' sake. I don't mind if you know, just as long as you don't mind. But my mom is so old-fashioned."

"I don't mind."

"Okay. Well, promise me we'll hang around more together now that school's started?"

"Sure."

They waved to a group of girls that they knew. Actually, they knew just about everyone and had known everyone since they were little kids. That was the beauty of living in a small town and going to a small school, but as with all places, people ran with certain crowds. Most of Vickie and Sarah's friends were also juniors, though some they were tight with simply from growing up in the same neighborhood.

"Ugh," Vickie said as they got to the door of the science classroom. "Make sure I don't blow anything up."

"You won't. That's chemistry."

"Oh yeah. Phew." What she didn't realize was that they were dissecting frogs for a special treat on the first day of school.

The stands were full of cheering fans, waving orange and black pennants. Seraphine, Mary, and the children sat together on the last two rows. Vickie was there, too, seated beside Sarah, and the two were laughing and joking—Vickie doing most of the joking, Sarah most of the laughing. Seraphine was glad to see Sarah in such a cheerful frame of mind. She was always so serious when they were home, and he was always afraid that she was lonely and studied too hard. She was quiet, like him, and he found it hard to know how she was feeling at any given time. He hoped that, also like him, her quietness only concealed contentment.

It was a brisk October day, and the people in the stands were bundled up in flannel-lined jackets and scarves. The men had their wool caps pulled down to their eyes and hid their necks in the collars of their jackets to shield themselves from chilly gusts of wind.

"Serry!" he heard Bill call nearby and watched as he and his wife, Sandy, waded through the people on the bleachers to sit next to Seraphine.

"Hi Mary. How are you?" Sandy said, sitting beside Mary while Bill sat beside Seraphine.

"Oh, I'm fine. How are you?"

"Great!"

"Where's Glenn?"

"He's running around here somewhere with a gang of his friends. He's at the age where he's too embarrassed to be seen in public with his mother."

"Yeah, Tommy's the—wait," Mary looked around after noticing the empty space in front of her, "where *is* Tommy?" Sandy laughed.

"Your boy's out there today, right?" Seraphine asked Bill.

"Well, Leo's fifteen, so he's just a grunt."

"What position's he playing?"

"Left bench!" Bill bellowed with laughter. Seraphine chuckled, though he'd heard that joke a million times. Bill wiped a tear from his squinting eyes. "Jimmy's going to be great this year, ain't he?"

"I guess we'll find out soon enough."

"Don't be so goddamn modest. You know your boy's the best out there. He's going to be a Cape and Islands All-Star. He's probably the best running back in the region."

"It's a team sport. He's only as good as the guys blocking for him."

"It's nice to be playing Nantucket at home, ain't it?" Bill said after a pause.

"Sure. Everyone wants to trounce their rival on home turf."

"Yeah, but the problem is if the home team get trounced!"

Seraphine nodded and said, "Nantucket's supposed to be one of the best teams this year. They've only lost one game so far, and that was to Barnstable."

"I heard that too. But those islanders don't have nothing on our boys."

"Nah. I hope we crush them today."

"Damn, Serry, I've never hear you so worked up before!" Bill laughed again.

"Eh, it's just 'bout Jimmy told me, last time they played them, they were giving them a load of crap. Saying things like, 'Hey, is that your boyfriend?' Things like that."

"Who was? The fans or the players?"

"Both, I think. But mostly fans. It was an away game."

"That's bullshit. Where do they get that crap from? That ain't normal heckling."

"Nah. I guess it's all the artists around here in the summers that give them the ideas."

"Those islanders are a bunch of in-breds anyhow. They like to act like they fucking invented whaling. Whaling was dead twenty years ago. They need to find a new claim to fame."

Seraphine snorted and looked over his shoulder to make sure no Nantucketers were sitting behind him. Bill had a habit of getting slightly off-topic. "You're one to talk, you old dory man. Anyways, I think our kids hear it at all the schools."

"Well, let them think what they want. Provincetown's gonna teach them how to play football today."

"Yep."

"You gotta admit, though, Serry, there's an awful lot of queers around here in the summers now." "Yeah. But it don't bother me so much," Seraphine shrugged.

"It don't?" Bill sounded a bit surprised. "At the rate they're coming. They're gonna take over the whole goddamn town."

"Let em. I'm not going anywhere."

"Me neither. Hey, I don't care as long as they're in the East End with the rest of the Commies."

Sometimes Seraphine didn't know how to handle Bill's bigotry. There were times when Bill could offend every creed and color in a matter of five minutes. Seraphine scratched his head under his cap. "You remember when the Portuguese weren't wanted, too, don't you? Remember when the KKK came and burned the cross in front of the Catholic church? I'd never want to hurt somebody like that. I don't pay much attention in church, but I know one thing, *Do unto others . . .*"

Bill seemed to miss the last part of what Seraphine said. "Hell, the Portuguese still aren't wanted, but we sure as hell are *needed*. Those damn Yankees can't fish worth a shit. If it weren't for us, there'd be no fishing industry."

Seraphine just fixed his gaze on the football field.

"Jesus Christ! Look at the size of those legs on number sixty," Bill exclaimed, for the first time noticing the game.

"Yeah, there's some big guys on Nantucket this year."

"But our kids are tougher."

Seraphine and Bill intently watched the competitive match. Both the size of the Provincetown team and the size of its players were comparatively smaller than other teams. It was hard to field an entire football team at such a small school with so few people, but they still could compete. The Provincetown kids just had more spirit. Perhaps it came from a sense of adversity simply because of their size, and perhaps it was because, mentally and physically, they were like men playing with boys. They were smaller in stature, but they were tough as nails because the Provincetown kids started working on fishing boats at such a young age. They spent their summers, and then some, helping out their fathers or uncles, and the trade made them stronger and more mature. They'd seen more and endured more than most men twice their age, and being used to the rigorous work on a boat made them plenty tough for football. That's why their mascot was the Fisherman.

The Fishermen quarterback was sacked hard. He was flattened on the ground by a defensive tackle twice his size, causing a nervous gasp from the stands.

"That looked like it hurt," Bill said.

"Yeah, Dory Plug's son."

But he got right up and kept playing just as hard. He passed the ball off to Jimmy for the next two downs, to the excitement of the crowd who'd waited for months to see how Jimmy would do. Jimmy was not the biggest nor the fastest running back, but he was strong as a bull and tore through the opposition with every ounce of energy he had. He was not easy to pull down, and the play often ended with four or five guys piled on top of him.

"Go Fishermen!" the cheerleaders shouted on the sidelines with their orange and black pom-poms. The score was fourteen to ten, Provincetown, when a miniscule marching band came onto the field for halftime entertainment.

"Between the football team, the cheerleaders, and the marching band, the entire school's on the field!" Bill laughed.

The crowd cheered loudly when the Fishermen came back to continue the rough game. Mary covered her eyes every time Jimmy got the ball. "Oh god, I can't watch this! Can't they pass the ball more?"

"Jimmy's their go-to. They're not going to risk an interception if they know they can just hand it off to Jimmy," Sandy said. She was a big football fan, always wore her orange and black, and hollered encouragement at the team. She was short and plump with sandy colored hair and round, red, puffy cheeks, but from this little body came a voice that could carry across the entire field. "That's okay John! Just shake it off! Frankie's open! Pass it! Would you look at that hit? Way to go P-town, way to go!" Sandy would stand up in her place, shaking her fists in the air, and clapping, her whole body wiggling with energy. So when the Fishermen won, she was elated. "Great job, boys! States this year!" Then she sat back down and wiped unruly hairs from her red face. "Wow. I need a drink now."

Bill, who had been entirely uninvolved is his wife's activity, heard the word "drink" and said across Mary and Seraphine, "Me too. Anybody want to hit the Governor Bradford with us tonight?"

"Nah, that's okay," Seraphine said. "I'm ready for a nap." Mary agreed and they said their good-byes and got up to leave, Mary waving for Sally and Joseph to follow. Sarah was going off with Vickie, and they figured Jimmy would be doing the same. Dory Plug stopped them on their way across the field. "Your boy's one hell of a football player. That's for sure!"

"So is yours," Seraphine said with a nod.

"He ain't too tall, but he's built like a brick shit house!"

"That's from working with his father," Mary said. "I feed him well, too. He's gonna eat me out of house and home."

"Hey, whatever it takes to keep him playing the way he does!"

Jimmy flagged them down as they continued toward the street. "Hey! What'd you think?"

"Great game, son," Seraphine said.

"You were excellent, dahlin'," Mary added. "You aren't hurt at all are you?"

"No, Ma, stop babying me," Jimmy rolled his eyes. "I'm gonna shower, and then I'm going to head off with the guys, okay?"

"Sure," Mary said. "Just don't get into any trouble, and if you see that brother of yours, will you tell him to get home by four? I can't have him gallivanting around like you high school kids."

"Okay," Jimmy said, grinning from ear to ear with sheer elation at the Fishermen having beat their rival. "See you later."

Seraphine, Mary, and the young children headed home through the crisp fall air. The blue sky was sprinkled with whispy grey clouds blocking out the sun enough to make the town seem shadowy.

"I love the fall," Mary said. "I love the way the leaves smell and people's fireplaces burning."

"Me too," Seraphine said. He'd heard her say this every fall for the last twenty years they'd been together.

The street seemed quiet, almost desolate, after a bustling summer. October always marked the end of the tourist season, and the town almost seemed to go to sleep. The people clung to last days of nice weather and stored up for the long winter ahead. The leaves were changing and beginning to fall, and Sally and Joseph kicked every pile they passed by. They ran in the street in circles and only got back on the sidewalk when the rare car would pass by.

Mary's flowers were turning brown, and the house was gray against the dim blue sky. She had put a pumpkin on the stoop to add a little color, and it welcomed them into a warm, cozy house. These were the days when one most looked forward to going home.

XIX

Rum Running and Train Jumping

Tommy, Art, and their usual gang of friends wove through the blueberry bushes and brush-filled woods. The scrub pines were spindly compared to what one would imagine to find in Sherwood Forest, but for the boys they were plenty big to create suitable adventure grounds. The dry leaves and pine needles crunched under their feet, and they frequently snagged their clothing and scraped their legs and arms on the tangles of brambles. They skirted around poison ivy when they saw it, but inevitably one of them would be seen covered in a rash by the next day, white with calamine lotion.

Tommy, leading the way, pushed low-lying branches aside, allowing them to snap back into the faces of the others. They picked up sticks and tossed them simply for the sake of doing so, grabbed cranberries and popped them into their mouths, making faces at the bitterness and challenging each other to see who could stand it the longest, and shook high branches with sticks in order to scare birds off of them. They continued in this fashion until they came to a clearing.

"All right, boys," Tommy said, his voice deeper than usual. "Let Tom's Pirate Gang begin to plunder."

"Plunder? What the hell does that mean?" Art asked, his already frowning face furrowing even deeper.

"It's a pirate word. I read it in a book. That's what pirates do. They plunder."

"So how do we *plunder*?" Frank asked.

Tommy thought hard for a moment, "Uhh, well . . . it means we have to make a fort. So we can hide from our enemies."

The boys considered this, but unwilling completely concede, Luke persisted, "Who made you the leader anyway?"

"Yeah, and who would come up with a stupid name like 'Tom's Pirate Gang.' That ain't what pirates call themselves," Rudy added.

"Well, you got a better idea?" Tommy snapped, but nobody did, so they went their separate ways to begin finding wood for their fort.

The boys were always playing pirate games, carried away by tales the old timers had told them of days before the town was inhabited and the peninsula was a place for pirates to stop, rest, and unload their booty. It was a wild land full of criminals and outcasts, lawless men with no religion. The Puritans of Truro wanted to claim these Province lands as their own, reform the ruffians, and make it their suburb. But the land could not be tamed, nor the people in it, and since long before its inception, the town had always had a life, a law, and a code all its own.

The pile of branches was getting bigger, and the "builders," assigned by Tommy, were beginning to give it form. The boys efficiently went about their duty, when Rudy's voice could be heard calling at a distance.

"He's found something!" Luke cried, and they all ran to see what it was.

Rudy was flagging them down as he stood beside a giant wooden barrel, piled on either side with leaves and drifted sand so that it appeared to have been there for quite some time.

"It's treasure!" Luke cried, his eyes wide with excitement.

"That ain't treasure," Timmy shot him down, and Art pushed through the crowd of gaping boys and commanded, "Let me at it."

They made room for Art, who had the presence of someone who knew what he was doing, and watched as he knelt beside the barrel and felt around until he appeared to have found what he was looking for. It took him minute, but he eventually pulled something free from the barrel. He gave the spot a sniff, stuck his little finger into the hole he had just made and licked it.

"Just what I thought," he said expertly.

"What?" inquired Tommy.

"It's a keg of whiskey!"

"Whiskey!" they all cried in unison.

"How do you know?" asked Frank.

"How do I know?" scoffed Art. "I've swiped plenty from my Dad's stash, but even he ain't got *that* much lying around. Hell, he'd kill himself if he ever got a hold of this!"

The boys were awestruck. "What do we do with it?" asked Rudy.

"Do with it?" Art was repulsed by these boys' naiveté. "We drink it!" He said it with such hurrah, the other boys couldn't help but cheer along, and they all lined up to put their mouths to the precious keg. One knelt beside it while two others helped tip it ever so slightly, just enough for some to pour into the other's mouth. Rudy was first since he had found it, and the others laughed as his face puckered in disgust at how it tasted.

"That's gross. Who would drink something like that? It might as well be motor oil."

"Ah, you'll get used to it," Art said and took a big swig like a pro.

Tommy who had never tasted whiskey before was also taken aback by its fiery flavor, but he tried to conceal his startled reaction so as not to embarrass himself in front of the rest of the boys. He was the Pirate King after all. "I like the way it tastes," he said, wiping his mouth with his forearm.

"Yeah, it ain't so bad, Frank added, though it was obvious he liked it no more than the other boys. They each forced down another mouthful and then another, until Frank said, "Hey, do you feel that? I feel all wobbly."

"Yeah," added Luke, "I feel all warm inside."

"I feel like I'm walking on air," Rudy said.

"I want some more!" said Tommy, and this time he meant it. "It don't taste so bad at all. I kinda like it."

"Nah. It's pretty good."

"Good? I say it's great!"

They all continued to take mouthfuls from the hole in the keg, and in just a short time, they were laughing and stumbling, trying to stand on their heads, but doing somersaults instead, dancing and spinning around, each going back for another swig.

Tommy fell on the ground, "Where do you think this stuff came from?"

"My dad says that during the Prohibition, when alcohol was illegal, rum runners used to smuggle booze into the country by stashing it in the woods out here or throwing it overboard into the harbor. Lots of times, though, they couldn't remember where they left it, or got caught before they could come get it," Art answered. "My dad's been looking for years to find an old whiskey barrel. It'd be like striking gold for him."

"Well, it's our treasure."

"Damn right."

By this point, most had fallen to the ground, and they all were sprawled out on the ground, some sitting, some leaning, some lying down, in an uneven circle.

"I'm sleepy," Frank said, and then nodded a bit before falling all the way backwards onto his back.

"I feel sick," said Rudy, and crawled to the edge of the clearing where he began to throw up in the bushes.

Tommy and the others began to laugh at him, until suddenly Tommy, too, felt nauseous and threw up. Art got dizzy but passed out before he got sick, and Luke was hiccupping and clutching his head. After hurling the remainder of their lunches, they each fell into a deep, dark slumber, spread out on the pine needle strewn ground.

In less than an hour, they were each awaking, one by one, clutching their heads, and moaning in agony.

"I've never been in so much pain in my life," groaned Tom.

The others agreed.

"Who ever thought it was a good idea to drink all of that stuff?"

"It's Tommy's fault. He's the leader," Frank said weakly.

"I didn't say any such thing. It was Art. He was the one who told us what it was," Tommy's voice was too pained to effectively argue.

"It ain't my fault. Rudy found it."

"I just wanna go home."

"Ma's gonna kill me."

"I'm gonna be dead either way. Might as well be in my own bed."

They stumbled, blindly home, each step sending pain into their throbbing heads. They didn't even say bye to each other as each boy, one by one, passed his door. All they cared about was getting home.

Tommy stumbled up the walkway and tripped to the front door, nearly crashing through it, and making a clumsy racket as he headed straight up the stairs.

"Tommy, is that you?"

The fear inspired by the sound of his mother's voice sobered him for a moment, but he quickly fell back into his stupor as Mary came out of the kitchen to see what all the racket was a about.

"Where have you been?" she asked as she rounded the corner.

"Nowhere."

"What have you been up to?" she eyed him suspiciously, seeing his disheveled state.

"Nothing."

"Is that alcohol I smell?" Mary's eyes snapped open wide with the discovery.

"No," Tommy said as innocently as he could, but by this time, he was slumped down on the bottom step, his chin lolling on his chest, his eyes half open.

"Oh yes you have! I'm not even gonna ask you where you got it from. It doesn't matter. I'm gonna find out after I sober you up!" Mary grabbed him roughly by the shoulder of his shirt, Tommy letting out a half hearted cry, and dragged him to the bathroom where she turned on the faucet and allowed a torrent of ice cold water to pound on him.

He gasped and sputtered and lay there in the cast iron tub looking like a drowned rat. Then Mary gave him a good couple of whacks on the rear with a wooden spoon and dragged him to bed without any dinner. "That'll show you to never let me catch you in this house drunk as a skunk again!" And she stormed down the stairs.

Tommy limply let his heavy head hit the pillow. It felt like a rock, and he closed his eyes wearily. The room felt like it was spinning and he hoped he would fall asleep before the nausea could fully overtake him again. Nothing his mother could do to him could possibly amount to the pain he was feeling right now or the pain he'd be feeling the next morning. He swore to himself he would never touch a lick of whisky ever again.

There wasn't a whole lot to do when summer was over, and Jimmy and his friends tried to figure out how to entertain themselves on this lazy Saturday afternoon now that their football practice was finished.

"Now what do we do?"

"I don't know. I'm bored as hell."

"Yeah me too."

"There ain't nothing to do here. It's too cold for the beach."

"Yeah and I'm tired of the food at Cookie's."

They sat in silence, scratching sticks into the ground and doing the typical fiddling of bored souls. Jimmy bolted up and said, "Hey, I got an idea."

"What?"

"The train comes at 12 on Saturdays, doesn't it? What d'you say we hop on and take a little ride up the Cape?"

"Sure!" they all agreed, less because they were going to go visit another town, and more because they were going to be sneaking onto a train.

JULIANNE PAPETSAS 2011

The passenger train to Provincetown had been established in 1873 in the hope of promoting a tourist industry now that whaling and mercantile shipping was on the decline. The railroad became the most popular mode of transportation to Cape Cod, much more comfortable than choppy, potentially dangerous boat rides across the Bay. But the boys surely weren't going to be sitting snuggly on the cushioned seats of the passenger cars. Instead they'd be hitching a ride on the back of the fish cars that came daily to pick up loads of fresh fish, straight from the docks, and some from the ice houses, to be shipped all over the state. The train's arrival was truly revolutionary for the town because it served as one more bridge to the outside world. Before, the only way to get to the town was by boat, but the coming of the railroad was a sign of more opportunity to reduce the sense of isolation. When the car grew in popularity, the primitive road that passed across the entire Cape was paved and turned into a driveable highway. Before that, it was unheard of to travel by land; it was not nearly as efficient as going by boat.

Still, many townsfolk did not have cars, or if they did, they didn't use them often. Everyone in the town walked to where they needed to go, and few felt any need or desire to go up the Cape. They had all they needed right in their own town.

But for bored teenage boys, getting out was essential, and they plotted a way to get onto the train, the best option being simply to hop on the caboose as it began to pull out of the station. They felt like they were bandits robbing a train, even though there was nothing to steal but fish. They waited by the New York Store for the train to roll by, and once it did they chased it and hopped on, grabbing onto whatever they could to hoist themselves aboard.

They rolled along and saw little more than the scrub pines that lined the tracks. They rolled through the dunes, the white sandy hills that shifted and moved with the blowing winds, changing shape and size. They rolled through the high hills of Truro, farmland with livestock and corn. At times they could see the bay and the curving shore, they passed Pilgrim Lake that had once been East Harbor, but was cut off with land fill for fear of a storm blowing through and making Provincetown an island. Occasionally they saw a modest wooden house or a general store or a person in a car, but for the most part, it was just trees. They felt the cool air in their faces as the train chugged slowly along, not much faster than a boat leaving the harbor.

It took quite some time to get where they were going, but the novelty of the adventure did not wear off, and their excitement grew when they saw houses beginning to become more frequent and, eventually, what was clearly the center of a town. The train stopped and the boys hopped off taking note that the last train to pass through Hyannis to Provincetown would be at five o'clock. They gazed around where they were. The main street was not as long or as crowded with shops and people as it was at home, but they enjoyed going into the stores. They went into a baseball card shop, a bookstore, and other novelty shops that were very different from any of the stores at home. They bought hotdogs and ice cream sundaes, but were in agreement that the Adams's sundaes were much better—Dottie put more fudge.

The people were relatively friendly, but the Yankees were more closed mouthed than the chatty Portuguese back home who would take any opportunity to weave a good yarn, whether one wanted to listen or not. The store clerks would ask where they were from and how they had gotten there, but otherwise, few questions were asked and little conversation was made.

The boys checked out Hyannis's beaches, as well, but were somewhat disappointed. Perhaps they were creatures of habit, but they just didn't seem as good as the ones at home. By the time they had seen all the sights and spent all of their money, it was time to catch the last train, otherwise they'd be sleeping in the train station for the night. The train was rolling by as they reached the tracks. The boys chased it down and just barely managed to grab on.

"We'll have to do that again," Chuck Enis said.

"Yeah, but it won't be for a while. It's gonna take me some time to make all the money back that I spent," Jimmy said.

As the train reached the final rise in Truro, the skyline of Provincetown and the harbor suddenly became visible. The town was like a mirage glimmering on horizon, the Monument against the orange evening sky, towering above the rest of the buildings, and the water of the harbor glistening, a few fishing boats still dotting the surface. The way the land curved, placing the town in the middle of the bay, Provincetown could have been an island, but the boys knew better as the train rolled down the other side of the hill, the trees and dunes again blocking the town from their sight until they were back in the middle of it.

There was nothing to be seen but scraggly scrub pines and sand until suddenly the wilderness faded away and the clusters of houses appeared. The boys hopped off the train at the New York Store, and parted ways. They were glad to be back home.

XX

Sarah

Most nights, after dinner was finished, Seraphine would sit in the living room in his rocking chair by the fire or open window, depending on the season. He often enjoyed listening to football games on the radio, but much of the time preferred the silence to sit and think. Sometimes, he would not even feel like picking up his violin. On nights like these, Sarah would come in, after helping Mary clean up the dishes, and read to him.

It was hard to deny that Sarah was his favorite child, though he loved them all, and despite the fact she was with her mother most of the day, Sarah's bond with her father ran deeper. Perhaps it was because she was the only one of the children who distinctly looked like him. The other children had mostly their mother's features, but Sarah was not so fortunate. What she lacked in beauty, she made up for in intelligence, and Seraphine was very proud of her for doing so well at her studies. He, himself, had barely any education at all. He was twelve when Josephine died, and from that moment on, he'd had to fend for himself. Even while his mother was alive, he was in and out of school, because he always had to work to help support the two of them. His knowledge was based on common sense and practical skills, but he was ignorant in most academic areas. His reading skills were elementary.

His desire to make up for all that he had missed and his natural curiosity made him look forward to Sarah's reading. She could say all of the big words and explain what they meant to him, and he would sit quietly and ponder everything she read.

"What will it be tonight?" she asked.

"I like that Emerson fellow," Seraphine said as he rocked slowly in his chair.

"Emerson? Are you sure?" she looked at him skeptically.

"Yes."

"But Emerson's so boring—*I* don't even understand him half of the time." Sarah was always amazed at the fact that he had taken such a liking to the dense, transcendental essays of Emerson.

"It forces me to think harder. Once in a while, I actually pick something up."

"Wouldn't you rather hear *Moby Dick*, or *Huckleberry Finn*, or something by Hemingway?"

"Later. Right now I want to hear some more of that essay you were reading to me last night."

"All right," she sighed and took the Emerson anthology off the shelf. She pulled up a stool beside her father, and began to read the essay *Self-Reliance*, slowly, and carefully so that she, herself, could digest the words and grasp their meaning. Seraphine listened attentively, his hands resting on either arm of his father's rocking chair, easing it slowly back and forth.

". . . *Thus all concentrates; let us not rove; let us sit at home with the cause. Let us stun and astonish the intruding rabble of men and books and institution by a simple declaration of the divine fact. Bid them take the shoes from off their feet, for God is here within. Let our simplicity judge—*"

"Wait," Seraphine held up a hand as though to stop her. "Read that last line again."

"Let our simplicity judge them?" Sarah asked.

"No, the one before that."

"Bid them take the shoes from off their feet . . ."

"Yes, that one."

". . . for God is here within."

Seraphine put down his hand. "God is here within," he inaudibly mumbled to himself, mouthing the words, more than once.

Sarah waited, looking at him expectantly, but all he did was wave his hand for her to continue. She finished the essay without him stopping her again, and she wasn't sure, from the blank expression on his face, that he had comprehended anything else she had read. She came to realize that her father enjoyed Emerson because, through all the incomprehensible gobledy gook, he once in a while picked up on a phrase or idea that meant something to him. It was like finding a piece of blue beach glass amongst the brown, green, and clear.

"The End," she always said when she finished reading something before closing the book. She placed it in her lap and was about to get up from her stool and say goodnight, when Seraphine spoke,

"So, how is school going?"

"Good. Great. I'm getting good grades, and I like my classes."

"You like your teachers?"

"Oh yes. Especially my French teacher, Mrs. Martin."

"French, eh?" he asked. "Is that your favorite class?"

"No, I prefer English. You know how I like books."

"What about friends? Do you have many girlfriends?"

"A few. I don't have a lot of friends, but I prefer to have a few close ones, anyhow. Vickie's my best friend. She likes going to parties and dances more than I do, but, for the most part, we're very similar.

"You don't like to dance?" Seraphine furrowed his brow at her.

"No. I like to dance. I just—I don't know—I just don't feel like going, that's all."

Seraphine chuckled a bit, "There are a lot of boys missing out, then."

Sarah shook her head skeptically. "No."

"No? Well, why not? There must be plenty of boys falling over themselves for you!"

"Dad, don't be foolish," she frowned.

"What do you mean? Why, any boy would be happy to be with a nice girl like you."

"I'm not even that interesting."

"Course you are! You're smart and kind and you work hard. You're one hell of a cook too! Your mother taught you that well. And you read good."

"Dad," she said, shaking her head, "nobody cares if I'm a good reader."

"I like it," Seraphine shrugged.

"Dad, look at me. You and I both know that I'm not nearly as attractive as any of the girls up at that school. No boys even look twice at me. I've got a nose the size the Mount Kilimanjaro. I'll bet every guy I pass in the hall says 'Oh look! There goes the girl with the Roman nose! . . . It's roamin' all over her face!'" Sarah said it bitterly, but Seraphine still couldn't help but laugh. It was one of his favorite jokes—he'd learned it from Bill. "You're no help, Dad. I wasn't trying to be funny. Why are we even talking about this?"

"No, no. I'm not making fun of you. You're beautiful. You look just like your grandmother."

"I'm n—I look like my grandmother?" Sarah's interest was sparked. Seraphine did not talk about Josephine often, but when he did, he made her sound like some kind of saint. Sarah was intrigued by tales of this divinely mysterious woman that she never met and never knew.

"Yes, you are almost the spitting image of her. That thick, dark hair, your eyes, your beautiful skin. You got that all from her." He paused and continued with a helpless grin, "And your *proboscis* . . . you got that from her too, I'm afraid. But, hey, we can't have everything."

Suddenly Sarah did not feel quite so disappointed about her nose. If Josephine could pull it off, so could she.

"Your grandmother was a strong and proud woman and that made her attractive in her own way. You are the same."

"I hope so." Sarah looked down at her hands. "Dad," she continued, slowly measuring her words. "I've been thinking. I know Ma wants me to get married and have twenty kids as soon as I graduate and move in the house right next door to you, and—well, you know. But I think I want to go to school instead. I know I want to go to school."

"But you do go to school," Seraphine said naively.

"Not high school. I mean, after high school. I want to go to college."

"College? Why?"

"I want to be a teacher. I want to teach English. I think I'd be good at it, and I need more schooling to be able to do it."

"Do any other girls at school who want to go to college?"

"Not really, but I don't care what the other girls are doing. I think it would be good for me."

There was another pause, and Sarah waited while Seraphine appeared to be thinking. "Will you go far?"

"No. Well, not too far. I won't go outside of New England. New York at the very farthest."

"*New York?*" Seraphine choked. "You mean you're going past the Cape?"

"Well, yes. There aren't any colleges around here." More silence. The chair was creaking as Seraphine rocked in it, staring hard at the wall in front of him.

Finally he said concernedly, "You'll come back, right?"

Sarah laughed a little. "Of course I will. Is that what you're worried about? This is my home. I'll always come back. You know, unless I become world famous or get whisked off to Europe by some handsome stranger."

"Those French better keep their filthy hands off of you!"

She grinned, even though Seraphine was only half joking. "So is it okay?"

"Well, it's fine with me, but you still have to ask your mother. You have some time to think about it. See what happens."

"Thanks, Dad."

He nodded in reply.

"Okay, then. Goodnight."

"Goodnight," he replied distractedly, rocking and thinking once again.

When Seraphine and Mary were getting ready for bed, he sat on his side folding his shirt, something he never did, and said, "You know, Mary. Sarah wants to go to school."

"She already goes to school." Mary was laying her head on the pillow and pulling the covers over her.

"No, she wants to go to college."

"College!" Mary bolted up in bed. "She can't do that!"

"Why not?"

"We can't afford to send her to college."

"Oh, we'll work it out. Don't worry about that."

"We can barely afford to keep the boat afloat and fresh paint on the house!"

Seraphine sighed and scratched the side of his rough, red face. "Things are a lot better than they were five years ago. Remember?"

Mary paused and thought, and gave a little laugh. "Yeah. Crackers and cocoa for breakfast. I don't know how my kids are as healthy as they are."

"What did we have for lunch?"

"I can't even remember! Whatever I could scrounge up."

"You did a good job. You kept us all well fed. We barely noticed we were in the middle of a depression. We've never starved."

"Not as long as there are fish in the sea. Heck, you kept the whole town fed. I remember when Milly and her three kids came to the dock looking for food. Her husband had died the spring before in a storm, and you gave her all the fish she wanted. They each came with a big bucket and you filled them right to the top."

"Well, it wasn't selling for much. I was practically giving it away anyways, so I might as well have given it to somebody who needed it."

"After that, everyone would go to the wharf with their buckets. It was like the soup line."

"I wasn't the only one that helped. We all did—all of the fishermen and the clammers and the lobstermen. We all did our part. I think that's why nearly all of us got through it." They both sat there smiling to themselves in reverie until Mary remembered what it had been they were talking about, and, annoyed that Seraphine had successfully changed the subject, she broached the topic again with even more force.

"Well, who's going to help me around the house and with the kids?"

"The kids will be old enough that they won't need looking after."

"Still, what use does she have for college if she's just going to get married?"

"She doesn't want to get married."

"Doesn't want to get married?" Mary exclaimed, flabbergasted.

"Not now, anyway. I don't see what difference it makes if she gets married or if she goes to college."

"It makes a huge difference! Because, if she's at school, she's gone, and I will never see her."

"We'd just have to visit."

"Visit?! An old salty dog like you with your waders on and your hat that's thirty-five years old, and a frumpy housewife like me who's never left this town? We'd be the laughing stock! No, no, it is out of the question."

"You just bought this hat for me for Christmas."

"Seraphine, that was at least six Christmases ago."

"It's what she wants to do," Seraphine said with a note of finality.

"If we always let our children do what they wanted to do, they'd be dead right now—especially Tommy," Mary countered

"You know Sarah is the most practical. She'll be fine."

"But, Seraphine," Mary said sadly. "I know she'll be fine, but she'll be gone, away from here in God-knows-where doing God-knows-what. I'll never see her again . . . I'll miss her too much."

"Ah, Mary," he put his arm around her shoulders, "She'll come back. Don't worry about that. It'll just take some getting used to, that's all. You have almost two years to prepare yourself."

"Oh god, I guess you're right," she huffed. "But please do not talk to me again about it until my two years are up."

"Deal."

They turned the lights out and settled under the covers, their backs to each other. After a few minutes, when Mary thought he was asleep, Seraphine said. "Oh, and by the way, you're not frumpy."

Mary snorted and buried her laughing face in the pillow. Seraphine chuckled too.

XXI

The West End Versus the East End
And a Close Call

For as long as anybody could remember, the West End and the East End were like completely different towns with different types of people; the artists and summer folk concentrated in the East End, while the native Portuguese populations tended to reside in the West End. Naturally, there was plenty of overlap and plenty of local children who lived in both ends. But the groups of children from either end of town had a deep-rooted disdain for one another, and this sense of separation and incompatibility manifested itself in gang warfare with sticks and stones. Each end had its own elementary school which further divided the children until they went to high school where they finally had to learn to get along and had matured past their differences . . . for the most part. But even then, with peace between them, they still had pride in their neighborhood and never forgot the years of animosity.

Seraphine's children were no different than the rest. Jimmy had long since outgrown the child wars, and Tommy still harbored childish animosity but only bothered himself with fights when necessary. Joseph, though, was at the prime age to go hunting for battles, and when a time was set, he was ready and armed with the biggest stick he could find.

Joseph was intently rummaging through a shrub beside the house, searching for the stick he had stashed there. Sally, standing behind him watching, her hands clasped behind her, asked, "Can I come, too, Joe?"

"No."

"Why not, Joe?"

"You're too little, and you're a girl."

"That don't mean nothin'."

"Yeah it does."

"What, then?"

"It means, if you get hurt, then Ma will give *me* a whoopin'."

"I won't get hurt."

"Yeah you will."

"How do you know?"

"Cause I told ya. You're a girl, and you're small."

Sally gritted her teeth, clenched her fists, took one, long, red look at Joseph's smug face, and then gave him a good, swift kick in the shin. As Joseph clutched his leg and hopped on one foot in agony, Sally stormed off. But little did Joseph know, Sally didn't go inside; she hid behind the shed and peered around the corner, giggling at the sight of Joseph's discomfort. Once he recovered and made his way down the road, she followed three houses behind. At each block, Joe picked up a couple more kids until there were around a dozen of them, rowdy with sticks, slingshots, and other weaponry.

The West Enders bravely walked to the center of town, the neutral ground, and then to the dirt lot behind the central icehouse. The East End kids were already there waiting.

"Thought you might chicken out," the biggest of the boys said.

"Nah, we ain't chicken.

The heckling went back and forth, until finally the ringleader of the West End boys said, "Are we gonna get this over with, or are we just gonna stand here and shoot the shit all day?"

The children raised their sticks, and then the two gangs merged into one, blurred frenzy of bodies and flying sticks. They clacked and clapped together, the children's woody version of swordplay. When a stick would fall, they'd resort to fists and teeth and feet and brute force, wrestling each other to the ground, punches and headlocks that stunned and caused bruises, bumps, fat lips, and nose bleeds. They were dusty from rolling the dirt, their hair wild from being tugged, their clothes ripped. Most didn't have shoes, so kicking tended to damage the kicker more than the victim, and stubbed toes comprised some of the worst pain.

The unruly mass was beginning to dissipate as the boys grew weary of the fight and their injuries were getting the better of them. Sally, hidden behind a bush, noted that Joseph was one of the smallest out there, but she was pleased to see that he fought hard. Nothing was solved, nothing was ended, nothing was won or lost or gained, except for some minor injuries and some extra holes in their already ragged clothing.

The retreat was on, in both directions, boys jumping behind turned over dories, dodging around pilings, running down the beach, and crouching behind peoples' fences, attempting to escape one another. A few hearty souls remained where the wild fray had once been, but not for long, and eventually, the sandlot was quiet. In all the activity, Sally had lost track of where Joseph had run off to, so she began to make her way home via the shore which was the route many of the boys had taken, hoping to perhaps catch up to her brother. She trotted across the beach, hugging the pilings of the shore-side houses when she caught sight Joseph in the distance, plodding along slowly in the direction of home, appearing weary from the fight. Sally hurried to catch up with him, when out of nowhere, three East End boys ambushed Joseph and began to pummel him with their fists, Joe collapsing onto the ground, rolled up in fetal position.

Sally, aghast, did not know what to do. She looked around for help, but there was nobody. Then she spotted a piece of driftwood, a tree branch that had been washed upon the shore. Sally mightily picked it up, the branch bigger than she was, and ran, full speed toward the mob. The boys didn't even see her coming until she clunked one of them upside the head with the branch, and swung it fiercely at the others. The first boy fell down while the others stumbled back in horrified surprise. Sally lunged at them with the branch, knocking another in the shoulder.

"You get out of here!" she screamed with her high-pitched voice. "You leave my brother alone!"

Unsure of how to react, the boy that had been hit in the shoulder said, "Come on, let's get outta here!" The three boys ran east down the beach, the first boy lagging behind while he clutched his head.

Joseph, spitting out sand, glared up at Sally, red in the face. "Why'd you do that?"

"Cause they were beating you up," she responded as she watched him struggle up from the ground.

"They weren't beating me up."

"Sure looked like they were."

"Now I'm gonna be the joke of the whole town. 'That big sissy Joseph's gotta keep his little sister around to protect him!' Great. Now the kids'll really wanna beat me up!"

Sally put her head down abashedly in response to this, and walked glumly alongside Joseph the rest of the way home. Joseph was bitter for the remainder of the night and lay sulking on his bed, but his bitterness faded in the years to come when no East End boy dared to ambush him. The word on the street was that he had one crazy sister that would put a boy in the hospital without batting an eyelash.

"Ready to go, Serry'?"

"Yep." Bill untied the *Halcyon* from the wharf and pushed off as Seraphine started the engine. The boat backed away from the pier, turning as Seraphine cranked the wheel hard to the left, the stern of the *Halcyon* engulfed in its own smoke. Seraphine steered her around the long breakwater. The black waterline that darkened the stones closest to the water signaled that it was about half tide, and the cormorants stood huddled together, their shiny black feathers soaking up the rays of the sun as they tried to stay warm on a chilly, late November afternoon. The tops of the stones were white from the offal of the birds, and the odor, pungent and overwhelming at times, was merely strong enough on this day to be a reminder of their presence. Seraphine deftly weaved the *Halcyon* between brightly painted lobster pot buoys, leaving a rippling wake in the steely blue water.

There was a breeze, but the sky was blue and the sun was shining, not as strong as in the summer months, but soft and warm and unassuming.

"It's a good day, Serry!" Bill called from the bow, taking a swig from his flask. "Wish everyday was like this this time of year." The engine of the *Halcyon* was loud but Bill and Seraphine had grown used to yelling to each other over it.

Paul and Frank lounged in the stern already eating the sandwiches their wives had made for them. Bill moved closer to the cabin so that he wouldn't have to yell quite so loudly, and leaned against the doorway, his wide feet firmly planted so that he barely swayed with the rocking of the boat.

"Hey, Serry, did you hear about the spook that's been around town?"

"Yeah."

"That sonofabitch is a goddamn lunatic, a real pervert, peeking in windows at night, calling raunchy things out to the people from behind bushes, stealing women's drawers from off clothes lines. Did I tell you how he came peeking around my house?"

"No."

"Well, me and Sandy were in bed, and the little girl comes in and says, 'Daddy, there's a man looking in my window.' Well, I know just who it is, and I leap out of bed—all I got is my underwear on. I grab my gun out from under my bed—you know, that big rifle I got—and I run right out the door and around the house to the window. That crazy bastard leapt out of the bushes and ran clear out the yard. I chased him, but the son of a bitch was fast, and he was gone by the time I got to the road. He ain't coming by my house again, I can bet you that. Just wish I coulda got a shot off on him. You know, taken off an ear lobe or something like that. He oughta be strung by his balls."

Seraphine gave the modest smile of his, and shook his head. "You better watch out you don't get arrested running around in your underwear at night with a gun. They'll think *you're* tederka."

"Wouldn't be the first time. Least I ain't sneaking around scaring the hell out of every little girl on the street."

"Rosie scared?"

"Well, she's smart enough to know it ain't the boogeyman, but hell, I'd be scared too if that sicko was looking in my window. She ain't having any nightmares over it, though—she know's her Pa's got a rifle that will blow that pervert's head clean off his shoulders."

Seraphine nodded. They were rounding Race Point, where the bay meets the ocean. At this point, the water appears to churn like a bubbling cauldron, creating a nearly distinguishable line between Cape Cod Bay and the Atlantic. They were in the ocean getting farther and farther away from the safety of the shore.

"How long we going out for, Cap'? Three days?"

"Yep. You bring enough food?"

"Course. Sandy makes me enough to last a week. Only thing I'm afraid of running out is my whiskey. You might as well throw me overboard at that point."

"I know."

"Lets hope these clear skies hold out for the whole trip. Hell, I could fish for a month straight in this weather."

Seraphine pulled his pipe out of his wool peacoat pocket and began to pack it with the tobacco he had taken from his other pocket, now that he did not need to focus quite so hard on his steering. He puffed and listened quietly to Bill's colorful stories, looking blankly at the vast horizon. He saw a gull flying toward shore, close enough to the water that he could make out its white and gray coloring. A minute later he saw two more birds. Then another group, and yet another even bigger. They were all headed toward land.

"Strange," he said pensively.

"What?" Bill halted his tale.

"See that?" Seraphine gestured with his pipe. "All those birds are flying toward shore."

Bill looked up. "Yeah, you're right. I don't think I've ever seen so many birds flying over the boat in all my life when there's no scraps to be had."

"That's what I was thinking. It don't seem right."

"You think we're heading straight for a storm?"

"Yep. I think we'd better head on back."

"Well, Serry, my guess is that the birds know better than we do, and you know better than I do. It's your call. You think we'll make it?"

"Hope so. We ain't too far out."

So they brought the *Halcyon* about and sailed her back toward land. The sky was beginning to darken as they passed Wood End Light, and once they got to the harbor, the sky was black and the sound of thunder was booming in the distance.

"Batten down the hatches, boys," Seraphine said, and the four of them made sure the boat was good and secure, tied snuggly to the side of the wharf, and everything locked up tight as a drum so that the boat would not get swamped.

As Seraphine walked briskly home, the rain began to pour down on him, and the thunder was right above. The occasional shot of lightning could be seen, but Seraphine kept his head down, his hat pulled low over his eyes, collar up, hands stuffed in his wool jacket. He was soaked to the bone by the time he made it to the front door of the house. The lights on inside were warm and welcoming, and he could smell Mary's cooking.

He opened the door, and stepped in from the rain, his sopping went clothing dripping onto the floor. Fluke was already there, wagging his tail so it beat against the stair post, and getting wet under Seraphine's stream. Mary heard him come in and hurried over, her apron greasy from linguica. "Oh I'm so glad you came back!" she said. "I was afraid you were caught in all of this." She pushed Fluke out of the way with the side of her leg, and he walked quietly back to his place in front of the wood stove. She helped Seraphine peel off his wet jacket and removed her apron to dry his face with. "You better get upstairs and put on some dry clothes before you catch pneumonia. I made clam chowder."

"You made chowder?" Mary never cooked a big meal the day that he left on a trip.

"Well, when I saw it getting cloudy, I had a feeling you might be back."

Seraphine smiled. "Good." Then he slowly made his way upstairs in his stockinged feet, the only part of his body still dry but getting wetter with each damp step. He heard Joseph and Sally playing in their room and Jimmy and Tommy bickering. He heard the sound of Mary's spoon against the cast iron pot, and he heard the storm raging outside, sounding far away now that he was within the small, warm, floater house.

JULIANNE PAPETAS 2011

XXII

The Holidays

As early as Thanksgiving, Provincetown was strung with Christmas lights and wreathes. The town was a buzz of festive energy unlike the hectic, crowded craziness of summer. The tourists had long since gone home and were celebrating the holidays with their families, leaving the locals to celebrate the holidays with theirs. The trees were bare of their leaves, but there was no snow on the ground. A white Christmas was rare, as the ocean kept the air too warm in December, and the best that could be hoped for was a gray, cold day, allowing for the fire to be lit and the doors and windows shut tight, locking in the smell of cooking.

Nobody had much money, but they did all they could to make a holiday meal big enough to feed an army. The grocers stocked up on turkeys and roast beef for one of the few occasions a family would extend itself to purchase such a luxury as a prime piece of meat, and a pleasure it was after a year of eating fish! The few cars that were not put up on cinder blocks for the winter had wreathes wired to the grills. Lights, ribbons, and shiny balls were hung in every store window, and Christmas carols blared on the radios.

Seraphine, Mary, and their five children walked to the Christmas tree lot, one gray December afternoon. They all were wrapped tightly in scarves, mittens, and hats knitted by the hands of Mary and Sarah, but the young ones seemed not to notice the cold. Joseph and Sally darted ahead of the group, excitedly racing to get their tree. Tommy tried not to act as enthusiastic as the other two, but his brisk pace failed to conceal his eagerness, and Jimmy and Sarah hung behind Seraphine and Mary, talking about what they wanted to purchase for their younger siblings.

"So what kind of a tree are we getting this year?" Seraphine said to urge on the children's excitement.

"A big one!" cried Sally.

"Yeah, a really big one!" chimed in Joseph.

"That sounds good."

"Let's just wait and see what they have on the lot," Mary said, forever the voice of reason.

"Hey, Ma, are we having a roast beef for dinner this year?" asked Jimmy from behind.

"Oh, I don't know. I was thinking we'd just do a turkey this year."

"Aw man, we have turkey every year," Tommy said in his tetchy way.

"You watch it, you *cudishka*, or else we might not eat anything for Christmas dinner," Mary pointed at him.

"Do you want a roast?" Seraphine directed the question back to Jimmy and Sarah.

"Well, we've never had one before. We just thought it'd be nice for a change," Sarah said.

"We'll have a roast then," Seraphine willingly accepted the proposal.

"But Seraphine, you know a roast is much more expensive than a turkey," Mary said lowly, though the older children could still hear her. "We can't extend ourselves that much this year."

"Oh, we don't have to have a roast beef, then!" Jimmy jumped in.

"Yeah, we didn't realize it was more expensive," added Sarah. "I like turkey."

"Yeah, me too."

"You all sound foolish," Seraphine said dismissively. "Of course we'll have a roast. Christmas is once a year. If I gotta catch a few more fish, then I've gotta catch a few more fish. And I've had a hankering for a good old roast myself for a while now."

Mary said nothing. Deep down, she had wanted a roast as well.

They got to the tree lot, and Joseph and Sally ran around, weaving between the trees, wanting each on they saw. Tommy struggled to restrain himself, but once he set foot in the lot, he enthusiastically cried, "I like that one! Oh, I like this one too," hopping from tree to tree. Jimmy and Sarah were more discerning, trying to find one that was the perfect size and shape, but, after some minutes, cries were heard from the corner of the lot.

"We found it! We want this one!" Joseph and Sally cried. They all went to the see the find, and were in agreement that it was a perfect tree. It was a bit sparse, but all the trees were. The town was lucky to be able to get any Christmas trees at all, and the kids had never seen a lush Christmas tree anyway. One thing was true, though, this tree was tall.

"Can we get this one? Please."

"Sure," Seraphine agreed.

"Wait, that tree's not even going to fit in the house," Mary said skeptically.

"Sure it will," said Seraphine.

"There won't be any room for the angel."

"Aw, who needs an angel?" said Tommy. "I like this one."

"It'll take up the entire living room."

"It ain't that big, Ma," Jimmy laughed. "Sometimes I think you've got more of Vovo in you than you like to admit."

Mary frowned at him.

"We'll make it work," Seraphine said, looking approvingly at the tree.

"Oh fine! You guys win again," Mary threw up her hands. "But you're the ones carrying it home!"

Seraphine fished around in his pocket for the cash to pay for the tree, and then he, Mary, and the kids left with their purchase and headed home. Jimmy carried the trunk, and Tommy lead with the top of the tree. Joseph held it at the middle, trying to help, and the others walked behind.

"Why can't Dad carry it some of the way?" Tommy moaned, already growing bored with carrying the tree.

"Because he paid for it, that's why," Mary retorted. Tommy did not push the question any further. Once they got home, they struggled to maneuver the tree through the door but managed to get it into the corner of the living room, where Mary had already put the stand, dug out from the shed. The trunk of the tree was too fat to fit into the stand, so Seraphine had to whittle it down to the proper size. The very tip of it was bent since it was hitting the ceiling, so Seraphine stood up on a chair and trimmed that as well. Now it just fit, but no room for the angel as Mary had predicted. When they let it go, though, it toppled over right onto Tommy, too heaven to be held by the stand, so Seraphine tied a few pieces of twine to it and nailed them to the wall. It strained against the lines, but it was secure at last and ready to be decorated. Tommy picked pine needles off of him and tugged at the sticky sap in his hair.

His part completed, Seraphine sat in his rocking chair, smoking his pipe and plucking at his violin as he watched the children decorate the tree. Sarah and Mary made cranberry and popcorn chains, the cranberries picked from the woods off of the highway, while Tommy and Sally placed the few ornaments they had randomly about the tree, and Jimmy held Joseph on his shoulders so he could put glass balls on the very top. They all sat back and admired their tree, though Mary and Sarah decided that they may have to make some more decorations for such a tall tree. "It'll look better once there's gifts under it," Joseph commented, and nobody disagreed.

That night, as Seraphine and Mary lay in bed, Mary said, "So what are we getting for the kids this year?"

"Not sure. You have any ideas?"

"Oh sure, I have lots of ideas, but the problem is which do I choose? There is so much that they need."

"I don't want to get them something they need. I want to get them something they want."

"Well, that narrows down my list a bit."

"If we can only afford to get them one thing, it might as well be something they can enjoy."

"That makes sense," Mary said, but she wasn't entirely committed to the idea. After a pause, she continued, "It's just so hard."

"What?"

"I wish we could give them everything they want. They're such good kids."

"We give them plenty. We give them the important things."

"You're right," Mary agreed. "The dolls and the games and the toys don't matter when all is said and done. But still, it'd be nice."

"Yeah it would. But enough about what we can't get. What *are* we going to get?"

"Well, I was thinking a book for Sarah. Maybe something like the *Complete Works of Shakespeare*. Something that she could read for a while."

"That's a good idea."

"And for Tommy, a new sled. It's a bit pricey, but he's been wanting one for a long time."

"Good."

"And the other kids will get use out of it too, I'm sure. I saw a precious doll set for Sarah. It comes with its own box of clothing and accessories. It think it might even have had a tea set. For Joseph, I thought a train set. It'd just be a small one, but I think he'd still have fun with it. And for Jimmy, I'm still not quite sure. I thought a nice fishing rod would be good."

"Those all sound like great ideas."

"You're going to come shopping with me right?"

There was a slight hesitation, but Seraphine said, "Sure." He hated shopping, but Christmas was the one time he would go.

As Seraphine and Mary headed home with their full shopping bags, they ran into a man dressed as Santa Clause coming out of Town Hall. He tried to sneak by them, but Seraphine's keen eyes picked out the familiar face from behind all the white hair.

"That you, Bill?"

His shoulders slumped. He'd been caught. "Yeah, it's me, Serry."

"What you doin' wearing that rig?"

"Sandy put me up to it. She's in charge of all the Christmas festivities this year, and she told me I had to be Santa." He pulled a flask from out of his red jacket and took a swig.

"You been letting kids sit on your lap with booze all over your breath?"

"It's the only thing that gets me through! This is like some kind of torture. That woman won't let me be. I don't bother nobody. I just sit in my chair and listen to my football games on the radio, and take a shot of whiskey here and there, and that's it. The way she yells and hollers, you'd think I was some kind of bum!"

"Oh, we know you aren't that, Bill," Mary said. "I think it's nice what you did. Did my kids come down by any chance?"

"Nah, and it's a good thing too. I'm sure they would've spotted me in heart beat!"

"Or smelled you."

Bill gave Seraphine a dirty look and then said, "Well, I best be going. See you folks got your Christmas shopping done."

"Oh yes. I've got my wrapping all cut out for me tonight," Mary said.

"Sure sure. I've got to get all my stuff done too. God knows what I'm gonna get my old lady, but I'll figure it out. So long!" Bill turned and strode down the sidewalk.

Seraphine had completely forgotten about Mary. How could he have done that! He had no idea what to get her. The rest of the walk home, he was silent in thought. A new stock pot? No, that'd be like giving her more work for a gift. A new dress or a pair of shoes or a shawl? But he didn't trust himself with picking out woman's clothing. Tools for the garden? No, still more work. He was stumped. Nothing seemed right.

As Seraphine headed to the boat the next day, he passed a store window and then doubled back to it. On display in *Oliver's* was a pair of beautiful sapphire earrings. He looked hard at them before finally going inside. "What can I do for you, Captain?" asked Oliver himself from behind the counter. The beauty of this time of year was that everybody knew everybody. Those who only had stores in the summer were gone, leaving the year-round clerks to help the locals. "What's the price of those earrings in the window?"

The cost was out of his range, and Seraphine thanked Oliver and left, contemplating what he was going to do now. He headed to the *Halcyon*, where he was planning to do just a few small tasks, but the more he thought, the more he knew that he had to get Mary those earrings. Nobody came to work that day, and Seraphine had not planned on voyaging to George's Bank until after the holiday. Without stopping to consider, Seraphine lowered a dory into the water and rowed toward the Point. Floating by Wood End Light, he cast out a line and tugged on it repeatedly, feeling the bounce of the jig. He had spent an hour without even a hit when suddenly there was a great yank on the line, so hard that the line cut his leathery palm. He cried in both pain and surprise, but jumped right back into action, grabbing a hold of that line with his bleeding hands and fighting against the force on the other end.

He reeled and pulled, paying out the line from time to time, so that he wouldn't lose the fish, letting it run, wondering what on earth could possibly be at the other end that felt so heavy and pulled so hard. He saw its back rise to the surface in the distance, and was shocked by the size of what he saw. He could not tell what it was. For all he knew, it was some sort of sea monster.

The fish was huge and heavy, but after its initial run, it didn't fight much. Big fish were like that. A little blue fish was nastier and had more fight in it than a striped bass four times its size, and Seraphine was thankful that all he had going against him was the size of this fish. If this fish had any fight in him, he would have pulled the entire boat under!

Seraphine pulled and pulled until finally the fish began to surface. What Seraphine saw would have horrified any other man. Up came the huge, gaping mouth of a giant halibut. He'd never seen a halibut this big in his life. It had to have weighed at least two hundred pounds, and here it was lolling right beside his dory, as big as the boat itself. There was no way Seraphine could get this fish in the boat, if he could even get it back to shore, so he secured it with more lines, so as not to lose it along the way, and rowed mightily back to the wharf.

It took him twice as long to get back as it had taken him to get out to Wood End, and his whole body ached from straining against the fish and oars. As soon as the first person caught sight of the giant halibut, caught by one solitary man, the entire town had heard about it and came running to see the prize fish. The photographer from the *Banner* took several pictures of Seraphine with his giant halibut, and everyone *oohed* and *ahhed* in amazement over its girth. They had no idea how Seraphine had reeled it in on his own. When they weighed it, it was two hundred and seventy pounds!

"He was just a big, lazy lug," Seraphine said modestly, though he could not conceal his proud smile.

Fish dealers were at his side offering him money for the fish, more money than he had received for whole boat loads of fish. He accepted the best offer without any thought or bartering, pocketed his money, and headed straight for *Oliver's* to make his purchase. He walked proudly home, his package already wrapped, thankfully, by Oliver and placed it in an inconspicuous place under the tree.

Mary made a feast to feed thirty people even though it was just the seven of them. The holidays were always a family time, and every cousin, uncle, aunt, grandparent, brother, and sister got together to share the holiday. But for Seraphine's family, it was just them. Seraphine had no living family besides his wife and children, and Mary's brothers had moved away. The only one left was Vovo who had an absolute fit when they tried to get her to come over and have dinner with them. Seraphine offered to carry her to the house if she felt she was too feeble to walk, but she screamed as though he were threatening to kill her, "You keep your goddamn hands off of me!" So they left her at her will, the children relieved they would not have to suffer in her presence, until, of course, they heard that it was their job to deliver Christmas leftovers to Vovo that afternoon.

The house was cozy and warm, the smell of cooking filling all the rooms, the wood stove keeping the kitchen warm, and a fire in the fireplace in the living room. Fluke lay sprawled on his side in front of the fire, and the kids huddled around the tree, excitedly opening their gifts and beginning to use them right away.

Mary had knit Seraphine a new sweater out of thick, gray wool, as well as a new set of gloves without any fingers, a scarf, and some socks. Her gift was the last to be opened, and her mouth fell wide open at the sight of the sapphire earrings.

"How—but—I—How did you get these? We—"

"Just a bit of luck, that's all."

Mary closed her mouth and looked down at the little box in her hands. "Oh Seraphine, I love them!" And she put them right on.

The rest of the afternoon was spent listening to Christmas carols on the radio (and some that were played by Seraphine on his violin) and eating Christmas cookies. They feasted on roast beef dinner until they thought their stomachs would explode, and even Fluke was given a rib bone for his Christmas meal.

Bill, Sandy, and their children stopped by for a moment on the way back from Sandy's parents' house. He brought with him a big bottle of whiskey with a red ribbon tied around the neck of it, and they laughed when Seraphine revealed the same exact gift for Bill. The children grudgingly took dinner to Vovo, keeping the visit as brief as they possibly could, and when they were all gone off to their rooms to occupy themselves with their gifts, Mary sat in Seraphine's lap as he rocked in his rocking chair, and wrapped her arms around his thick neck. "You did too much this year," she said.

He patted her on the knee, and continued to rock slowly back and forth. "Christmas comes only once a year."

XXIII

Ice Harvest

"Seraphine, get up." Mary shook him on the shoulder vigorously.

"What?" he groaned and tugged the lumpy pillow under his head.

"Come on. Get dressed." She leapt off the bed and began to pull on her wool undergarments under her nightgown.

"Why?" Seraphine put the pillow from Mary's side of the bed over his face with a muffled moan.

"We're going out." Mary was still quickly pulling on several heavy layers of clothing.

"It's freezing out," Seraphine stated from under the pillow.

"Not as cold as it could be."

"I don't feel like going out."

"You're a bore."

Seraphine slid the pillow to his forehead and peered at his wife from under it.

Mary stood, her hands on her heavily padded hips, her blue eyes looking as though they would burn a hole right through Seraphine's head had the pillow not been shielding it. She broke her serious gaze and waved her hands in annoyance. "You know, the kids aren't the only ones allowed to have fun. I want to be able to do something fun once in a while too."

"You don't find cleaning out the firebox fun?" Seraphine said.

"Don't be a smartass. Get your pants on."

Seraphine sat up and began to methodically pull his extra layers on, struggling to overcome his sleepy haze. Mary, impatient with his slowness, hurried over to his side, yanked his jacket sleeves over each of his arms, and buttoned it shut with the deftness of a mother of five. Then she grabbed his hands and pulled him to his feet with a groan. "Come on, old man, let's go."

He began to walk with his heavy, rolling gait across the room, but before he took three steps, Mary turned and shushed him. "You'll wake the kids with those clodhoppers." The two continued along on tiptoe.

Halfway down the hall, Seraphine gave Mary a quick, hard pinch on her side, and she grappled behind her, stifling a yelp and turning an angry eye on him. Seraphine chuckled under his breath as they continued on. They struggled to put as little weight into their feet as possible to prevent the stairs from creaking. It was virtually hopeless, and at every dry crack, they would halt in panic, look at each other, and continue on, their hearts in their throats.

"I don't know how Jimmy sneaks out to see his girlfriend without waking the entire house," Mary said when they got to the bottom of the stairs.

"He goes out the window," Seraphine responded absentmindedly.

"How do you know that?" Mary flung an accusing glare at him. Seraphine pretended to be absorbed in his boot lacing.

Mary felt something hot and damp behind her leg, and she turned to see Fluke giving them a panting grin. "Go lie down," she ordered him in a loud whisper. "You're not coming with us!"

Fluke lowered his head and his tail and walked back into the kitchen with glum obedience, returning to his place in front of the wood stove.

"Ready?" Mary asked Seraphine.

He nodded.

They carefully opened and shut the front door with only a click of the latch sounding and stepped onto the front stoop. Jimmy had shoveled it and the walkway earlier, but the bricks were still slippery and a fine layer of fresh snow covered them. Mary clung to Seraphine's arm for stability as they both slid toward the gate.

"Where do you think the sled is?" Seraphine asked her.

"It's got to be around here somewhere. The kids just toss it in the yard when they get home. Think of the place where you are most likely to trip over it."

Sure enough, it was right inside the fence, to the side, but still sticking out enough to trip an unsuspecting visitor passing through the gate. It was hidden under a pile of snow. Jimmy had dumped his shovelfuls right on top of it. Seraphine yanked the sled out of the wet, heavy snow and shook the rest off of it.

"Great. Let's get a move on." Mary grabbed his arm again and pulled him out onto the sidewalk and up the road.

"What's the rush?" Seraphine struggled to keep up with her. "You act like we're meeting somebody."

"We are. Sandy and Bill."

"Bill? He didn't tell me anything about getting together tonight."

"He didn't know about it. Sandy and I said we'd get you two *lumsones* out of bed and to the bottom of Monument Hill by midnight."

"You two are a couple of sneaky bastards. Me and Bill work hard all day while you two plot how to tire us out even more."

"Oh, come one. You know you like this as much as I do." And Seraphine did. He just wished she would slow down a bit.

The snow of the recent storm still clung to the trees. Their branches were weighed down with the white, their nakedness concealed. The few cars that were parked along the curb were piled with snow, and it was obvious nobody had made any attempt to dig them out. It was easier to walk as plowing was inefficient. The pavement and sidewalk were indistinguishable and the houses stared out from under their white wigs, curls of smoke rising from their buried chimneys. After tomorrow, the clean, white snow would be muddy from foot traffic, but for now, it was still untouched aside from the slick, packed paths that had been carved through the drifts by the few wanderers who had made it out of their houses on this wintry day.

Once they got to Gosnold Street, Bill and Sandy were already there, Sandy's layers accentuating her plump figure and Bill standing with his hands shoved in his pockets and his hat pulled down low over his eyes.

"Mary! There you two are. We were scared you weren't going to make it!" Sandy cried.

"You were scared, not me," Bill wryly responded from behind her left shoulder. "How's it going, Cap'?" He nodded toward Seraphine.

"I'd like to be sleeping right now."

"Me too, me too," Bill rolled his eyes.

"Oh Mary, you just wouldn't believe the time I had getting this one out of bed," Sandy elbowed Bill in the side. "He never wants to do anything with me."

"That ain't true. There's lots of things I like to do with you. You just never want to do 'em!"

Sandy ignored the comment, and said to Mary, "The kids went to bed hours ago, so hopefully they didn't hear us. It's kind of fun, isn't it? Sneaking out like a bunch of teenagers and going sledding. I just love it. I feel like a kid again!" Mary smiled at her friend, who, years ago, had begun turning gray. Sandy always dyed her hair herself, which resulted in it being an abnormal orangey color. She led the way up the hill, chattering ceaselessly to Mary.

"Now I see why you talk so much to me," Seraphine eventually mumbled to Bill. "She won't let you get a word in."

"You think I'm bad! That woman's a professional talker. I don't know how your wife can listen to her for so long."

"I guess it's nice for her to have somebody to talk to once in a while."

They all climbed up the steep, snowy hill, a precarious task, but they did it. Other couples gradually arrived, the younger husbands and wives considerably more animated. They wrestled and laughed and chased each other up the hill, dragging their sleds behind them while the older couples took slow, measured steps. Seraphine and Bill were hot and winded by the time they got to the top of the hill, grumbling about not being in bed.

Sandy, ready to go, snatched the sled away from Bill and tossed it down right where the hill began to slope downward. She plopped herself on it, and looked up at Bill impatiently. "Well, are you coming?" Without saying anything, Bill squeezed on behind her. He held onto her tightly and they pushed off, flying down the hill. Seraphine and Mary watched until the two were little more than a speck, and then Mary said, "Well, it's our turn, I guess. The two sat on the new Christmas sled that had already gotten considerable wear from the children's abuse, and braced themselves to go.

"It sure feels like a long time since we've done this," Mary said a bit nervously.

"Let's go." And with that they pushed of and went flying down the steep hill at a remarkable speed. They barely saw the high school as they whooshed by it, the halfway point marker. The snow was already slick and packed down from the kids who had been enjoying their snow day by sledding every hour they would have been in school. Mary was yelling with the thrill of it as the cold air brushed through her hair, her scarf flying back and flapping in Seraphine's face. "I hope you know how to steer this thing," Seraphine said, as he squeezed her tightly to him.

As they neared the bottom of the hill, the momentum they had picked up was incredible. "How do we stop this thing?" Seraphine asked.

"We don't," Mary said. They reached the bottom of the hill and flew across the Back Street to Gosnold. It was a level road, but their momentum carried them, barely slowing down. They passed the Adams on the corner, flew across the Front Street, and continued down a narrow alleyway between two shops all the way until they were slowed down and eventually stopped by the snow-covered sand of the beach. Mary and Seraphine toppled over with the halt, and lay in the cold, snowy sand, breathless.

"Still alive?" Mary asked, gasping for air.

"Barely," Seraphine wheezed. They began to get up and saw Bill and Sandy grinning at them from down the beach. "You two were going like a bat out of hell!" Bill cried. Their faces were red and flushed.

"Gonna do it again?" Sandy asked eagerly.

"That was fun, but that might be as much as we can take," Mary said.

"Yeah, anymore fun and I'll have a heart attack," Seraphine added. Mary and Seraphine looked at each other. "Want to go again?" she asked, regaining her composure.

"Sure," he agreed with little hesitation, and the four scrambled back toward the hill, laughing and tripping around like the young couples they had seen earlier. Seraphine and Mary flew down that hill several times until their noses were so numb they forgot they were on their faces, and their eyes were glassy from the cold. Their noses ran and their fingers were stiff, but, somehow, they were still enjoying themselves. Finally, it was time to go home, and Mary and Seraphine made their way back down Front Street to their house, their arms wrapped around each other, and laughing, tripping, and stumbling the whole way.

"Sandy was right," Mary said once they made it, breathless, to the door, the hot air from their mouths making smoky clouds in front of their faces. "It makes me feel like a kid again." Seraphine just smiled.

When they woke up in the morning, they were so stiff they could barely move.

The rest of that winter was absolutely frigid. It had been several years since there had been a winter so cold that the harbor froze, a rare phenomenon, as it required painfully low temperatures for a long period of time. To see the harbor frozen on these rare occasions was a remarkable sight, as it did not freeze over smoothly like a pond would, but it was ever shifting and changing from the waves and the changing tide, building great, white chunks of ice.

Seraphine had told his men to take some time off until the ice cleared away, but he still went to the *Halcyon*, moored against the wharf, to make sure everything was all right. As large as the icebergs were, they rarely crushed the boats moored safely in the harbor, and Seraphine found the *Halcyon* rugged as always, resisting the pressure of the ice that crowded around her and piled up along her sides. What did result in the demise of many ships was the weight of the ice that crusted over them. The spray of the ocean would instantaneously freeze in weather as cold as this, and the weight could grow to be so much that the ice would drag the ships right underwater. Seraphine had taken with him a hammer and chisel to chip off some of the icy coating.

The biggest problem the icy harbor posed to captains was whether they could get their boats out around the Point, or worse, if they could bring them back in. Some captains tried to navigate their vessels through the chunks of ice, which often resulted in getting trapped by a barricade of ice and having to turn around and come back. Occasionally, others managed to make it past the Point but were unable to get back into the harbor on account of how thick the ice was. Extremely cold weather like this was a dangerous time to go out fishing, though catches tended to be good. A captain had to always be alert of icebergs hidden under the water, and at night it was nearly impossible to see them. Serpahine felt it was best to leave the *Halcyon* where she was for the time being. There was no great urgency to go out.

Seraphine spent an hour chipping away at the ice until his hands were numb, and he decided that a sufficient amount of weight had been taken off to protect the *Halcyon* for another day. He sat with his legs hanging over the side of the wharf, his wool peacoat buttoned tightly around him. He was accustomed to the cold, but on days like this, ten layers still could not keep him warm. Fluke sat beside Seraphine with only his thin, honey-colored coat as protection from the cold. Seraphine watched the white harbor move and break to pieces. The tide was rising now, and he could hear the ice cracking as it broke apart against the pilings of the wharf and against the side of the *Halcyon*. Other than this, there was silence.

Seraphine, after some time, stood, Fluke doing the same. The sky was dim and gray, and the lone seagull that flew in a circle above his head blended with the clouds nearly completely. Turning back toward the town, whose colors, too, were dim, Seraphine walked slowly down the wharf, his hands in his pockets. He chose, today, to walk back home via the beach, which was hardly recognizable. As the tide came in, it pushed the hunks of ice onto the shore until the entire beach, from the shoreline to the foundations of the houses, was piled high with ice and snow, rugged like the arctic. Seraphine struggled to climb over the craggy icebergs that rose up from the sand, and maneuvered his way around the particularly large ones that were nearly as tall as him. Fluke athletically hopped over some ice chunks and up and down others with ease, but he would pause and wait for Seraphine to catch up, whose two legs were far less limber for such rough terrain. But even for Fluke, many of the icebergs were too high to leap over, and he struggled to find an easier path around.

Eventually, Seraphine came to a hunk of ice that was even more impressive than the others. It was at least eight feet high, and smooth on the top. Seraphine stopped at its base and looked up, feeling as though he were looking up at Mount Everest. He began to climb up it, stepping on lower chunks and then fitting his hands and feet in ridges that jutted out or holes that were carved into it until he made his way to the top. Once upon the smooth surface of the iceberg he stood and looked over the white harbor, unable to discern where the water began and ended. He was filled with a tingling sensation of being on top of the world, a world that looked very different from the one that he was accustomed to. He looked down and saw Fluke staring helplessly up at him, so he slid back down, and the two continued on their way home. They cut up the Gosnold Street alleyway where they saw an ice truck backing down it.

"Hello 'Cap," Ricky Lambrou gave a big grin and a nod out the window of his truck. "Can you believe this weather?"

"No."

"I haven't seen the harbor look like this in probably ten years!"

"Been a long time."

"It's quite a sight, ain't it?"

"Yep."

"We're gonna go cut up some of those big hunks of ice out there and take them back to the icehouse. Why get it shipped if we've got it right here in our very own harbor? Save a few bucks!"

"Sure."

"You have a nice day, Cap'. We've got our work cut out for us." Ricky gave a wave and continued backing his truck up.

Seraphine continued home with Fluke following closely at his side, his hands in his pockets, his jacket collar pulled snuggly up around his neck, and his hat to the wind, ready to sit by the fire and smoke his pipe.

XXIV

Jimmy

Slowly and carefully Jimmy eased the window up inch by inch. It was heavy and stiff in its tracks, and despite his efforts, the window let a low, dull, painful creak halfway up. *Crap*, Jimmy thought when he heard Tommy's voice loudly whispering behind him, "Where are you going?" The moonlight filtering through the paned glass of the window made a dim blue circle of light on the floor right where Jimmy was standing. It reflected off his face, giving him an ethereal appearance, the only lit object in the dark room. He felt guiltily exposed as he turned and strained through the shadows of the night to see Tommy sitting up in bed, the covers fallen away from his red, plaid, flannel nightshirt. "Nowhere. Go back to sleep!" Jimmy kept his voice low, but spoke with a tone of severity.

"I know where you're going," Tommy smirked mischievously, forgetting for a moment the level of his voice.

"Shh!" Jimmy flung an index finger to his lips.

Quickly adjusting back to his loud whisper, Tommy continued, "You're going out to see your girlfriend."

"Yeah, what's it to you?"

"God, Jimmy, you're crazy. You go out almost every night to see that girl of yours. Snow, rain, it don't matter. You're nuts!"

"If I want to go out in the rain, that's my problem."

"Well, I want to get something out of it."

"Oh come on, Tom," Jimmy said pleadingly. "Can't you just let it go this time?"

"No way. There's school tomorrow."

"So? There's school everyday."

"Well, if I've got to go to bed early and stay in the house all night and cover for you while you're running around with your girlfriend, then I want to get what's coming to me."

Jimmy sighed dejectedly. "Fine. What do you want this time?"

"Cold hard cash," Tommy replied, holding out his hand.

"I ain't giving you money!" Jimmy raised his voice almost to normal speaking level.

"Then I want a bag of penny candy."

"Again? You're gonna get fat from all the candy you eat."

"And whose fault would that be?" Tommy said challengingly, a smug look on his face.

"Okay, fine. I'll get it for you in the morning," Jimmy turned back to the window.

"Goodnight shnookums," Tommy said in a mockingly high voice.

"Aw, get lost!" Jimmy shot behind him and climbed out the window, easing his way down the lattice and ivy Mary was growing on the side of the house. Then he hurried down the street to the Coast Guard station where Vickie was waiting for him, a red cardigan wrapped over her navy blue dress. Without saying hardly a thing, they grabbed each other's hands and hurried toward the beach.

It was a mild spring evening, compared to the bitterly cold winter they had had, and the full moon lit a path for them. In silence, they walked to the breakwater, its stones taking on a silvery appearance, while the crags that separated them gaped black. The water of the harbor lapped near the top of the breakwater, the moon tides exceptionally high and making the breakwater feel low and like a part of the ocean. Jimmy and Vickie gingerly made their way across, Vickie hanging heavily on Jimmy's arm for fear of falling and trusting his instinct more than her own. They could see little around them aside from the white, sparkling, snowy-looking sand of the Point in the distance and the harbor that reflected the moon's light like a great, rippling mirror.

The two shadowy figures stole through the night, hopping carefully from stone to stone, until, finally, they touched sand. Vickie carried her shoes in her free hand and dug her toes into the soft, cold sand, enjoying the sensation for the first time since winter had ended. They walked until they reached the Point, unable to see a piece of driftwood in front of them until they were practically on top of it, and looked up to where the beach grass grew, but were only able to make out the faint motion of it blowing in the breeze. They could tell where Long Point Light was only by the light that shined to safely escort seamen home and young lovers to her base for an innocent rendezvous.

Jimmy and Vickie plopped down in the sand and lay on their backs, pleased with themselves for safely making it the entire way. They crossed their hands over their chests and looked up at the stars in the clear night sky. Across the harbor, the shore was sprinkled with the lights of the town, and it seemed they were standing in the wilderness, looking back at a solitary piece of civilization. The lights looked lonely; not lonely for want of others, for there were plenty of lights in the town to create a community, but lonely in an isolated sense. The lights were as numerous as the stars and as separate from the rest of the world as those in the sky.

Vickie sat up causing her skirt to fall away from her legs, revealing a dark bruise and scrape on her left knee.

"How did that happen?" Jimmy asked, sitting up himself.

"Oh, I scraped it climbing down the drainpipe," Vickie said matter-of-factly.

"Why were you climbing down the drainpipe?"

"Same reason you do."

"I climb down the drainpipe because my room is on the second floor, and I have to walk past my parents' room to get out and go down those god-awful creaky stairs. My mother's like a hawk; she hears everything. I thought your room was on the first floor."

"It is."

"So why'd you have to climb down the drainpipe?"

Vickie huffed. "Really, Jimmy, what fun would it be *not* to climb down the drainpipe?"

"You'll get yourself hurt for absolutely no reason. That's foolish."

"Jimmy, stop worrying about me. I've been climbing down the drainpipe since I was a little kid."

"What were you sneaking around at night for when you were a little kid?"

"Do you really want to know?" Vickie remarked.

Jimmy realized he didn't. "Well, it looks like it hurts."

"Aw it's okay." Vickie dismissed the topic. "At least I didn't rip my dress. My mother'd kill me."

"She'll kill you anyway when she sees that and realizes you've been sneaking around at night."

"I'll just tell her I tripped over the dog in the morning. She'll believe me. She's done it plenty of times herself."

Jimmy lay back down and the two were silent.

"I can't believe you're graduating in two months, Jimmy," Vickie said quietly.

"Yeah."

"Time sure flies."

"It does."

There was another long silence. "You aren't saying much tonight," Vickie continued.

"Do we always need to talk our mouths off? I see you almost everyday. Nothing's changed. There's nothing to talk about."

Vickie sighed and lay back down, uncomfortably, staring blankly up at the sky. It seemed an eternity had gone by before Jimmy, said, "Sorry."

"It's okay," she said softly but didn't look at him.

"I've just been thinking a lot."

"About what?"

"About after graduation."

"Yeah?"

"You're probably not going to like this idea, but . . . well," Jimmy cleared his throat, "I'm thinking of joining the Navy."

"Joining the Navy!" Vickie sat bolt upright and looked at him hard for the first time.

"Yeah. What's so wrong with that?"

"Have you been reading the paper or listening to the radio or anything?" she said exasperatedly.

"Yes. So?"

"Well, don't you see how bad things are in Europe with Hitler and all? There's going to be another world war."

"I know that."

"Well, you'd have to be crazy to enlist now! You'll get shipped over to Europe and get yourself killed over there!"

"America's not in the war yet."

"No, but in all likelihood we will be." Jimmy's tone was still calm and matter of fact, but Vickie was agitated. Her whole body shook with frustration, and her brown curls were beginning to fall back into her face.

"Whether or not I enlist now, I'll most likely get drafted if America joins the war, anyway."

"Jimmy," Vicky moaned, placing her face in her hands. "Why are you doing this? I thought you were going to work with your father when you graduated."

Jimmy didn't respond right away. He was sitting up again, his arms laid over his bent knees and one hand gripping the opposite wrist. He was staring at his bare feet that looked dark against the white sand.

"Vickie," he began, calmly and gently, to explain, "do you really want me to stay here my whole life?"

"What's wrong with staying here? I'm here. You're family's here. This is your home."

"I know that, but think about all the opportunities being in the Navy will give me. Think of everything I'll get to see. I'll get to be on a boat, like I've been my whole life, except this boat will take me around the world! Wouldn't that be great? I'd get to see everywhere. Think of all the people I'd meet and the things I'd get to do. I'd get to go to Tahiti and see those women with the white painted faces."

"Those are Geishas—they're Japanese."

"Then I'd go to Japan. I'll see elephants in Africa and go to Italy and eat spaghetti and meatballs until I get sick! I'd probably go to Brazil. They speak Portuguese in Brazil, you know."

"Yes, I know that, but you hardly speak any Portuguese."

"That doesn't matter. Wouldn't it be great?" Vickie looked glumly at her lap. "I'll send you a postcard from every port I stop in. I promise. And I'll buy you the best Indian silk and the sweetest Chinese tea! I'll write you a letter every day and send you a picture of me with the Maharaja."

"Who's the Maharaja?"

"I don't know, but I'll meet him and send you a picture."

"Sounds great." But Vickie's tone was far from enthusiastic.

"It will be!" Jimmy was still caught up in his excitement, but when he noticed Vickie's downcast expression, he halted his enthusiasm and put an arm around her. "Aw, Vickie, don't be sad."

"I can't help it. I thought we were going to get married!"

"We *will* get married," he assured her.

"But you're leaving me."

"I'm not leaving, just, I'm just going on, well, let's call it a vacation."

"But I can't come."

"No, but I promise I'll stay in touch, and I promise I'll come back. I'll only do it for a few years, and then you'll want to marry me even more because I'll be so damn cultured!" He tried to make light, but his charm fell short.

"You're going to forget all about me, who are you kidding?"

"Now you sound foolish. Of course I'm not going to forget you. You're my girl!"

"You'll meet all kinds of girls while you're gone *seeing* the world," she said bitterly.

"Nah. The only kinds of girls guys meet in the Navy are prostitutes."

"That makes me feel a lot better. Not only are you going to run off for god-knows-how-long, but you're going to come back and give me syphilis or something like that."

Jimmy stifled a laugh. "Come on," he said rolling over onto his side and wrapping his arms around her stiff waist. "It's going to be fine."

Vickie softened a bit, but he saw that with it came a tear down her cheek. "What if you die?"

"I won't die."

"You might."

"Well, if I do, be glad you didn't marry me."

"What's that supposed to mean?" she snapped angrily, her brows furrowing hard.

"It means," Jimmy swallowed, trying to find the right words to say. "It means—let's not get married just yet."

"But when? When will we get married?"

"After I get done. After the war, if there is one."

"That's awful. Then I really might lose you! I think that's a terrible idea."

Jimmy squeezed her hand, "Vickie, if anything does happen to me, I don't want you to be a young widow. I don't want you to be tied down by anything. I want you to be able to get married and be happy. I'll just feel better about all this if we leave it like that."

"No. You're terrible. You're just trying to find a nice way to get rid of me!"

"Vickie, please! Listen to me," Jimmy was frustrated, but he made his tone gentle again and looked hard into her face. "Vickie, it'll give me something to look forward to. It'll give me a reason to come back. If there's a war, and if I have to fight, it'll give me the will to live. Do you understand?"

Vickie's eyes were wide and glassy as she nodded slowly up and down. "Do you think your parents are going to mind?"

"No. Well, I hope not," Jimmy considered the other obstacle. "I don't think my father will mind. He fought in the Great War. He's proud of being a vet and fighting for his country."

"Didn't he almost die?"

"Well, I'm not sure. I think so. He doesn't really like to talk about it. I just know that he has a couple nasty scars. He's got a really big one on his thigh that I've only seen once because he always tries to hide it. Never wears shorts or anything."

"I see."

"The biggest problem is my Ma. She'll probably have a fit. She did when Sarah told her she wants to go to college. But I'll deal with them. Telling you was the hardest. Now it'll be easier to convince them."

They both lay back down in the sand, Vickie lying in Jimmy's arms, and both looking up at the sky.

"Just promise you won't forget about me," she said quietly.

"I won't.

XXV

The Fire

Seraphine was just about to lower his head to the pillow, when he heard the furious clanging of the Town Hall bell and could feel its vibrations cutting through the still, warm, late May air.

Without thinking twice, he bolted up, sprung from the bed, rushed down the stairs, and pulled on his boots that had been sitting by the door. As he did this, Mary walked quietly down the staircase, pausing in the middle, and asked, "What's all the commotion about?"

"It must be a fire," he replied bent over. There was no professional firehouse in a small town like Provincetown and emergencies were remedied by organized volunteers.

Jimmy came down the stairs only a second later. "I'll come too."

"No. You stay here," Seraphine put up his hand as though to stop him and pushed the door open.

As he stepped onto the sidewalk, Gordon Blue, who lived three doors down, came rushing by. "There's a fire at the Catholic church!" he cried. "Come quick, before the whole town burns down!" And with that, he rushed off.

Jimmy stood in the doorway, looking at Seraphine. "Please, let me come."

Seraphine said nothing but waved him along, Jimmy jumping at the opportunity and grabbing an over-shirt that hung near the door. They briskly walked up the road together, and within a couple blocks, they were able to smell the smoke and see the flames rising above the roofs of all the other houses.

As they neared the vicinity of the church, they could see a crowd of people circled around it; women, children, and old folks, staring helplessly up at the flames. Many were crying as they saw the place where generations had been married, baptized, and laid to rest burning, while ash floated in the air like snowflakes, raining down on them without melting. It clung to their clothes and created a dusting at their feet, yet none seemed to notice. They were awestruck by the fury of the uncontrollable flames.

The volunteer firefighters were there with hoses and small fire engines, but every able-bodied man was helping as best he could. The white church was completely engulfed in flames making it glow like a giant birthday cake.

Seraphine approached Eddie Costa who was just walking from the church, wiping soot off his sweaty face. "What can we do to help?"

"There ain't nothing anybody can do now," he sighed as he rubbed his sleeve across his forehead, making the blackness worse.

"But is everybody all right? Is everybody safe?"

"Sure is. Thank God for that! There wasn't anybody in the church, except the priest, and he got out just fine."

Seraphine followed Eddie's gaze to see the priest sitting on the curb with a gray, wool blanket flung over his shoulders. He was cradling his damp face in his hands and appeared to be crying.

As Seraphine observed the disheartened man, there was a sudden crash as one of the stained glass windows shattered from the extreme heat. Colored glass flew everywhere, and the three men ducked and hid their faces from the scarring spray.

"Keeps happening. There's no saving this church," Eddie said. "All we can do now is stop the fire before a wind picks up and burns the whole town down."

"Well we can help with that," Jimmy said eagerly.

"Then grab a hose, grab a bucket, grab whatever you can get with some water in it. I'm gonna do the same thing myself," Eddie responded and began to go off.

"I'll come with you." Jimmy began to follow, but then turned and asked, "okay, Dad?"

"Just be careful," Seraphine replied, somewhat distractedly, and watched his son run toward the mass of men fighting the fire. Before he could take action of his own, he heard the wails of the priest and saw the people around him trying to cosole him. Seraphine quietly stepped closer as though daring not to be seen or heard.

"It's all gone! Gone! We'll have nothing with which to deliver Sunday mass," the priest cried.

"It's okay, Father. We've still got God and we got each other. We salvaged you from the fire, and that would have been the biggest loss," a woman tried to comfort him and gave him a squeeze on the shoulder.

"But it can't burn. It's sacred!"

"I know, it's a shame, but God has his reasons."

"But the tabernacle. And the . . . Oh Lord. I don't even want to think about everything we've lost," he moaned.

"When this is over we'll get everything brand new. It'll be just fine," another woman soothed.

"But there's so much history in there. You can't replace history. There are so many memories attached to each of those objects. What will be left to remind us? And the tabernacle, it was a gift from the bishop himself. I should have at least tried to save that."

"It's impossible, Father. Look at those flames!" an elderly man gestured.

"I know. It's lost—all of it," the priest complied placing his tearstained face in his hands. "We will have nothing left of our precious church. Not a single thing. Let God's will be done." And he sat there resignedly and watched the place that he loved most burn bit by bit, all the windows having burst by this point and the flames taking their place.

Seraphine, still some distance away and unnoticed by the group of people, stepped forward and said, "I'm gonna go get it."

The priest looked up bewildered. "What?"

"I'm gonna go get the tabernacle," he said simply.

"Are you crazy?" one woman cried.

"You'll cook up like a conkerinkle on the end of a stick!" another hollered

Seraphine smiled a little. "This Portugee skin of mine's a thicker shell than those snails have. Besides, it's a bit chilly out. I could use some warming up."

Before the people could protest, Seraphine was jogging toward the flaming church. He covered his face with his arms and jumped through the black, gaping door of the church like a circus lion leaping through a ring of flames, ignoring the cries of the men fighting the blaze to not go in.

Once inside, his eyes burned and watered from the heat and smoke. He immediately broke into a drenching sweat and could barely make out where he was in relation to the altar due to the blinding fog. He bent as low as he could so as not to breathe in too much of the toxic air and made his way toward the altar.

There were few flames in the middle of the room as the flames were climbing along the walls and up along the ceiling at a rapid pace. Bits of plaster and wood were falling from the ceiling, and the paint on the walls was curling from the heat, reflecting pink in the light of the flames. The floor and the, once pristine, wooden pews were littered with ash and glass, and the hoses of the firemen had not yet been able to dampen the roasting contents of the burning shell.

Seraphine could just make out the silhouette of the bust of Jesus that marked the altar, being accustomed to squinting through fog, but he relied mostly on instinct and memory to get there. He stumbled along, but all went relatively smoothly, aside from the time he tripped over what must have been a large piece of fallen wood. He did not take the time to observe what was around him, but aimed simply for the object he desired, and in the not so far distance he saw the gold of the tabernacle glimmer. He rushed toward it, stepping up onto the altar, which at this moment was unscathed. Everything was in tact as though it were waiting for the weekly mass, but a thick and unfamiliar haze of smoke hovered over it.

Seraphine dashed to the tabernacle and impulsively grabbed it with both of his hands. He instantly jumped back with a cry of pain as the searing hot metal scalded his bare palms. He ignored the pain and ripped off his flannel shirt, wrapping it over his burnt skin, and latched on, once again, to the scorching tabernacle.

It was nailed to the altar! He could not budge it. He pulled and pulled, but he was unable to move it from the shelf it sat on. He used all his weight against it, the salty sweat running down his forehead and burning his dry, red eyes. He panted and stopped in frustration at his own weakness, resting his hands on his knees and coughing toward the floor a couple times. Only when he looked up did he notice that the flames had begun to attack the altar as well. He looked behind him, down the length of the church and saw that he was surrounded by walls of flame. On all three sides, and the ceiling, all that could be seen was the fire as though the church were painted with it. He was awestruck by the ominous sight, so bright that he was tempted to shield his eyes.

So this is what hell is like, he thought to himself, and miserable, turned back to the altar. The flames had traveled along the floor and caught on the wine colored curtains that immediately ignited. He gazed fearfully at how rapidly the fire was sweeping near the altar and destroying everything it touched.

I've failed, he thought, and was consumed with anguish at the futility of his endeavor. *It is impossible. I'll be lucky to get out of here alive.*

But it seemed that the raging flames had come to a standstill at the foot of the altar. It seemed that they were traveling no farther. This was impossible, Seraphine considered, and assumed it was just a trick of his weary imagination. Yet even the smoke, oddly, had seemed to clear, and before him was depicted the image of Saint Peter walking on water. The flames had climbed up the wall via the drapery and along the ceiling, but it did not pass the line into the altar that was backed by the giant, concave mural of Saint Peter.

Through the dispersing smoke and the frame of flames, Seraphine gazed upon the altar with the magnificent mural of the patron saint of fishermen. He was drawn in by it. It was all he could see. The saint could not be overcome by water or fire.

As he gazed, his mouth open in awe, Seraphine began to feel some reassurance. He knew not why, but the strength and confidence seemed to be returned to him again, and he felt prepared to give it one last try. He rewrapped his hands in his shirt, and laid hold of the tabernacle. All he could see was the image of St. Peter before him, seeming to grow bigger and more lifelike every moment and drawing him toward it with an indiscernible force. Seraphine's heart throbbed in his chest, and his mouth was agape at the wonder of what he saw. Within him welled a warmth that was not the burning sensation caused by the heat of the flames, but, rather, a warmth of growing energy and power, as he saw Saint Peter making his way lightly across the indigo blue water. Then, with all his might, Seraphine pulled on that metal box until he heard a slight creaking, and then a cracking, and then a snap as the tabernacle ripped from the surface of the shelf, causing Seraphine to stagger backwards with the precious relic cradled in his arms.

It was as though, in that instant, he remembered where he was. He could hear the roar of the flames. He was choked by the smoke and burning from the heat. His eyes burned, his throat swelled, and his clothes were drenched with sweat, the same sweat that coursed down his face into his eyes and mouth, tasting more salty than the water of the ocean.

He began to run blindly through the church to where he could best estimate the location of the door, or any safe way out he could get to. As he ran, there was a deafening snap as a whole beam came crashing down behind him from the ceiling. It was covered with flames. The debris from the ceiling was falling in larger chunks, now, and much more abundantly. He dodged the raining flames and disintegrating ceiling, and soon he was able to see a safe exit. He ran with all his might, cradling the tabernacle against his chest, but before he was within ten feet of the door, the building gave a great shudder and there was a loud gong and the sound of cracking wood. Before he could get out the door, the bell and the entire steeple crashed down and landed on the floor only feet beside him. The ground shuddered, the building shook, and Seraphine felt the vibrations of the ringing bell as it clanged to an earth-shattering halt on the floor of the remnants of the church, the vibrations pounding through his dizzy head. Seraphine skirted around the bell, and leapt out the doorway, through the smoke and flames and onto the cool, damp ground and fresh air.

He was on his stomach, face down, shielding the tabernacle with his body. He did not notice the people quickly rushing to his side and dragging him away from the burning church just as the entire roof caved in, leaving the church a gaping, uncovered box.

Seraphine did not know who it was that lifted him to his feet and led him to a bench to sit on. Somebody brought him a cup of water, another brought him a blanket, somebody was asking him if he was all right, somebody was patting him on the back and congratulating him. But he did not hear them. He did not see them. They were merely a whirl of unintelligible sounds and images that left no impression on him. He did not notice as they pried the golden metal box from his arms. He did not feel it when they cleaned his burnt hands and wrapped them in clean bandages. He did not even hear the grateful exclamations of the priest who called him a savior, an angel, and a miracle. There was nothing in his head but the image of the altar and his bewilderment at the sudden strength he had obtained. He did not understand from whence or how it came.

Finally a voice in his ear snapped him out of his trance. It was distant at first, but it soon became louder and clearer as though he were being awoken from a dream. "Dad. Dad? Dad, are you all right?" It was Jimmy with his hand on Seraphine's shoulder, looking down at him with grave concern.

"Dad, talk to me. You okay? Dad."

Seraphine blinked twice, what seemed to be the first movements of his eyelashes he had made in ages, and then turned his head and slowly looked up into the worried face of his son.

"I'm fine."

Jimmy released a great sigh of relief, though he was not entirely convinced. "Do you feel okay? Are you hurt anywhere else? Can you walk?"

"No, no. I'm fine," Seraphine assured him, his voice still dreamy and distant. For the first time he noticed his bandaged hands and was beginning to feel them throb. He winced, but the adrenaline he was still experiencing from the ordeal prevented a full onslaught of pain.

"Do you need the doctor? How about some water?"

"No," Seraphine interrupted Jimmy's concerned queries. "Let's just go home."

Jimmy was slightly taken aback, but he did not argue. He placed one arm of his father over his shoulder and placed his own arm around his back, bearing the brunt of most of Seraphine's weight and lifting him to a standing position. Seraphine let the gray, wool blanket fall off his shoulders onto the ground, and the two men, soot-stained and weary, hobbled their way back home, feeling a mixture of great loss and accomplishment.

Before they went in the house, Jimmy asked, "Dad, why did you do that? It was just a metal box."

"I know it was just a metal box."

"Then why?"

"I don't know. I just felt I needed to go in there."

"I don't understand."

"I don't either. But it had nothing to do with the tabernacle. None of it did."

The next day, after the flames had finally been put out and the embers cooled, the priest, a couple of volunteer firefighters, and the president of the Knights of Columbus went to survey the damage. There was little left but a holey, crumbling shell. The four walls still stood, but the beautiful stained glass windows were nothing more than gaping openings. The roof had completely caved in and littered the floor and charred pews with giant, black beams. It was dangerous moving around, as there was nothing there remotely salvageable, until they got to the altar which still stood nearly unscathed. The statues of Jesus and Mary, the table, even the Stations of the Cross were recognizable and practically complete. But what was most remarkable was the mural of Saint Peter which still stood, soot-stained but whole.

Book II

The Changing Tide

I

Life Moves On

Jimmy graduated from high school, and immediately enlisted in the Navy, never expecting America to join the war so soon but realizing that it was inevitable. The unrest in the world outside of their country and their town had only been half acknowledged as life continued to move on in its normal fashion, until the attack on Pearl Harbor, precisely six months after Jimmy's graduation, shook the town and the entire country to its senses, suddenly turning the distant war into a tangible reality. Their boys, excellent seamen for their ages, superior candidates for the Navy, were now in true danger, and while being in the military had always been deemed an honor to the proud townsfolk, they now carried a genuine, unshakable anxiety for the welfare of their own. The fear clung to them—fear for their families and friends, fear for their country, fear for their own harbor, fear for all the liberties their land represented. But instead of shrinking at the thought of a foreign enemy, they became angry, stirred by patriotic sentiments. Boys from sixteen to twenty-five lined up outside of Town Hall to enlist. They put their studies on hold, even those who had just a few months to graduate. They told their fathers to find other help on the boat, and some even left young wives and children to join the war.

Mary and Sandy Buckets sat on the benches outside of Town Hall and watched as the boys lined up.

"My Jimmy's been in the Navy for just six months and already he's going off to war. I don't think he ever imagined this would happen. Now look, everybody's going."

"I think Jimmy'd be in that line right now if he hadn't already joined. Jimmy would never sit back and watch all the others do the dirty work. That's not how you and Seraphine raised him. I'm just glad my boys are still too little for all this. But they're already picking up sticks and pretending to shoot at each other with them. Whatever happened to using sticks as make believe swords or fishing poles? It's a different world."

"You got that right. Sarah is graduating from high school in June, and she wants to go off to college. Can you imagine? College? My Seraphine didn't even get past the sixth grade."

"Bill neither."

"I got through high school, but I never even thought about going off anywhere—too many responsibilities at home."

"Is Sarah going, though?"

"No. We can't afford it. I told her that."

"That's too bad, she's a smart girl."

"Yeah, but there's plenty for her to do around here. With the war starting, I figure she can join the Red Cross and help out with the war effort."

"That's a good idea. I'm going to help too."

The two women sat and sipped on their coffee from Adams. It was a chilly December afternoon, but the women had wool coats, coffee, and ceaseless conversation topics to keep them warm, as they watched the line get longer by the minute.

"Can you imagine our boys leaving us to go get killed?" Sandy shook her head.

"Is it really so different?" Mary replied.

"What do you mean?"

"Than what we go through everyday. Is it really so different? Everyday our husbands and sons leave us to go out fishing, and everyday we have to fear that they may not come back alive. Do you really think fighting a war is anymore dangerous than going out on the ocean in a little, wooden boat? You never know if they're going to get caught in a storm, lost in the fog, drowned at sea, or wrecked on the shoals. We fight a war everyday."

"But who's the enemy?"

"The ocean, nature . . . God." Sandy squinted at Mary. To hear such words come out of her devout friend's mouth sounded like utter blasphemy. "Our town sits here at peace, but we never know when the ocean is going to rise up and swallow us all. We rest beside a sleeping monster. How or when or why it happens, I don't know. I just have to trust that it happens because God wills it to and that it's happening for a reason."

"I never really thought of it that way. I guess I've just always been used it being there," Sandy considered.

"The ocean?"

"The fear."

The two women sat in silence for a moment.

"But it's part of life," Sandy continued. "Everything happens for a reason, like you say."

Mary nodded. "Besides," Sandy added, "you just don't like the water 'bout you get seasick. If I was the only Portugee on the planet who got seasick, I guess I'd be kind of bitter about it too."

Mary laughed and went to take another sip of her coffee, when she started, nearly spilling it all over herself.

"What is it?" Sandy asked.

"My God."

"What's wrong?"

"I must be seeing things. I *better* be seeing things!" Mary bolted up from her seat and marched toward the line, ignoring Sandy's confused expression that halted once Sandy saw what Mary had already noticed. The most recent addition to the line was Sarah. Mary went up to her, grabbed her by the arm, and pulled her out of the line.

"What are you doing?"

"I'm enlisting."

"Why?"

"Because I want to."

"Not a good enough reason!" Mary was livid.

"Mom, I want to get out of this place. I want to see the world."

"But *this place* is your home."

"Yes, but this place doesn't let me see and do and be all the things that I want in life."

Mary gritted her teeth looking for a response. "There is plenty that you can do right here without getting your head blown off!"

"Ma, I want to help my country. Besides, they don't even let women fight. I won't get my *head blown off.*"

"Well then why don't you just stay here and help?"

"But, Ma, don't you understand? I want to be more educated. Being in the Navy is an education itself. And on top of that, if I enlist, the government will pay for me to go to college as soon as the war is over."

"Is that it? Is that what this is all about? If you want to go to college, there are other ways to make it work. We can do it. Your father and I can figure something out."

"No. It's not just about going to school. It's about making something of myself, something worth being proud of."

"But I'm already proud of you."

"I know you are, but this is something I have to do for myself. I've thought about this a lot."

"And you never told me about it."

"No."

Mary was completely dismayed. "What is your father going to say when he hears about this?"

"Oh he doesn't mind."

Mary's fury rose up again. "He doesn't *mind*. He already *knows*?"

Sarah put her head down. "Yes."

"I don't believe this. I don't believe this! You two have been going behind my back all this time. When were you two *cadishes* planning on letting me in on the big secret?"

Sarah didn't respond. Mary clenched her teeth.

"Please, Ma, just let me do it."

Sarah's pleading struck a cord with Mary, and her face softened.

"Sarah, I don't know what to say."

"Just say it's okay."

"But it's not okay. What if you die?"

"Ma, are you listening to me? They just started letting women into the Navy. Do you really think they're going to have us on the frontlines with guns? Most likely, they'll have me stuck behind some desk in a tiny cubicle."

"Well that just sounds like a great time," Mary said sarcastically, but then her tone changed again. "This is really something you want to do?"

"Yes."

"And your father says it's all right?"

"Yes."

"And you promise you won't get yourself killed?"

"Yes."

"All right; I guess that's good enough for me. But there is going to be hell to pay once I get home to that father of yours."

Sarah gleefully got back in line, and was one of the first women to join the Waves.

In just a year, both Sarah and Jimmy were gone. Tommy was in high school, desperately trying to fill the void his brother had left on the football team, and Joseph and Sally were growing faster each day. The house felt bigger without Sarah and Jimmy around, but Tommy, Joseph, and Sally were still capable of creating enough mischief to keep Mary occupied.

Seraphine thought about the growth of his children as he walked to the pier one hot, summer day. He wondered where Sarah and Jimmy were and what they were doing. It seemed like long ago that he had fought in the Great War, and less than twenty-five years later the world was caught in a second major conflict. In many ways, being in the Navy had been great for

Seraphine. He got to see the world, meet many people, and do things he had never done before. It was an education he would never have received in school. But then, there were also hard times, dangerous times.

Seraphine was broken from his reverie by a man on a bike who nearly ran him over. "Get out of the middle of the street, old man!" he cried as he rode recklessly by. Seraphine had not seen him coming, and it wasn't like he was the only one walking in the middle of the road. Now, when Seraphine looked around him, it wasn't stubborn townsfolk boycotting the sidewalks that filled the street, but people he had never laid eyes on. They were like ants, weaving through the cars, on the sidewalk, off the sidewalk. He, personally, had no problem with using sidewalk, but felt compelled to move himself into the road after bumping into people eating icecream, pushing strollers, walking dogs, and swinging shopping bags.

He began to take note of all the t-shirt and gifts shops that seemed to have sprung up from nowhere, pausing in front of one window to see a table piled high with shot glasses that donned a fish, paperweights that said "Cape Cod," a snow globe of the Monument, and wooden cutouts of lobsters. There was a rack of postcards and calendars and a shelf of ashtrays. He never remembered there being so many trinket shops, but perhaps it was because he rarely left the house this late in the day. He was probably out before they opened, he figured.

Even though it was just after eleven o'clock, he decided to stop and get a cup of coffee, but when he got to the counter, Dottie was frantically making ice cream cones for a line of hot people. "What'll it be 'Cap? The usual?" she asked over her shoulder.

"Yep."

Dottie managed to finish an ice cream cone and pour Seraphine's coffee at the same time. He left his money on the counter and squeaked through the crowd of people to the door, where Fluke waited for him. He had grown so accustomed to the dog following him, he hardly noticed anymore. He went to sit down on the bench, which was packed with people, and had almost given up looking for a spot to sit when a group of three got up to leave for the beach, chatting jollily, their totes packed with beach towels, lunch, and an umbrella.

3Seraphine uncomfortably sipped his coffee until he spotted Ernie Gobo heading toward him. Seraphine never would have believed that he could feel so happy to be begged for money.

"You out late, Cap'," Ernie said from halfway across the street. "Strange seeing you mixed in with all these people."

"Yep. I feel like a fish out of water."

"None of the cheap bastards will even spot a guy a quarter or let him bum a cigarette."

"Maybe they're onto something there."

Ernie laughed as he leaned back comfortably on the bench, his body accustomed to spending many nights on it. "You know Cap', I was thinkin', as I layed here on the beach this mornin', watchin' the boats comin' in and out of the harbor. I thought, 'now that's a beautiful sight.' And I heard the weir boats goin', and I thought to myself, 'that's a beautiful sound.' But then I thought, 'it's quieter than it used to be.' And then I thought, 'there ain't as many boats as there used to be.' And from time to time I think things like this, and I'm beginning to think that one day, I'm gonna be lying here and there ain't gonna be no sound, and there ain't gonna be no fishin' boats."

Seraphine nodded pensively, and then said lightly, "When'd you become such a thinker?"

Ernie laughed. "Well, you got a lot of time to think when you don't do nothin' . . . But I'm serious Cap'. You remember when Provincetown Harbor was the biggest fishing port in the country. The whaling was right up there with Natucket's."

"Sure I remember. It wasn't in my lifetime, but the fishing fleet was certainly a lot bigger when I was young."

"That's right. And every year it gets smaller. For every boat that's taken out of the water, another hot dog stand opens. I mean, I like hot dogs when I got the money to buy one, but there ain't no need for that many goddamn hot dog stands! I mean, I remember during the real hard times when we had nothing to eat."

"Have you ever had enough to eat?" Seraphine said drolly.

"That ain't the point. Now, it's a choice; then it wasn't."

"We never starved. The ocean kept us alive. Fish kept us alive. Hell, it still keeps us a live."

"It's our bread and butter, Cap'. It don't matter if you fish out of those boats or run the general store; that fish keeps us all alive.

Seraphine nodded slowly.

"How 'bout you, Cap'? You gonna sell the house and go off to South Carolina? Leave me here with nobody to beg money off of."

"What'm I gonna do in South Carolina? I ain't goin' nowhere. This here's my home. It'll always be my home no matter what happens."

"Well, in that case, you got a quarter for the old man? For old time's sake."

Seraphine shook his head and handed him a buck. "You really want something from me, why don't you come down to the boat this afternoon and get a fish? It'll feed you for two days, at least."

"Nah, Cap'. This'll do me. Thanks, gov'na," and Ernie made a gesture of tipping his greasy cap.

Seraphine stood and headed to the wharf, Fluke trailing close behind.

II

The Lady in the Water

Tales had been told of a lady in the water. She lurked just below the surface, and on clear, calm days, her fair face, framed by wavy brown hair and green eyes gazing longingly toward the sky, had been spotted. Many men swore she was a mermaid, a siren, calling to them to find her, to rescue her and bring her to land. Myths had told of many seamen lured by the songs of the mermaids and captured by their allure forever, never to escape their ageless beauty and hypnotizing promises of love. Those who had spotted this lady in the water, just a brief glimmer of her, became determined to find her again. Those who had only heard of her longed to see her just once. Young men and old could never rest on land; they went to sea, not in search of fish, but in search of the lady. None had yet brought her back, none had touched her, none had seen her but for a moment, and many were tortured. Or so the story went.

It was a popular tale told in the bars or to young children listening, wide-eyed, to the old salt on corner, his cane gesticulating in fantastic pantomime. But aside from the hashing of local lore, the lady in the water was forgotten and considered nothing more than a myth of the past.

The dories were rowing back toward the *Halcyon*, bringing with them the final catch of the day. Seraphine had long since been on board and was surveying the catch and preparing for the long trip home. His keen ears heard a distant cry in the only dory still in the water. The men in the boat raised a signal, and Seraphine quickly lowered a dory and rowed out to them.

"Cap', you gotta see this," Frank Medeiros said, and pointed into the water.

Seraphine lashed his dory tightly to the other and squinted down into the rippling water. At first he could see nothing through the haze of blue-green. He leaned over the edge of the dory and peered hard into the water until he finally saw what appeared to be the silhouette of a woman's body. The sight sent him reeling back into the boat as though he had been kicked square in the chest. Quickly recovering from his shock, he cried as he started to pull off his jacket, "Jesus Christ, it's a woman! I've got to get her." His reason was clouded by his impulse to dive into the water and save the woman barely within sight of the water's surface, but his men, in an equally serious tone, said, "That ain't no lady." Those simple words were enough to sedate Seraphine's reflex, and he quickly came to his senses. "Sure it's not, but what is it?"

"I think it's part of a boat. We got hung up on it—nearly lost our entire line. We were trying to figure out what we'd hit, when we saw her. Old Codinha, here, thought she was a mermaid or something."

"Did not!" Bobby Codinha, a new recruit, interjected defensively.

"I thought, like you did, 'Cap, it was some kind of body, but then I thought, no body that's been floating under water would look that good!"

Seraphine nodded. "Let's bring her up."

He pulled the *Halcyon* to where Frank and Bobby were marking the spot, their line still hung up on the wreckage. He, Bill, Paul Careiro, and Scooda Morris lowered ropes down and then managed fish around and hook onto the painted lady. Then, with a pulley and the brute force of eight hands, the other two men guiding the lines, they began to raise the giant piece of wreckage. They could not see the rest of what the lady was attached to, and though she was heavy, she broke off cleanly with just the piece of bow she was built into to. The lower portion of her body grew right into the frame of the boat, so she had no figure below the hips. Her head and shoulders were free from the boat, and from the mid torso up, she could stand alone as her own piece of sculpture.

The men heaved on the line, but as the body came out of the water, her sheer size and weight was truly felt. Not only was it a massive piece of wreckage, but it was completely waterlogged from decades of being under the ocean's surface. The pulley began to creak and the ropes and rigging began to strain.

"Cap', we're gonna lose her. That gear's never gonna hold," Paul said.

It was futile to get the entire piece onto the boat; they did not have the strength nor the proper equipment. Seraphine grabbed a handsaw from the cabin and tossed it down to Frank. "Cut her off," He said.

After a brief questioning glace, Frank did as he was told and began to saw away at her torso until the rest of the bow, her body, fell off and sunk back deep into the water, out of sight forever. The men, without too much difficulty, were able to pull the remainder of her aboard and surveyed their catch. Her paint was faded and worn in many places, but the artistry was apparent. The details of her features, hair, and bodice, were carefully carved and carefully painted. The wood was in perfect condition, soft from the water, yes, but no chips or gouges. With a little paint, she would be as good as new.

"What're you gonna do with her Serry?" Bill asked taking a swig from his flask as they began to sail home.

"Not sure," Seraphine replied.

"Bobby, there, seems to have taken quite a liking to her." He gestured to the man who was making an extra examination and scraping off a few barnacles.

"Well, he found her."

When they got to port and unloaded her along with the fish, the other men on the dock quickly surrounded the body. They fawned over her and mumbled amongst each other, "It's the lady in the water . . . That ain't the lady in the water; she had brown eyes . . . Nah, that's her. Blue, I always heard they was blue . . . I saw her once when I was just a boy; just for a second. Don't seem so special now that I can see her in plain light . . . How old you think she is? Hundred, two hundred years? . . . You crazy? Nah, she looks too good to be that old . . . All those men who died for her. She made 'em crazy, she did. And for what? She's just a rotting piece of wood. After all that. Just a rotting piece of wood . . . Where's the other half of her? Said they cut it off. Goddamn shame . . . She finally made it . . . What you talkin' about? . . . She's here. On land. Somebody finally saved her."

An art collector from Boston had caught wind of the find and pushed his way through the crowd holding out a wad of cash. "How much you want for it?" Seraphine have him a hard look. "It ain't for sale."

"I can give you a hundred dollars for it. That'll feed you for a month."

"I said, it ain't for sale."

"But this should be in a museum. This should be on display for all people to see." Seraphine knew perfectly well that this man wanted it for his own, private collection, or to peddle it off to some historian for even bigger bucks.

"Oh she's goin' to be seen by everyone, don't you worry about that," Seraphine said, irony in his voice and a smirk on his face. "She ain't goin' in no museum. She's been trapped behind glass her whole life. Bobby here is gonna nail her above the door of his house. Ain't that right, Codinha?"

"Sure am," he grinned widely.

"Ain't no better spot to be seen.

They loaded her onto a cart, and Bobby Codinha proudly wheeled her on home.

III

A Death in the Family

The men were busily making repairs to the *Halcyon* after she had been battered by an earlier storm. Bill was working on the engine, Paul was tarring the hull, Bobby Codinha was working on the roof, and Seraphine was supervising, checking the rigging and looking for weak spots in the wood.

"Hey Serry!" Bill called from the engine room. "Can you bring me the wrench? I forgot to grab it."

"Sure," Seraphine said and went to the tool box in the cabin only to find the wrench missing. *Bobby must have it*, Seraphine thought, annoyed, and headed toward the cabin door to ask him. Just as he stepped on to the deck, there was a cry from above and a body came falling right on top of Seraphine, flattening him to the deck. Hearing the loud thud, Bill came rushing over.

"Holy shit! You okay?" he asked as Bobby rolled off of Seraphine's back and Seraphine raised himself to his knees. "Christ, nice boy," Bill continued, "you nearly took out the captain!" He laughed heartily now that he knew they were both all right. Seraphine gave him a look that was far from amused.

"Oh my God!" Bobby cried. "Thank God you were there! I would have broken my neck for sure if you hadn't been there to break my fall."

Bill laughed harder, and Seraphine said with a twinge of sarcasm in his voice, "Yeah, good thing." He stood up stiffly. "What happened anyway?"

"A seagull, that's what happened. That big bastard swooped right down and knocked me clear off the roof."

"How do you get knocked off the roof by a seagull?" Paul asked skeptically, just arriving at the scene.

"He went for my face, that's how. Tried to peck my eyes right out, that nasty bastard."

They all laughed at that.

"You okay Cap'?" Bobby asked with genuine concern. "I'm real sorry I fell on you."

"That's okay, nice boy. Just glad you're all right." Seraphine hobbled to the bow to take a seat.

"You're gonna be stiff tomorrow," Bill said.

"Yeah, I think it might be best if I call it a day," Seraphine said rubbing his back. "You fellas know what to do."

Seraphine hobbled home, slowly, getting sorer with every step, but all his pain vanished when he walked into the house to see Mary sitting in the rocking chair sobbing.

"What's wrong?" asked Seraphine, immediately concerned something had happened to one of the children. She kept crying.

"Is it Jimmy or Sarah? Has one of them been hurt?"

Mary shook her head and Seraphine was instantly relieved.

"My mother is dying," Mary finally found the composure to say.

Seraphine was not quite sure how to react. He might have cracked a bit of a smile had it not been for Mary's distress. That woman hated him.

"Oh, I know my mother is downright mean to you," Mary said as though she could read his thoughts, "but you have to understand that she is *my* mother."

Seraphine remembered how he had felt when his own mother died and softened, "What happened?"

"I just got a call from my bother that he stopped by to see her today and found her on the floor by her rocking chair. She had a stroke or something and can barely move. They don't think she'll make it." Mary paused. "Oh

271

I know I should have gone over there more often! God knows how long she was like that for!"

"It wouldn't have made any difference. I know she couldn't have been like that for very long."

"We have to go see her," Mary stood up decidedly.

Seraphine hesitated. Philomena was bad enough on a good day, let alone on her death bed. "Can she talk?"

"I don't know. She's bad though."

That was not very reassuring, but Seraphine told himself that perhaps she couldn't. On the way, Mary told him Philomena was home in her own bed. She didn't want to be taken anywhere else if she was going to die anyway.

Hmm, Seraphine thought, *she must be able to talk*.

When they got to the house there was a couple of nurses and Mary's brother Fudgey. Mary went straight into the room, but Seraphine stayed outside the door, peering in at the sleeping old lady. She looked so helpless and frail lying there. Her body was so emaciated, it hardly protruded through the covers, and her hair was white and curly like a little snowy wig. A glimmer of drool shone in the corner of her mouth, and her thin hands rested lightly on the bed at her side. Seraphine had never seen her look so vulnerable and stepped into the room.

As soon as he did, the old lady's eyes shot open, and she began to holler, "What the hell are you doing here? I'm on my deathbed, and I have to look at your ugly face! I don't want that goddamn bastard here!"

Everyone was frightened. It was like the corpse had risen from the grave, except all she could move were her eyes and mouth. *God help me*, Seraphine thought.

"Ma, calm down," Mary said. "It's fine. It's just Seraphine."

"I know goddamn well who it is! That good for nothing . . ."

"Ma, relax. You'll give yourself another stroke."

"Good. Maybe I'll actually die this time!"

Seraphine was uptight and eased his way out of the room.

"Where do you think you're going?" her dry, crackly voice screeched.

"I-"

"Get back in here."

Seraphine was incredibly confused. They all were. Mary pulled another chair beside her and Seraphine sat himself gingerly on it.

"Whatsamatter with you?" she asked snidely.

"Nothing."

"It ain't nothing. Answer me in a complete sentence, you fool."

"Just a guy at work fell off the cabin and landed on top of me."

"Oh yeah?" Philomena was amused.

"He did?" Mary asked in surprise. "Why didn't you tell me? You could have broken your neck."

"Humph," Philomena laughed sinisterly. Seraphine just shot her a look.

"That's enough, Ma," Mary mediated. "Are you all right?" she asked Seraphine.

"I'm fine. Don't worry."

"Yeah. Enough about him. I'm the dying one. This doesn't happen everyday, you know. Give me my time in the spotlight."

"Have you confessed?" Mary asked.

Philomena sputtered sardonically. "If the priest gets here in time."

"Don't say that, Ma."

"I don't care! If I'm gonna go to hell, I'm gonna go to hell. If I wasn't sorry then, what difference does it make if I'm sorry now?"

"Ma."

"Don't *Ma* me. I'll say what I want to say when I'm damn well ready."

Mary dropped the subject, and they all sat in awkward silence for what felt like an eternity.

"I want to talk to you," Philomena demanded, locking her piercing gaze on Seraphine.

"Me?" Seraphine asked, flabbergasted.

"Yes you!" She widened her eyes nastily at him and then mumbled audibly to herself, "Idiot."

Everyone sat where they were, unsure of which way to move next.

"Alone!" she shrieked.

"Oh, okay," Mary and the rest said rising and leaving the room like skittering mice.

Seraphine was alone with the old lady for the first time in God only knew how long. Perhaps ever. She just stared at the ceiling while Seraphine sat timidly in the chair.

"What I say stays in this room. You got that?"

"OK."

"Do you?" she looked at him severely.

"Yes."

"If you tell Mary, I swear I'll torture you from the grave."

Seraphine could not imagine how much worse that could possibly be than what he was enduring at that moment. Philomena paused again as though struggling to muster the gumption to say what she intended to. The silence was agony.

"You're all right," she mumbled.

"What?"

"You're all right!" she cried. "Christ! Don't make this harder than it already is." Seraphine shut his mouth. "I haven't always been so nice to you, and I know I give you a hard time, but the thing is, you're all right. Now, I really wish my foolish husband had left one of my sons the boat, but now that I see what you've done with it, I don't really mind. And, I know I've always said that you're not good enough for my Mary, but, really, you are. You're the homeliest bastard I've ever seen, but your kids look like their mother, thank God. I just wanted to tell you to take care of my Mary. I know you already do, so keep doing what you're doing. I know I've always been hard on Mary and that you never liked me much because of that, but believe me when I say that she is my favorite, always has been.

She was the apple of her father's eye, but she's mine too. Just thought you should know that."

Philomena stopped and Seraphine waited expectantly. "There, I said it. So long, and may I never see you again." She turned her eyes from the ceiling and saw that Seraphine's thick hand was gripping her frail one. She could not feel it, but she knew it was there, and Seraphine saw a tear trickle from the corner of her eye. She could not bring herself to look at his face gazing intently upon her, and after a short time, Seraphine got up and left. He never saw Philomena again.

IV

The War Effort

The people watched as the naval ships streamed into the harbor, huge, shining, steel vessels, so unlike the quaint, wooden fishing boats. The sun reflected blindingly off their sides, and the American flags were raised and flapping proudly in the wind. The townsfolk cheered, their patriotic sentiments aroused by the sight of these steel giants, despite how out of place they looked in the middle of the picturesque harbor.

It was not the first time the town had been the site of military activity. The navy had set up a base in the town during the First World War. Out on the Point, two large hills could be seen. These were the locations of two forts that had been put up during the Civil War, and during the Revolutionary War, the British had used the harbor as a base for their prolific navy. Such a deep, well-enclosed, natural harbor was hard to come by and the perfect place for a naval base.

The inn way in the West End had become a command base, and there was another located near the wharf. Soon the streets were filled with officers and sailors, walking proudly in their starched uniforms. The townsfolk treated them with the utmost politeness and, in return, were treated fairly.

The young sailors, though, were a loud and raucous bunch, rowdy as they came in and out of the bars, raising Cain in the streets, drunk and fighting. They sought desperately after the young Portuguese girls, much to the dismay of the mothers who struggled to keep their daughters confined to the house in the evenings, and rarely succeeded.

"What a bunch of floozies we have in this town," Mary said to Sandy as they passed a sailor with a town girl on each arm, the girls giggling and leaning into him.

Sandy rolled her eyes, "Regina must be beside herself with her daughter out like that, all made up and acting like a common whore."

"Regina could sugarcoat it all she wanted—I always knew that girl was no good. I saw the way she'd eye up Jimmy. One day she came to the house looking for him, and I had to fight her off the stoop with a broom! She never came back, but I still have that broom behind the door, just in case."

Sandy laughed. They were almost to the Community Center where they were to meet up with a couple dozen other town women. Mary and Sandy each had their knitting bags and walked into the room to see the ladies sitting in chairs and on the floor, knitting away. They were of all ages; elderly windows, middle-aged mothers, and young girls whose boyfriends and brothers were off in the war.

In the center of the room there was a huge wooden crate of army-issued yarn that the women were using to knit socks for the soldiers. Mary and Sandy made their way to the crates, greeting everyone they knew and chatting the usual small-talk, until they finally got their balls of yarn and found their closest friends to sit and knit with, Kitty Murphy and Betty Roderick.

"Hi girls," Betty said. "I've already finished two pairs. You've got a lot of catching up to do."

"Oh please," Mary responded. "I didn't see you here yesterday."

"Had a doctor's appointment. My back's been killing me."

"Well, that's what you get for moving all that furniture by yourself," Kitty reprimanded her, no sympathy in her voice.

"Hey, somebody's got to make a few bucks. My husband can't go out fishing nearly as much as he normally would; not with the warnings of German subs out there."

"I think it's all bull if you ask me!" Kitty said. "They just want to keep us scared at home, so we keep supporting the war even though we can't get a goddamn thing to eat."

"Yeah, the war rations are ridiculous. You have to sell your soul for a piece of beef around here," Sandy said.

"Well, it's not like it's the first time we haven't had meat. I mean, all we eat is fish most of the time anyways. We poor Portugees can't afford prime rib," Mary said, casting on her stitches.

"True, but I guess now that we really can't have it, we want it more," Sandy commented.

"I heard that Cookie's is the only restaurant in town that has any meat," Kitty said.

"How's that?" asked Betty.

"Brown nosing, that's how. She puts up the soldiers, makes 'em special meals, provides breakfast on the house. They love her for it! When the soldiers' rations come in on the boat, they toss her a load of meat out of gratitude, which she sells to us for top dollar," Kitty shook her head bitterly.

"Hey, she's a business woman," Mary said.

"I say she's a sneaky bastard. She doesn't even have a son in the war."

"Yeah, Mary's got a son *and* a daughter in the war," Sandy added.

"Doesn't look like my other kids are far behind. Tommy and Joseph are determined to join as soon as they're old enough."

"Let's hope the war's over by then," Sandy said.

"At this rate, who knows," Mary sighed. "I really hope nothing happens to my kids. I know they're fighting for their country, but I want my children here with me. It's awful not knowing where they are and if they're okay or if they're dead or alive at any given time. I get a letter from each of them, maybe once a month, and that's all I have to go by. It's really awful, you know."

Kitty nodded knowingly. She had a son in the war as well. "Many sleepless nights. But I keep knitting these socks thinking he might end up getting a pair. I think about my Peter all day every day." There was a moment of silence.

"The soldiers here in this town are a rotten bunch, don't you think?" said Betty trying to change the subject. "I mean, it's one thing if the old salts want to come home from fishing and stir up trouble in the bars, drunk as skunks. At least they pay taxes!"

"Oh, I think the soldiers are paying dearly for this town," Sandy said.

"I wish our boys could be stationed here instead of these strangers," Mary said, still thinking about Jimmy.

"That would be too easy. The boys would never be able to focus if they were still home while they trained," Sandy said.

"Things are just so different now," Mary said. "I mean, it used to be impossible for people to get here, and now it's like this war has opened up the floodgates. Our kids are leaving home, other people's kids are here and causing trouble. I mean, I haven't seen so many strangers here in this town in all my life, and I don't just mean military men," Mary said. "There's more artists and tourists here than ever before. I've never seen anything like it before in my life!"

"It's kind of nice, though," Sandy said. "I mean it's interesting seeing all the different people and, I mean, why *wouldn't* people want to come to our town? It's beautiful."

"I know. I just hate feeling like my home is being taken over. How'd you like to come home and find some stranger sleeping in your bed? Well, that's how I feel," Mary said. "Somehow having those battleships in the harbor makes me feel like we're being taken over, not the other way around."

Kitty said, "Ah, we couldn't be isolated forever. Who wants to be shut off from the rest of the world? There have always been all walks of people here; it's just that there's more of them now. You used to have to work to get here. Now it's much easier."

"When you think about it, this really is a very cosmopolitan little town. It always has been. I don't see how you couldn't be when you're a major port. You never know who or what is hopping off the next boat."

"No, it's great. I love that about here," Mary said. "I guess I'm just being selfish. I want it all for myself."

The women's hands never stopped their knitting and their voices hummed through the hours.

Seraphine sat on the *Halcyon* with Fluke, watching the naval ships practicing drills on the other side of the Point.

"Hey Serry, how's it goin'?" Bill sat down next to him. "No fishin' today?"

"Nah, too much commotion out there. They almost took out Mealy's weir nets on the way out."

"Christ, you'd think they'd know where they're going better with all that fancy navigation equipment they've got."

"Ah, you can't beat a Portrugee's instincts. *No* machine can match that."

Bill grinned. "I tell ya, we're all gonna lose our shirts this year. You can't get no rations in this town, and yet we can't go fishin'. It's ridiculous. How'm I supposed to feed my kids? Those sailors are some friggin' cocky too. They look at me like I'm some old, washed up fisherman while they're in their big fancy boats. I yell at them I'm a navy vet too! I know what it is to fight in big war ships, and you do a hell of a lot less on one of those than you do in a little, old fishin' boat. They can all kiss my royal Portuguee ass. I ain't taking it."

"Ah, they're just kids. Jimmy's somewhere causing the same trouble."

"I support the war effort, but I can't wait for them to get the hell out of here." Bill took a swig from his flask. He stretched and said, "Well, if we're not fishing today, I guess I'll go clamming. Tide's low at one thirty. You want to come?"

"Nah, I'll just do some things around here."

"All right then. I'll see you later," and Bill left.

Seraphine pulled out his pipe to light it and saw it was cracked, so he tossed it overboard and pulled out a new one from inside his jacket.

"Excuse me," he heard a voice behind him. He turned to see a young woman standing on the pier with a wooden case in her hand.

"Yes?" Seraphine looked at her inquisitively.

"Well, I just came over from Boston. I am attending the Fine Arts Work Center over in the East End." Seraphine nodded, not taking his eyes off her.

"I was wondering if I could do a portrait of you?"

Seraphine gave a little laugh. "What would you want to paint my ugly mug for?"

"Oh no! You have a great face for a portrait. You're exactly what I've been looking for." Seraphine looked at her skeptically. "This town's beautiful. It's the perfect place for an artist to find inspiration. I understand now what all the fuss is about. But I've really wanted to paint a *character*."

Seraphine didn't know whether he should be insulted by this comment or not, but he shrugged it off. "Well, there's plenty of those around here. Why me?"

The girl hesitated. "Well, I can't quite explain it. Words aren't my forte or else I'd be a writer. It's just the way you're sitting there on your boat. You look so comfortable, so accustomed to it. You're calm and relaxed as though you haven't a care in the world. But in your face, in the lines of your face, I can see a man who has experienced many hardships and done many great things. You seem to embody in your face the human struggle, the history of man's battle against nature, and yet you are serene."

Seraphine hadn't expected such a thoughtful response, and somehow it made him appreciate the girl more. Had she not so eloquently addressed him, he may have resisted her desire to paint him, but now he said, "Well, what the hell? I've got nowhere to go."

The girl excitedly unpacked her things and began to paint. It took several hours but Seraphine didn't mind. He was comfortable where he was. At first he felt odd and exposed, awkwardly raising himself for the pose, but the girl told him to just relax and act naturally. She'd do all the work. So he sat back, puffing on his new pipe and let her paint. The battleships cruised in the background, a stark contrast from the man on his modest, wooden fishing boat.

Though Seraphine was hesitant to see it, the girl insisted on showing the finished painting to him. His apprehensive face relaxed once he saw himself looking back at him. For the first time, he did not cringe at his homeliness. Instead he was surprised to feel that he looked . . . good.

"You doctored it up too much. You made me look too good."

"No I didn't. I pride myself on how realistic my portraits are. I don't want to toot my own horn, but I really think I captured you quite well."

Seraphine did not want to admit it, but the girl was right. There wasn't a line out of place. It looked like him in every way except there was a pride and intrigue about the figure in the painting that was truly a marvel to behold. The girl watched him attentively as he studied the portrait. She could tell that he was filled with doubt and surprise that his face translated in such a way upon a canvas.

"This is the way people see you. Maybe you don't see yourself this way, but this was done through my eyes. So you are seeing yourself the way I see you and the way, I am sure, most others see you. Not bad, huh?"

Seraphine's modesty got the better of him, and he did not respond. "So what are you going to do with this?"

"Well, I am having an exhibit in Boston in a couple of months, but I really don't know if I want to sell this. I think this may be my favorite painting yet."

Seraphine shook his head and smiled. "Well, it's your wall, I guess."

"I feel bad that I have taken so much of your time. I really ought to be going. Thank you much for doing me this honor. I hope you are pleased with the result."

"Yes I am. Good luck." Seraphine nodded at her, and she went on her way never to be seen by Seraphine again. He leaned back in the *Halcyon*, and decided to smoke one more bowl full of tobacco. Maybe these artist folks weren't so bad, Seraphine thought. Maybe they understood more than the townsfolk gave them credit for. Maybe they understood what the townsfolk took for granted.

V

The Great War

Seraphine awoke with a start, his shirt damp with sweat. He rubbed his shoulder, feeling the raised skin of the scar that marred it, and squeezed his eyes tightly shut as though he could somehow force out the images that were circling around in his head and through his dreams.

He stood on the deck of the great naval battle ship, much bigger than the boats he was accustomed to being on, far bigger than Glory's *Halcyon*. He gripped the rail and wondered when they might be able to do something. They'd been out at sea for nearly three months and had encountered no opposition. It seemed as though there was no plan whatsoever except to float along and wait until something arose that they could do.

Seraphine watched as the anxious young men joked and horsed around. They were a mouthy bunch and devoted their spare time and spare energy to boxing and wrestling, which Seraphine preferred to have no part in. He kept his distance as the young men laughed and jeered at each other and pushed each other around. The men on the boat had long since become indifferent to Seraphine. His introversion was boring to them, and they decided it was not worth the energy to try to assimilate him into the group.

There was one young man, Micky Tucker, who had taken a liking to Seraphine. He was a tall, slender, freckle-faced, red-head from Boston with a thick Southie accent.

"Hey, Seraphine, why don't you come on over with me and the other guys? We aren't doing nothing. Just fooling around a little. Come on."

"Nah," Seraphine said.

"I know you like to keep to yourself, but it wouldn't hurt once in a while to hang out with the other guys."

Seraphine scratched his neck, and without saying anything began to walk toward the group. The men looked up from their card game, expressionless, when Seraphine stood in the circle, and one nodded at him while the others masked their surprise.

"You play cards?" a dark haired, serious fellow asked.

"Sometimes."

"Want me to deal you in?"

"Aw, Christ, man, there's enough players as it is," a big, dirty blonde, lug of a guy named Martin said. "We don't need this fool joining in. He hasn't wanted to be a part of it before!" Martin was, by far, the biggest man on board the vessel, and Seraphine had witnessed him using his brawn to bully the other guys on numerous occasions. Many didn't tolerate him, but others were scared enough by him to let him push them around. Seraphine had already developed a bitter taste in his mouth for this man, disliking his way of treating others. Martin was the boxing champion of the ship. He was able to beat anyone who was brave enough to face him, and by this point, there were few who still would.

"What're you scared you're gonna lose, Martin?" the dark haired guy said, clearly one of those who cared little for Martin's roughness. "He probably won't win anyways. He says he only plays sometimes."

Martin just scoffed and said, "Deal him in."

All the men put their cash in front of them, and the game commenced. The game went at a steady pace with little excitement, but they began to notice that with every hand Seraphine's pile was getting bigger, and eventually, it became plain the Seraphine was winning. He was winning it all! Seraphine won another hand, and Martin turned red, and looked up at him, "What're you some kind of cheat?"

Seraphine just looked back at him coldly with his crystal clear eyes. Martin bristled, uncomfortable at having so little to react to, chilled by the silent stare.

"Say something, you quiet fuck!"

"I didn't cheat."

"My ass you didn't! You know what people who don't talk are? They're liars. Big fucking liars. I haven't trusted you from the moment we got on this goddamn boat, always sitting there by yourself, getting all your work done, not saying nothing, like some friggin' goody two shoes. You think just because you got that ugly fucking face, people'll leave you alone? I got a mind to lay a lickin' on that face and make it even uglier."

Seraphine's stone cold expression gave the hint of a smirk, and Micky jumped in, "I'd like to see you try."

"Shut your mouth, you fucking faggot!" Martin yelled and gave him a rough shove, sending Micky falling to the deck of the boat. Seraphine stood up, his fists clenched, his stout, thick body, erect. His chest rose and fell with his measured breathing but the rash on his face glowed red with anger.

"Oh! So the quiet man's gonna challenge the boxing champ of the *USS Massachusetts*," he laughed sardonically. "I'm game for that, but I want my money back after I beat your ass!"

The rest of the men opened up into a great circle, buzzing over the excitement and thinking that Seraphine was about to receive a harsh beating from the gargantuan man. The two men took off their white, uniform shirts, Martin revealing his big, white, rather flabby, hair covered back and chest, and Seraphine revealing his broad shoulders and neck, his thick harms, and his olive complexioned skin. Seraphine was far more muscular than Martin, but he was just so much smaller!

The fighting began, and Martin came at Seraphine with a heavy, reckless fist, that Seraphine easily dodged and retaliated with a hard uppercut to Martin's abdomen, knocking the wind out of him. Martin bent over from the pain and loss of breath, but he quickly recovered and drove at Seraphine again in the same uncontrolled fashion, Seraphine responded with yet another hard blow, a left hook to the ribs. Martin faltered, and Seraphine nailed him again with a quick one-two, right-left, jab-hook, sending Martin off-kilter, but instead of finishing the work with what could have been an easy final blow, Seraphine stepped back and let Martin regain himself. He clutched his side and looked bitterly at Seraphine. He could not take a punch, because he had never really been hit before. All the fights he had ever been in were quick knockouts, and he had never encountered a truly powerful puncher. He had never felt the damage of what a strong man could do. It was not size or even speed that won, but coordination and power.

Martin, furious at being crippled so, his anger rushing to his head, stumbled after Seraphine again, managing to catch Seraphine on the side of the face. Seraphine didn't make a sound and recovered quickly, pivoting and landing two more blows on Martin's soft torso. Martin gripped his right hand, crying in agony, for the bones had snapped against Seraphine's hard jaw. Yet he came back again, this time flailing with an uncoordinated left hand, and Seraphine gave him a stiff, fast uppercut right under his chin pushing his head up and sending him falling backward onto the ground. Martin lay, sprawled on the deck, completely knocked out.

The men cheered and slapped Seraphine on the back who stood quietly looking over his conquest. He did not smile, he did not gloat or cheer, but turned and walked away to go sit alone again on the bow of the boat. A day passed and Seraphine's jaw had swelled and bruised, but he looked much better than old Martin who walked around in a daze, a broken man. Micky sat by Seraphine, congratulating him over and over again, but Seraphine just sat there.

"He had it coming to him," Seraphine finally said, unable to avoid the comments anymore. "Somebody was bound to do it sooner or later. It just happened to be me."

"But Martin's so strong! He's the biggest, strongest guy I've ever seen! I don't think anybody else could have done what you did!"

"Nah, he's weak."

"Maybe to you he is!"

Seraphine shook his head. "Size isn't a sign of strength. Only a weak person hurts others to make him feel good about himself. A strong person doesn't hurt anybody. A strong person lifts up the weak, doesn't put them down."

Micky grinned and began to walk back down the deck when there was a great explosion. The boat shook and flames and debris burst out from every point. Seraphine was sent flying from the force and flattened against the deck. He blinked his eyes open and began to try to raise himself onto his hands and knees. He saw that a hole had been burned on the right thigh of his white trousers and that the area was sticky with blood, as was his shoulder on which he perceived a great bloody gash. He stood dizzily, the boat reeling around him, too delirious to notice the pain, the world spinning, smoke in his nose. He could hear nothing, and the chaos whirled around him like a dream of which he was merely an observer.

Men were running and crying, "We've been hit by a U-boat! Get to the lifeboats!" But to Seraphine it sounded like nothing more than muffled moans. The able-bodied men scrambled across the deck, loading into the boats, but a weak cry off to the side of the flaming ship caught Seraphine's attention and jolted him from his daze. He hurried toward the hand he saw sticking out from a pile of debris, seeming to struggle to find something to cling to. He fell to his knees and began to shovel the wood and metal away with his hands, not noticing as the hot remnants of the boat burnt his palms. It was Martin, who, remarkably, was still conscious, though badly cut up and bruised. "You gotta help me. I think my leg's broken. I can't move it." Afraid that Seraphine would not help him, he gave another desperate, "Please."

Without hesitation Seraphine bent over and lugged Martin up onto his shoulders. The man was twice his size, but Seraphine supported the weight in a fireman's lift, and bore the limp, heavy body as though he were carrying a giant fish, except this time, the slickness that covered his hands was not from smooth wet scales, but from sticky, hot blood. He did not know if the blood that oozed down his neck and saturated his sooty, burnt clothing was his own or Martin's. Likely, it was both, but it made no difference to him, as he took one heavy step after another toward the lifeboats, bending forward and laying, as carefully as he could, Martin into the hull of the little lifeboat. Seraphine turned as though to leave again.

"What are you doing?" a man asked. "Get in. Save yourself. The ship's going down quick. We've got to get out of here."

But Seraphine just turned and ran up the deck, looking for more bodies to collect. He stopped and scanned the burning, wretched sight. The smell of gas and smoke burned in his nostrils. Suddenly, he noticed to his right a limp rumpled body lying amidst burning debris. He went toward it and discovered the body of Micky. The side of his face was badly burnt and his clothes were covered in blood. Seraphine clumsily felt around his neck, and when he could feel nothing, he placed his ear to Micky's bloody chest, quickly pulling away, for there was a large wound, a jagged piece of shrapnel lodged right in his heart. Seraphine put his hand to the side of his face and let out a choked gasp. His face contorted with pain and sadness, and the tears squeezed out of the eyes of his crying, wretched face. He put his hands under Micky's armpits and lifted him up to his chest, cradling the limp, lifeless body as though it were that of a small child or a lost a puppy dog. He held it tight and wept as the ship sunk lower and lower into the water. He felt the cold ocean wash over the deck and wet his knees and realized the imminence of his deadly plight. If he were to save himself, he had to go now, and he lowered the body of Micky slowly back to the deck and watched as the water encircled it, turning red as it came in contact with the bloody carcass.

Seraphine looked up and could see the lifeboats in the distance. He jumped into the water and swam nearly a hundred yards before somebody spotted him. The men rowed toward him, and several strong hands reached down and lifted him into the boat.

"You okay?" a voice asked. It was the dark-haired fellow, who had invited Seraphine to the card game, and Seraphine nodded and placed his face in his hand, exhausted and in pain. The man took off his shirt and ripped it into two pieces. The larger of the two he tied tightly around Seraphine's thigh, the other, around his shoulder. Seraphine did not wince or grimace at the pain. He simply thanked him before closing his eyes and waiting for help to come.

It was two days before they were discovered. The men's toungues were swelled with thirst, and their skin was burned and blistered by the sun. They had only some canned rations to eat, though they had little appetite for it since what they craved most was water. Seraphine's complexion had gone chalky white with loss of blood, and he lay in the boat in agony, thinking that, at any moment, he would surely die. But he did not. Help arrived in time, and Seraphine was kept in a small, hot, fly—ridden hospital in France during his lengthy convalescence. He longed for home.

VI

The Old Colony

It was a chilly November evening, and Seraphine and Bill docked the *Halcyon* and readied themselves for the evening's walk home.

"What're you up to tonight, Cap'?" Bill asked.

"Not much."

"What'd the wife make for dinner?"

"Not sure. She's got one of those meetings tonight; those Red Cross something or others. She left something for me in the icebox."

"Why don't we hit the Old Colony, then?"

"No thanks."

"Come on. It'll be fun. Like the old days before we had the shackles put on. We used to have a great time. Remember? We hit that place every night."

"Sure," Seraphine remembered but without any warmth.

"Come on. Just for old time's sake."

After a few more minutes of Bill's persuading, Seraphine finally assented, and the two continued on their way, but instead of turning left to go home, they went right, three doors down to the Old Colony.

"Too bad you don't have your violin with you," Bill said as they entered through the dark doorway. "I know you don't like to play any of the peppy stuff, but with a few drinks in you, I'm sure you'll be a riot!"

The tavern was dim with only an oil lamp hanging above each table, their light barely able to shine through the soot-caked glass. Scrappy, the owner, keeper, and bartender preferred to maintain the old-time ambiance than move into to the modern era of electric light. The dull glow of the lamps could not reach to the extremities of the room so the corners were dark. The floors were a dull, dark, grimy brown, slick and shiny from years of traffic and spilled booze. Benches ran along all the walks, and there were about a dozen heavy wooden tables, their surfaces marred with cigarette and pipe burns, gouges from knives and stains from messes of liquor. The chairs were weak and rickety (Scrappy couldn't afford to buy nice ones, because they were always being broken in brawls or from men toppling over backward in a drunken daze), but the glasses were solid and the booze was good, which, really, was all that mattered. The bar was to the left, the bottles lined against the wall, and the large brass handle of the tap sticking up in front. A mirror separated the shelves of bottles, saloon style, and the countertop was the only polished thing in the entire room. Even the widows were foggy with fingerprints and grungy smudges.

Eight or so men were already there, their pints of beer in their hands, and their empty whisky shots in a line on the table in front of them.

"Hey Scrappy!" Bill shouted with the familiarity of one who still regularly frequented the bar. "Give us a couple of drinks! What'll you have, Cap'?"

"Just a beer."

"Give us two schooners of beer!"

"Coming right up," Charlie hollered back. "That'll be fifteen cents for each of you."

"Best deal goin'," Bill grinned and then waved his hand at Seraphine who was rummaging through his pants pocket. "Put your money away. This one's on me."

Seraphine and Bill sat at their own table with their mugs of beer. They knew all of the other faces in the room, gave their greetings, made their small talk, exchanged a few jokes, and by the time a few other souls came in, Bill and Seraphine had already sucked down their entire pints.

"Hell," Bill said, "that went down too easy. Hey Scrappy! Give us a whole pitcher, will ya, Pard!"

"That'll be a dollar!"

"Best deal going, Pard. Give us a couple shots of whiskey, while you're at it. This beer ain't strong enough for the likes of me. I told you, put your money away; they're on me, Serry!"

Bill kept the liquor coming fast, and in no time, Seraphine had a pleasant buzz. He was laughing more than he ordinarily would, and he lost track of who was coming and going, though hardly anybody was going. Eventually, he realized that the room was almost full. There were men at every table and seated on every chair, laughing uproariously. The air was heavy with the smoke of tobacco. Many had cigarettes stuffed in their mouths, the ashes falling all over the tables. Others, including Seraphine, were sucking on pipes. The room rang with the sounds of schooners being clanked together in the air and shot glasses being slammed down on the tables.

The captains of ships and mates alike were all sitting together having a casual drink after a long day, for some, a long month, of work. Those who had just gotten back from a long trip at sea shared their tales of what they caught and what they encountered with the color and exaggeration of men with great enough imaginations to fill their monotonous time at sea. All of the town drunks were there, as always, this being the closest thing they had to a rooted home, even going so far as to have their mail sent to the bar care of the Old Colony Tavern. These men included Ernie, who was positively elated when his mind cleared sufficiently to realize that Seraphine was there. Finally, there were the naval sailors who sat in their own corner of the tavern, wearing their issued blue and white uniforms. Some mixed with locals, but they predominantly kept to themselves.

Potts walked in with a five gallon bucket, a brownish green claw sticking out from the top.

"Hello folks!" he hollered as he stepped into the room. "Will ya look what I've got!" He reached down into the bucket and pulled out a huge fifteen pound lobster. Its naked claws moved around lazily in the air.

293

"Jesus Christ! Put some rubber bands on that thing before it bites somebody's toe off!" a voice yelled.

"I ain't got any rubber bands big enough!" Potts called back with a proud grin. He was used to being nipped by angry lobsters.

"A lobster that size calls for a free drink!" Scrappy said, already three sheets himself from taking nips behind the bar. It was by this time of the evening that Scrappy always began to lose money, being in such jolly drunken spirits that any occasion prompted a free drink.

"Ah, I've seen bigger," someone said dismissively.

"So have I!" Potts nodded back in mild offense. "But these are hard to come by in the traps. They don't usually fit. I've gotten ones twice, three times this size, diving for 'em, but it ain't the time of year for diving. Too damn cold. I got pictures! I pulled from the water, with my very own hands, the biggest goddamn lobster this town's ever seen!"

Nobody argued. Many people went diving for lobsters, but Potts was particularly good at it. He had an instinct for lobsters. They were his specialty.

Potts sat down in the last open chair with the bucket containing the lobster beside him. In no time at all, he was as drunk as the rest of them, pulled the lobster out of the bucket, and set it loose in the middle of the floor. It skittered backward around the room slowly enough to be avoided, but occasionally it would sneak up on a drunken, unsuspecting victim and latch onto the end of his boot with its giant claw. "Jesus Christ!" The man would holler, giving his foot a good shake and sending the lobster skidding across the room, much to the delight of the onlookers. Some, who were paying more attention to the creature made bets as to who it would go after next, exchanging bills, change, and drinks to the winner, the men the lobster attacked never realizing why some people were cheering and yelling.

Eventually, the novelty of this creature wore off, and most everybody forgot about it until there was a momentary lull in the noise of the room and the scraping and scratching of the legs of the lobster could be heard.

But even that noise ceased, as the lobster became weary and found some dark corner to settle itself in; the same corner where a man sat passed out, hunched over his half empty schooner with his cigarette still burning in his mouth.

There was the sound of clopping down the road, a steady clip-clopping of some heavy hoofed beast. The volume of the room lowered as the men who knew the source of the sound paused to listen in uneasy anticipation. They held their breaths as the sound grew louder with each passing moment, but no matter how much they waited and listened, they were still staggered when the sound made itself known.

Through the doorway stepped a great, black horse, its owner leaning forward into its mane in order to clear the top of the doorway before sitting up straight and erect in front of the awed crowd.

It was Bos'n, the town's most infamous character. He sat on top of his black steed, bareback, the large nostrils of the cart-sized horse flaring, releasing two clouds of steam. Its black eyes were clear and shiny, but a little crazy; almost as crazy as those of his owner.

Bos'n's hair was long and curly. Black with chunks of white and silver streaked through it. His beard was nearly as long, blending in with the rest of his hair. His upper lip was clean, and his face was furrowed with deep, coarse lines, but his eyes were clear and sharp, and they made every man they came in contact with uneasy. They were shifty eyes, alert eyes, that darted from side to side, as though the body they were set in was ready to pounce at any moment, but his body was calm and still. The movements were slow, but calculated. He wore a thick naval officer's jacket opened with a dingy, white, button-up shirt underneath. It was open at the chest, and he kept a red bandana tied around his neck. His patched, gray slacks were stuffed into the tops of unpolished, black boots, and though his face was damp with sweat and his clothes were old and dingy, he looked to be far more than a dirty bum from off the street. He carried himself with the authority of a king, which far outshone his greasy appearance. He had a scarlet cloth tied around the top of his head, over which he wore a big, black, felt hat. He came close to being the spitting image of a pirate—the only things he lacked were the peg leg and a hook for a hand.

What was most odd about this man's appearance (as though sitting in the middle of the tavern atop a giant, black horse were not sufficient) was a little monkey he had sitting on his shoulder. The monkey wore a little red vest with gold embroidery on it, the only thing that covered his fuzzy, ticked brown body. It, too, had black beady eyes, and its long, thin tail snaked in the air behind it as it sat comfortably on Bos'n's shoulder, even as he carefully and easily slid himself off the back of the horse.

Bos'n handed the rope he used for reigns to a young boy who was there to clean the tables without saying a word. The boy knew precisely what to do, and lead the horse back outside to be tied up. Bos'n stood in the middle of the room, his monkey on his shoulder, his rotund belly hanging over the gold buckle of his belt. He had his hands on his hips and surveyed the room, his gaze cold. The men sat, expectantly watching.

"Well what are you all sitting around for with your mouths open like a bunch of dead codfish?" His voice was scratchy, but it carried through the room. "It's like a goddamn funeral in here!" And with that he let out a bellowing laugh, setting the room back at ease, almost, and everyone went back about their business. A chair was given up at Seraphine and Bill's table for Bos'n, and he sat down easily in it, letting the monkey hop off his shoulder. It sat on the table, licking its paws, but when Dory Plug stuck a finger out to pet it, it gave it a good, swift bite on the tip. Dory Plug yanked his finger back and sucked on it, wincing with pain.

"Ah, you don't want to do that, Pard," said Bos'n. "Dr. Foo's a bit irritable today. Got a bit of a hangover from last night."

"A hangover?" Dory Plug asked incredulously.

"Yep. He's taken a bit of a fancy to the sauce. This here creature can out-drink me! But you know what I say; the only way to get rid of a hangover is to drink more! Ain't that right, Dr. Foo?" and he let out a loud laugh as the monkey jumped excitedly on the table clapping its hands.

"What'll it be, sir?" Scrappy asked.

JULIANNE PAPETOAS 2011

"Give me a bottle of whiskey. Two glasses. I got a chunk of change in my pocket that's burning a hole in it." He poured himself a couple shots, savoring the burn, and poured himself another one before taking up the bottle.

"Okay, Dr. Foo. Hold your horses. Your turn's comin'! Open up."

The monkey sat right down on its hind quarters, tilted its face toward the ceiling and opened its mouth wide. Bos'n began to pour the whiskey down its throat, and just when the onlookers were shocked that the monkey had consumed as much as it did, it put up its arms, latched its hands around the neck of the bottle, and tugged on it for more. Between his own shots, Bos'n would pour more down the throat of the monkey. Eventually he called for another shot glass and filled it up so Dr. Foo could have his own. The monkey sat on the table, his head nodding and rolling around, his hands around the brim of the glass that sat between his legs. He would pick it up and take a sip, and Bos'n looked lovingly at his little friend with the air of a proud father.

Bos'n slammed a fist on the table. "It's too damn quiet in here!" he hollered. "Somebody play something!" Everyone looked about helplessly until Bill said, "Seraphine plays the violin!" Everyone cheered.

"I don't have it with me," Seraphine said, happy for an excuse, but Scrappy reached behind the bar and pulled out an old, beat-up instrument. "Will this do ya?" he asked, placing it in Seraphine's hands.

Seraphine played a screechy note on it, and nodded. "I think I can get something out of it." He began to try to tune it, sending chills up the spines of the cringing men. Finally satisfied, to the relief of the others, Seraphine began to play.

"And none of that slow, sad shit," Bill said. "Something we can tap our feet too."

Everyone watched to see Bos'n's reaction, afraid that if he didn't like what Seraphine was playing, he'd take the instrument and crack him over the head with it. At first, his face was blank as he was listening, and then he began to tap his foot, and then he stood up all the way and began hopping and turning and skipping around more lithely than anyone would have expected from him. That was the signal to go, and the men were dancing around the floor and on top of tables and chairs. Some were swinging each other around, others remained sitting but clapped and cheered and stomped their feet. Bos'n was wild, making his way all around the room. Even Dr. Foo arose from his drunken stupor and hopped around on the table, screeching with delight and brushing the faces of sitting men with his tail.

Seraphine's fingers were flying, the bow moving swiftly back and forth, up and down. He kept time, tapping his foot, and his whole body moved with the rhythm of the music. The lamps were swinging, the floor was creaking, glasses were clanking, and everyone had a great time. Seraphine only knew a couple rousing songs but it was enough. Everybody was too drunk to notice the redundancy.

When Bos'n became tired, so did the rest of the room, but Seraphine kept playing lightly, enjoying himself, and glad for an excuse to desist his drinking for a time. Bos'n, in the heat of the dance, had pulled off his jacket, tossing it to the floor, and exhilarated, slammed his elbow down on Seraphine and Bill's table as though he wanted to arm wrestle. His shirt sleeve was rolled up, and he leaned his drunken face in low, his eyes still sharp but glassier than they were before, as though he were about to tell them a secret.

"Take a look at this, boys," he said, and pulled up his sleeve farther. "Get that lamp down here!" he ordered, "Nobody can see!"

The lamp was placed beside his arm, and he straightened it out, the underside raised to reveal a series of brown rings marking his skin.

"Do you know what this is?" he asked rhetorically for effect. "These here marks are from the suckers of a giant squid! Have any of you seen one of those before in your lives? I doubt it!"

"Where'd you find a giant squid?" Dory Plug asked.

"Well, if you shut your trap, I'll tell ya!" Dory Plug leaned back in his seat like a dog that had just been kicked. The rest of the men in the room hushed and moved in around Bos'n.

"This," he continued, keeping his arm exposed for effect, "came from a fifty foot long squid that I came upon in the Pacific. We were sailing across the globe in a big merchant schooner. I'm a bit of an explorer, you know. I started out in the Navy, and then I moved on to bigger things. The Navy was boring as hell." He turned to the sailors in the back of the room, "Yeah, that's what I said. Boring as hell! Didn't do nothing for me. I've been through the jungles of the Amazons. I've ridden elephants in India—that's where I found this little fella here," he said, nodding to Dr. Foo. "I've fought with cannibals in the South Pacific, and I've been chased by panthers in South America. But nothing, and I mean nothing, has ever scared me so damn much as that goddamn giant squid. The thing's tentacles were longer than a pickup truck, and it had a beak on it sharp enough to take a man's head clean off.

"It was your average day, a little calmer than usual. We were sailing at a good clip, when all of a sudden the boat came to a halt. The jolt was so bad most of us fell right over. We looked over the side and saw the tentacles of a squid wrapped around the stern of the boat. We didn't know how to get her loose, so I offered to jump down and cut the boat free. Everybody said I must've been out of my goddamn mind, and, well, of course I am, but I didn't listen—I never listen to anybody. I grabbed a machete, tied myself to a rope, and jumped overboard right onto its back. I hung on by squeezing my legs tight around it. It was like riding a gigantic, bucking horse. I began to hack away at its tentacles, but that didn't last for long 'bout as soon as it noticed, it took a few of those things and turned them on me—wrapped them around my whole goddamn body. Nearly choked the life out of me. The pressure was incredible, like being wrapped all the way around by a giant cobra. (I've had that happen to me too.) But this was worse. I just kept chopping away. It tried to suck me under water, and several times it succeeded, blinding me with thick, black ink, like tar, and trying to lead me to its mouth. Christ, did that shit stink! But I fought, nearly drowned to death, but I fought. I gave that bastard a real tough time of it. It was so angry at me, 'bout I must have cut eight of its tentacles off, that it forgot almost completely about the boat. It let go of the boat, but grabbed onto me with all the able tentacles it had left. Sucked me right under, all the way.

"I could barely see a thing 'bout the water was so thick with ink, but I swam as hard as I could to stay away from its mouth. I cut and kicked and slashed and butchered the son of a bitch, and once I cut one loose, I was able for a moment to fall down toward its belly where I gave it a good stab with my machete. It weakened a bit, and its tentacles loosened their grip on me, and I was able to slide down and slice it clean up the middle so all its innards came spilling out.

"In the process the rope had come undone, but fortunately, the ship was caught in irons because the boys were too busy watching the scene below. I swam to the side of the boat and managed to climb up. Nobody helped me, of course, 'bout they all thought I was dead, and I rolled myself over the rail, all wet and black with ink and covered with the huge sores and panting, ready to have a heart attack, and those fools were looking over the stern with the end of the rope in their hands, crossing themselves and saying their prayers. I hollered at them 'You goddamn idiots!' and then I passed out. Those men thought they'd seen a ghost! I woke up three days later covered with these scars and still stinking like squid ink. Sometimes, if I get caught in the rain, I still get whiffs of it!" Bos'n let out a loud cackle and leaned back in his chair proudly. He looked at the rest of them as though challenging them to rival the tale, but nobody dared.

For the rest of the evening, Bos'n told the men tales of his worldly exploits, nearly dying of starvation in the Arctic, resorting to cannibalism while floating in the middle of the Pacific in a lifeboat, hunting bears, wolves, and bison. The stories were endless, and nobody could vouch for or against their legitimacy. Nobody cared. The stories made for a highly entertaining evening, right up until Scrappy signaled that it was closing time for the bar and that all had to go on their merry, drunken ways. Bos'n coaxed a inebriated, unsteady Dr. Foo onto his shoulder, hailed to all a good night, hopped on his naked, black horse, and rode back down the street. The rest walked. The bums went to the docks they slept under on the beach, Scrappy and the boy began to somewhat clean the mess that had been left, and the sailors went back to their ships. Seraphine was glad he had gone, though he already had a searing pain in his head, and when he lay down on the bed and closed his eyes to sleep, he could feel the room whirling around him. He did not plan on doing this again anytime soon.

VII

Josephine

Cleaning houses was the only job Josephine could find as a young widow in a new country unable to speak the language, but she did it willingly. Her hands were always rough and red, and her body always ached, but she never missed church on Sunday and said her rosary every night before bed and in the morning before she got dressed. People on the streets called her Josie Mops because they always saw her walking across town with her bucket and mop, going from house to house, and then to the public toilets in Town Hall. She kept her head up, and her eyes were always determinedly focused on her destination. She never spoke to anyone, and her silence was the source of much coffee gossip.

"I hear that woman's deaf and dumb," a man would say as he looked out the window of Adams, blowing onto his steaming cup.

"Nah, she ain't dumb. She just don't speak English," his friend would reply.

"You call what *we* speak English?" The two men laughed.

"She speaks Portuguese."

"So do I—*panalla*." The man roared with laughter.

"I oughta beat you with a *panalla*. I ain't talking Portuguese slang. I mean the real thing."

"There's plenty of people in this town who still speak Portuguese. Plenty of first generationers. I speak it a bit, but my parents wouldn't let me most of the time. My father'd give me a good whack if I ever used it. Wanted me to be American."

"Yeah, but it doesn't make any difference. She just don't want to talk to nobody. You know, she's Carlos' wife."

"Which one?"

"The one who used to sail with Captain Cook."

"The one who died in the gale of 1898?"

"Yeah, him."

"Really? I didn't know that."

"Yep. She was a widow pretty much from the moment she set foot in this town."

"That's a shame. He was a hell of a nice guy. Didn't know him too well, but he seemed all right."

"Yeah, she's got a little boy too. He must be ten or eleven. I don't know. Quiet like his mother. I offered to buy him an ice cream one day—poor kid don't look like he's ever had a treat in his life, but he said, 'No. My ma says I'm not s'posed to take anything for free from nobody.' I said to him, 'It ain't charity. It's just ice cream.' But he shook his head, thanked me and took off. What kind of kid refuses ice cream? It ain't normal. And he don't talk to nobody either. Just walks back and forth to school with his books. I never see him play."

"Wait. Is he the kid with the rash on his face?"

"Yeah. I don't know what it is. Poor kid. Maybe a birthmark or something."

The other man shook his head and looked down into his cooling cup of coffee. "The whole situation is sad."

Everyday Seraphine went home to their little, one room studio after school and cleaned up. After Mrs. Francis died a few years earlier, he and Josephine had to leave, because the family was selling the house. They had to downsize to a studio apartment because nobody was willing to rent them a one-bedroom as cheaply as Mrs. Francis had. Seraphine would sweep the floor, make the beds, wash dishes, and set the table for dinner. He would do laundry and hang it up on the line outside, and if he had time, he would even take his little spool of fishing line out with a hook and catch a fish or two for dinner. Then he would sit down at the table and do his homework by the light of a sooty oil lamp.

"Studying again?" his mother would say when she walked wearily through the door.

"Yes."

"You should try playing once in a while."

"No."

"Why not?"

"There's too much to do." Seraphine at no point removed his nose from the book he was studying or lifted his pencil from the vocabulary problems he was doing.

"Don't worry about the house, Seraphine. Really. I can clean up. You should make some friends. Go outside. Be a kid."

Seraphine continued to look down at his book, but the pencil stopped moving. "I caught a fish today." At first Josephine thought that he was trying to change the subject, but then she realized that Seraphine was trying to tell her that fishing had occupied his allotment of fun for the day. Though it seemed like work to Josephine, to Seraphine fishing was a productive way to have a good time, and this subtle comment was his way of assuring her that he was not deprived of all of life's enjoyments.

"Did you? You're quite the fisherman, my *Boyzine*. You caught it with just a hook and line?"

"Yes."

"Well, that sure is something," Josephine proudly encouraged Seraphine's skills and diligence. "When I save up enough money, I'll buy you a nice fishing rod."

"I don't need a rod."

Josephine smiled and ran her hand across his red cheek. She had taken him to so many doctors, spent so much money on ointments and medicines to clear up his face, but none of it worked. She, at last, had given up, accepting that this was the way God made him. Her *Boyzine*. Her precious little boy.

After dinner, Josephine would collapse on the little bed, a mattress on the floor covered with tattered blankets, and Seraphine would curl up beside her after making sure that everything in the house was in its place and that his school books were put neatly away. The two would sleep, dreaming only of the day that had just passed and the day that was to come, never pining for the things that they did not have and never taking for granted those that they did.

Seraphine was so quiet and introverted that he went unnoticed by most of the children at school until he was about the age of eleven when his peers were finally observant enough to take note that he did well in school, always completing his homework and getting good grades, which made him a prime candidate to bully. It was with this realization that many other observations were made, and the taunting began and persisted daily for quite some time.

"Hey Boyzine! Isn't that what your mother calls you? Her precious little boy."

"Ooh my precious little boy," another boy jeered.

Seraphine just kept walking across the schoolyard toward the road.

"Come on, Boyzine, say something."

"Whatsa matter? You dumb, Boyzine? Like your mother. You both dumb?" One boy stuck his foot out and tripped Seraphine. He stumbled forward but caught his balance on one hand, clutching his books to his chest in the other.

"Don't lose your books, Boyzine. Don't wanna get a bad grade or something."

The boys laughed and jeered.

"Hey Boyzine, what's the matter with your face? You got the ugliest mug I've ever seen."

"Yeah, you got some kind of disease?" Another boy tried to yank the books out of Seraphine's hand, but he pulled them away and held them tightly. The boys began pushing him around, trying to pry the books loose, but he would not let go. He fought them off like a pack of wolves, elbowing them away from him as he turned in circles, shoving them off to the side with his weight, shielding his possessions. One boy grabbed onto his shirt and a ripping noise could be heard. Seraphine was horrified by the sound, knowing that his mother could not afford another, but he did not falter in fending off the cruel boys, because he knew even less could his mother afford to replace damaged books.

"Hey!" A voice called loudly from the side of the yard. "What are you doin'?"

Seraphine saw a tall boy, at least tall compared to the rest of them and probably a couple years older, step forward. His hair was a thin, lighter shade of brown. He was already developing the gut of a fifty year old man, but it only added to his overall huskiness, allowing him to considerably outsize the rest of the boys in the yard: a man among children.

"Nothing, Bill," said one of the boys nervously.

"We're just trying to get his books."

"His books? What do you want those things for? It ain't like any of you study." Some of the boys hung their heads, while the others made sheepish faces. "Leave that kid alone. He ain't botherin' nobody."

"Okay, Bill," they aquiesced and dispersed as Seraphine straightened up and began to head toward home.

"Hey, where you going?" Bill called and hustled to his side. "I just saved your life, and that's the thanks I get?"

"Thanks," Seraphine mumbled and kept walking, not looking at him.

"You don't talk much, do you?" Bill said, still trying to coax conversation.

Seraphine kept walking.

"Well, you gonna say something?"

"Are you just here to taunt me more?"

"No. Just thought I'd try to make a new acquaintance." There was a note of facetiousness in his voice.

"Didn't know you was such a friendly guy." Seraphine countered the sarcasm.

"Actually, I'm quite charming. That's what my mother says. The ladies say so too." Bill chuckled. Seraphine gave Bill a sideways look. "I've seen you in class and around the streets. How come you don't talk to nobody?"

"What's it matter if I talk to people or not?"

"Don't matter. Just wonderin' if there was a reason why."

"Don't feel like it."

"I get it. Some people don't shut up, and some people just like to be quiet. But, you know, the kids would probably like you a lot better if you talked a bit. It just seems kind of strange when somebody never says boo like you do." Bill paused briefly, waiting for a reply, and then continued on, "You're smart, though, huh? Not like me. I hardly even go to school. Been held back two years. I'm about ready to give up on it. Got a job on Captain Glory's fishing boat. Just swabbing decks and stuff like that. He'll have me fishing soon."

"How old are you?" Seraphine finally spoke.

"Fourteen. You?"

"Twelve."

"Seem older than that. You should come out with me and the boys sometime. You know, get in some trouble."

"Can't."

"Why not?"

"Gotta help my Ma."

"You really are a mama's boy, aren't you?"

"You got a dad?" Seraphine challenged.

"Yeah."

"Well I don't. It makes a big difference."

"All right, all right. I hear you. It's hard enough for us to make ends meet, and I've got a dad." Bill's tone was still so good-natured that Seraphine was not sure he had truly won that argument. "Hey, I'd love to keep shooting the shit with you, but I gotta go. You take care of yourself, now. I'll do my best, but those fellas might try coming after you again."

Bill and Seraphine parted ways for the first time, Seraphine assuming they would never speak again.

Seraphine went into the house to find his mother in bed already. He quietly set his books down.

"That you, *Boyzine*?" a voice asked weakly from the bed.

"Yeah, Ma. You okay?"

"Oh sure. Just tired." Josephine coughed. Seraphine sat down in a chair and began sewing the hole in his shirt.

"What are you doing?" Josephine asked hoarsely.

"Nothing."

"What happened to your shirt?"

"Nothing. It's fine."

Josephine struggled to sit up in bed and reached over to grab the shirt. Seraphine saw that her skin was pasty white. Seraphine held the shirt out of her reach. "No, it's fine. You're sick."

"Just a little cold. That's all."

"Well, you better get some sleep."

"Of course. I'll feel fine in the morning."

But the next morning Josephine was not fine. Though Seraphine tried to stop her, she forced herself to go to work, but every evening when she returned, her condition had worsened until, one day, she could not lift herself to get out of bed. She spent more time in bed than out, too weak to get up, and Seraphine began to miss school in order to accommodate the many jobs he had to take on in order to support himself and Josephine. He delivered newspapers for *The Advocate*. He swept the floor at Adams and cleaned out the ice cream bins and coffee pots. He stocked fish in the ice houses and salted fish at the salt fish lots. He did numerous menial tasks to help pay the rent and put food on the table, and eventually, he had to stop going to school altogether.

"I noticed you ain't been in school lately," Bill stopped him on the road one day. "Not that I've been much either. So I know something must be wrong if I've been there more than you. You quit?"

Seraphine nodded.

"Yeah, me too. They're just going to hold me back again, anyway. I can't possibly move onto the next grade if I don't go more than once a week, so I might as well just give it up altogether. But you like school. Why'd you stop?"

"Don't like it anymore."

"I ain't no fool, Boyzine."

"My name's Seraphine," Seraphine shot angrily.

Bill wasn't too bright, but he was perceptive enough to put the clues together: Seraphine not going to school, his sensitivity to being called Boyzine, the fact that he was working like a slave, and the fact that nobody had seen Josie Mops around for weeks. "Okay, Seraphine. Is it your ma?"

Seraphine hesitated. "Yeah."

"She's sick, ain't she?"

"Yeah." Seraphine put his head down, his voice softening.

"Serry. If you need any food, my ma's a real good cook, or to help clean the house or something. She goes to church all the time. One of those do-goodery people."

"So's my ma, for all the good it's got her," Seraphine said bitterly.

"Well, if you ever need anything . . ." and Bill walked off.

Seraphine got home to find his mother with a terrible fever. She was drenched in sweat, her face on fire.

"We better call the doctor," Seraphine said.

"No! We can't afford one."

"Yes we can," Seraphine said. He called the doctor despite his mother's delirious pleas, and the doctor came quickly. He checked all of her vitals, her temperature, felt her glands, and turned to Seraphine, "You're mother is very sick. She needs medicine. How long has she been like this?"

"Almost two months."

"Two months! Why didn't she call?"

"We couldn't afford to. I don't think I even have enough to pay you today, but here's what I've got." Seraphine pulled a handful of change and a couple bills from his pocket.

"It's okay, nice boy. Don't worry about it."

"I'll pay you back as soon as I can. I promise. I'll have it by the end of the week and the money for the medicine."

"Don't worry about it," said the doctor and told him it was ten dollars for two bottles even though it was supposed to be ten dollars for each. He took pity on boy who stood before him, just a child with the face and speech and mannerisms of a man. A boy whose hands were already callused from work, shoulders stooped as though under the weight of the world.

Seraphine worked day and night to pay the doctor's bills and the rent and to put a little piece of chicken and a few vegetables into the thin broth he made every night. While other children played, he worked, and he never thought twice about taking a day off. Playing was childish to him compared to the great responsibilities he now had.

He walked wearily home one evening after yet another long day of work, when a boy called to him, "Hey, *Boyzine*. Oh, is that your mummy's name for you? Where is your mummy? Heard she's been sick."

"Yeah."

"Old Josie Mops, sick in bed. Everyone's houses are gonna get dirty."

"Don't call her that."

"Why not? Cleaning up other people's messes was all she was ever good for."

"Take it back! Don't you say that about my mother! Clearly, your mother ain't no good if she's got a rotten son like you."

"Who you calling rotten?" The boy turned red. "You and your mother are just a couple of greasy, good-for-nothing foreigners. That's all you are. You don't belong here. You and the rest of the stupid Portugees."

Seraphine was so tired, he was beyond anger. Though he was bothered by what the boy was saying, he did not have the energy to feel complete rage, and his desire to lash out was a result of his fatigue more than anything. The pressures of life were weighing him down, and he had this ignorant Yankee harassing him on top of it all. He was tired of everything and wanted to make it change, wanted to make this kid go away.

"I'll bet your dad ain't even dead. I bet you're ma's just some big whore."

At that statement, Seraphine came at the boy with a large heavy fist, catching him right against the temple. The boy, not expecting the strike, was stunned and teetered back, almost falling down. Angrily, he came back at Seraphine, who dodged a couple of lazy swings, but as Seraphine wound up for another punch, the boy came up and popped him right on the nose. Seraphine heard the crack and felt the blood splatter onto his face. He tasted it in his mouth, but he felt no pain, the adrenaline was running so high, exhilaratingly high. He felt like he was alive for the first time in months, and he landed two more hard blows on the boy, who fell down like a prize fighter. After hitting the ground hard, the boy rolled around, clutching his head and wailing. Seraphine spat blood and turned away. The boy never bothered him again, nor anybody.

"Seraphine, what happened?" his mother cried when she saw his disheveled state as he walked through the door, but he just shrugged away her exclamation and began to blot the blood from his swollen, painful nose.

"It must be broken. You have to get it fixed."

"No. It's fine," he said, and he never went. His broken nose healed crookedly, but he didn't care. It was an ugly nose to begin with; a big, ugly nose.

He saw Bill the next day. "Heard you lay a good beatin' on the Winthrop kid. That bastard deserved it." Seraphine didn't respond. "Don't think he'll be bothering you again."

"It don't matter."

"How's your ma?"

"Bad."

"Really?"

"The doctors said this medicine would make her better, but it doesn't make any difference. I've been working my tail of, and it don't make no difference."

"Well, my ma wanted me to tell you that she's praying for her."

"Prayers don't do nothing either. If prayers worked, my ma would be better by now."

"Hey, Serry, don't get so down. That kind of thinking don't help."

"How'm I supposed to feel?" Seraphine said and walked off.

His mother was saying the rosary weakly when he walked in the door.

"Go to sleep Ma."

"Not before I pray."

"It ain't doing any good Ma, don't you see! It doesn't do a goddamn thing!" It was the first time he had ever raised his voice to his mother. She let the beads drop to her side.

"Come here," she beckoned him toward her, and he did so reluctantly. "I don't ever want to hear you talk like that again. Okay?"

Seraphine was silent.

"I know it's been hard on you, but soon it will all be over." Seraphine put his head down. He was not reassured at all. "I know it seems bad now, and I know it seems unfair, but just remember that God has a plan for all of us. He has great things in store for you, I know. I wish I could be here to see it, but I'll be watching from above."

Seraphine gripped the covers aggressively and buried his face near his mother's side. "But I want you here with me!" he wailed.

"I know you do, but you have to be strong. You've been so strong all this time. Don't weaken now. Stay strong. You don't understand how special you are. I knew when I brought you into this world that you would be unlike anybody else."

Seraphine kept his face buried so his mother could not see the tears running flowing from his eyes. He did not want to be different or special. He hated God, the great God who was taking his mother away from him, who took his father away from him and left him with nothing. No one to love him, an ugly face, a life of scrimping and scrounging to make ends meet. This was what the great God left him?"

As though she could read his thoughts, Josephine said, "Have faith my *Boyzine*. You have God's strength in you. You just don't know it yet."

Josephine covered his hand with hers and the two stayed beside each other all night. In three days she was gone, and Seraphine was alone. He sat in his father's rocking chair, rocking back and forth, clutching his knees, unsure of what to do from now on. He was just shy of thirteen years old and alone in the world.

VIII

The Submarine

Seraphine and Bill were fishing only a few days before the holidays. They had been warned by officers stationed at the wharf to be careful because the S-8 submarine was patrolling for German U-boats on the backside. The *Halcyon* was not rigged with any navigational devices to keep watch for military vessels, so all they could do was be extremely cautious. It was a cold day, and Seraphine decided to fish close to shore, a quick catch to get them through Christmas. He and Bill lolled lazily in their dory, watching the sub in the distance, submerging and resurfacing over and over.

"Can you imagine being in one of those things?" Bill said, taking a swig of whiskey. "It's like being in an underwater tomb." He shuddered. "Glad I never had to get on one of those while I was in the Navy."

"Me too," Seraphine nodded, sucking on his pipe. "They've been going back and forth between those buoys all afternoon."

"Yeah, you'd think they'd have figured it out by now," Bill gave a laugh and Seraphine straightened up.

"Well, time to call it a day. Not much biting anyway." So they rowed toward the *Halcyon*, raised the dory into her, and signaled to the others to join in as well.

"Would you look at that cutter over there rounding Race Point? Those ships sure move," Paul Careiro noted.

"Yeah, I wouldn't want one coming after me," Bill responded.

"Say, do you think they realize there's a sub out here? They're flying."

"Course they do. The Coast Guard nowadays has all that fancy radar stuff. They synchronize tying their shoelaces," Bill said.

"Yeah, you're right," Paul assented. Seraphine tied down one of the dories, but his eyes were turned toward Race Point Light where the cutter was quickly nearing. Something didn't seem right, and then he saw it. The water began to churn where the sub was resurfacing. It was only half a football field away from the Coast Guard vessel.

"Jesus Christ!" Seraphine cried. "They're gonna collide." The rest of the crew scrambled to the side of the *Halcyon*.

"What can we do?" Frank Medeiros asked, but it was too late. The cutter had already made contact, a spray shooting up from the S-8 like a whale spouting.

"They're gonners!" Bobby Codinha gasped.

"We have to radio the life saving crew," Bill said, but the Coast Guard men of Race Point had witnessed the horrifying events themselves and were already rushing out in their small lifesaving boats. They soon found that there was nothing they could do. The sub had already disappeared into the deep, the only sign of it ever having been there being some air bubbles and a thin slick of oil. They floated in their lifeboats beside the cutter talking to the men to see if everything there was all right and trying to get to the bottom of what had happened, but men in small wooden boats could not possibly bring up a sunken submarine.

Seraphine turned the *Halcyon* toward the harbor, driving her faster than he had ever done before. They hastily docked her and leapt off the boat crying, "The S-8 has sunk off of Race Point! Somebody get help!" They were surprised to see all calm on the wharf as though nobody knew a thing about what had happened.

Seraphine hurried to the base to alert the naval captains of the horrible accident that had just occurred, but the dispatching officer said they were aware of the situation and that all of the capable ships had gone to the front or back to Boston to load. They'd have to wait for a ship from Boston to come.

"But they can't wait that long. They'll all be dead, if they aren't already," Seraphine said.

"Captain, if they survived the crash, there is enough oxygen in there to sustain them for several days. A ship from Boston that is equipped to handle this situation will be here in a few hours."

"You mean there's nothing you can do *now*? You haven't even checked to see if there are any survivors! If there are, you can't let those men stay down there all that time."

"We're going to get them out as soon as possible, Captain, but there's nothing we can do about it now. We don't even know where the sub is located precisely. We don't have any boats equipped to find it."

"No boats equipped? You're the friggin' Navy! If that's your excuse, you don't need some fancy boat to find something underwater. Christ, I'll find it myself. Ain't no different than trawling for a big fish. I saw it sink with my own eyes. I have a good sense of where to look," and without waiting for the officer's response, Seraphine left the little office.

Bill had already told half the town and was eager to help Seraphine find the S-8, so the two headed out and began dragging lines across the bottom of the ocean floor. They were out there for hours without any luck, alongside the Coast Guard and some other local fishermen.

"Maybe the rope's not long enough. I know it was right around here," Bill said.

"Nah, I'm getting a good bounce. It's long enough. We just haven't gotten lucky yet."

Back home, the town was all abuzz with nervous energy. The sun had gone completely down, and by now the news had spread like wildfire. Everyone had heard about the disastrous accident, and it was all anyone discussed.

"I heard there were thirty people on that submarine."

"Me too. There's no way they all could have survived that, no way."

The townsfolk went to the church, lighting candles in prayer. Some stayed all night, sitting in the pews, the hot wax melting on their hands. Others came praying to Saint Anthony, and then leaving to see if anymore news had been revealed. But there was none—no word except that the *Halcyon* was out helping the Coast Guard of Race Point locate the sunken submarine.

"It's been hours!" one man said to another, standing on the corner next to Adams Pharmacy. "Why hasn't anyone come to help yet?"

"Beats me. Said somebody had to come from Boston. Said they didn't have the right equipment here to lift the sub."

"Well they better hurry. If anyone's alive, they don't have much time."

Three old salts sitting on the end of Railroad Wharf, smoking pipes and little brown cigars looked out toward Wood End.

"Wonder if Seraphine's found the sub yet."

"If anyone can, it'd be him. Give that man a hook and line, and he'll find anything."

The third man sniffed and spit on the dock. "Wind's picking up."

The others nodded that they had noticed too. "Gonna be a gusty one."

Seraphine and Bill also noticed, out in the dead of night with only one spotlight to show their way.

"Figures," Bill said as the waves began to rise. He's a real bastard sometimes."

"Who?"

"God. Always gotta make it hard on us."

"God's got nothing to do with the ocean. That's nature. Nature does what it wants to do. God just watches. God's worried about people because it's people who are supposed to handle nature. That's what we're here for. Humans are Nature's keepers."

Bill just looked at Seraphine. "Jesus Christ, Serry, you're one smart bastard. I don't know what the hell you was just talking about, but it sounded good. God, Nature, whatever the hell it is, all I know is we've got a hell of a time on our hands." Just as he said that, the line caught something and they put the boat in neutral. They dropped more lines to get a sense of the dimension of the object and sure enough it was the submarine.

Seraphine went to the light and flashed it on and off signaling for help. The lifeguard boat came close to them, bobbing up and down on the growing waves. "Found it, Cap'?" Glenn Jason, the captain of the Coast Guard called as a wave splashed over the bow of the boat, drenching him.

"Yep."

"We gotta send a diver down. Eddie's, all suited up here. We better do it before the waves get any bigger. Can we dive off of your boat? Ours is too small to battle against these waves, and we've got to do it before the wind picks up even more."

Seraphine agreed, and the Coast Guard men tied up to the *Halcyon*, secured Eddie, and sent him down. Five eternally long minutes later, Eddie tugged on the line signaling that he was ready to be raised. They pulled and heaved, the waves trying to separate them and the diver, but he finally surfaced, and they were able to pull him into the boat.

"What happened?" they asked.

"Six of them," Eddie gasped. "Six are still alive."

"How do you know?"

"Taps. They tapped. Morse Code. I asked them, and they tapped six times. I said help was on its way." Glenn dropped a flag to mark the spot, and Seraphine steered the *Halcyon* toward port to call in the news and get help.

Glenn walked into the Naval captain's office and announced, "We've found the sub. There are six men alive, and they need to be evacuated immediately."

The Captain responded, "I told you, there aren't any available ships. They've got to come from Boston."

"But it's been hours! There are men in there, and we need to get them out. They're buried alive in a steel tomb! They're running out of oxygen every moment we sit around here with our hands on our asses!" Glenn cried.

"Help was just sent twenty minutes ago. We don't have the equipment here to do it."

"That's a bunch of bullshit," Glenn said and stormed out.

Seraphine and Bill were waiting on the dock. Frustration was written all over Glenn's face. Then he slammed his fist hard on the side of the building and cried, "Goddamn it! When are they going to pull their heads out of their asses?" Looking up after his outburst, and with a defeated tone in his voice he said, "You fellas can go home now. There's nothing more we can do tonight."

Seraphine and Bill were reluctant to leave, but they did not argue and headed home. The people in the church thanked God that at least six were alive. It was better than all thirty perishing. There was still hope.

The next morning Seraphine went to the wharf earlier than he usually did and was relieved when he saw that three small naval ships had arrived. He stepped into the naval quarters to see if anybody had any news. He found Glenn and the Captain, surrounded by several seamen, in a heated argument.

"What do you mean you can't go out there and raise the sub? You've got all this help you've been waiting around for!" Glenn cried.

"It's too choppy," the Captain said calmly, but visibly bristling over the fact that his authority was being questioned. "We can't do it with the waves this high. There's just no way."

"No way!" one fisherman cried. "These ain't high seas. Hell, it's a beautiful day for fishin'."

"Then go fishing!" The Captain snapped defensively.

The fisherman got red with anger. "Yeah, I'll go fishing, you rotten sonofabitch. Least I ain't scared to do my job when there's a few gusts of wind."

"Watch your mouth, sir. I could have you court-marshaled."

This infuriated the fisherman more, but his companions standing by quickly tried to calm him.

"Now, let me get this straight," Glenn continued. "You're just going to leave those men down there?"

"Yes, until the wind dies down."

"Nobody knows when that'll be. They could be dead by then!" a voice cried from the back.

Annoyed, the officer said to Glenn, "What are these people doing here anyway?"

"They're just concerned townsfolk who want to help."

"There's nothing they can do."

"So *you* say!" another man cried from a corner. "I ain't about to stand here while you worthless sacks of shit sit on your hands. I'm going out there."

"You stop right there," the officer rose from his seat and pointed at the man, "or I'll have you arrested." The fisherman looked at him smugly and left, slamming the door behind him. A few others followed.

"I've never experience disrespect quite like this," the Captain snootily complained.

"You ain't the boss of us, just because you've got a fancy uniform on," another voice said.

Glenn jumped in, trying to mediate the scene. "Everyone just calm down. Let's get back on track here. You're all missing the point. Officer, I get it, you can't bring the sub up until the waves settle down, but there has to be some alternative, something else has to be done until then. I'm going to send divers down to try to hook up an air hose so we can feed them fresh oxygen. Do you have a problem with that?"

"No, but I don't think it will work."

"Well, I'm willing to give it a try." Glenn was agitated as he headed toward the door, but he stopped when he saw Seraphine and said, "Can we use your boat again?" Seraphine silently nodded a slow assent.

Men were already heading out in dories and fishing boats, not sure of what they were going to do, but determined to do something. They were quickly halted by naval officers, calling out over megaphones that they were not to go near the submarine, and if they did, they would be arrested. The fishermen were furious, but reluctantly obeyed.

Seraphine, though, headed out with the Coast Guard men to the marked spot. Glenn sent Eddie down. He was under the surface for some time before the tug was felt on the line, and he was carefully raised. He pulled his mask off, and though his face was wet, they could see tears in his eyes. "They're still alive," he said. "But they say that the air is getting bad. They want to know when help is coming. I told them not much longer."

"Well, let's do it," Glenn said, "Let's send down the air hose."

The waves were crashing against the boat sending it rocking and reeling. Seraphine struggled to hold it steady. Eddie came back up with the end of the hose still in his hand. "I can't do it. I'm getting yanked around too much."

Another diver went down with no more success. "There's nowhere to feed the hose in that I can see."

The waves were getting even bigger, and it was getting more and more treacherous for the divers. They'd been out there for several hours with little success, and now it was too perilous for all of them. The *Halcyon* headed dejectedly home.

Two more days had passed, and still the Navy had been unable to make attempt at saving the men. The wind still blew, but to the fishermen, the weather was just fine. They had no qualms going out fishing on days like these; why couldn't the Navy do what they had to do?

Several women sat in a dimly lit room, knitting socks for soldiers. "How can they just leave those boys down there like that?" one woman said. "This is the most terrible thing I've ever seen."

"It's like my own boy is down there," another sniffed. Tears streamed down her face. "What if it was my boy?"

The others empathized. These were women whose sons were in the Navy and whose husbands were fishermen. They understood how the ocean so easily claimed its victims. They knew the fear of losing a loved one to the sea and the pain when it finally happened. To them, there was a possibility to save these men, possibilities that were never there to save their own kin. This was the biggest tragedy of all—to just sit by and do nothing while hope still existed.

But the wind never died, and none of their efforts ever succeeded. Glenn sent Eddie down again, and when he returned Glenn asked, "Are they still alive?"

"Yes," Eddie said, but this time his crying was obvious. "But the taps are much weaker. They say they can't go on much longer."

"Goddamn it!" Glenn kicked the side of the boat. "If we could just get a hose down there!"

"They asked if there was any hope. I didn't know what to say. It's over, Sir."

"It's not over!" Glenn shrieked. "It's not over!" He threw is hat down on the deck of the *Halcyon*.

"Yes it is, Sir. Unless the wind lets up, and they can bring that submarine to the surface within the next three hours, it's over."

Glenn squatted defeatedly, his face buried in his arms, his hands gripping the roots of his disarrayed hair, and sobbed like a child, his frustration and disappointment coming out in exhausted wails. Seraphine and Bill looked quietly on, merely spectators of this tragic scene.

The next day they went one last time, but Eddie's taps were received by nothing but silence. The whole town mourned the loss of the sailors, the women cried, more candles were lit, and the men sat looking vacantly at their hands. Three days later the wind died, the sea was calm, and the submarine was finally raised.

IX

Things Happen in Threes

Seraphine and Bill sat at Cookie's sharing a large breakfast together that consisted of, they could not say what. With food shortages and rationing the way it was, Cookie had gotten creative using the scraps fishermen brought her. All they knew was that it was battered, seasoned, and fried enough to be edible.

Everyone was eating merrily and talking jovially when David Cabral walked in, his somber appearance casting a shadow upon the entire place. All eyes turned to see what he was about to say.

"Well folks. We just got some bad news. The *Scully Joe*, Captain Silva's ship, went down last night out on George's Bank. They got caught in a squall, and the whole crew was lost, including the captain; all five of them." He then proceeded to list the familiar names, and everyone in the establishment took off their caps and put their heads down in reverence. A few wiped tears from their eyes, and others mouthed silent prayers.

"The service will be held at St. Peter's at ten o'clock Thursday morning." On that short note, he left the people in the diner to their thoughts. Only two bodies had been recovered, and for the others who were buried at sea, wreaths and flowers were thrown from the end of the town wharf into the water to be carried out to the lost.

For several days, the townsfolk walked around in quiet solemnity. The squall had produced five more widows, a dozen, at least, fatherless children, and Captain Silva even had two grandchildren. The entire town felt the tragedy of the loss.

"The waters are real dangerous to be fishing in these days," Bill said to Seraphine, as they pushed their cold, half-eaten meals away from them. "The waters are filled with German Subs that just shoot everything down. They think we're transporting goods. They say that the *Victory's* wreckage had a huge hole in the side like it had been blasted open by a missile. It wouldn't surprise me if the same thing happened to the *Scully Joe* too. They just don't want to tell us that 'bout they're scared none of us will go out fishing."

Only two weeks earlier, the *Harpoon* had also gone down. Two boats in two weeks was a massive loss and frightening to any fisherman. "Things happen in threes, Cap'," Bill said, and Seraphine nodded. "It's only a matter of time before somebody else goes down."

Seraphine went home to Mary's angry outcries over the sinking of another boat. "Those goddamn Nazis. They just love killing innocent people!"

"We don't know it's from that. It was probably just a strong storm out on the ocean. There are storms out there that we never know about. Even Glenn said it was from a squall."

"Storms, Nazis, sea monsters . . . I don't care how they're sinking; all I know is that they sank, and men died, and I don't want you going out for a long time. I don't want you to be that third boat."

Seraphine grimaced. "That's foolish. I can't stay docked just because of a superstition. I've got a family to feed. Christ, it's almost as bad as things were during the Depression. We can't afford to eat anything but the fish I catch, and how can I get us any fish if I can't ever go out fishing? The kids have holes in the knees and elbows of their clothing. We have to burn the woodstove constantly because we can't afford to pay the oil heat. The kids are down on the beach finding driftwood to burn. It's terrible!"

"I know it is, but everyone is in the same bad way. My point is, you don't need to risk your neck for a few pounds of fish. It's the middle of winter, anyways. Only crazy people fish in the middle of winter."

"Then I'm crazy."

"Yeah, and a stubborn Portugee!"

Seraphine dismissed the comment and went back to eating his watery soup.

Seraphine, Bill, and Bobby Codinha were doing maintenance work on the *Halcyon* when the *Provincetown Princess* pulled in alongside of them. "How's things?" Seraphine called from his deck to theirs, and the captain came to the side of his boat.

"We had a close call out there, Cap'."

"What happened?"

"Well, we went out farther than we usually do to do a couple of trolls. The fish haven't been too good on the Bank, so we went about fifty miles deeper. It was windy, and the waves were real high, but I swear I saw something black in the distance. I'm staring right at it, and it's looking right back at me, and it looks like a small battle ship, one of those patrol boats, way in the distance. Every time we rolled to the crest of a wave, I could catch a glimpse of it. Then it'd disappear when we went back into the trough. I didn't know if it was German or American, but I didn't want to wait to find out. So we pulled in the nets as quickly as we could and began to hightail it back home.

"I kept checking behind us, and I swear that ship's coming right after us. I take my binoculars and see pictures on the side that sure don't look American so we head back toward home full throttle. That boat keeps getting bigger so I know it must be gaining on us, and if it wanted to blow us to pieces it certainly could of. I don't know why it didn't, but eventually it hung back, and we lost sight of it. I guess they decided it wasn't worth wasting ammo on a crappy old fishing boat. Can't say I blame them."

"Wow," Seraphine said. "I thought it was all just a load of malarkey."

"I thought so too. I keep hearing about fishing boats getting blown up, but nobody really knows for sure. I mean, they say the *Harpoon* was blown up, but nobody is positive of that. All I know is I'm sticking close to home, Cap'. One close call is enough for me." He waved goodbye.

"Wow! That's one hell of a story, Serry," Bill said, amazed and shaking his head. "Maybe we ought to take a tip and stay docked for a while, too."

Bobby, who had been nearby going about his work, looked up and said, "Aw, I ain't scared of a few German boats. I need some money. My wife's seven months pregnant, and I can barely afford to clothe it. We're still going out ain't we, Cap'?"

"Sure. In just a week."

"You crazy, Serry?" Bill frowned. "We'll be sitting ducks out there."

"Well, we can't just sit around here doing nothing. God knows when this goddamn war is going to be over. We'll all be in the poorhouse by then."

"I don't want to pressure you, Cap'," Bobby persisted, "but I need to start making ends meet. It's too goddamn hard with this war. I'm beginning to think I would've been better off enlisting."

"We're all having trouble, nice boy. It ain't easy times for any of us," Seraphine said, trying to persuade the young man that there was no argument coming from his end.

"Sure ain't," Bill said. "We've all got bills to pay and kids to feed. Just sometimes I ain't sure if the risk is worth it."

"What else are we gonna do?" Bobby asked.

"I'd let you know if I had an idea. Unfortunately, it seems that fishing is all we can do, dangerous or not."

The three stood in silence. "Well, let me know when we're gonna leave," Bill said. "We'll be hard-pressed to get anybody else to go out with us."

"We don't need anybody else," Bobby gave a cocky grin, and Seraphine looked at Bill gravely.

X

Those Empty Winter Streets

Seraphine pulled on his boots and buttoned his jacket to leave for his three day trip to George's Bank, a mid-winter's fishing trip. The day was not as bitter cold as the previous few weeks had been, but he was still sure to bundle up in the wool socks, sweater, and scarf that Mary had knitted for him of thick homespun. The collar of his navy, wool pea coat was popped up around his neck, concealing the lower half of his face, and his cap was pulled down low over his eyes. He picked up a sack of food and necessities that Mary had packed for him and hauled the remainder of his gear over his shoulder.

Tommy, Joseph, and Sally had distractedly said good-bye earlier in the day since his leaving on a trip was not an unfamiliar occurrence. Mary, on the other hand, followed him to the door. She was apprehensive about him going.

"Maybe it would be best if you waited for a few days," she said, a pleading look in her eyes. She subconsciously wrung the hem of her apron in her hands as she waited for his response.

"The boat is ready to go," he answered simply.

"Yes, but it isn't going anywhere," she argued quietly. "I mean, it will be just as ready three days from now."

"I promised the men. They need the money. It's the middle of winter, and there isn't much opportunity to be had."

"Yes, but what will a few days hurt?" she began to push harder. "They can wait, can't they?"

"Mary, it's not just them. *We* need the money. Don't you realize how difficult this winter has been on us? The last half-dozen trips I've made, we've come back with barely a quarter hold of fish."

"But we're not starving."

"I know. But I don't want it to get worse."

"But it's so dangerous out there right now! Between the war and the weather, how can I be sure you'll come home alive?"

"Are you ever sure?"

"I've never felt as bad as I do now."

Seraphine put his head down. The terrible images running through his mind were not of wind and waves or battleships and explosions; they were of Sally's thinness, the patches on the knees of Joseph's pants, the holes in the toes of Tommy's shoes. These were the visions that plagued him, that made him fret throughout the day and sleepless at night. "The men on the wharf say that there are plenty of fish out there on the Bank. If I can make big on this trip, it will help get us through the rest of the winter."

Mary sighed and decided not to pursue any further argument. Once Seraphine had made up his mind, that was that, and there was no point in frustrating him with her anxious and, probably, unnecessary concerns. In three days' time he would be back, a hold full of fish and ready to rest by the fire.

"I'll see you soon then," she said, but it sounded more like a question.

He nodded in assent, and as he turned to leave, she grabbed his hand and squeezed it between her own. Seraphine paused and turned his head back over his shoulder to look into her worried face, his serious furrow softening at the sight of her troubled expression.

"Don't worry about me, Love. Everything will be just fine," and he turned back around and stepped out the door, Mary still desperately clutching his hand. As his thick fingers slipped from hers, a deep coldness washed over her, and it seemed as though they were already separated by a great ocean.

The moment that Seraphine stepped out the door of his warm, cozy house, he felt greatly alone. There was barely a soul around to greet him, and the town was like a ghost town as he walked up the empty street. The sky was gray. The cold pavement slapped under his feet and seemed to echo in the silence. The townsfolk had relegated themselves to the sanctuary of their warm, little houses with fires burning and soup on the stove, but, oddly, on this day he did not even smell the comforting, woodsy scent wafting from the chimneys. It was as if there were no more life within the houses than there was without, and this thought made Seraphine shudder in his heavy wool clothes.

"Mary's nervousness has gotten the better of me," he thought. "This day is no different than any other gray, winter Sunday. People do not want to leave the comfort of their homes. They want to sit and read in a nice comfortable chair. The children would rather play with their toys than have their noses nipped by the frosty air. What man goes to work on a Sunday? Only a crazy one!" Seraphine stuffed his hands deeper in his pockets.

He told himself that there was no need for him to have such a foreboding, melancholy feeling as he continued on his way to the wharf; the emptiness was typical of wintertime in Provincetown. The masses of people had all left and gone back to wherever they came from originally: Connecticut, New York, Boston, wherever. They all left, and many would come back but only when the weather was at its finest and when the town was bustling with energy and life. It seemed as though, to them, life no longer existed in this place as soon as the sunny days became fewer and the water was too cold to swim in. Thus, only the locals had a true understanding of what winter in the town was like.

With the departure of the warm weather went all the tourists and souvenir shops. The stores and restaurants that the locals had no use for shut their doors to wait until the next season. The craziness of bicycles flying in every which direction, the constant crowding of the streets and sidewalks, the honking horns, the blasting music, the dancing and drinking and riotous activity was over for the season. Those who made their living from the people who visited the town finally had leave from their hectic summer schedules to sit and count their money. Those who did not were just plain happy to have their town back. It was like they could breathe again.

For the most part, the townsfolk enjoyed the visitors, the new faces, the endless activity that diverted them from their day to day lives. It was exciting and gave them a window looking out on the rest of the world that many of them had never had opportunity to experience. They accepted the people who came, embraced them, and were willing to share their small piece of the world with them. They did not judge, they did not discriminate, they just opened their doors, and let those on the outside share in what they held so precious.

Still, it was a relief when it was all over and the strangers left. Each year there was an increasing sense that what they valued about their little town was not the same as what those who came here valued. There was a time when those who came did so to admire the beauty of the little fishing village, the quaintness of its people, the sense of unshakable community that is difficult to find anywhere else, but more and more it seemed that few cared about these things. It seemed that the people forgot that this town belonged to someone even after summer had passed and the leaves had fallen off the trees.

The locals never turned anyone away, and the town itself was becoming increasingly dependent on the influx of visitors every year. But it did not seem quite fair that for three months out of the year, their town was taken from them and laid at the mercy of those who did not seem to care nearly so much. The locals stood their ground and held onto their right to the town, seeing how they supported it all year long, not simply for a week or a day or a month out of the year.

Seraphine recalled a time, as he walked down the now desolate winter street, one of many recurring conversations he had had with tourists who stopped to gaze at his boat, an intriguing backdrop to the bustling summer crowds. Seraphine sat on a wooden crate, mending a trawling line, quietly passing his time as if he were untouched by the hectic nature of the summer. He was, concurrently, separate and one with the town. While he was clearly distanced and uninvolved in the seasonal madness, he was imbedded in the ebb and flow of the nature of the town. His place here on the end of the pier with his boat and his crew of fellow locals was where, for him, the heart of the town was preserved, regardless of what was happening elsewhere.

He looked tranquil as he sat there making his knots, and, as separate as he was from the whirlwind of energy, he looked more like he belonged than anyone else. It was not that he did not know what was happening or that he was pushed away by it; it was just that he was entirely apathetic and was not going to change his routine, regardless of the season. The stranger was intrigued by the air of indifference in this man and his unaffected appearance, which caused him to stop.

"Good afternoon," the man said brazenly as though he had known Seraphine all his life.

"Afternoon, Sir," Seraphine looked up coolly, giving a small smile which put the man even more at ease.

"Do you live here?"

"On the boat? Nah. I have a house in the West End," Seraphine said, uncomprehending the simplicity of the man's question and gesturing with his head toward his left.

"Oh, I meant, do you live in town, but it is obvious that you do! Pleasure to meet you, Sir." The man stuck out his hand, but Seraphine was too intent on his mending to notice.

He replied, though, with a, "Pleasure to meet you, too, Gov'na," but never missed a stroke in his mending.

"So, do you live here all year?"

"Sure. Where else am I gonna go?"

"Well, I just can't imagine what it's like here in the wintertime . . . What is it like?"

"What's it like? Same as this just with less people. And colder," he added.

"That it, eh? Well what about that tower there? What happens to that?"

Bill, who had overheard the question, and couldn't help himself when it came to teasing the tourists, seized the opportunity to make a wise crack at this question.

"Well, dontcha know? We take it down."

"Really?" the man was fascinated

"Yeah. There's a big pole that goes up the middle of it, and when we pull it down, the whole monument collapses in on itself, brick by brick, until it is folded up like a big umbrella."

"You don't say," the man sounded skeptical, but didn't want to be rude by questioning the truth of this statement.

"Yep. Then at Christmastime, we put it back up and string lights off it and decorate it like a giant Christmas tree."

"Is that so?"

"Aw, Bill, leave the poor fella alone," Seraphine said.

"Yeah," another voice from the boat interjected, "That's the stupidest thing I've ever heard, Bill. They don't even make lights that long!"

"It ain't stupid!" Bill shouted back, mildly insulted. "I thought it was a damn good idea."

"Bill, you're full of malarkey."

"Hey, you never know, one day there might be lights long enough to string off the Monument. Just you wait!" The crew was laughing, and Bill went back to his work satisfied with his response. Boy, did he laugh when his prediction turned out to be true, and every year after, lighting the Monument became a Christmas tradition.

The tourist also laughed, trying to mask his initial gullibility, and decided to continue his interrogation of Seraphine. "Is Provincetown really quiet in the wintertime?"

"It would be to you, I suppose, but for me, it's normal."

"Really? But what do you do when there's no one around and nothing going on?"

There was a pause as Seraphine raised his face, and, for the first time, he looked the man square in the eye. "I work."

"That's it?"

"It? What else am I supposed to do? I have to survive. Life ain't easy. Especially when you got a family to feed."

"Ah, what is it your children do?"

"They go to the school, like everybody else."

"Wait, there's a school here?"

"Course there's a school here! It's a town ain't it?" Seraphine was beginning to become exasperated with the foolishness of this man's questions. One would think the man had just landed on Mars.

"I'm sorry, of course there is. I just forget-"

"You forget that this is a town where people live all year long? You know, it doesn't all shut down after you summer folks leave. There are people who make their bread and butter here. It ain't all fun and games. We still gotta work, sun or no sun, rain or no rain. We got families to support and houses to keep up. We've got jobs we've got to keep working and taxes we've got to keep paying. Winter, Summer, Spring, Fall—it's all the same, just the weather's a little different, that's all. We still keep doing what we're doing whether you are here or not. We make our lives here. You know what your home is like and what you do in your home. Well, it's the same here. For some people, this is the only place they know. They've never been outside of it, nor do they intend to. We aren't just visiting. We're here for the long haul, and when you come back next summer, you can be sure the town will still be here because it never went away." There was nothing scolding or harsh in Seraphine's voice as he told the man all this, but he used the enlightening tone of a teacher speaking to a pupil.

The man had heard all he needed and smiled, for he was not disappointed by Seraphine's response or shamed in any way. "Well, thank you very much for your time, sir. It was a pleasure having the opportunity to talk with you this fine afternoon."

"And you, Gov'na. You take care now, and come back sometime."

334

"I certainly will," the man grinned.

"You know what they say:" Seraphine added, "Once you get sand in your shoes, you always come back."

The man gave a knowing smile, and said lightheartedly, "Take care of her while I'm gone."

"I'll be here," Seraphine chuckled, and the man went on his way, and Seraphine went back to his work.

People came and went, and the saying was mostly true that they usually came back. They snapped their photos and collected their shells, fished and swam and had a grand old time, and there was something appreciable in this. It made the townsfolk proud that the people who came here could fall so madly in love with such a small fishing village. They were proud that this little world the visitors could not get enough of was theirs and that they were the reason it was what it was and had its charm and its endearing nature. They were proud of the fact that this town was a major part of their identity, and they were melded in body and spirit. Anyone else who was not born and raised here could not say the same. They could buy property, live here for years, love and appreciate the town more than the natives did, but it still could never quite be in their blood as it was with the natives who were born of this land.

Even Seraphine was not quite attached. Oh, he was close for sure, so very close, but even he was not born in the town. He was born on the sea, and something about this made him different from the rest. He teetered on the line between the town and the old world, but he belonged fully to neither. Portugal meant little to him. It was some distant land that he had never seen nor knew anything about. He understood his ancestry was there, but what did it matter when his life was here in this little town at the tip of the continent? It was all he had known and everything that he loved was contained within its three mile border. The only thing that could draw him away was the ocean, and it held him with all its power and majesty. It was the only place where he felt, with his complete sprit, that he belonged, and the ocean called to him, beckoned him into her arms that would cradle and rock him or beat him and slap until he felt he could weep like a child. The torment was worth the wonder, and he accepted the ocean and all her many faces, but only God knew what mood she would be in during the following three days, and he tried not to be concerned.

Seraphine was nearly to the wharf, having made good time, lost in thought and without a living soul to disturb him. Normally he would be grateful for that, but today the quiet, the solitude, and the emptiness filled him with unexplainable loneliness and gloom. He felt as though he were the only man alive on earth, and that he'd never see another soul again.

But then he felt something soft brush the side of his hand, and he looked down to see the top of Fluke's head. How long the dog had been following him, he did not know, but he was comforted by the presence of this loyal creature.

"Fluke, where did you come from, fella?" Fluke looked up at him with a panting smile and then rubbed his face on the side of Seraphine's thigh. He followed him the rest of the way to the wharf, and when Seraphine arrived at the *Halcyon*, Fluke sat and watched as Seraphine greeted Bill, who was already there.

"How you doin', Cap'?" Bill grinned, but then seeing the solemness on Seraphine's face, his smile faded and he said, "You okay? You look white as a sheet. I ain't never seen old leathery skin like yours turn that color."

"No, I'm fine. It's just the cold."

"Cold don't make a man white. You having second thoughts about this trip, 'bout I ain't the one concerned about money. That fella there is," he said pointing to Bobby. "You give the word, and I'll go home."

"No. We'll go. Bobby needs the money, and I could really use a good trip, myself."

"I ain't complaining. I'm as ready as you all are. I ain't rich either. Just wanted to put your health first, Cap'. We all know these aren't the safest days to be out fishing."

"Thanks, Bill," Seraphine said, his discomfort eased with the support of his closest *compard*.

It would only be the three of them on this trip. Bill was right; they were hard-pressed to find anybody else who would want to go out this time of year in the cold with the risks of storms and enemy ships. Others were sick, or had other jobs, or were satisfied with their financial state and saw no purpose in bothering. Bobby came because he was a young man starting out and wanted to prepare himself to settle down with his new wife and unborn child. Bill came, mostly, out of loyalty to Seraphine and the thrill of an adventure.

They loaded on all the gear and supplies, made sure the engine was in working condition, and that the dories were strapped on well and had no visible damage before pushing out into the harbor. Fluke sat on the edge of the pier watching intently until the boat rounded the breakwater. He then rose, and turned for home.

The fishing boat chugged along, disturbing the gray, still water with its churning, white wake. A couple lonely seagulls flew overhead as the *Halcyon* motored out into the middle of the quiet, empty harbor. As they rounded the Point, Seraphine gave one glance back at the serene little town. It was as though it were only a photograph in a book, two dimensional, and unreachable. It looked lonely and far away, and his chest seized with emotion at the simple beauty of the town and the eternal anxiety that he might never see it again.

The boat rounded the Point, and the town was blocked from sight by the strip of land that protected it. After several minutes, only the very top of the Monument could be seen peeking above the brown beach grass of the land. Seraphine eventually gave up his attempts to get one last glimpse of his home. The boat traversed along the shore until it reached the Race where the bay meets the ocean and the waters churn as though boiling from the depths of hell. They were at the mercy of the ocean.

XI

Widow's Walk

Mary stepped onto the stoop and watched as Seraphine walked steadily up the sidewalk, the trawling lines over his shoulder and his sack of food at his side. He gradually became smaller and smaller until he was merely a black spot in the distance. There was not a soul on the street and very few parked cars on this cold, lonesome day. He was the only living, breathing object in sight until he reached the top of the shallow rise in the road and disappeared down the other side.

As soon as she was sure she could not see him anymore, Mary reluctantly shut the wooden door and sunk down on the bottom step of the staircase. Placing her face in her hands, she felt the dampness of tears spring into her eyes, and as the first tear reached her hand and streamed along the crease of her palm all the way to her wrist, she began to sob uncontrollably. She buried her fingers in her hair, gripping it at the roots and doubling over onto her knees. Her whole body shook, and she could feel her tears soaking right through her apron and housedress. Her hands were sticky, and strands of hair were falling into the path of tears and becoming stuck to her skin.

"Please don't let the children hear me," she thought to herself, for she was still trying to believe that she had no reason to be afraid and that there was no need to cause her children alarm.

She continued to cry until a cold, soft dampness pressed against the backs of her hands and began to sniff through her hair, causing more strands to fall onto her forehead and rustling the rest into disarray. She lifted her

339

tear-stained face to see Fluke's black nose, nearly pressed against her own. As soon as she revealed herself to him from behind her hands, he sat down at her feet and looked her square in the eyes. The two black pupils gaped before her, an infinitely long tunnel, a black hole, a dark abyss that she could walk into and disappear forever.

There was something comforting about the calmness of the dog's face, the stillness and tranquility she saw in his eyes. Mary's mouth fell open slightly, and she sat, mesmerized before the serene, friendly face. She felt warm inside and comforted as though, with just a look, he had transported her to some safe haven, she knew not where, but could be sure that nothing would harm her there. She looked hard into those shiny, black eyes of his; so hard that she could see through the translucent darkness and down, far, far, down that tunnel, all the way to some white light at the very end. What was it? She wanted to reach out and touch it, but she didn't dare move. She felt frozen in space and time.

An unexpected paw landed on her knee, and she was jolted from her hypnosis, blinking a few times. She gave a soft laugh, partly nervousness, partly relief, partly at her own foolishness, and she wrapped her arms around Fluke's neck and scratched his sides. It was nothing but a mere reflection; a trick of light and tears.

"What a good dog you are. A very good dog," she said in a soothing voice, though it was she that needed the soothing, and having Fluke there made her feel safer and less alone. She got up to attend to her afternoon's chores and begin to prepare dinner for the children.

Mary had spent a restless night in bed, tossing and turning, frightful, stormy images flying through her head. At times she felt like she was falling until she stopped right before hitting the ground. Other times she felt she was drowning and her arms were too weak to propel her to the surface as her lungs restricted from lack of air. In other instances, she was trying to run but her legs felt like gelatin, and she was glued to her spot. She thought she heard a scream, sometimes crying, sometimes a groan. She saw flashes of lightning, dark clouds, and crashing waves. She shivered with cold, broke into a sweat, tossed the covers off to escape the heat. There was no peace for her until she lurched up in bed with a gasp, as though the wind had been knocked out of her. She clutched at her chest and looked straight out the window before her. It was just after dawn and the sky was blazing a fiery red. *Sailor's warning* . . . she thought to herself.

She briskly rolled out of bed, her bare feet touching the cold, wood floor, and grabbed her pink, flannel robe off the back of the chair. Without losing a stride, she stuffed her arms into it and pulled it tight across her chest, hugging her arms close to her.

Down the stairs she rushed, and into the kitchen. She did not know from what or to what she was running, and as though she could not think of anything better to do, she slammed the kettle onto the stove to boil water for coffee. She began banging through the cabinets and rustling through the drawers. She opened the icebox, then slammed it shut, then did the same with the oven. She pulled apart everything on the counter, then put it back, then rearranged it. All of this she did with no particular purpose in mind, and between the rattling and clanging and the whistling of the neglected kettle, she was creating quite a racket.

Tommy quietly came up behind her. "Ma . . ."

Mary whipped around to face him, nearly dropping the coffee mug she had been tightly clutching in her hands, her eyes wide and startled looking.

"Gee, Ma, you okay? You look like you saw a ghost."

"Me? What? Oh. No, Hon, I'm fine," she shook her head as if his statement were ridiculous and turned back to the stove, changing the subject. "You're up early. You don't have school today."

"I was just wondering where Fluke was. He usually comes to me and Jimmy's room when Dad's gone. He isn't there this morning."

"Well, maybe he is in with Joe and Sally," Mary suggested.

"Nah, I just checked in there. I checked all over the house. He ain't anywhere."

"Oh, I wouldn't worry. Maybe he just let himself outside to go to the bathroom or something. He'll be back." But Mary was very worried. Tommy was right. This was a strange behavior for Fluke, especially on a cold, gray morning like this.

Tommy went back upstairs, unsatisfied with the answer he'd received from his mother, and Mary began to go about her housework, making breakfast, sweeping the floor, stoking the wood stove. This turned into a complete cleaning frenzy, as she scrubbed the floors, dove into the bathrooms, and dusted every square inch of the house.

Two o'clock arrived, and she was on her hands and knees cleaning out the fireplace when she noticed a shadow come over her and turned her head to see Tommy, Joseph, and Sally standing in a huddle above her, looking down at her with concerned and confused faces.

Sparing their mother the embarrassment of acknowledging her odd behavior, Tommy came right out and said, "Fluke is still missing. He hasn't come back yet. Maybe we should go out and look for him."

Mary pulled herself up from off the floor and brushed her sooty hands on the front of her housedress. "Yes, that sounds like a good idea. Why don't the three of you go and ask around town? Maybe walk down the beaches and look on the wharves. I'll do the same."

The three willingly agreed, and they went off without saying goodbye. Mary pulled on a clumsy pair of rubber boots, her dress reaching just to the top of them, and wrapped a large crocheted blanket over her shoulders.

She trudged down the sidewalk westwardly until she came to the breakwater. The air was brisk and cool, but it felt good to be outside and get some fresh air. The outing was more to clear her head than to look for Fluke. She knew he would come home when he was ready to, and if anyone could take care of himself, it was that dog. Still, it was odd that he would just take off like that, and it only reinforced her feeling that something was terribly wrong.

The grassy moors lay tranquil before her. There wasn't a breath of wind today; not a blade of grass blew or the water ripple until a bird's wing

342

brushed it. It was so still, so peaceful. Not a spot of snow or patch of ice, though Mary had to pull the blanket tightly around her to shield herself from the cold. The sky was a solid gray sheet above her head, and the whole town took on a flat appearance with no light, no shadow, and not a hint of movement.

She carefully stepped onto the first stone of the breakwater, then the next, and then the next, until she was about twenty yards from the shore. It was a full moon so the tide was extremely high, and she looked upon the flat harbor, so calm, so still, so deceptively peaceful. The gray sky, the gray water, the gray stones, and there she stood, a black speck in this immense, gray world. The water had about reached its maximum height yet it seemed it was going to well up at any moment and swallow her, wrap its wet claws around her and pull her under its surface. She heard a steady trickle and looked down to see the water pulling itself through the stones only inches beneath her feet. She had never before been this close to the surface of the water without touching it, and she was filled with a sudden sensation that she was walking upon the gray pool.

She crouched down on one knee and barely had to reach to dip her fingers into the still water, only to pull her hand back as though it were scalding hot. The water was frightfully frigid, and her heart began to race. *Cold, so cold,* she thought. She frowned, stood up, her hands at her sides, and faced the water defiantly.

You, you great bully, she thought. You cruel being who cradles and lulls the innocent only dash them away and destroy them. You lure us in. You welcome us into your arms before you swallow us whole. You give us hope with calm, clear waters reflecting a sunny sky. Then you torture us, injure us, beat us with your waves and wind and wrath. Men who only want to support their families are destroyed. Women waiting patiently for their husbands have their hearts crushed to find that you have taken our loves and our breadwinners from us. Who are you to use your insurmountable size and strength to shatter the lives of those who live on your shores; who survive by yielding a small harvest from your depths? You are not a body of fruitfulness and prosper; you are the maker of widows, orphans, wreckage, and destruction. You do not fool me. You sit there like you are harmless, when you are only a beast waiting to be released from your cage, ready to reach out and strike me down. Dash my life away in one fell swoop . . .

But you will not ruin my life. No. Nothing you can do will destroy me. You will not take my husband from me. You will not devastate my family. You will not swallow me up and drown me. I will cling to my small strip of land, and when you try to swallow that up, I will rise above the floodwaters and walk upon you, over you, across your surface to my deliverance. And my husband, though he is even more at your mercy with nothing to cling to save his own heart and his own strength will do the same. He will battle you and match your might, for he will not let you take him from me. He will come back, whole, after having faced your fury, and overcome it. Of that I am sure.

Her heart pounded in her chest, her face was red and beads of sweat were forming at her temples though the day was cold. She had not spoken a single word aloud, though she felt sure the entire world could hear her cry. She turned round in a full circle on the flat stone upon which she stood and took in, completely, her surroundings. She saw the marshes to the west with the fine blades of grass peeking just above the surface of the high water, and the land hook around before her, a thin strip of sand that was both protective and vulnerable. She saw to the east the harbor, ominously calm, like a gray sheet of glass that would shatter as soon as it was touched, and behind her was the town that sat as though waiting for some earth-shattering occurrence. Everything was calm, so calm. There were no birds; there was no wind; there was hardly a sound except for the trickle of water beneath her feet. It was all calm, too calm, and Mary knew this would not last. She knew it would change for the worst and dreaded it deep down in her heart. She choked down her fear.

Mary turned back to the town and walked steadily home, the skies ominously darkening at every footfall.

XII

The Storm

The *Halcyon* made good time in getting to George's Bank. She was running well, and once they were there, they had enough time to do a quick trawl before night rolled in, and they could rest themselves for three long days of hard work. The initial catch was a successful one, especially for only three men. Bobby stayed on the boat, while Seraphine and Bill set out the lines from a dory.

The water churned from the light breeze, but the afternoon remained gray without any drastic changes in the weather. Seraphine pulled on the cold lines with his bare hands, hardly having to strain against their weight and seeming not to notice the bite of the cold wind on his back. He and Bill worked with the efficiency of six men, and soon their dory was full of fish.

When the sky was beginning to dim, and the men were weary from their toiling, they prepared themselves for dinner and a good night's sleep. They all sat in the cabin, chewing on pieces of bread and eating linguica and beans that their wives had stocked them with. They drank a whole bottle of whiskey between the three of them, Bill drinking most of it, since Bobby hadn't quite developed a fisherman's appetite for hard liquor, and Seraphine preferred not to have his senses dulled by the foggy head whiskey gave him. Still, they drank enough to warm themselves from chilly night and ease their aching joints. Seraphine sucked placidly on his pipe, and Bill, beginning to slur a bit, told several of his various tall tales.

"Did I ever tell you about the time I saw the sea monster?" This was meant to be a rhetorical question, for Bill had every intention of telling Seraphine and Bobby the story whether they liked it or not.

"Yes, and I don't want to hear it ever again," Seraphine responded.

"What do you mean? 'Course you gotta hear it. It's a classic. Bobby here hasn't heard it, have you, nice boy?"

"No," Bobby shrugged not seeing any harm in hearing Bill's story, but Seraphine put up a hand, and said, "Believe me, you'll have plenty of chances to hear that one."

Bill masked his insult by taking another swig from the bottle of whiskey and, feeling much revived by the pleasurable burn of liquor in his mouth and the heat of it spreading throughout his body, he said, "Well, if you ain't gonna listen to any of my stories, I want to hear a bit from Bobby here."

"There ain't nothin' to tell," he shrugged. He became shy now that he was alone with Seraphine and Bill, two men he had grown up admiring. "You already know that I just got married last spring, and my wife is pregnant with our first kid. She's certain it's gonna be a girl, but I'm hoping for a boy."

"Ah, don't knock the girls. They're worth more than you know," Seraphine said between drags on his pipe, leaning casually back on the bench.

"Oh, I know, I know. You just know how it is to want a son you can go fishing with and do things like that. But I don't care as long as it's healthy and has all its fingers and toes. Whether it's a girl or a boy, I'm sure there will be plenty more to come."

"Now, that's the right thinkin', nice boy!" Bill held up his whisky bottle and laughed. He passed it to Bobby who took another swig himself and relaxed, prompting further talking.

"I'm just scared that I won't be able to provide for her. My wife and me, we don't have any money, and with the baby on the way, I gotta make sure we got something so that we can at least feed it and put clothes on its back."

"Don't you worry, nice boy," Bill said, "Cap'n Seraphine'll lead us to a real honeyhole. We'll come home with a cargo of fish to make the richest men jealous. You'll have plenty of money for that new baby and that pretty wife of yours."

"Well, I know my chances couldn't be better than with you two. I'm just beginning to realize how much responsibility I have, though. I mean, my wife and my children, they're all going to be depending on me, and what if I fail? What if I'm a bad father and a bad husband?"

"Well, you're out here now, ain't ya? Not many men are willing to go out fishing in this kind of weather. You can see it's just the three of us sitting here. You've made a damn good start."

"I'm doing my best," Bobby said, and then looked over at the silent Seraphine. "What about you Cap'n? Do you have anything interesting to tell?"

"Yeah, Serry," Bill jumped in, "I'm so sick of you always making me do all the talkin'. It ain't easy to carry a conversation, you know."

Seraphine looked up from his pipe, not smiling, but his eyes giving a friendly twinkle, the lamp on the table lighting his large, dark face so its irregular redness seemed to glow. His narrow eyes sparkled, and his stump of a pinky twitched as though trying to reach the clay pipe he held in his complete fingers.

"Bill has all of the good stories."

"Nah, Cap', that ain't true. You went to war."

"You went to war, too, Bill."

"Yeah, but I didn't have my ship blowed up."

"You're ship was blown up!" Bobby exclaimed.

"Nah. It wasn't no big thing. I don't like to talk about it."

"You don't like to talk about nothing!" Bill said exasperatedly. "You ain't got nothing to hide. Why don't you just tell us a story? Everybody's sick of mine. Hell, I'm even sick of mine."

"Yeah, come on Cap'n," Bobby chimed in.

"War stories are typical. Everyone has them, and every one tells them, and they're all the same. You're going to make me out to sound like Frenchie."

"Yeah, but the difference is Frenchie never did a goddamn thing. He just gets all liquored up and then shoots his mouth off all night."

"And day," Bobby added.

"Cap', you're beginning to make me feel bad. Haven't we been working together on this here boat since it belonged to Cap'n Glory?"

Seraphine didn't respond, just pulled the end of his pipe from his mouth and stared hard at it, his gaze vacant and unseeing. The room was silent except for the sound of the waves beating against the sides of the boat and the lantern creaking on its rusty nail. The two men waited, barely breathing, for Seraphine to respond.

"I ain't gonna talk about the war," he finally stated, his voice ringing clear in the silence of the boat. Seraphine lowered his pipe to his knee and without looking up, began his story.

"Quite some years ago—I was just a kid then—a boat, a Spanish frigate, went aground on the shoals, just past the Race during a storm. The boat sank, and all the men died, but word had it that a horse, one of those fancy Spanish pure-bred types, escaped and managed to swim to shore. Men in town all talked about this ghost horse that ran around in the dunes. It lived out there. They said it was the primest specimen one could look for in a horse—a white stallion. They said this horse had a spirit like the wind and when it ran through the dunes, its mane billowed like the sails of a ship, and it barely left a mark in the sand. Every fella in town wanted to get his hands on that horse, but hardly anybody had ever seen it. We all thought it was just a myth. You know, people would see it when they least expected it, when they weren't looking.

"Well one day, a party was going out there to hunt down that horse and catch it and bring it to town. They asked me to go with them, and of course I said yes. Who wouldn't? It was like hunting for a legend. The men had a plan, a good one, to surround and trap that horse, and we lay low in the bayberry bushes. We could hardly breathe for fear of scaring him off. I was just about to shut my eyes and fall asleep, since we'd been waiting for hours, when, only maybe ten yards in front of me, came the stallion. What a horse that was! It was white and had a long, thick mane and tail that was blowing in the wind. It rose up on its hindquarters, and you could see every muscle in its body ripple. Its fur was pure white, clean like the snow, not a mark on it, and I thought I could almost see through it, like a really thick fog. I remember my jaw nearly hit the ground when I saw that horse, and I just lay there on my stomach and stared at it. It was so free, so strong. I was in awe, sheer awe, and then I heard the call and saw the men run up with ropes and flung them around the horse's neck. The horse reared up and bucked and twisted its body around in every direction. It neighed so hard—it was the most painful thing I've ever heard, almost like a scream, but worse. I could see the whites of its eyes as they rolled back in his head in fear and frenzy. That horse was so damn strong, though, that it just flung those men off like fleas. They were falling all over the place, not strong enough to hold him down.

"I just sat there. I couldn't move. I don't know why. I guess I was just too scared. The horse, the ropes still attached to him, took off across the sand, over the crest of the dune and down the side to the beach. The men chased after him, and so did I. I wanted to see what would happen. I got to the top of the hill just in time to see the horse run straight across the shore into the ocean. The waves were big that day and white and they swallowed the horse up before I even knew what was happening. The white of its mane and its tail just blended right in with the whitecaps, and it was gone, swallowed up by the sea."

Seraphine paused. His eyes were wide and sad and distant. They were not looking at the lantern swinging before him or the two men who sat gaping, but at that horse that had run into to ocean. He blinked away the glassiness that was growing in his eyes and looked down at his pipe about to stick it back in his mouth. "I guess that horse just preferred to be dead than captured. It was the bravest thing I've ever seen and the saddest. It was so beautiful and innocent and free. That's what got to me. The freedom that horse had, running around in the dunes all day. It was sadder to see those ropes put around his neck than to see it drown itself in the ocean. I think I'd do the same thing. Sometimes I'm not sure I believe I even really saw it, but other times I see that horse in my dreams, and it's real as hell. It's so real, it almost scares me."

Bill and Bobby sat silently, not quite sure what to say. They were left somber from the emotion of the story and the sound of their captain's voice for the first time in any great length. Seraphine put his pipe down, breaking the silence and dismissing the heaviness that hung over them with the command, "All right men, it's time for bed. I'll take the first watch, and let you two get some sleep."

The two men did not argue with the order, as sleep was always short and interrupted on a boat. Their weary bodies welcomed what sleep they could get before they had to take their shift manning the boat. Seraphine always took a longer shift allowing the others to get more rest, for he did not mind staying up in the black silence of the night. He could muse and suck peacefully on his pipe.

Nothing could be seen all around, for they were in the middle of the ocean, and even the ocean could only be felt as the waves gently rocked the boat. The light on the *Halcyon* reflected off the immediate surface, one lonely, little spot in the blackness. Seraphine leaned against the wheelhouse, seated on a crate and looked up at the clear sky. The full moon shone, surrounded by thousands of sparkling white stars. His breath blew out smoky in the cold air which smelled salty and fresh, and he felt at peace, alone, a mere speck on the vast ocean.

Seraphine also had the last shift, which he always took, for he loved watching the blazing sun rise over the horizon, but this morning it was particularly bright. The sky was a blend of red and magenta and deep orange. It seemed to be on fire, more brilliant than any sunset he had seen, and an anxious feeling crept over him. As beautiful as the color of the sky was, it was an ominous sign, and he was tempted to call off the trip and turn back.

Bill and Bobby rose and joined him on the deck shortly after the first light peeked through the dark curtain of night.

"That sky's quite a sight, ain't it?" Bill said without speaking his true thoughts.

"Yep," was all Seraphine could muster to say.

"My God," Bobby looked wide-eyed. "I've never seen anything so beautiful before."

"Don't be fooled, nice boy," Bill said more gravely than had been intended. "It don't bode well."

"I think it might be best if we head back," Seraphine said.

"But we've barely a fifth of our hold full," Bobby objected. "We haven't covered the cost of the gasoline it took us to get out here."

"That's true, Cap'," Bill agreed. "Me and Bobby won't be any richer from this voyage, but you'll be even deeper in the hole. I can't live with that."

"Don't worry about me. I always make out just fine," Seraphine assured him, not wanting the men to feel obligated to stay out on the ocean.

"Cap'n, I need the money from this trip real bad," Bobby said. "I can't go home empty handed. Please, can't we get in at least one more day's worth of fishing? I've got to put food on the table. It will seem like such a waste."

Seraphine sighed, his concerned faced softening with empathy. He had already made up his mind, but turned to Bill anyways, "What do you think, Bill?"

Already knowing Seraphine's thoughts as well, Bill responded, "Well, even if a storm is on its way, I sure don't think we're gonna beat it home. Might as well fill up this boat before we fight it out. You know me; I'm always ready for an adventure." Seraphine could see the reluctance on his face, though Bill tried to sound encouraging, and he gave him a slow nod that only two men who have worked together for over twenty-five years could understand.

"Well, that settles it then. Come on men. Let's catch us some fish."

The fish that day were more plentiful than the day before. The sky quickly became overcast, but there were still no dark, storm clouds. The waters were relatively calm and the air warmer than usual for a winter's day. They went about their work with little anxiety over what was to come, knowing that already they had given themselves to the mercy of the ocean and the sky and the elements that flowed between them.

The sky was turning a gunmetal gray color by the time they called it a day, and the darkness was both from the increasing clouds and the setting sun. Night was coming upon them with all its cruel tricks.

The three men ate quietly with no stories and little laughter. Seraphine told them he would again take the first watch so that they could rest. "We may have a busy night ahead of us."

But he did not call them. He let them sleep and sat, allowing the hours to pass. He dozed off himself from time to time, but remained seated in his spot against the wheelhouse until what must have been the very wee hours of the morning. Three o'clock or so, he looked up at the sky, and a clear patch in the cloud cover opened revealing to him the shining moon. An aura of light glowed around it, fuzzy and white, and then he could see dense, black clouds roll over it and blot out the moon and its light completely. With the clouds came a gust of howling wind, and Seraphine felt the first drops of rain. The storm had finally arrived.

He stood and hurried to where the men were sleeping, the waves already growing larger and the boat rocking more. "All hands on deck!" he called. "The storm is here!"

Bobby and Bill rushed to the deck, pulling their clothes on. The rain was already falling torrentially, and the wind was wailing. The whole boat shook, as the wind seemed to blow right through every stitch of wood in it, and it was tossed by the growing waves. The water turned foamy and white, the wind churning it into a mass of whitecaps.

Seraphine manned the wheel, desperately trying to hold the boat steady over the waves, trying to prevent it from capsizing, but he had little control in such a storm as this. Bobby was to keep an eye below deck to make sure that everything was secure, that the engine was running properly, and the boat was not taking on too much water. Bill made sure the dories were well strapped down and that they would not lose any of their gear.

With every passing moment, the fury of the storm increased. The wind blew stronger, the rain fell harder, and the waves grew higher and higher. On every great wave the *Halcyon* reached its peak and seemed to be flying in mid air, the men's chests tightening with anticipation. Then, as the boat careened down the side of the wave, their hearts leapt in to their throats, and the *Halcyon* crashed to the bottom with a bang that felt as though the vessel would shatter. The men's bodies felt stretched and compressed with every rise and fall, and they feared the *Halycon* was weakening from the force. Each wave they rode over seemed higher than the first.

The waves crashed over the side, and the boat spun and rolled, tossing the men from one side to the other. Seraphine gripped the wheel with all his might, using the wheel more to balance himself than to keep the boat on course, since steering was useless. Bill fell to floor and rolled on his side, sliding until he hit the wall of the cabin.

"Hang on, Bill! You okay?"

"Yeah, Cap', I'm okay!" They yelled to each other over the sound of the pounding waves and the rattling boat.

"Find something to hold onto, and don't let go!" Seraphine advised him.

Bobby scrambled up the ladder from below deck, breathless. He clung for dear life to its rungs for fear of being flung off with a sudden jostle of the ship. "Cap'n. She's taking on a lot of water."

"Has she sprung a leak?"

"Can't tell. It might just be from what's washing over the side."

"Just try to make sure there aren't no leaks. There's little we can do about the rest."

"Aye Cap'," Bobby said, and carefully went back down. His face was pasty white with fear and from the icy coldness of the water.

A short time later, Bill cried, "Looks like one of the dories is sprung lose. I better got batten it down," and rushed out to it, clinging to whatever he could so as not to be flung overboard.

The wind blew the water against him so that it stung his skin like bullets and soaked his jacked clean through. He flung himself onto the dory, not yet completely free of its restraints, and tried to hold it down with the weight of his body, as his cold hands fumbled with the wet, icy ropes. After what seemed like an eternity of struggle, Bill got the dory secured and pulled himself back to the wheelhouse.

And so it went for nearly an hour. Seraphine and Bill took turns at the wheel so that each would have to suffer the wrath of the storm first hand. Seraphine went down to inspect below, and Bobby had not exaggerated; the boat was full of water, more than simply could have come in from crashing over the side. There had to be a leak, and Seraphine knew that with each pounding of the boat, the leak would grow and the hull would weaken. He hoped to God this storm would end soon, for he did not know how much longer the boat would hold up.

As soon as one stepped outside of the cabin onto the deck, he was drenched from the vicious spray of icy water. It was impossible to tell whether it was the rain or the waves that was getting them the wettest. The two mixed from above and below into one great torrent of icy water that was blown against them with such a force as to knock a grown man over.

The water froze before it could drip off the cabin, and the boat was covered with frosty ice that got thicker by the moment. It was impossible to see out of the windows of the wheelhouse because the ice had grown so thickly encrusted on it, and the deck was slick and slippery as the water continued to layer on and freeze. Everything was coated in a white sheet, and Seraphine felt that they must look like a great ghost ship.

Suddenly a wave, greater than any Seraphine had every experienced, came upon them. The boat keeled almost entirely to one side, and as the water was about to crash over them, Seraphine cried, "hang on, men!" and he gripped for dear life onto the wheel. He felt as though he were floating in the air, hanging only by the wheel in his clenched arms, as the water burst through the windows, shattering them, and gushed down upon the men. Bill too, had managed to hold onto something, but Bobby was not so lucky and slid across the floor, running his body into the wall of the cabin as a large hunk of loosened wood cracked down on his head.

Seraphine, soaked to the bone and still unsure of what position he was in, whether upside down or sideways, scrambled to the side of the injured man. Bobby was knocked out cold, but Seraphine could tell the blow had not been fatal and could see that Bobby was still breathing.

The water was rising fast, and Seraphine knew that the boat would sink at any moment. The water had nearly come to the top of the hold and bubbled in the opening of the floor, frighteningly, like black, bubbling tar.

"Quick!" he called to Bill. "Grab whatever is left from that cabinet over there, and let's get to a dory."

Bill crawled as quickly as he could on his hands and knees to the cabinet and yanked whatever contents out. "There's just some wool blankets!" he called, but took them up in his arms as Seraphine beckoned him to follow.

Seraphine dragged Bobby's dead weight across the leaning deck of the sinking *Halcyon* with all his might. Bill quickly got to his side and helped him cut the dory loose and flip it over. Together they flung Bobby, who felt like he weighed five hundred pounds, into the dory and then jumped in themselves, as they pushed it into the raging sea. Bill, though, missed as a wave pushed the dory away from him just as he attempted to jump in. He was swallowed by the black, foamy waves, and Seraphine, from within the spinning dory, saw that his mate was not beside him and reached down into the water. He had acted quickly enough to manage to grab a hold of Bill's jacket sleeve and from there was able to grip onto Bill's arm which eventually grasped the side of the dory. Bill weighed considerably more than Seraphine did, and it was nearly impossible to get him into the boat between Seraphine's insufficient strength and the violently churning waters. Bill hung on for dear life, Seraphine helping in what way he could until, finally, there was brief calm in the storm that allowed him to get a better grip on the half-submerged man. By this point, Bill was losing consciousness, his cold, stiff hands that grasped the side of the boat were nearly immovable. Seraphine managed to pry them off as he, with all his strength, hoisted Bill into the dory as though he were a lobster pot or a giant fish, and then fell back into the boat himself.

The storm stirred up again, and the water continued to beat on them from the sky and the ocean. All the men were soaked to the bone, shocked from the coldness of the water, and Seraphine saw that he was helpless with two unconscious men. He began to drag Bobby to the bow of the boat, and wrapped a damp blanket around him, for all the help it was. He crawled back to the side of Bill, and as he was about to wrap his arms under his chest, Bill's eyes cracked open, and he said in a weak and distant voice, "Don't throw me over, Cap'."

"You're crazy. I'd never do that."

"Nah, Serry. I mean it. When I die, don't throw me over."

"You ain't gonna die." Seraphine tucked a blanket around Bill.

"It's over, Cap'. But when I die, don't throw my body overboard. Keep it in the dory to add load. I'm a big man, Serry; I can help keep this here boat from flipping over."

Seraphine did not know what to say. He was stunned as he saw his best friend and partner, with a sudden burst of life, drag himself to the bow of the dory beside Bobby and prop himself up, right there. He crossed his arms over his chest, resolutely, and closed his eyes.

Seraphine hoped that the combined warmth of the two men's bodies would be enough to keep them from getting hypothermia, but deep down, he knew it was too late. He then wrapped the last remaining blanket over them, and then he, himself, laid his body over theirs as though to shelter them and keep them warm from the fury of the storm. He hoped to God the waves would not swallow this helpless little dory, but he was at the storm's mercy, and there was nothing more he could do.

Suddenly, he was struck by the bitter coldness that overwhelmed his body. His vision blurred and he felt the life draining from his limbs. He could not move, could not stir in the slightest, as a black dreamless sleep crept over him. He and his two mates lay unconscious in the dory that rode through wind and waves and torrential rain, a tiny ark on a great watery world.

XIII

The Laden Dory

Seraphine attempted to open his eyes, a difficult task, as an icy crust had formed on his eyelashes. He found himself still sprawled over the bodies of his mates and moved his arm stiffly, trying rub and blink away the frost from his eyes. He lifted his sore, battered body into a seated position, his damp clothes frozen rigid and frigid cold. He looked around him and could tell that the storm had finally subsided. The waves had calmed considerably to a normal choppiness, and the wind no longer blew so harshly. The rain had stopped, and there was little water crashing over the side of the boat.

The sky was still a dark, steely gray, but Seraphine could tell that it was daytime now, though he had little idea of how long he has been unconscious. It could have been for several hours. The amazing thing was that he had awakened at all, and for that he was grateful.

He checked Bill and Bobby, but he could not tell whether they were alive or dead. Everything was so cold, and even his own heart felt as though it were beating at a frightfully slow rate. He knew that all he could do now was try to get them home. He began to reach for the oars which, thankfully, were still there, and as he did so a misty light began to show through the clouds. The deep, dark storm clouds were beginning to diminish, revealing thinner, less ominous, cloud cover. Seraphine could see the sun trying to burn through the thick, gray covering. It peeked through the clouds right above the dory floating on the choppy black water. The light filtered from the sky through the cloud cover in heavenly rays upon the boat, lighting up the dory and the immediate circle of water surrounding it. Seraphine looked up toward the sun, to the hopeful bit of light above him, and was filled with an overwhelming feeling of strength. He was awed by the sudden sense of warmth and life that flowed through his body, that started in his toes and welled up through his chest, right out to his tingling fingertips. He felt whole again and capable of fulfilling the task at hand.

As he experienced this powerful sensation, the beam of filtered light shining dimly upon him, he saw a bird fly between the rays as though it were flying toward the sun, and Seraphine's heart leapt. They must be near land, for the birds would not be out nearly so far in the ocean after as great a storm as the one they had just encountered. The wind and waves must have pushed him toward shore while he lay unconscious in the dark, stormy night.

Seraphine, with his new found hope and vivacity, grabbed his oars and began to row in the direction he was sure to be home. He rowed and rowed, unaware of time or place, but his energy was unfaltering, and as soon as he could smell the sweetness of the land, he rowed faster and harder, desperately trying to get his mates home in time to save their lives. The water of the choppy waves sprayed upon him, the cold nipped at his face and hands and burned through his clothing, but he did not pause, failing to notice his own suffering. He was blind to any and all pain and was driven simply by the fulfillment of his mission.

Mary awoke at three thirty in the morning with the first signs of the storm. The wind rattled the windows, and rain beat against the glass. She could hear it pound on the roof above her head, and pulled the covers close to her. She was frightened, so very frightened.

Soon, she saw the silhouette of a body in the door. It was Joseph.

"What is it, *dahlin*'?" she asked trying to sound calm, and he walked cautiously to her side.

"I'm scared."

"Of the storm?"

"Yes." He was trying to sound brave, knowing he was too old to be afraid of storms, and it was obvious he was struggling to hold back tears.

"I didn't think you were afraid of storms anymore." Mary extended her arms to him and pulled him to her. Tears began to fall from his face, and she could feel them dampen her nightgown.

"I know, Ma, but usually Dad is here."

"Oh honey, Dad is going to be just fine. Don't worry. Nobody knows how to handle a storm the way he does. He would never let anything get between him and us. I guarantee he'll be home soon."

"I know, Ma. But what about Fluke? Who will take care of Fluke? I don't know where he is, and it's cold and rainy outside. Dad has his boat, but where is Fluke living? Won't he get sick? Isn't he lonely? He should be here with us."

Mary gave a little laugh at the innocence of her son. His fear for his dog overshadowed his fear for his father's life, simply because of his confidence in his father's own strengths and abilities. To him, his father was nearly immortal, a Portuguese Hercules.

"Oh, *dahlin'*, don't worry about Fluke. He'll be just fine. I know that dog knows how to fend for himself. He'll come back home when he's ready."

"I hope so, Ma, and I hope Dad will come home soon, too." And with that Joseph began to sob uncontrollably into the folds of his mother's nightgown. She pulled the covers over him and let him sleep with her for the rest of the night. Sally was a sound sleeper and could sleep through even the wildest storms, and Tommy was too "brave" and grown up to go to his mother's room.

Mary remained awake all the rest of the night listening to the storm and fearing the worst. The storm lasted well into the morning, the skies remaining dark. She and the children went about their morning routine as best they could, trying to shake away their fear that Seraphine might not come home.

Around noon as the storm was finally subsiding, Mary told the children she was going out to get some groceries, but instead she made her way to the Coast Guard dock.

She looked wild and unkempt, a woman who had spent a wretched, sleepless night, and Glenn Jason tried to hold back his shock at seeing the most beautiful woman in town appearing in such a state. She had an old, rumpled housedress on and her gray knit shawl was wrapped around her. Her feet had been shoved into an old pair of rubber boots, and she had dark circles under her eyes. Her cheeks were sunken and sallow looking.

"Have you any word of my husband?"

"Why, no," Glenn said. "He wasn't out in this storm, was he?"

"Of course he was!" she cried. "He left Sunday morning on a three day fishing excursion."

"Why, who was with him?" Glenn asked, greatly concerned.

"Bill Buckets and Bobby Codinha. Please tell me they're all right."

"I have no idea and no way of knowing. But Mary, I hate to break it to you, but I don't think anyone could have possibly survived that storm."

"You're wrong. My husband could have survived it," Mary contradicted him resolutely.

"If anyone could have, it would be Seraphine, but I have to warn you of how unlikely that is. I don't want you to get your hopes up."

"Get my hopes up?" Mary put out the palms of her empty hands like a beggar woman looking for change. "But that's all I've got. I have to hope. It's all I can do. It's the only thing that will keep me sane. He has to come back to me. I can't live without him."

"I know Mary. I'm wrong; don't give up hope. We'll do the best we can. I'll send a search party out for them, but it could take a long time, and by then it could be too late. Our boats took a real beating in this storm, and I only have a couple of small ones still functioning. We'll do the best we can, I swear."

"Thank you," Mary said weakly, and then let her hand fall to her sides. "Thank you so much. I've got to go take care of my children." Then she turned and left, a broken woman.

The sun had set, and Mary had sent the children to their rooms to do their homework and get ready for bed. Tommy had not put up much argument to stay up this night, and she was grateful for that. She was wearily lowering herself into Seraphine's rocking chair, when she heard a bell ringing frantically on the end of the coast guard dock. They had found something!

She leapt from the chair, grabbed her shawl off of the hook by the door, jammed her feet into her rubber boots, and rushed out the door. As she neared her gate, a neighbor who lived on the harbor side of the road hurried toward her and said, out of breath, "It's Seraphine."

She did not pause to hear anymore or ask a single question, but bolted toward the beach. She ran as fast as she could, her rubber boots slapping the pavement, and her hair whipping across her face as she clutched her shawl close to her chest. She got to the beach and ran down it, her feet crunching the hard crust of frozen sand and then sinking into the soft that lay underneath, causing her to stumble and trip. The sky was finally clear, and the moon and stars glowed brightly, reflecting on the placid harbor as did the few remaining lights of the town. She saw the dory pulled up to the shore, and a body being pulled from it.

It was Seraphine's. The men had trouble getting him from the boat, for his cold, stiff hands were frozen to the oars. They had to warm them and pry the knuckles apart to loosen the steadfast grip on those pieces of wood that had brought him home.

Mary got to the dory as soon as the men had freed Seraphine's hands and pulled him out of the boat. She collapsed onto the sand, sliding like a base runner and pulling the stiff body of Seraphine into her lap. She cradled him there like a baby, wrapped her shawl around him and rocked him in her arms.

She pulled off his stiff hat, still jammed tightly on his head, and tried to wipe the frost away from his hair, but when she did, she realized that it wasn't frost at all. His dark, salt and pepper hair was nearly completely white. She began to weep softly, as she stroked his snowy hair, not sure if he was dead or alive.

His eyes opened slightly, treading a line between conscious and the unconscious. "I did my best," he said, and then his eyes shut and he was unconscious to the world. Mary leaned over him and wept uncontrollably, sobbing and kissing his face over and over again, squeezing him with all her might.

The doctor arrived, and told Mary that they had to get Seraphine home immediately and warm him up before he could die from the hypothermic shock. She reluctantly let the men pull him from her arms and carry him to the house and up to his bed. The children came out of their rooms, wanting to see their father, but Mary sent them back to bed, the strictness in her voice warning them not to pursue the request.

While the doctor did his examination, Mary holding Seraphine's hand, she got the full story from Glenn. "We didn't see him until he was already halfway into the harbor. As a matter of fact, it wasn't even one of our men who spotted him. The night watchman had fallen asleep, and it was Zappa who spotted him."

Zappa was also in the room with them, and he recounted his own part of the story. "I was going to bed and took one last look out my window, just to see what was happening. Well, out there in the middle of the harbor I see a body in a dory rowing to shore. I said to myself, 'who in his right mind would be out there at a time like this, on a night like this, rowing?' And I realized there was something funny about this rower, so I ran out to see what it was, and as soon as I get to the beach, I see it's Seraphine, and he's in real bad shape, and I holler for help at the top of my lungs. That's when everybody wakes up, and the bells start ringing. Well, I didn't even think about it. I ran right into the water and waded up to the side of that boat to pull it in. 'It's okay, Cap',' I said. 'I gotcha.' And as if he heard me, he slumped back into the boat and was finished. Some other men came and saw me struggling to pull him in, so they ran into the water, too, to help me, and we managed to get him in to shore. That's when you arrived."

He was grave, and it was only during his story that everybody finally realized Zappa was wet to the chest. He didn't seem to realize it himself.

"You get home now," the doctor said. "We don't need another sick man on our hands.

"Thank you, Sir," Zappa said. "Seraphine'll be in my prayers as will the two others less fortunate."

"Wait," Mary's eyes snapped open, suddenly remembering that her husband was not the only man in the boat. "What happened to Bill and Bobby?"

"Oh, Mary," Glenn said. "They died. I think they died long before Seraphine got that dory to shore."

Mary began to weep for sorrow and for shame at the death of those two men and how she was so selfish to only think of her own husband. "Oh, poor Bill," She said through her tears. "And that poor boy. What will his wife do with a baby on the way and nobody to provide for her?" Mary wept into her hands, while the doctor applied hot compresses to Seraphine's frozen limbs.

"There is nothing we can do now. You husband did all that he could, and we must get him well so as not to lose another. We will help Mrs. Buckets and Mrs. Codinha out as best as we can, but you just worry about Seraphine for now."

"Yes doctor," she said, and he gave her instructions as to how to properly nurse Seraphine back to health.

"Call me if there is any sign that his condition is worsening, but I am confident that he will get better. I will come back tomorrow to check on him again. Take care, Mary."

He put his hand on her shoulder as he turned to leave, and she said, "Thank you doctor." Glenn left too and the others that she had not noticed.

She sat by Seraphine's side all night. Much of the time, she squeezed herself onto the bed next to him and held him tightly, trying to warm him with her own body and not wanting to be too far from him again.

The ocean had claimed two more victims. It had made two more widows, four more fatherless children, and one more lost vessel. It had baited them, caught them, and swallowed them whole. It had tricked them with its calm and raped them with its fury, and then somehow, somehow, it had delivered her husband back to her whole. Or rather, he had delivered himself. Mary did not know if it was the mercy of the sea, the goodness of God, or the sheer miraculousness of Seraphine's own abilities that kept him alive. Perhaps it was all three. All she knew was that he was here now, helpless as a child, his hair snow white, she knew not how, but she touched it with her fingers as though it were something other than hair. She kissed his fiery cheek and placed her head on his shoulder.

The sun rose, a white natural light. No red skies this morning. It filtered through the windows, and Mary rose from the bed, and knelt on the floor at Seraphine's side, looking hopefully at his face, but there was no sign of him waking. She turned and began to straighten the room, hoping that the children would sleep late this morning.

"Mary," she heard a weak, scratchy voice come from the bed. She turned and was at his side in two strides, kneeling on the floor, once again, and grabbing his outstretched hand. She did not know what to say.

"Did they make it?" he asked flatly, little hope in his voice. Her heart broke to tell him the truth, but she knew he would have to know sooner or later.

"No."

He stared at the ceiling as she clutched his hand in both of hers, and she saw one tear trickle out the corner of his eye and run down the crease in his face to the pillow. "I didn't think so," he said simply, and she wiped the tear away with her hand, Seraphine hardly seeming to notice.

She wanted to say more, but there was nothing to say. She sat with him for a little while, and then said, "I'm going to make you some soup, okay? You must be starving. Then I'll get you good and cleaned up." Seraphine did not say anything but turned his face sadly toward her.

Mary went dowstairs, and began to prepare the soup. She pulled out all of the ingredients and put the pot on the stove. She was beginning to dice some vegetables when she heard a scratch at the door. She looked up, confused by the sound, and would have ignored it had it not persisted. She wiped her hands on her apron and walked to the front door. She opened it and could not believe what was before her eyes.

"Fluke!" she exclaimed at the sandy and disheveled, but whole, dog. She barely got a look at him before he bolted through the door and up the stairs to Seraphine's room.

"Don't your dare get on that bed being as dirty as you are!" she called after him, though not really caring.

Fluke went directly to Seraphine's side, wagging his tail and licking Seraphine's hand. Seraphine patted the dog on the head, and said, "Good dog. You've been looking for me, haven't you?" as the dog lay down beside to bed. And there he remained until Seraphine was well again.

XIV

Recovery

Seraphine lay in bed for several days, barely touching his food. Mary brought him the local newspapers, but they just piled up on the floor beside him. She brought him his violin, but it stayed in its case. She offered to read to him like Sarah used to do, but he just gave a slight shake of his head. When the doctor came to see how he was feeling, he said he was fine, even though the stethoscope said otherwise.

"You have a lot of fluid in your lungs," said the doctor. "Have you been coughing much?"

"No," replied Seraphine and then immediately began low, phlegmy hacking. "See not much. The first time I've coughed since you've been here."

"You can't take this lightly, Seraphine," the doctor said firmly. "You have pneumonia. I am sure after the hypothermia you just experienced that your lungs will never be quite the same. I'm going to give you some cough medicine, but you have to stay in bed and rest for at least another week."

"Another week?"

"Yes."

"Doctor, I've got to work. I can't stay in this bed all day."

"You can't do any strenuous work for another month . . . if all goes well. It could be longer."

"Longer! Absolutely not! I've got to feed my family. I'm not staying laid up for another month. It ain't right for a man to spend his life in bed."

"I know it's hard, Seraphine, but think about how it will benefit you in the long run. Now, I want you to stay in this bed for another week. You aren't to leave the house, you aren't to work, you aren't to pick up a thing. Oh yes, and no smoking. You stay right here and let your wife wait on you. It'll be like a nice vacation. Get some reading done, listen to the radio, sleep. There's plenty to occupy your time with."

"Vacation," Seraphine grumbled sourly.

The next morning Mary came upstairs to find Seraphine sitting on the edge of the bed, fully dressed and leaning over to pull on his socks with Fluke lying beside watching him.

"What are you doing?"

"What's it look like?"

"I see, but where do you think you are going?"

"It's Bill's funeral today."

Mary's shoulders fell. She had hoped she would be able to sneak out to pay her respects to Sandy without Seraphine noticing. She did not even know how he knew it was today. He must have taken a glance at those newspapers after all.

"Seraphine, the doctor said you need to stay in bed. You're too weak to go."

"I'm going!" he slammed his fist on his thigh and began to cough. Mary hurried to the bedside table to pour him a glass of water from the pitcher and handed it to him. He took a sip and then shoved the rest back to her. Still coughing, he raised himself from the bed and made his way shakily across the floor. He picked up his fisherman's cap from off the bureau and pulled it snugly over his white hair, placing his hand on the surface of the bureau for a moment of support, and then, as though he hadn't faltered a step, continued to walk slowly toward the hall and down the stairs, leaning heavily upon the railing. Fluke followed, and Mary cried, "Wait, Seraphine! Let me get ready so I can go with you." But he pulled on his boots as though he hadn't heard her and headed out the front door with Fluke following behind. Mary sighed, knowing that she could not fight against his stubbornness and his determination to get out of the house.

But when she had gotten her black dress and hat on and headed down the road, she saw that Seraphine had not made it very far. She caught sight of him gripping a picket on the fence of a house only about six doors down from their own. As she got closer, she could see that his back was heaving from his labored breathing and walked briskly to catch up to him. Fluke was sitting beside him looking up at Seraphine's red face and his hand clutching his chest. He recognized Mary's footsteps long before Seraphine realized she was nearing.

"Seraphine, are you okay?" she asked, trying not to sound too concerned, for fear of affirming his certainty that she was trying to baby him.

"I'm fine. Just give me a moment."

"Is it your chest?"

"Feels like it's on fire," he wheezed.

"Are you sure you want to do this?"

"Yes." The vehemence in Seraphine's voice was enough. Bill was his best friend, a fine fisherman, and a fine person. It would be wrong to not pay respect at his funeral. Mary also understood that Seraphine felt some guilt. He was the sort of man who would take an event, completely out of his control, and blame himself for it happening.

"Well, there's still plenty of time before it starts. We'll go slowly." She took his arm so that he could put some of his weight on her, and they eased their way at a snail's pace down the road.

They could see a crowd gathered at the chapel on the hill of the cemetery. Mary felt Seraphine stiffen as they made their way up the incline. "You okay?" she asked, barely above a whisper.

"Yes," he replied but his voice was hoarse and low, and Mary detected a note of anxiousness in his tone.

She paused to measure her words, finally saying, "You know, Seraphine. It wasn't your fault."

"I know," but it was clear that he did not feel that way. He straightened himself as best he could, lifted his head, and let go of Mary's arm once they reached the top of the hill and neared the crowd. Everyone turned their heads and looked at him, hushed their stories about Bill and their subdued discussion of the weather. But as soon as Seraphine began to make his way through the parting crowd, the first person he came upon nodded and said, "hello Cap'," in no unfriendly way whatsoever. The next person shook his hand and said, "Good to see you, Cap'." The next person did the same and then the next. From each person in the shifting crowd came a nod, a handshake, or a pleasant greeting. They all looked upon Seraphine fondly and with respect, something Seraphine had never anticipated. The blame he had placed on himself he thought would be projected by everyone else, but all they cared about was the fact that Seraphine had rowed for miles in a little dory, in the bitter cold, to bring his mates back home. He had accomplished a miraculous feat that had only ever been dreamed up in romances and epics. For that, he obtained more respect from his fellow townsfolk than he had ever had before, and that was saying a lot.

At the end of the clearing crowd, Seraphine saw Sandy, and immediately seized up again. She looked up from her grief-stricken pose over Bill's coffin, and Seraphine beheld her red, puffy eyes. Her simple black dress tugged at her belly, and her straw colored hair was limp and undone. She was not crying. She was all cried out. But when she saw Seraphine, her vacant face suddenly softened with recognition, and she walked over to him, stopping only a foot before him, as though not quite sure what to say or do until she collapsed, her arms around him, burying her sobbing face in his chest.

"Thank God you're here," she cried. "Bill would want you here. You're the reason he's here. You're the reason he's back with his family, the reason I could see his face one last time. This is where he belongs. Not out there buried in the cold water. He belongs here. Seraphine, he loved you so much. You were the world to him. There was no person on earth he respected and adored more than you. He'd give his life for you if you'd ask him to. But you never would. No, you never would. You'd give your life first. That's why he loved you. You are selfless."

Seraphine placed his hand on the top of her head, as she gripped tightly onto the front of his coat. He could feel her tears begin to seep through his heavy layers to his skin. Tears were soaking his collar as well. And then he realized that they were not Sandy's tears at all. They were his own. The tears were flowing from his eyes, filling every crease of his face, and rolling down onto his jacket collar. There was nothing he felt bold enough to say, so he just stood there and cried with her. Mary looked on, crying too, and then Seraphine placed his hands on Sandy's shoulders and said, "You'll be all right." He eased her away from him, the tears now halting their flow, and looked at her with the strength she needed, as though he could transfer it from himself onto her.

"Thank you, Seraphine," she said, wiping her face with the back of her hand, and turning slowly to return to her family.

It was a military service, since Bill had fought in the Navy in World War I, just as Seraphine had. The veterans shot off their guns, and Sandy was presented with the American flag as "Taps" played on a solitary bugle. Sandy and their two children looked sadly on as the coffin was lowered into the ground, emblems of grief amongst a crowd of friends, distant family, and townsfolk wishing to pay their respects. It was a sad day for all.

As they headed home, Seraphine said, "I wish I hadn't missed Bobby's."

"You couldn't have helped that," Mary said. "They buried him right away. You had still barely recovered from the hypothermia by then."

"I know. I just don't feel right about not being there."

"At least you made it to Bill's. I'm glad you went . . . even though you weren't supposed to." She had to add that extra jibe in an attempt to lighten the mood.

"Me too. Can you send Bobby's wife some food or something?"

"Already did. I sent her a blueberry pie—used my best preserves. And a stuffed codfish, clam chowder, and stuffed sea clams. I figured that should last her some time."

Seraphine cracked the first real smile he had made since he'd been home. It was a weak one, but a smile no less. "I should have known better."

"Yes. And I'm knitting some clothing for the baby. I told her I'd help her out with anything she needed."

"That's good." They walked on, slowly. It was cold, but the sky was blue. The naked trees shook in the wind, and the streets were empty of cars and people.

"They'll always have food," Seraphine said, still referring to Bobby's wife.

"I know," Mary said softly.

Seraphine was happy to be back in the nice, warm house, get out of his heavy boots, and crawl back into his comfortable bed. But Tommy, Sally, and Joseph bombarded him as soon as the door shut behind him. Sally gave him a big hug and Joseph cried, "You went out today!"

Tommy said, "Yeah, we thought you'd never get out of bed."

"Yeah, Dad. We kept peeking in, but you didn't seem to notice, and we didn't want to bug you. Ma said you were too sick to be bothered, so we left you alone. But we wanted to come see you!" Sally was gripping his arm, her eyes wide and smiling.

Tommy wanted Seraphine to listen to his favorite radio program with him, and Joseph wanted him to eat dinner at the table tonight, but Mary stepped in and said, "Come on now. You're father had a busy day today. He's still not quite himself, so you should let him go rest in bed for a while. He'll be better soon. They all looked at her, and listened but were insistent that they follow their father up to his bed. "I don't want him to fall down the stairs or nothin'," Tommy said wryly.

"I ain't that old, son!" Seraphine laughed.

"You sure look it with that white hair."

"Yeah, Dad," Sally asked. "How'd it get so white?"

"I don't know," Seraphine shrugged. "The doctor said that happens sometimes in stressful situations."

"Will you tell us about it, Dad?" Joseph asked. "Everyone at school says you're a big hero. Tell us!"

"Another time," Seraphine replied. By this point they were in the room, and Seraphine was sitting on the edge of the bed, his chest burning again.

"Glad you're feeling better, Dad," Tommy said, and the rest agreed. Seraphine held out his thick arms and huddled Joseph and Sally into him, burying his face in their hair, and giving them each a kiss on the top of the head. He went to shake Tommy's hand, but Tommy moved in for a hug, and Seraphine preferred it that way. As old as Tommy thought he was, he was still just a kid.

Seraphine sent them off and lay down in his bed, bracing himself for a long recovery. He felt pain everywhere.

XV

A Happy Return

As Seraphine neared the end of his long convalescence, the ill in the world had also begun to dissipate, and the war finally came to an end. Seraphine was sitting at home when he heard the news that the war was over, rocking in his rocking chair with the radio beside him. The town cheered right along with the rest of the world, happy at last to have their harbor empty of naval ships and to see the returns of their children. The family had not heard from Jimmy in some time, but they told themselves that no news was good news.

The next day Mary was in the kitchen cleaning, when she heard the front door creak open. She turned, astonished to see Jimmy standing at the bottom of the stairs, and unable to say anything but, "What are you doing here?"

"Gee Ma, thanks a lot. I thought you'd be happy to see me," Jimmy laughed.

"No, I—" Mary gave her head a shake and blinked her eyes a few times to ensure that what she was looking at was not simply a figment of her imagination. When Jimmy was still there, she jammed her fist on her hip, put on her sternest motherly tone, and scolded, "You didn't tell me you were coming home! Why didn't you send a letter? The war just ended yesterday. How did you get here so fast!"

It was Jimmy's turn to be confused. He had not anticipated this kind of welcome. "Well, I—I didn't realize I was going to be getting done so soon, so I figured I'd surprise you."

Mary's stern face broke into a smile, and she tackled Jimmy, smothering him with kisses and squeezing him so hard, he thought he'd break a rib. Still with Jimmy in a stiff arm-lock, Mary called upstairs, "Jimmy's home!"

Tommy, Joseph, and Sally rushed down the stairs to greet him, asking him a hundred questions at once, breathless and excited, and hanging all over him, but Jimmy was not ready to give them the full details of his adventure just yet. Disregarding the swarm of siblings, Jimmy asked, "Where's Dad?"

"He's working out back in the shed," Mary said.

Jimmy was about to head out the door, when Mary grabbed his arm and pulled him into the kitchen, asking lowly, "Did you get my letter?"

"About the shipwreck?"

Mary nodded.

"Yes, I did, but I just got it a couple weeks ago. I was so angry when I realized that it had been dated from nearly six months ago—the mail is so goddamn awful."

"Well, at least you know."

"Is he feeling better?"

"Much, but, Jimmy, he's still not the same. I don't want you to be too surprised when you see him. He's becoming more like his old self, but it's taking a while."

"Well, I'll see for myself," and he turned to go to the backyard. There he spotted his father sitting on a wooden crate, mending a trawling line. He was dressed much the same as he always had, with the hat pulled low over his face, but Jimmy was able to detect that the once dark hair that peeked out from under the cap was now snow white.

"Dad," he said hesitantly, standing straight and tall before Seraphine, his naval uniform crisp and clean, the medals on his chest shining.

Seraphine raised his head, and Jimmy saw it was the same rugged face with the red complexion and the weather-beaten skin that he had always known, but now the lines seemed deeper. Seraphine's skin hung looser, and his once tough façade, now appeared beaten and tired. But what bothered Jimmy most was Seraphine's eyes. They had little sparkle left in them, little life. They were filled with grief and exhaustion, and Jimmy's heart broke at the sight of his father, his hero, in such a frail light.

But on seeing Jimmy, a smile broke across Seraphine's face, and for a moment, Jimmy saw a glint in his eye. Seraphine raised himself from the crate and walked over, more steadily than Jimmy had expected, but still with that rolling fashion of an old, rocking boat.

Seraphine asked no questions, but simply smiled and gave his son a brief hug, placed his arm around his shoulders and said, "Come in the house. Tell us about what you've been doing over dinner. It's nearly time to eat, and your mother will be sure to make a feast now that you're home."

Seraphine led Jimmy toward the house for the first real meal he had had in ages.

The family gathered around the table, nearly complete again. "Jimmy, do you know where your sister is?" Mary inquired. "We haven't heard from her in a few weeks."

"Ma, just because we're both in the Navy doesn't mean we know each other's whereabouts."

"Well your sister certainly knew where you were! Every time we got a letter from her, she'd say, 'Jimmy's ship is docked in Hawaii,' or 'Jimmy's stationed right off the coast of the Philippines.' It was quite a relief knowing she could track you down at any moment."

"Well, that's because she became an officer in the WAVES. That gave her access to all kinds of information that grunts like me couldn't get. I wasn't supposed to do anything fancy but fight."

"Did you fight, Jimmy?" Tommy asked eagerly. "How many Japs did you kill?"

Mary gave him a quick glare over her dinner plate, but Jimmy said, "I don't know how many I killed, if I killed anyone. I'm sure I did, but it was impossible to tell. Our ship was attacked by fighter planes many times."

"Really? What'd you do?" Joseph asked, wide-eyed.

"I was one of the gunners. I had to shoot those anti aircraft machine guns. They let hundreds of bullets fly per minute, and if I didn't hang on tight, I'd get flung around real bad. Those things shook so hard, my brains would feel like mush by the time the battle was over, and I wouldn't be able to hear right for days. They'd get some hot. I'd have to wrap my hands in rags sometimes just so they wouldn't get burnt on the metal."

"So how many planes did you shoot down?" Tommy asked still reaching for the hard numbers.

"It's hard to say. There were many guns like the one I shot, and we all rained bullets at the same time. There was no way of knowing who actually shot the bullet that brought the plane down, but I'm sure we all made contact at some point."

"Man, I'd want to know. I'd want to know just how many planes I shot down so I could brag all over town about it."

"Ah Tom, it ain't like you read in the books. It's better not knowing. It helps your conscience. When you're out there, all you're supposed to do is kill the bad guy. But they ain't bad guys; they're just like us. They've all got wives and kids and families, and when I saw many of my shipmates die, I realized that that had to have been the way all of the people we'd been killing felt as well. It's not a game; it's people's lives. So, really, I'm glad I don't know. As far as I know, I might never have killed anybody, but then again, maybe I killed them all. There's just no way to be sure, and I'm glad of that. I never had to see the faces of the men we killed, and I'm glad about that. It was bad enough seeing people die that I knew."

"How many of your friends died?" Sally asked, growing less fond of these war stories.

"Well, we were lucky compared to other ships that experienced kamikaze attacks. Kamikaze attacks are real scary 'bout you've gotta shoot them down before they crash into you. You can see them coming straight at you, and all you can do is fire as fast as you can. Fortunately, my ship didn't encounter too many kamikazes, but we did fight off plenty of air raids. A couple of my really close friends were killed."

"You must wish that this whole mess had never happened," Mary sighed.

"No, not at all. For the most part, it was great. We did a lot of exporting of goods and supplies to the soldiers stationed on the islands, so I got to visit tons of islands in the South Pacific. The fruit is great. You can pull coconuts and mangoes and bananas right off the trees. The island folks are really friendly and welcoming, and they have a completely different way of living—it's great. It was a real education. After the bombs were dropped, lots of my buddies got to go into Japan and see all of the tea houses and Geisha women. I hear they're some beautiful, all painted white with red lips and black hair. Wow! I wish I could have seen then, but I was already on my way home. I collected a few souvenirs from all the places I went to; tried to get something to help me remember each island. They're small but they're enough to refresh my memory.

"Can we see them, Jimmy?" Sally asked eagerly.

"Of course. I got a couple things for you guys, too."

"Where?"

"In my bag." The kids were about to jump out of their chairs, but Mary halted them, "Wait 'til after dinner. Jimmy hasn't had a good meal in a long time. There's plenty of time tonight for him to tell us all about what he did and saw and show you his things."

Mary had every kind of seafood she could scrounge up spread across the table. Clams of every variety, scallops, squid, three kinds of fish, shrimp, and lobster, all cooked in rich, spicy Portuguese red sauces, stuffed with onions and linguica, fried, baked, broiled. It was all there.

"God, Ma, I've never seen so much seafood in my life. You must have raked the docks clean."

"I've got connections."

"I know, but what'd you think, the entire ship was coming home with me? There's no way we'll be able to eat it all."

"What we don't eat we'll have for leftovers tomorrow night. You've gotten so much bigger, I figured your appetite had grown too, but apparently not. You're eating like a bird. What, did they only give you tiny rations?"

"No, it wasn't bad; just different. We weren't ever hungry, but the food on the boat wasn't so great. Everything on those battleships is out of the can, but at least we didn't starve. The food was great when we got to land though. Pork and rice and beans and fresh fruit and fish. It was great."

"Well, I'm sure it wasn't as good as my cooking," Mary said and poured another spoonful of squid stew onto Jimmy's plate and pushed him a stuffed clam.

Jimmy clutched his expanding stomach and tried to mentally make more room in his gut for the fifth helping his mother had just given him. Jimmy had always been broader than the average teenager from working on the boat with Seraphine and playing football, but Mary and Seraphine could see that his forearms had gotten thicker and more sinewy. His shoulders were solid and broad, and his chest puffed out. His face was more chiseled, more like a man's; the soft features of his formerly boyish face had disappeared. He was clean shaven, but the shadow of a dark beard was already beginning to peak through his skin. His hands were thicker, the fingers wider, the knuckles more swollen, and marred with a few dark scars. They were a man's hands. In his dark eyes there was an air of knowing and a glint of wisdom. No more carefree, boyish twinkle, but the depth of a man who had traveled around the world and seen many beauties and atrocities.

"The years really flew by. I missed home, but, lord, what an experience it was. I could never have seen and done the things I did if I had stayed here. It's good to be home, though."

"It's good to have you home," Seraphine said, the first words he had spoken since they had sat down at the table. The food on his plate had only been picked over, and his finger was working steadily at the crack in the table as he watched his family. Things were starting to seem right again.

The next day, Jimmy and Seraphine left the house together. It took them considerably longer to get into town than it normally would have, because nearly every person they encountered stopped to say hello to Jimmy and ask him how he was. At first Jimmy basked in the attention, but eventually he found himself trying to hide behind his father in hopes of going unnoticed, a futile endeavor seeing how he was so much taller than Seraphine.

"It's nice that they're all going out of their way to say hi to me, but I'm getting kind of tired of answering the same questions over and over again," Jimmy said to his father.

"You're a hero."

"From what I hear, *you're* a hero," Jimmy grinned, but Seraphine did not respond. Jimmy paused to remark at each store that had changed and each establishment that had disappeared.

"Where's Tilly's bait and tackle?"

"Gone. Said there was too much competition."

"Too much competition? But this is a fishing port!"

"There doesn't need to be ten tackle shops here anymore. There ain't as much fishing going on."

"So, what, they put a gift shop there instead with *pictures* of fishing boats and fishermen?"

"Yep. For the people who come to visit."

"Wow! They're painting Arby's house."

"Yeah. New owners."

"New owner?"

"Yeah. Arby died, didn't you know?"

"No. When?"

"Oh, must have been a year ago, at least."

"Didn't his family want the house?"

"Nah, they're all uprooting and going elsewhere. Say they can sell the house and live like rich folks wherever it is they're going.

"That's strange. I thought they fished, though."

"They say they want out of the whole business. Too dangerous. After last winter . . ." Seraphine paused and cleared his throat. "Well, it just ain't worth it to them."

"Hey, let's stop in Adams."

All the men and women sitting at the counter looked up from their coffees and conversations to give Jimmy a warm greeting. Dottie was behind the counter and gave them a big grin. "Well look who it is. I thought I heard you were back in town."

"Finally. First full day back"

"And you come in here! I'm flattered."

"Still the best cup of coffee around."

"Well, let me get you one." She filled the cup and passed it to him, as Jimmy and Seraphine lifted themselves onto the spinning brown stools. "Still take cream and sugar?"

"Yep."

"How about a hot fudge sundae while I'm at it? To my knowledge, these are also the best around. On the house. For old time's sake. Want one too, Cap'?" But Seraphine shook his head.

"On a diet or something? Trimming down that waistline?"

"Tryin'."

Dottie laughed. Her dark hair had streaks of gray in it, and she had more lines around her eyes, but otherwise, Jimmy felt, she looked the same. It was like he had never left, but the ice cream tasted better than ever.

Seraphine and Jimmy finally arrived at the wharf, walking farther and farther into the harbor, leaving the town stretching along the shore behind them. They sat down at the end, with their legs dangling over the side, not fearing the water below. They sat in silence for some time, just breathing in the salt air and watching the seagulls overhead, scavenging around the fishing boats just coming into port. The weir boat motors were running and the cormorants were flying back and forth from their nests on the breakwater. Potts was pulling lobster pots, mightily yanking them out of the water and into his little skiff. The sky was blue, and the breeze was strong.

"So, Dad, I know you probably don't want to talk about it, but Mom wrote to me about the storm," Jimmy finally said. "She didn't give me many details but just said that Bill and Bobby had died, the *Halcyon* was gone, and you were really sick for a long time. What happened out there?"

Seraphine didn't speak for quite some time, as though considering whether he wanted to recount the events of that night, that night he had relived over and over again in his mind, trying to figure out if he could have done something differently. Just as Jimmy was deciding that he should never have broached the subject, Seraphine began to plunge into the story. He spoke quietly and told Jimmy exactly what had happened without the fishing tale flourishes.

"We never would have made it back in time. I keep trying to find some way we could have made it out of that storm alive, but the more I think about it, the more I realize there was no hope. That storm was going to get us. The only way is if we had just stayed home."

He continued on about the *Halcyon* sinking and loading Bill and Bobby into the dory. "Bill knew that was it for him. He knew he wasn't going to make it, but I still hoped. I just wanted to get them both home, dead or alive. I wasn't going to leave them out there. All I could think was to get them home. For all the good it did."

"How'd you do it, Dad? How did you not freeze to death yourself?" Jimmy asked, finally breaking his polite silence.

"I don't know. I was just numb I guess. I passed out for a while. I couldn't do anything in that storm. I was frozen solid, and we were getting tossed around in the waves so bad, I just collapsed. It's amazing the boat didn't get swamped. When I awoke, I thought at first I was dead. But then I realized I was still in the dory, and it was just me and the sea and the sky. I felt so helpless, but I knew I wasn't dead yet. I couldn't feel anything, my hands, my face, my feet, nothing. Then I saw a bird fly out of the clearing sky and the sun try to break through, and that gave me hope. Then I could feel my heart beating, and I felt my body begin to get warm, and I picked up the oars and I rowed. I just rowed. Kept rowing for dear life. Kept rowing 'til I got home. I didn't even think about it. I just did it. My body just moved those oars as though it wasn't my body at all. I don't know how; it just happened.

There was silence, and Jimmy knew the story was finished. He could get the rest from his mother.

"I'm sorry I lost the *Halcyon*. She was a good boat."

"Yeah she was, Dad, but maybe this is a sign that it's time for a new beginning. We can get a new boat. A better boat. I mean, think about it, the *Halcyon* was old. Now they make new boats with faster engines and modern navigation equipment. We could get a trawler, Dad, that's what everybody's doing nowadays, that's what everybody's been doing for the past ten years."

"Except for me. I don't want a trawler. I don't want a new boat."

"Why not? What, are you just going to give up now? You're a fisherman, that's what you do. But this is a sign that it's time to progress. It's time to put the old style away and try something new. Don't you think? Isn't it a great opportunity?"

Seraphine kept looking at the water in front of him, not responding.

"I know you're skeptical, Dad. You're a stubborn Portuguee like all of us are, but you've got to dream a little too. Maybe you don't want to do it, but I do, and I'm going to do it. I'm ready to start my own life, and it's up to you whether or not you want to join me. We can be partners on it. I'll get my own boat, and you and I can go fishing together like we always have. You can captain it like you always have. I don't mind. But I want to do this. I want to fish. It's in my blood. I've been gone all these years, and all I could think about was how I wanted to go back home and fish. Get married and fish."

"Get married?"

"Yeah, that's the other thing. I'm going to ask Vickie to marry me."

"Have you seen her yet?"

"No, I've only been home a day, and I fell right to sleep as soon as my head hit the pillow last night."

"No sneaking out the windows for old time's sake?"

"Nah, but thanks for covering for me all those times."

Seraphine shrugged. "I know what it's like. I wasn't about to give you a hard time for it."

Jimmy laughed. "Vickie and I wrote to each other a lot, and it's all we really talk about, so I'm sure she'll say yes. I hope so. Otherwise she's just been stringing me along!"

"Nah, no girl's willing to waste that much time."

"That's what I figure. Anyways, I'm going to go see her tonight and ask."

"Good luck. She's a beautiful girl."

"Thanks, Dad. Hope Ma won't have a fit."

"Nah, she's ready to be a Nana I think. Tommy's only got a couple years left in school, and the other two are getting up there as well. Things are changing."

XVI

Things Keep Changing

Sarah was home for the wedding but did not stay for long. She arrived at the door of the little floater house in her long, navy, wool coat decorated with stripes and medals. She'd received the highest rank a woman could hold in the Navy, and now that she had fulfilled her duty to her country, she was now ready to fulfill her duty to herself.

Mary reeled backward in her chair when Sarah told her she'd been accepted to Wellesley College and would be leaving in just one month.

"Why didn't you tell us you were going off to school! We didn't even know you'd gotten in!"

"Ma, you always knew this was the plan. It's one of the main reasons I joined the Navy."

"I forgot," Mary grumbled, when all she really meant was she'd hoped Sarah would change her mind and be dying to come back home once her journey abroad had reached its end. "But it's so far away. It's in Wisconsin or something, isn't it?"

"No, Ma, it's right outside of Boston."

"That's just as bad."

Sarah put her head in her hands, her frustration building. "Ma, I am so tired of you always trying to stop me from going places and doing things. This is not all there is. Here is not all there is. Why don't you realize it? You have always been content to stay here, and that's great! You are fulfilling the life you set out to fulfill, but my aspirations are a little different from yours. I love it here, just like you. This is my home; it

388

always will be. Being away from it makes me love it even more, but I have to educate myself in order to feel satisfied with myself as a person. My life will be a disappointment if I don't go."

"Your life isn't a disappointment to me."

"No, but it will be to me. If I don't pursue my education, I'm going to regret it for the rest of my life. I want to become more than here allows. That means I have to go to school, see more of what's out there, and then, if I want to come back, I'll come back. I'll always come back; you don't have to worry about that. Provincetown is in my blood. It's my identity, but so is school and being a student. Don't you see? I can have the best of both worlds."

There was no sense in arguing any further. Mary knew that her children had to expand their horizons past the little town at the end of the world. Or perhaps, it was actually the beginning. You could stay rooted to where you were, insistent that there was no place left to go, or you could turn around, go in the other direction, and see what the rest of the world had in store. No, Mary knew she had to surrender. Sarah was the least like Mary of the entire tribe of children. Mary didn't want to let her go again. She wanted her family near her, but she knew that she had to.

Mary sighed and said, "You know I wasn't about to let you go without a fight, but you win. Just don't forget your decrepit old mother."

"Of course I won't. You know this will be easier than me being in the Navy. At least the mail will come quicker."

The wedding was small and humble, though Vickie's family was quite large, and naturally, they all came bearing generous gifts. The service was quiet, a traditional Catholic wedding, and an intimate gathering at the end with plenty of homemade food from the combined efforts of Mary and Vickie's mother.

Sarah, shortly after, left for her school and the big city, and before Seraphine and Mary knew it there were grandchildren. Tommy had also joined the Navy, Sally and Joseph were late in their high school years, and

Sarah had graduated college. Where had the time gone! Seraphine felt that he was caught in the middle of a whirlwind of time that never paused to slow down and let him take a breath. He'd always worked and worked hard, but once he was grown and married, he always had the comfort and security of knowing that his family would be waiting there for him at dinnertime. Now three kids were gone, and two were leaving. They had their own families and their own lives.

Seraphine didn't mind the change so much. The holidays were always big, everyone home, and like it was before, yet he felt less needed. He did not have to support his children anymore, though he was always generous where he could be. Even his boat was not his own; it was his son's, the *Phoenix*. It was a trawler, and Seraphine never felt at home on it. They raked the bottom of the ocean and dumped the contents on board. No more catching each fish by hand. It was still dangerous and laborious work, but it was not for him. Seraphine found himself going out less and less.

He sat on the dock and looked around at the harbor filled with yachts and pleasure crafts. He enjoyed the sight of the masts of the many sailboats clustered together on their moorings, like a flock of gulls, but when he turned back to the wharf, he saw fewer fishing boats.

Times were tough for fishermen. The fish were more scarce. They had to go out farther and longer to fill their quotas, the same quotas that got smaller each year. The Russians were clearing out the Atlantic, coming with their huge vessels that sucked every last fish out of the ocean. Grown fish, baby fish, edible fish, trash fish, it all came out, leaving nothing left for the local fishermen. More and more Seraphine heard complaining about how bad the state of fishing was, the harsh regulations, and the lack of plentiful schools, instead of excitement over a great month of full holds. Seraphine could hardly stand to pick up his coffee at the Pharmacy, for he could not bear the weary looks on his fellow fishermen's faces, but he still went. He was one of them too, and he shared in their struggle.

"I'm done with this. I'm done with fishing, at least for a while. I just can't make enough money with it to support my family. I've got to do something different. I'm going to do sightseeing tours—you know, for the tourists. They love that kind of stuff."

Many were doing the same thing, running chartered fishing trips, renting out boats and moorings to out-of-towners, some even opened up stores. Hot dog and ice cream stands sprouted up all over the place, more gift shops, more clothing stores; the tourism industry was growing as rapidly as the fishing was failing. Several got into the trades, but many people simply left the town altogether, finding no more lucrative opportunities than to sell their homes and go.

"What has happened to my town?" Seraphine thought as he was witness to shrinking populations in the winter and vastly growing ones in the summer. More houses on the street were dark and uninhabited, having turned into summer homes, and many of the neighbors he'd always known had become unfamiliar faces. Serpahine felt out of place in the bustling summer streets, and lost and alone in the empty winter ones. Everything was changing around him, and more and more he was feeling like an outsider.

The only thing that never really seemed to change was Fluke. He appeared ageless. Seraphine did not know just how old he was, but he knew he had to be getting up there, having had Fluke for twelve years himself. Yet the only signs of aging that Fluke demonstrated were some graying hair on his face and his slowness in getting off of the floor. Otherwise, he still followed Seraphine everyday to work, and he was still in top health, unlike Seraphine whose health had weakened. He did his best to hide it, but he had lost a good deal of strength since the night the *Halcyon* sank. Though he overcame the initial bought of pneumonia, his lungs were weak, and he was always plagued with a chest cold of some kind. He got winded walking from home to work, but stubbornly pulled his pipe out of his pocket and began to puff on it.

Seraphine sat on the town hall bench as he always did, Fluke curled up under his feet in the shade, when Ernie Gobo came by.

"Well, hello, Cap'," Ernie said.

"Hello, Ernie," Seraphine replied

"You retired now?"

"Nah, just don't go out as much as I used to. Getting too old for this fishing life."

"Ain't we all," Ernie grinned and took a deep breath, leaning comfortably back against the bench. "How's it feel to be part of a dying breed?"

Seraphine looked at him as though unsure of what he meant.

"You know better than I do that every year there's less and less of us."

"Sure, the fishing industry's gone way down."

"Oh, not just fishermen. I mean locals, real natives. They're all leaving. Your own kids are leaving."

"They'll be back."

"Oh sure, but only to visit. There's nothing left for them here."

"It's not that bad. There's plenty of opportunity. It's just different opportunity."

"I sure hope you're right, because soon there won't be any of us left. We're slowly getting pushed out."

"No one's being pushed. They choose to leave. If they wanted to stay, they could. It's not like the Germans kicking the Jews out of their homes and into ghettos. It's a choice."

"So, I take it you won't be leaving, will ya, Cap'?"

"Like hell I will. I'll be gone when my cold, dead body's in the ground."

"Glad to hear it, Cap. We need you around," Ernie nodded his head up and down. Then, after a pause, he said, "It's a tough place to shake, ain't it?"

"Yep."

"No matter where you go or what you do, you always want to come back. Why, in my day, I did plenty of traveling. I've seen lots of places, beautiful places, great places, places where I could have done and become whatever I wanted. Yet, always, I just wanted to come back here. I couldn't stand the thought of ever making a permanent move away. What do you think it is, Cap? Is it the water, the way the land curves, what is it?"

"It's home."

Ernie leaned back on the bench and tilted his face up toward the sky in contemplation. "Sure is, Cap'. Do you think it's like that everywhere, for all people?"

"Don't know. I've never lived anywhere else."

"I don't think it is. Not so much anyway. I think this place has a profound effect on everybody that comes here. It's like the saying, 'once you get sand in your shoes, you always come back.' I mean, they keep coming back, they always come back. Can you imagine? If such a lasting impression is made on people who only come here for one day or one week, what must be the connection between the land and the people born and raised here?"

"You say it as though you don't know."

"Oh, I know. I just don't like to take things for granted, so I think about them a lot. You know me; I have a lot of time to think. And you know what? Nobody ever gave me a hard time about it. Nobody ever said, 'nice boy, you just sit there and think day in and day out,' but nobody ever tried to stop me either. They just accepted that that is the way I choose to live my life. Oh sure, I can work hard when I need or want to—I'm Portuguese!—but I don't need to and I don't want to and that's also a choice. Maybe that's a reason why so many come back. They can be who they want to be, be who they are, just as God made them, without having to hide or sacrifice themselves to get everybody else's favor. When was the last time you ever saw anybody given a hard time for what they were wearing or doing?"

Seraphine shrugged.

"Me neither. There's been plenty of times I've thought people looked funny or were acting strange, but hell, I look funny too!"

"Just never thought about it much, I guess," Seraphine said quietly. "People are people, and they can do whatever they want so long as it don't hurt me any."

Ernie nodded like a proud teacher speaking to his pupil. "They all come here because nobody throws any judgment on them. We're all a bit tappy. Hell, before this town was even a town it attracted outcasts and rebels. Those damn Puritan hayshakers in Truro wanted to reform us, make us their suburb!" He laughed. "But look who's the suburb now! Nobody can take our freedom away, our right to be who we are and what we are. It's the American Dream in the flesh, I say."

Seraphine was silent, contemplating Ernie's statements.

"You don't agree with me, Cap?"

"Nah, I agree with you, Ernie," Seraphine said as he watched the colorful people move by, men in tight clothing holding hands, an old salt with a bucket of clams, Skunk with a bottle of booze in a paper bag stumbling up the road, kids running barefoot and brown, an artist with an easel and paint-spattered trousers. All walks of life.

"I'm proud to live here. I'm proud that our town accepts everyone. It's ain't like that in most of the world," Seraphine finally answered.

"No it ain't, Cap'."

"But I don't know if we can survive all this freedom."

"What do you mean?"

"I mean, what you were talking about before, about us getting pushed out. I mean, those who want to stay, stay. They make the effort to change their way of life so that they can stay, but it's getting harder and harder to find possible changes. The face of the town is changing because of it. It don't look the way it used to, and if people keep selling out and moving away, how can it possibly stay the same?"

"That's what I was trying to say. One day, there ain't gonna be anymore of us left. It'll be a summer town, and that's it. That ain't why people started coming here. They came for the fishing village. That's why the artists are here. They want to paint boats and fishermen, people doing their work, toiling, fighting the elements. Now that's a story, Cap'. But one day it's gonna be all gone. It's gonna be lost, and people will forget that we were ever here."

Seraphine clutched his knees with both hands and slowly stood up. "I best be goin'," he said under his breath.

"So soon, Cap'? I didn't mean to bum you out. It won't happen for a long time. We just have to change with the times."

Seraphine nodded slowly and gave a subtle wave goodbye as he headed toward home. He didn't want to change.

XVII

The Hurricane

The storm raged outside the shuddering little house. Wind and rain beat against the rattling windows, and sand pitted against the shingles.

"I sure hope this old floater house can weather this storm," Mary said as she, Seraphine, Joseph, and Sally huddled around the fire in the living room.

"She's survived many others," Seraphine said, and coughed a little.

"Did you take that cough syrup the doctor gave?" Mary demanded.

"Nope."

"Oh, Seraphine! You have to take it or else you'll get really sick again."

"It doesn't work."

"How would you know? You don't take enough of it to make it work." There was a giant gust of wind that made the family start as the house shook. "I sure hope Jimmy's boat is all right."

"He put it in the lea by the breakwater. He was going to try to ride out the storm, but—"

"Absolutely not! Not with that little boy of his. To hell with that boat! Let the goddamn boat sink!"

"Well, that's what he said too."

Joseph and Sally played checkers on the floor but yawned and said they were going to go to sleep. They huddled up with blankets on the floor. Fluke lay between them, and the three stayed warm together in front of the fire. Seraphine plucked at his violin and then played a soft melody. Mary curled up at his feet and placed her face on his knee as he rocked, slowly and gently, in the rocking chair his father built. She too fell asleep, but Seraphine stayed awake to wait out the storm.

When it was over, he went outside to inspect the damage. Several shingles had blown off of the house. The street was littered with debris, there were several fallen tree branches, and some houses had experienced considerable damage—flooding, collapsed roofs, and shattered windows. But the most damage could be seen in the harbor. Seraphine stood on the town landing, and his heart sank. Dozens of boats had washed up on shore, battered by the pounding waves. Several of the small wharves had toppled right into the harbor, and the rest had sustained a great deal of damage. Lobster pots, buoys, and old boat wreckage littered the beach. Many boats had sunk right on their moorings, and Seraphine knew that this was yet another major blow to the fishing industry.

He took Joseph with him to find Jimmy who had already discovered his boat washed up on the shore and was inspecting the damage. It had blow right off of the mooring but hit a sandbar before being pushed all the way into the beach. The waves had battered it, doing a number on the paint job and breaking some windows, but the damage was minimal considering the state of many other vessels. There was a weak spot in the hull but the wood had not been completely punctured, so the boat had not been swamped. Jimmy said to Seraphine and Joseph, who had waded out, "the tide is going down, fortunately, but that only gives us a couple hours to work before she begins to float again."

"Well, let's make her tight." Seraphine sent Joseph to get wood and nails from the shed, and they all got to work reinforcing the hull, just finishing in time for the tide to reach them. Then they checked the engine and the rigging. The engine was fine, just needed a bit of tuning, but the rigging had incurred some serious damage, so Jimmy and Seraphine knew it would be a while before she could go out fishing again. Though not in fishing condition, the *Phoenix* was at least in a good enough state to become part of the cleanup crew, and Jimmy was happy to lend a hand.

He and Seraphine spent days towing swamped boats and helping to clear out the wreckage of the collapsed wharves. They pulled pilings out of the water and other debris, moving it to the town pier, which still stood, to be toted off to the dumps. Crews cleaned up the beaches, cleaning out all of the wooden wreckage and whatever else was washed up on shore. After the cleaning was more or less done, it was now time to start rebuilding, and this began with the weir traps.

Nearly the entire weir boat fleet was wiped out, completely paralyzed by the storm. The nets under the water were destroyed and washed up on shore or out to sea or left in one, great, tangled mass. It was a beautiful, warm, sunny day, and Jimmy and Seraphine volunteered to help repair what was left of the weir nets. Jimmy suited up in a black wetsuit, having grown accustomed to diving since he was in the Navy. He enjoyed diving for clams, lobsters, to repair boats—pretty much everything—so he was excited for the opportunity to do some real diving work.

Seraphine sat in a small motored dory, paying out lines and passing tools to Jimmy; whatever he could do from above the surface of the water. His cough had gotten worse since the storm, and his stamina for such physical labor was vastly lowered. Still, he and Jimmy were enjoying themselves with the lightheartedness of the old days when Bill was around.

Jimmy floated to the surface and pulled back his mask. "There," he said breathlessly, "finished that one." As he tread water to catch his breath, Seraphine noticed something black swimming behind him. Seraphine's still keen eyes squinted into the sunlight, trying to make out what was behind Jimmy.

"Jimmy!" he called. "There's a shark behind you!"

"A what?" Jimmy called back.

"A shark!"

"Yeah sure, Dad. That's really funny."

"No, I mean it, Jimmy. There's a shark behind you." Jimmy shook his head, frowning in disbelief. "It's getting closer. You'd better move it."

Jimmy still frowned, but finally turned to look behind him, and on seeing the black fin sticking out of the water, his eyes opened wide with terror, and he swam frantically to the side of the boat. Seraphine helped pull him in, and the two fell back into the boat, Jimmy gasping, and Seraphine bellowing with laughter.

"I've never seen you swim so fast!" Seraphine said, his face contorted with hysterics.

"Yeah, real funny. I'm sure you'd really be laughing if that shark had taken a big hunk out of my ass."

Seraphine just laughed harder, pausing only to cough in between. "You can't blame him. You look just like a nice, plump seal in that rig!"

Jimmy, having overcome his initial fear was beginning to see the humor in it all and began to laugh too.

"You better not sit on the Point dressed like that. Some old Portuguee might club you over the head and sell your nose for five dollars."

They wailed with laughter.

"Thank god nobody does that anymore," Jimmy said.

"You kidding? Stingray still does. He can't understand why the town hasn't paid him yet for all his hard work. Says they owe him one hundred and fifty bucks. I'll bet he's over on the shore, yonder, plotting how he's gonna get you!" They laughed until the tears fell from their eyes and decided to call it a day from the dangerous waters.

But over at Town Hall, more serious matters were being discussed. The Town Manager addressed the hall of people: "There were nearly fifty wharves in this town and nearly all of them have been destroyed or rendered to a state of utter disrepair. It will cost, possibly, millions of dollars to fix them all, and this town cannot afford that kind of money."

The hall was filled with low voices commenting and grumbling over the harsh reality. For most of them "millions of dollars" was a term not even dreamed about.

"The fishing fleet is crippled. Eighty percent of our boats went under. It is the owners' prerogative if they want to fix their vessels or buy new, but my feeling is that the fishing industry in this town has already been in decline for the last several years, and this is just one more blow. Why should we bother to invest all this money into fixing up all of the wharves when the fishing fleet is as diminished as it is?" There was a wave of more whispers and grumbles. "I do not think the fishing economy can possibly come back as strong as it once was after a storm like this and with the new regulations being put in place."

The floor was open to anybody who wanted to comment, and many were furious with the Town Manager's feelings. They dug in their heels and cried, "But fishing is what made this town what it is!" to the cheers of the audience. "What are we supposed to do from now on? Fishing is our livelihood. It's all we know. Are we just supposed to give that up? And what? Feed this town to the tourists?"

But many knew that these were the futile cries of a few stubborn Portuguese set in their ways. Nobody wanted things to change, but they knew, inevitably, that change would come, that change was here. This was just another mark of the fishermen's decline, and they knew that no matter what was decided today, it would not change what inevitably was going to happen in the decades to come.

XVIII

Violins and Rocking Chairs

Seraphine dug a crowbar into the wood and plaster, ripping away the flimsy, rotting walls. His hands had already grown thick and large, his shoulders and chest broad, and his nose evermore prominent. He had the body of a man at fifteen years old, and the strength of three. The debris crumbled at his feet like the broken life he'd lead up until now—no father, no mother, no home, no friends, no education, just work. Hard work was all he knew.

The physical labor never exhausted him, and he found he felt best while he was working with his hands. He invested his mind and body into his work, but once he got home, weariness overcame him. He sat in his only chair, the wooden rocking chair his father had built before he died, and looked around the empty room, a room void of warmth, comfort, and people; a room filled with loneliness. He felt so empty, he could not feel. He was hungry, but he didn't feel hungry. He was tired, but he didn't feel tired. He was cold, though he didn't feel cold. And he was lonely, but that he felt.

He would look at his reflection in the window and hated what he saw. He hated his big crooked nose, and his ruddy red complexion. Why had God cursed him like this? His mother had heartily believed in this so-called benevolent God, but all Seraphine could see was that this God had cursed his life, cursed his face, taken all he loved away from him. He never went to church, he never prayed, and he never turned to God for assistance. He believed that all he had to rely on was himself and that, through hard work, he could someday right these wrongs.

Seraphine moved through his work quickly, stepping over the debris at his feet, moving from room to room. He came to the corner of what had once been a study and mechanically began to tear through the wall with his crowbar. He was about to move to the other wall, when he thought he'd caught a glimpse of something, and for the first time that day, let his crowbar lower. He peered into the gutted wall and saw a black case resting between the studs, half buried in the debris.

Seraphine lowered himself onto his knees and pushed aside the plaster, revealing a leather case. He took it out of the wall and held it in his hands, turning it over to inspect the cracked leather and the rusty hinges and brushed the dust and cobwebs off of it. He was about to open the case when a voice from the other room called, "Hey Seraphine, you all right?"

"Yeah," he called back.

"Just heard it get quiet all of a sudden. That doesn't ever happen."

"No, I'm fine." Seraphine concealed the case between the wall and his body lest the other crewmen walk in.

"Well, take a break, for god's sake, if you're tired. You're entitled."

"Thanks!" Seraphine called back and decided he'd better do something with the case. He snuck outside and found a bush to stash it under so nobody would find it and then went back to work. He struggled to push the case out of his mind as he worked frenziedly to make the time go faster.

"Good job today, Seraphine," Flinn said when the day was over, putting a five dollar bill in Seraphine's hand.

Seraphine nodded and thanked him as he wrapped his fingers around the measly earnings and stuck it in his pocket. He felt, deep down, that his real pay was hiding in the bushes. He dug the case out and wrapped it in his jacket. As soon as he got to his little, one-room studio, he sat in his father's chair and slowly opened the lid.

He was shocked by how smooth the hinges were, considering their condition, and looked into the case to see a honey-colored violin. It was not fancy by any means. It had a dull finish and no designs carved into it. Yet to Seraphine, it was the most beautiful thing he had ever seen. The strings had snapped from dry rot, but Seraphine was sure somebody could fix that. He lifted the violin out of the faded, purple velvet-lined case and found that there was also wax and a tuning whistle. He took the bow from the lid and rubbed the horsehairs that were also falling apart with his fingers. This too he could get fixed. He looked inside the base and saw etched, "Samson 1807." Why, this violin was over a hundred years old!

Seraphine put it to his face and sniffed it, the moldy mustiness of its long concealment filling his nose. He placed it to his nose again and smelled deeply. This time he believed he could smell the saltiness of the sea and the freshness of the ocean air. There was one string still whole on which he plucked a single note, but in that note he heard the waves crashing, the wind blowing, the birds calling. He rubbed the smooth finish, in perfect condition, and felt as though he were running his hands along the surface of the water.

He was immediately filled with warmth and yearning, a yearning to go out to sea. What was he doing on land when he lived in a world surrounded by water, a world where people made their livings on the ocean? His father was a seaman, Seraphine himself had been born on the ocean. His mother had always said that Seraphine could catch a fish with anything. He sat in the chair his father had made of driftwood and boat wreckage—salty seasoned wood.

Seraphine stood up with the violin and took it outside. He walked down the road until he came to Front Street. Then he crossed that onto the beach. There was an old dory there that he turned over, dragged to the shore, and pushed out onto the water. He placed the violin in the bow and began to use the old oars to row. They felt familiar in his hands, like his hands were made to hold them.

He stopped rowing, and let the boat drift in the middle of the harbor. He felt it sway back and forth, leaned back in it and looked up into the starry sky. He took the violin in his arms and held it against his chest plucking the one string. He closed his eyes and smelled the air, listened to the water slap against the side of the boat and the splashes of fish jumping in the water. He felt at peace.

When he opened his eyes, the sun was rising, and he knew there were three things he must do today. He rowed back to shore. He first dropped the violin off at the music shop in town. "Can this be fixed?" he asked and the man replied, "Yes. Easily. I can have it back to you by tomorrow."

"Good. How much will it cost?"

"Five dollars."

Seraphine pulled the money he'd earned the day before out of his pocket and placed it on the counter. He then went to the Town Hall and approached the man at the records desk.

"What can I do for you, Seraphine?"

Seraphine was taken aback that the man knew his name, but then he reminded himself that this was a small town and everybody knew everybody.

"I was wondering if you had any records of a person named Samson?"

"Samson? Of course!" Seraphine had expected him to have to consult the files behind him before giving a response.

"You mean the Samson of Chip Hill, right?"

"I think so."

"Douglas E. Samson. Why, that man's a legend. The first great explorer to come out of these parts."

"Really?"

"Oh yes, he traveled everywhere—the Arctic, the Antarctic, Alaska, South America, Asia, everywhere! He began as a merchant but then began to go on excursions just for the sake of exploring. In the basement, we've got a store of stuffed animals he left behind: wolves, polar bears, lots of Indian artifacts too. Boxes of stuff! He left it all to the town when he died. We'll have to stick them in a museum one day." The man shrugged. "So what do you want to know?"

"No, that's good, actually. I was just curious. Do you know if he played the violin?"

"Oh, I don't know about that. I suppose anything's possible. He was good with his hands—left a lot of wood carvings that he'd made, soapstone, whale bone, all kinds. He had to do something, spending all that time on a ship."

"He was gone a lot?"

"Oh yes. They say the majority of his life was spent on the sea, traveling from one place to another. It's remarkable that he died at home in his bed. Almost tragic, really. It seems to me that a man who has spent his life on the ocean, the way that man did, should die on the ocean. He never had any wife or children. It was just him and the sea."

"How do you know all of this?"

"My grandfather knew Samson. He actually went on a couple of expeditions with him. He liked to tell me stories about him from time to time. I wish I had asked more questions, listened more closely. Once the stories are gone, they're gone. They die with their keepers. They die with the past. Everything is forgotten eventually. My grandfather could have told you if old Samson played the violin."

"It's okay. You've told me plenty. Thank you." Seraphine nodded appreciatively and left. He was glad he had covered up the etching in the violin before he gave it to the man at the music store. They may have taken it from him and stuck it in a museum!

He thought about what the man in Town Hall said as he walked up the street. That violin must have traveled around the world. That violin must have seen more places than any man alive had. It had traveled to the ends of the earth, but it ended up in a wall. Samson must have treasured the violin above all things to have put it in a wall instead of giving it to the town with the rest of his belongings. It was not meant to be put behind glass. It was meant to be played and to sing of grand adventures on the sea. This violin was Samson's time capsule, not the artifacts stored in the basement of Town Hall. This was the one thing that contained all of his journeys and exploits. It contained the man's spirit. Seraphine was sure that Samson had made the violin, carved its wood with his own hands. The wood must have come from everywhere, anywhere. Seraphine could only guess. And he hid it for a hundred years until it would be gotten by another man, the right man. Fate had brought Seraphine and the violin together.

Seraphine's third and final stop for the day was the wharf, where he approached Captain Glory's *Halcyon* and began his journey.

XIX

Seraphine

Seraphine got out of bed coughing painfully and leaned over to pull on his socks. He dressed himself, pulled on his wool cap, and took one glance into the mirror. He saw his aged, lined, leathery face, his crooked nosed, his rough, red cheeks, and the white tufts of hair that stuck out from under his cap, but he did not mind what he saw. He remembered he used to be disgusted by his reflection in the mirror. He had thought himself homely, but now he realized that he was just a man, an ordinary man who had seen many miracles happen, and he counted his blessings.

He walked shakily down the stairs, coughing violently once he got to the bottom.

"Where are you going coughing like that?" Mary asked.

"Work."

"No sir. You aren't working in that condition. You need some rest and a doctor."

"I don't want to see any doctors," Seraphine retorted, and he left the house.

Everything felt different and looked different to him. It was still his home, but home had changed so much. Ernie was right; he was a man of a dying breed.

Fluke followed him to the wharf where he sat and gazed at the small fleet of fishing boats, only a fraction of the size of the fleets of his youth. He had missed Jimmy, but he didn't mind. He was tired. The toil of the sea had finally caught up to him. He was only a man. What more could he do?

A boat came in, the *Nancy II*, and Dunlop hopped off. "How are ya Cap'?"

"Oh fine."

"Good day for fishin', Cap'. Flat-ass calm out there. Surprised you ain't out there with the boy. Don't get many days like this."

"No. Just taking it easy today, but I'll help you unload."

"Thanks, Cap'," Dunlop said, and Seraphine began moving crates of fish. He was still a strong man, could still carry heavier crates than most, but in the midst of a load, he went into a coughing fit. He dropped the crate, and coughed uncontrollably. A couple of the mates came over to ask if he was all right, but he waved them off, trying to catch his breath. His hands had blood on them, and his chest burned like it was on fire. He tried to straighten up, but his head spun and his eyes blurred. Next he knew, all was dark.

Seraphine awoke in bed with Mary looking concernedly at him.

"Oh thank God," she clutched her heart. "Here, take some of this."

He wanted to ask what it was, but his voice came out hoarse, a mere croak, and Mary quickly stuffed the spoon into his mouth. The red syrup tasted disgusting, and he began to cough again. As soon as the fit subsided, Mary asked, "Hungry?"

"No."

"I made soup," and she left as though she hadn't heard him. His hand dropped over the edge of the bed, and he felt it land on the smooth coat of Fluke. Fluke was always there.

In two day's time, he was trying to get out of bed again, much to Mary's vexation. His cough was as bad as ever, but he could not sit still. He had to do something. He eased his way down the stairs which seemed to spin and blur. He couldn't shake the fogginess out of his head.

Mary approached him, but he evaded her complaints with, "I need fresh air."

The cool air burned his lungs, but he found it much more invigorating than lying in bed all day. The town looked foggy to him, though. His head ached, and his stomach felt queasy. He was almost run over by a man on a bike that he didn't see coming. Fluke walked slowly by Seraphine's side as he continued his way determinedly up the road.

Seraphine stopped at Adams and bought his cup of coffee. He rummaged in his pocket for the thirty-five cents but dropped the change as he handed it to Dotty. He scrambled to pick it up, but his fingers were like jelly.

Dotty looked at him pityingly. "You all right, Cap'?" she asked gently.

"Yes, fine." He put his hand to his spinning head. "I just-" He was out of breath. "I just—I'm fine," and he stumbled toward the door, forgetting his coffee.

He sat on the bench and closed his eyes. What was wrong with him? He'd never felt like this in his life. He walked to the pier where Jimmy was just pulling in and reached out to grab the line, but he missed the toss. He reached over to pick it up and wrapped the rope around the piling, but his weak fingers could not tighten the knot.

"Dad, you all right?" Jimmy asked, a worried expression on his face, hopping from the boat to help him.

"Fine! I'm fine!" Seraphine declared frustratedly.

"You shouldn't be here; you should be in bed."

"I can't. I have to," Seraphine choked on his words, "do something. I can't—I can't go back there. That house is swallowing me. I have to be here. I have to-" Jimmy put his arm on Seraphine's shoulder. "It's okay, Dad. You'll be better soon. Just give it a week or so." Seraphine looked down at the ground. Jimmy seemed to tower over the shrinking frame of his father, and his heart truly ached for the first time in his life. Jimmy gave the mates their orders and then walked Seraphine home. Fluke followed.

"I have to head back to the boat," Jimmy said, stopping at the gate. "You know how Ma is. She'll force me to eat something if I go in. She's convinced Vickie doesn't feed me well enough. But you go in and go straight to bed."

Seraphine simply nodded and headed to the door. The house was quiet and empty. Mary must have gone out, but even when she was there, it was quiet. The sounds of children's voices were gone. All his children had grown up and were making their own lives, their own stories.

Fluke followed as Seraphine pulled himself wearily up the stairs and had another violent coughing fit. He looked at the bottle of medicine on the table but climbed into bed without touching it. Mary came home a while later and asked, "Did you take your medicine?"

"No."

"Well take it. You're supposed to take it three times a day." She stuck the spoon in his mouth. "What would you do without me!" she cried.

Seraphine gave a tight lipped smile. When Mary left, he spit the medicine into the cup of coffee he'd left untouched on the bedside table.

The next morning when he awoke, he felt considerably better. The cough was still horrendous, but his mind was clearer. He felt more like his old self, sharper, more alert. He moved to get out of bed, and he felt the weakness of his body. The coughing was taxing, but the room no longer spun, and that was all that mattered. Fluke wagged his tail and watched intently as Seraphine pulled on his boots. He knew what today was.

Seraphine made his way to the wharf with a five gallon bucket and filled it with fish from Jimmy's latest catch. He and Fluke then walked to a little house on Court Street and placed the bucket on the front stoop. Seraphine didn't knock or ring the doorbell but turned back down the road, passing a mailbox with the name *Codinha*. People had often seen Seraphine walking up the road with his dog at his side, toting a bucket full-to-the-brim with fresh fish, but nobody ever stopped to consider what he was doing with it. Seraphine had been taking fish to Bobby's wife every week since the sinking of the *Halcyon*.

When Seraphine walked through the door of his house, Mary asked him how his day was and how he was feeling, to which he responded, "Much better."

"Good, then the medicine's working. You better take your afternoon dose."

"No."

"No what?"

"No. I don't want any."

"But you have to take it."

"No, I don't. It makes me sick."

"You're already sick."

"It makes me sicker."

"Of course it doesn't."

"It does. My cough's as bad as ever. It doesn't help."

"That's because you're not taking it enough."

"No. It doesn't work. I keep coughing, and I can't think to boot."

"Come on Seraphine. Just take some." Mary came toward him with the bottle, and he took it from her and threw it with all his might across the room.

"I don't want any goddamn medicine!" he yelled at the top of his lungs. The bottle shattered as it hit the wall, the red syrup spilling everywhere.

Mary stood, horrified. Seraphine had never raised his voice like that. Seraphine put his head down, ashamed and frustrated, as he lowered himself into his father's rocking chair.

"I'm sorry," he said quietly. "But don't you see? I can't work with that stuff in me. I can't think. I'm dizzy and nauseous and weak and clumsy. I can't live like that. I'm not myself."

"But I want you to live. That's why you should take it."

"What good is being alive if I'm nothing better than a vegetable? I'm useless. Believe me, if I believed that stuff was working, I'd take it, but it's not."

"But the doctor said it was the last kind of medicine he had to fix your cough. It has to work."

"If it doesn't work, Mary, it doesn't work. All things have to end eventually."

The tears were streaming down her face. She was still a beautiful woman. Not a hint of gray in her hair thanks to Clairol, and her face looked ten years younger than her actual age. She looked at him with her vivid blue eyes, "But I need you here with me."

"I am here with you. I'll always be here with you." He reached out his arms for her to come to him, and she curled up at his feet, her head in his lap as he rocked in the rocking chair.

"Don't you know, Mary, that every time you look at the ocean, you're looking at me. My life is connected with the sea, the way yours is connected with this town." Mary just cried. "And this," Seraphine said as he reached for the violin case and took out the beloved instrument. "Smell it."

Mary's sobbing stopped long enough for her to look up and give him a confused expression.

"What?"

"Smell it, just smell it." Mary did so. "What do you smell?"

"I smell wood."

"No, smell harder." Mary breathed in deeply. "Now what to you smell."

Mary was quiet for a moment, and then said, as though in disbelief, "Why, I, I swear I could smell the ocean."

"Yes."

"And, it smells like you."

"Yes."

"Really, it's like the same thing, isn't it?"

Seraphine silently nodded. Mary reached out and touched the violin. She rubbed her hand along its smooth surface. She plucked one of these strings, hearing the sound as it vibrated under her fingertips. She said nothing more, but Seraphine knew she could hear what he had always heard. She understood.

Seraphine looked down at her sad face. "You know I always played for you."

"I know," she said, the tears running down her cheeks, and then buried her face against his knee and wrapped her arms around his legs. They stayed like that for a long while.

Seraphine went to bed. His mind was clear. He didn't want to be useless, he thought. He didn't want to live in a world that didn't need him anymore, a world that kept changing and, with every change, distanced him farther and farther from what he felt was his purpose in life. He was no longer compatible with this world, this place he'd called home, but he knew he would not be around long enough to see many more changes. Life had at last gotten the best of him, and he too would soon become a figment of the past. But at least it was a past he belonged to. He knew he'd be forgotten like the countless others who'd died before him. He, like them, would take his story with him. Nobody would want to hear the story of a simple fisherman anyway.

Seraphine sighed and pressed his hands to his burning chest. An ordinary man with a wife and a dog and children. A man possessed of no great wit or intelligence, of no great skills besides his ability to fish, of no wealth or beauty. Who cared about the story of a simple, hard-working man?

And yet, somehow, he felt this wasn't true at all. It was his life, his story. His life mirrored those of countless other fishermen who had passed and faded into the past, their memories kept by the deep, blue sea. He represented all of them just as they represented him, and now as he lay here on his deathbed, he felt proud to be a part of such a forsaken group. No, forsaken was not the right word. Blessed, that was the word. They were blessed. No one was closer to God than the toilers of the sea. Jesus' apostles were fishermen, and though Seraphine didn't know precisely why, he could make a good guess. To know struggle and hardship and still persist in doing what one must do to provide, to face death everyday unflinching and without fear, to withstand physical strains and hardships without breaking, to harness the sea as it harnesses you, and to toil and struggle and fight everyday for your life and never complain or brag or gloat. These were true servants of God.

Seraphine did not fear death, not now, not ever. He realized, lying here, that his death was something he had never before considered. It would come when it was ready, and for everyone, the timing was different. He wondered if everyone knows when their time comes. Bill knew, Glory knew, Philomena knew, his mother knew. He knew. There was nothing left for him in this life, and he accepted that.

XX

Home

Seraphine lay on his back in bed looking up at the shadows of the trees dancing along the ceiling in the pale blue moonlight. He had a handkerchief clapped over his mouth in an effort to suppress his violent coughing and to disguise the red spatters of blood that escaped. Never had he felt so weak and so helpless. It didn't seem right, he thought to himself, that a man should die like this. Isn't it better to be struck with a pain in the chest and fall, dead before you even hit the floor? Isn't it better to be caught in a tempest and die in the middle of the ocean in a rickety little boat, pounded by waves and rain, like what happened to Bill? Or to die as the last of your kind, like his father, Carlos the whaler? Or to die for a cause like all of those men who died when his ship went down in WWI, or like all those men who had just died in WWII?

But not this, he continued to think. Not here in bed, lying on your back suffering, enduring pain, while the rest of the world moves and changes and lives around you. He winced more from pain at the thought of it than from the burning in his chest. The world was so different now. Perhaps in a good way—he hadn't quite decided yet—but different nonetheless. And he would never live to see this change evolve, experience this change. He would not survive this change, if he even managed to survive the night.

What had transformed this world he once knew? Was it the war that brought sailors in their warships to the harbor and the boys of the town out into the rest of the world? Was it the new highway being built that let more and more strangers come to see the town? Was it the new technology that

417

made little wooden fishing boats a thing of the past or that his children were grown or that his wife was older? Or maybe, it was just him. He seemed to not belong anymore. The world had changed around him, and he remained the same. And now he lay here dying in his familiar bed and the home he'd made with his wife that now felt like it was suffocating him. He had to get out.

Mary had taken to sleeping in the other room, afraid of disturbing him with the presence of an extra body in their bed. He didn't really understand why she felt that way, but he didn't argue, figuring that his coughing kept her awake anyhow. Fluke stayed with him, though, lying on the floor beside the bed.

Seraphine sat up slowly. His whole body ached from fever and from being sedentary, but he began to slowly dress himself in his usual garb. He tried to stand, nearly falling back onto the bed, his legs feeling like rubber from lack of use. He shuffled his way across the floor to grab his hat on the dresser, and as he leaned to grab it, caught his reflection in the mirror. He straightened, and looked at his silvery white hair and his gray face still marred by the ruddiness of that damn skin condition. His skin hung loose around his cheeks and bagged under his eyes, further accentuated by deep, dark circles. But it was his eyes that bothered him the most. They no longer shined like polished pieces of onyx but sat there like dull pieces of coal.

He sighed deeply, pulled on his hat, and began to carefully navigate his way down the hall to the stairs, leaning on the wall and railing for support. He sat at the bottom of the stairs pulling on his boots as he always did while Fluke watched him, ears perked but his tail not wagging. Seraphine opened the door and closed it quietly behind him and Fluke.

He slowly made his way up the sidewalk to the street but was feeling a bit more agile now that he was up and moving. Fluke followed closely behind, aware that something was much different about this walk. By the time Seraphine made it to the beach, his lungs were burning excruciatingly. His chest felt tight and restricted and his breathing was labored. He struggled not to cough, for each hack cut through the air loudly enough, it seemed, to wake the entire sleeping town. He nearly collapsed when he reached the sand but restrained it to a stumble.

The beach was bare and cold. The sand was silvery in the moonlight and smooth from the rising and falling of the tide, no living being having walked across it since the tides had changed. In the middle, though, only some feet from the water's edge, was a small dory. It was old and rickety and abandoned in the middle of the empty beach. Seraphine shakily made his way toward it, and found that it was sturdier than it had looked from the distance. At least it appeared to have no holes even though the wood was rough and unpainted. He sat on the side of it to take a breath and ease his beating heart. Fluke watched him.

Seraphine looked back up the beach at the town. There were hardly any lights on, but the rooftops were bathed in the evanescent glow of the moon. He loved this town, this place, his world. He loved the people, the smells, the life he'd had here. In those houses slept his family, and his friends, and everyone he'd ever known. Tomorrow they'd all rise as they always did; the storeowners sweep their stoops, the wives cook their soup, the fishermen mend their nets, the children go to school. Life would continue even though he would not be there. Life would continue, yet it would be different. He knew it would be different. As with life, Provincetown would change and grow and evolve, for nothing stays the same. The change was happening presently as he sat on the side of the dory watching the town, and he could do nothing to stop it but shut his eyes tightly and turn away from it.

But he did not shut his eyes. Instead they began to shine with the light of the moon reflecting off the glaze of tears. He preferred things the way they were, the way he knew them to be. His children would experience change and so would his grandchildren and his great grandchildren. He thought about the generations that would come after him, of his blood, and of this town. His blood was made of sea and sky and sand and fish. It was of pieces of driftwood nailed together to make a house and broken bits of clay pipe that were dropped into the water to wash up again on the shore. It was of the exhaust of rusty boat motors and the seagull droppings that rained down on them as they cleaned the fish. It was of the past, of his ancestors, of the Norse who first set foot on the land, the Pilgrims who landed here in search of freedom, and the Portuguese in search of a new life. His blood was of this town and everything in it, and he ached to leave it behind.

But the inevitable was happening, and he could do nothing to stop it. Provincetown had changed and was no longer his, so he turned back to the one place that would always be his and that would never change. He stood, gave the town a final look, and turned to the harbor and boat that waited for him. He was steady on his feet now, and when he expected to cough, he realized he couldn't, wouldn't. The burning in his chest had subsided, and he knew that this was his chance to do what he must do. He leaned over and began to push the dory to the water's edge until he felt it begin to float. As he was about to swing his leg over the side, he turned back to see Fluke standing at the water's edge, just barely getting the tips of his toes wet.

"You stay here, boy," Seraphine said quietly as he laid a hand on the dog's head. Fluke immediately sat, never taking his eyes off of his master. He watched as Seraphine climbed into the boat and began to lean back on the oars. Seraphine focused his attention on the strenuous activity at hand, but looked up once, when he was already to the middle of the harbor, to see the black spot of Fluke still sitting at the water's edge watching him go, the silhouette of the town as his back drop and then the great expanse of stars and sky. Seraphine looked back down for fear that he would not finish his task and for fear that the pain would return.

He rounded the Point with its solitary lighthouse, and pulled himself, only a bit farther, before lifting the oars from the water and allowing the boat to drift. He could not row anymore. The last of his energy was spent, and he no longer needed it. So Seraphine lay down, warm, without pain, and completely content, in the hull of the gently rocking dory and closed his eyes, a faint smile on his lips.